BEYOND THE LIMIT

LINDSAY MCKENNA

WHEELER PUBLISHING

An imprint of Thomson Gale, a part of The Thomson Corporation

THOMSON

GALE

Detroit • New York • San Francisco • New Haven, Conn. • Waterville, Maine • London

THOMSON

GALE

LIBRARY OF CONGRESS CATALOGING-IN-PUBLICATION DATA

McKenna, Lindsay, 1946–
    Beyond the limit / by Lindsay McKenna.
        p. cm. — (Wheeler Publishing large print romance)
        ISBN-13: 978-1-59722-497-0 (alk. paper)
        ISBN-10: 1-59722-497-9 (alk. paper)
        1. United States. Marine Corps — Fiction. 2. Man-woman relationships —
Fiction. 3. Afghanistan — Fiction. 4. Large type books. I. Title.
    PS3563.C37525B49 2007
    813'.54—dc22   2006102278

Published in 2007 by arrangement with Harlequin Books S.A.

Printed in the United States of America on permanent paper
10 9 8 7 6 5 4 3 2 1

Dear Reader,

I love MORGAN'S MERCENARIES as much as you do. There is no other family in saga history like them, thanks to you and your loyal readership! *Beyond the Limit* is Pete Trayhern's story, and you'll get to see how life has dealt with him. As you may know, children often don't walk the path of the parents — even if the parents want them to! Pete comes from a military dynasty, but he's a builder, an engineer who revels in creation and transformation.

Engineers are a breed apart and very interesting personalities, I think. I'm married to a civil engineer, and have followed Dave around from one building site to the next. Engineers have a true "fix-it" mentality. Here you'll read about Pete's dilemma . . . and I hope you find it fascinating how he dances on the edge of the sword, between what he desires versus protocols and unbending steel rules of conduct found within the engineer's world. The story heats up when Pete meets one of the few women in his field: Cali Roland. I love hearing from readers, so please visit my Web site at www. lindsaymckenna.com. Happy reading!

Warmly,
Lindsay McKenna

To my loyal readers who inspire me, thank you.
And to my husband, David, who is a civil engineer and graduate of Ohio State University —
Go, Buckeyes! — for his help and experience in creating this novel.

CHAPTER ONE

"Major Trayhern, your orders to Afghanistan are either going to be a career killer or a career maker." Colonel Ronald Waskul laid down the olive-green file folder and stared across his desk at the twenty-nine-year-old Marine Corps officer. Waskul liked how the major's gunmetal-gray eyes focused like a laser as he absorbed every word. As it should be.

Tapping the report, the colonel added gruffly, "This construction project is important. You will be there for two years, laying the groundwork and facilitating the building of a historic building of a small coal-fired power plant in that country. Afghanistan has very little electricity and has no power plants inland because there are no lakes and rivers. The U.S. government at the highest levels of the State Department are working with an international consortium of construction companies to provide more energy to this region."

Pete Trayhern was sweating heavily in his dark green wool uniform. He could see it was snowing outside the window behind Colonel Waskul's gray head. A late and unexpected April storm had dumped two feet of the white stuff on Washington, D.C. Pete had just arrived off a transport that had flown him in from Germany. Despite the crazy weather, perspiration beaded his upper lip, and he had the wild desire to wipe it off with the back of his hand. But he didn't dare. According to his father, Morgan Trayhern, the colonel was a king maker in his own right. They had worked on many covert projects together over the last decade, and Pete knew his father idolized the rough-hewn Marine officer.

"Yes, sir, I got a briefing on it before I left my old construction job. I'm sure it shows in my personnel file. I served as an assistant company commander in Kandahar for a year, so I'm not unfamiliar with the country. I'm gung ho on these new orders, Colonel Waskul, and I'm the right man for the job." With his background as a mechanical engineer, graduating from Annapolis four years earlier, Pete had since made a name for himself as an assistant site-construction superintendent. And yet he wondered if his highly influential father, who ran a CIA covert group, had anything to do with this latest development. Pete had known that his two years at the German construction site were up and that he would be transferred, but he hadn't known where. Until now.

Waskul grunted and opened another folder. His thick gray brows turned down. "Yes, your assignment to Kandahar as an assistant company commander is part of the reason you're here. I've carefully gone over your construction record, Major Trayhern. We ran the requirements through the Pentagon computers and came up with five finalists. You were first on that list." Tapping the folder, he added, "You've got a background in bringing electrical substations online, and your last job was building a power plant in its start-up phase near Berlin. You kept that job on schedule and on budget. In today's environment, the U.S. government is *very* concerned about meeting all these goals."

He stared at Pete. "Colonel James Flint, your past supervisor, has glowing remarks about how effective you were in liaising with civilian construction companies and getting their work completed within the contract requirements."

"Yes, sir, the old carrot-and-stick routine." Pete started to smile, but quickly wiped it

11

off his face when Colonel Waskul frowned even more. Pete hated these "official" meetings with superiors. Truth be known, he'd rather be out clomping around in the field with D9 Caterpillars, growling earthmovers and noisy backhoes than sitting in the stifling, stuffy confines of a Pentagon office. He yearned to be out in the cold, crisp air, drawing it deeply into his lungs. Fighting jet lag and no sleep in the last forty-eight hours, Pete felt rummy. As he held the colonel's icy blue stare, he did his best to remain alert and appear interested.

"Well, you're going to need every carrot, stick and donkey you've got up your sleeve to coordinate this mission, Major Trayhern," Waskul growled, handing Pete the folder. "This time, you are going to head up the project. You're no longer the assistant. And this isn't Italy or Germany. Afghanistan is a third world country. You speak fluent German and Italian. But where you're going, Farsi and Pashto are the languages spoken, along with a multitude of tribal and regional dialects. Your workers are going to be Afghans, as well as other hard hats from around the world." His brows rose and he sat back. "You've got your work cut out for you."

Looking down at the overflowing file on

the power plant project, Pete murmured, "Yes, sir. I understand this is a very different and difficult project." As he looked back up, he smiled just a little at Colonel Waskul's bulldog features. "I'm confident that I can handle it, sir. And I appreciate the confidence the Navy has in me to do just that."

Now the Marine Corps was a sub-branch of the U.S. Navy, although no Marine liked to admit it. Still the Navy construction branch was well known as a "can-do." Pete was sure this was partly responsible for him receiving this assignment. Pete was one of many officers from various military branches that were sent interservice, to projects around the world. Although he was a Marine, he had worked for the Air Force at his first job, in Italy, and for the U.S. Army in Germany on his second tour. Specialties such as his were shared among the branches.

"That's youth talking," Waskul muttered, giving him a cutting, one-cornered smile. "You have seven days of leave, Major. I suggest you get a good night's sleep and show up here tomorrow morning at the Pentagon. Fill your Blackberry and laptop with information you're going to need and then your father is expecting you home."

"Yes, sir, I'll be here at 0800 tomorrow

morning to pick up the details of the project."

"Give my best to your dad. He's one hell of a Marine, and it's always a pleasure to work with him and his companies." Standing, Waskul watched as the major sprang to his feet at attention. "At ease," he said, thrusting his hand across the desk to Trayhern. "I can't stress enough how critical this project is, Major. If you do this right, you'll be in one helluva position for early lieutenant-colonel's leaves. The Afghan government is hinging a lot on this power plant and it's political as hell. If people start getting electricity inland, the government feels the regional tribal sheiks will be more cooperative, rather than fomenting uprisings to tear that country apart again. Got it?"

Pete relaxed and shook the tough Marine's callused hand. "Yes, sir, I got it. I'll make you proud of me, sir. That's a promise."

Nodding, Waskul released his grip. "In my late twenties I thought I could conquer the world, too, Major. Just remember, you're going to be working with an international mix of construction companies. Everyone speaks different languages and does things their own way. You have to weave them into one machine, with one heart, one mind and one focus on the goals you set for them. Your father says you have what it takes. I'm counting on you. . . ."

"Pete! Welcome home!" Laura Trayhern's voice sang through the hall as her son stepped in the doorway.

"Hi, Mom." Pete grinned and opened his arms as she dashed toward him.

"Welcome home, sweetheart! We've missed you so much!" After hugging her second son fiercely, she planted several kisses on his clean-shaven cheek.

"Sorry I couldn't get home sooner," Pete said, pulling back so that he could get a good look at her. Simple and elegant in black slacks and a white blouse, Laura Trayhern was in her fifties, but to Pete, she seemed so much younger.

He hung up his coat and lifted his nose in the air. "What's that I smell? My favorite meal cooking? Am I in time for lunch?" He grinned widely, his heart expanding as his mother took his arm and drew him down the polished, golden-red cedar hall and into the bright, airy kitchen.

"Yes, your favorite. Beef stroganoff. Your father will be here any minute. I decided to make it for lunch instead of dinner."

Pete felt the tension he'd been carrying in

his shoulders dissolve. He'd hitched a ride on a commercial flight from D.C. to Anaconda, Montana. From there, he'd rented a car and driven to Phillipsburg, a very small town nestled deep in the Rocky Mountains. The weather had cooperated; it was spring here, with patches of snow left, but greenery and wildflowers popping up after a long, severe winter.

"Where's Kammie?" Pete asked, looking around. She was the youngest of his sisters. The table was set to perfection with sparkling glassware, colorful china plates and glistening flatware. His mother was one hell of a cook, and Pete always appreciated the homey nest she'd made for all of them growing up.

"She's in school. Normally, she doesn't come home at noon." Laura smiled as she pulled the casserole out of the oven and placed it on a trivet in the center of the table. "You'll see her tonight."

"I've missed her. She's really grown up in the last two years." Kamaria Trayhern was the fifth child in their family. Pete recalled the infant girl being brought back from Los Angeles after a deadly earthquake had devastated southern California years earlier. Kamaria had been found beneath the body of her dead mother. Pete's own mom had suffered a broken ankle and been trapped in the rubble of a hotel for days.

After being rescued, Kamaria had been flown to the Camp Reed Marine Base to recover. Many children without parents had been cared for at the huge medical facility. Laura, who had been bedridden, had volunteered to help out by bottle-feeding little Kamaria. And had fallen in love with the little black-haired tyke.

Pete had been a teen then, and he recalled the phone call from his parents to him and his fraternal twin, Kelly, about bringing the baby home and adopting her. He'd thought it was a great idea. And through the years, as Kammie grew up, she'd been a continuous blessing to the family. Pete and Kelly had been especially close to their adopted little sister. He always appreciated the e-mails and pictures she sent from her computer. Kammie was a photo bug of the first order. Two years ago, Pete had given her a cheap digital camera for her birthday, and a photographer had been born. Ever since, Kammie took pictures of the family and routinely sent them to him so he wouldn't feel homesick. She wanted to grow up and be a professional photographer who worked for a major international news organization, wanting to follow in Kelly's footsteps and lead an adventurous life. Kammie idolized her big sister. Kelly had left the Marine Corps aviation as a helicopter pilot and had been flying the Sirkorsky Sky Crane for Shaheen Aviation. Kelly fought wildfires across the globe with her helo that could fly in 3000 gallons of water on a raging forest fire. Kammie doted on red-haired Kelly's brave acts and dreamed of an adventurous life when she graduated from college someday.

"Can I help with anything?" he asked his mother now, looking around the kitchen.

"Nope, just sit down. Want some red wine with lunch?" Laura grinned. "You're out of uniform and on leave."

"Vino for lunch. Very European. Not a bad idea, Mom."

Over in Italy, Pete had had to get used to the idea, but as a military officer he couldn't imbibe. Putting the finishing touches on a salad in a cedar bowl, Laura pointed to the end of the counter, where an unopened bottle of red wine stood.

When Pete heard the front door open and close, he knew it had to be his father. After opening the wine bottle, Pete set it on the table and headed toward the foyer. His dad, Morgan Trayhern, was one of the most revered military figures in the country. After his stint in the Marine Corps, he'd had to prove to his superiors and to the world that he was not a traitor who had run out on his men when his company had been attacked and decimated in the closing days of the Vietnam War. Once he'd proved his innocence, Morgan had seen the need for the organization he'd subsequently created, Perseus. He had gathered together top-notch ex-military men and women and sent them on missions around the world, helping people in trouble that governments could not — or would not — help. Later, Morgan sold his companies to the CIA but continued to run them for the U.S. government as a supersecret black-ops unit. Pete admired how his father had overcome such incredible adversity.

Walking down the hall, he saw Morgan hanging his black raincoat on a wooden peg. "Hi, Dad!"

Morgan turned and smiled. "Hello, Pete. Welcome home." As he clasped his tall, lean son in his arms and hugged him, he couldn't help noticing Pete was the spitting image of himself at that age. Pete had a square face and large, widely spaced gray eyes. His irises were ringed in black, giving him a hawklike look similar to Morgan's.

Pete's full mouth hitched in a wry, teasing

smile as he slid his arm around Morgan's shoulders. "Wait till you see what Mom made for lunch!" he said as the two of them walked down the hall to the kitchen.

"You mean we're not just having sandwiches?" Morgan said with a wink.

"I heard that," Laura called, laughing.

Rounding the corner, Morgan beamed at his wife, who was placing the salad on the table. "Guilty as charged." He patted Pete and released him. "Let's eat. You can fill us in on your new assignment as we chow down."

Pete stuffed himself like the proverbial turkey. His mother's cooking was a welcome relief from military chow. As he wiped his mouth and took a sip of wine, he saw his father's eyes dance with mirth. Throughout lunch, Pete had, between bites, been telling them about his latest construction project.

"So, are you happy with your new orders?" Morgan inquired as he slathered butter on a slice of some Italian bread.

"Yes, I am. Stunned, sorta. I mean . . . I expected another construction assignment, an intermilitary kind, but not this. Not a power plant to call my own."

Laura smiled. "Well, we're proud of you, sweetheart. Ron Waskul called your father one evening about two months ago. They talked for about an hour." She gave her husband a warm look before going to fetch dessert.

"Talking about me?" Pete asked. He stood up and carried the plates and flatware to the kitchen sink. "I thought you might have something to do with this assignment, Dad."

Morgan shrugged. "Let's just say Ron and I go back a long way. He wanted to know a lot more about you than what was in your personnel jacket."

"Uh-oh," Pete said, laughing. "So, what did you do? Extol my virtues and not tell him about my bad side?" As he waited for his father to answer, Pete spooned dollops of whipped cream on his butterscotch pudding.

"Well," Morgan hedged, "I told him how you were the quarterback of the football team in high school and that you took them to state championship three years in a row. That you were a good leader and you knew how to get diverse background people to work for a common goal."

"That's a skill you've always had," Laura said, pride in her tone. She dropped a spoonful of whipped cream on her own serving of pudding. "And in construction you're like a puppeteer with a hundred strings, trying to get a hundred different construction companies to come together for a common goal."

Pete glowed internally from his parents' praise. He knew they meant it. "Well," he murmured between bites of the tasty dessert, "I had two great teachers. Mom, you taught me patience, and Dad, you taught me about maintaining strong boundaries and keeping my eye on the ball."

Nodding, Morgan put his empty dessert bowl aside and took a sip of hot coffee. "You and Kelly are very different from your older sister and brother, Cathy and Jason."

"Opposites, almost," Laura agreed, smiling softly. "I know Jason's looking forward to seeing you while you're here, Pete."

"Likewise. I'm going to visit Jason, Annie and their two tykes later today." They lived twenty miles away, up in the mountains above the small town, Phillipsburg. Annie had just given birth to a little girl, Rachel Ann, six months ago. Kammie had sent Pete digital pictures via e-mail to keep him up to speed on their niece. Kelly had wanted to be home for the birth but was on a wildfire assignment instead, much to her disappointment.

"They're hoping you'll stay for dinner tonight. If you're not too tired?" Laura murmured.

"No, that's fine. I'd like to spend an evening with them and catch up. And hold Rachel Ann. Finally." Pete knew he'd been gone far too long from his family. The construction job in Germany had been brutal on him because he hadn't had any time off. Due to several site problems, he never got to use his thirty days' leave. Understanding that his family missed him as much as he did them, Waskul had given him seven days to catch up.

Pete grinned. "So, what will I be missing here tonight for dinner?"

Morgan chuckled. "Son, you think with your stomach. Your mother is making macaroni and cheese. But there will be leftovers, don't worry."

"Hey —" Pete held up his hands "— guilty as charged. I just like home cooking when I can get it."

"Annie's a wonderful cook, too," Laura noted.

"Oh, I know she is. But . . ." Pete slanted a glance at his mother, whose blue eyes danced with happiness ". . . there's no cookin' like Mom's. I know that for a fact."

"Well, thank you, dear. We've called Cathy and she's not going to be able to make it home to see you. She's undercover with her husband in an Alcohol, Tobacco and Firearms unit down in South America right now."

"I got an e-mail from her a week ago," Pete said. "She's really happy, and I'm glad for her and Mac."

Morgan scraped his chair back from the table. "Right now, our family is stable and growing." He gazed down at Pete. "When are you going to get interested in finding the right woman, Son?"

Feeling heat flow up into his face, Pete cleared his throat. He glanced over and saw his mother's hopeful look. Laura delighted in being a grandmother. She had planned Jason and Cathy's weddings. More than once in e-mails over the past two years, she'd hinted that she'd love to plan a wedding for him. "Well, I just guess it isn't the right time," he told them. "Besides, Dad, you told me that a later marriage was a smart one. Getting married really young wasn't the brightest lightbulb thing to do."

Morgan rubbed his jaw. "That's true, I did say that."

"You were older than me when you married Mom," Pete pointed out.

Laura nodded. "Yes, and it has been a marriage made in heaven."

"And Cathy and Mac were older when they got married, too."

24

"Okay," Morgan conceded, "truce, Son. Your mother and I know the benefits of a solid marriage. We just want you to find that special someone out there and be as happy as we are."

"And as happy as Jason and Cathy," Laura said in a pleased tone. "You're so special, Pete. You're drop-dead handsome. When you played football, you had girls hanging off your arms."

"My job keeps me too busy for a social life now," Pete said, trying not to sound defensive. Getting up, he gathered the empty dessert bowls and spoons. "Being on a construction site 24-7 doesn't give me any time to go out and woo women like I might want to."

"You had Brandy Wilson as a steady in Germany," his mom said wistfully. "I wish that had worked out. I really liked her, Pete."

Wincing inwardly, he took dirty dishes to the sink. "Now, Mom. Brandy just wasn't the right woman, that's all." No woman was, as far as Pete was concerned. He wasn't lucky in love.

Laura sighed as she got up. "Maybe you'll meet a special woman over in Afghanistan. Your father said it would be a big project."

"Mom," Pete said, turning and leaning against the counter, "construction sites are male dominated by nature. The only women around are usually secretarial assistants, if that. Where I'm going, I'll probably end up with some guy as my office assistant. In an Islamic culture it is frowned upon for a woman to work outside the home. So I'm expecting mostly men on the site. This plant is going to be built out in the middle of nowhere. There are villages nearby, but women are married and have families." He shook his head. "So don't go there, okay? I'll meet Ms. Right when it's time." And Pete knew it wouldn't be on this project, but didn't want to dash his parents' expectations.

Morgan clapped his hand on Pete's shoulder. "Don't mind your mother, Son. She just wants to see you happy."

Pete bit back the stab of pain he felt when he thought of his past relationships. None of them had worked out. He tried to analyze why he couldn't find a woman who was compatible. He wanted someone smart and curious, who was just as adventure oriented as he was. Like his fraternal twin, Kelly whom he idolized. But no woman had the courage, brilliance and chutzpah his twin had. And Pete had given up on ever finding that kind of gutsy freedom-loving woman. Maybe he was being too picky, he decided as he helped his mother rinse the dishes. Well, where he was going there would be little chance of meeting any women. And truth be known, with the enormity of this project and what it meant careerwise, he didn't want to focus on anything but his work. Finding a girlfriend in Afghanistan would be impossible, and he wasn't looking, anyway. Women had always meant trouble with a capital *T*. And he'd been too hurt in the past to want to try again. He seemed to draw women who lied. And something he couldn't stand was a lie. Maybe Kelly was too good of a role model that he'd grown up with. She had an in-your-face, rather blunt personality. Pete had lived with that, went out into life expecting all women were like Kelly. Had he been in for a rude awakening! Pete had found women coy. Their communication with him, confusing at best. No, he had absolutely no expectation of ever finding a plain-spoken woman, that was for sure!

Chapter Two

After emerging from a battered, dented green taxi, Pete tried to shake off the fatigue from his fogged brain as he headed for the U.S. government office in Kabul. Except for the mouthwatering odors of curry, coriander, turmeric and onion filling the crisp morning air, the town seemed like the Dodge City of the Middle East. Desert-camouflaged Hummers moved slowly up and down the boulevards, manned by U.S. Army soldiers with M16s or machine guns. The capital of Afghanistan was bristling with firearms, with danger and spies. Perched at an altitude of six thousand feet, it gave new meaning to "Mile High City", the nickname of Denver, Colorado. Kabul teetered on lawlessness due to terrorists striking out of the shadows and killing Americans at any opportunity.

As Pete hurried down the cracked sidewalk, he passed several men dressed in astrakhan hats or turbans, loose-fitting, long-sleeved shirts, vests and baggy trousers. Hearing snatches of many languages, he felt as if he were at the United Nations without a translator. In his Kandahar assignment, Pete got used to this situation. He kept his focus on the white stucco building before him, the U.S. government headquarters, surrounded by Marine Corps sentries. Once he arrived, Pete produced his ID and was allowed through the security perimeter.

Inside, he went through a metal detector and another series of blockades designed to tell friend from foe. How he itched to get rid of his flak jacket. But he was on official business and needed to be wearing his Marine Corps desert-camouflage utilities.

The sentry nodded to him as Pete picked up his 9 mm Beretta pistol and tucked it back in the holster strapped to his right thigh. No one went anywhere in Afghanistan without carrying a protective firearm.

"Can you point the way to Mr. Elliot's office?" Pete asked the short, thickset sergeant in charge.

"Yes, sir. Take this elevator up to the fourth floor. Mr. Elliot has his office there."

"Thanks, Sergeant." Pete gave him a brisk nod. His desert boots thudded on the polished white linoleum floor leading to the elevators. He caught a whiff of strong, rich coffee in the air and wished he had some. Maybe Kerwin Elliot, a U.S. liaison officer overseeing in-country projects, might offer him a cup. Pete tried to forget his eighteen hours in the air and his failed attempts to grab some badly needed sleep in the cargo hold of a C-9 Starlifter. The aircraft had been crammed with equipment for the war effort.

Entering the elevator, Pete glanced down at his watch. It was 0830. Good. He was half an hour early for his meeting with all the major players in building this power plant. Excited despite his exhaustion, he gripped his black leather briefcase and exited the slow-moving elevator when the door opened.

At the end of the hall was a middle-aged woman dressed in a springlike lavender suit. As he approached, she looked up and smiled.

"Major Trayhern here to see Mr. Elliot," he told her as he halted in front of her.

"Ah, yes, Major. Welcome to Kabul. I'm Betty Johnson, his assistant." She held out her hand.

In her midforties, Betty was a good-looking woman, Pete decided. Shaking her hand gently, he said, "I'm sure I'll see a lot of you in the next two years working on this power plant project." He smiled.

She laughed lightly and rose. "Oh, I'm sure you will, Major Trayhern."

"Call me Pete. I don't like standing on protocol."

"Okay, Pete," she said, smiling back, "just call me Betty. And yes, you'll be interfacing with Mr. Elliot and his group probably on a daily basis by telephone, fax or e-mail. Would you like some coffee?" She gestured toward the station behind her desk. "Black? Cream? Sugar? What's your pleasure?"

Grateful, Pete looked around. "Yes, ma'am, I'd love some hot, black coffee."

"Betty, remember. You don't have to 'yes ma'am' and 'no ma'am' me."

"Got it." Pete nodded and glanced at the large wooden doors to Kerwin Elliot's office. They each had a rearing Arabian horse carved on them. Unsure what type of wood it was, he stared admiringly at the artwork. "Is anyone else here yet?"

"Oh, yes. They're all waiting for you. But don't look so devastated. They've been in-country, and you just got here after a long flight. I've kept them plied with pastries from our bakery next door, and I think they're doing just fine."

So he was the last to show up for the 0900

meeting. *Great,* Pete thought. He didn't want to be the final one in the door, but there was no way to change this situation. Technically, he wasn't late, but as the superintendent on this project, he needed to make a good impression on his team . . . and his supervisor. What kind of opinion would Kerwin form about him?

The receptionist handed him a paper cup of steaming black coffee. "You're an angel, Betty." He lifted the cup in a mock toast to her.

Betty grinned and stepped around her desk. With brisk efficiency she opened the doors. "Go right in, Pete, and meet your boss. You'll see Mr. Elliot and the Roland Construction management team straight ahead."

Girding himself emotionally, Pete smiled at the kind assistant and entered, his boots silent on the colorful Oriental rug that stretched all the way to the large maple desk where silver-haired Kerwin Elliot sat. Surrounding the desk in a semicircle were four other people.

Pete's attention focused right away on a red-haired woman in the waiting group. Kelly had red hair, too. Pete loved that hair color, a sign of an independent woman. Frowning, he wondered who she was. According to his data sheet on Roland Construction, C. Roland was the site project engineer. His gaze roamed to the woman's right. A big, beefy man with buzzed brown-and-gray hair sat next to her. *Must be C. Roland,* Pete thought. Maybe the red-haired babe was his assistant? Not bad looking, either, but Pete reigned in his appreciation of her.

"Ah, you've arrived," Elliot stated, rising and nodding toward Pete. "Welcome, Major Trayhern. We're glad you could make it."

Pete noted the man was dressed conservatively in a dark suit and tie. Kerwin Elliot appeared to be a smooth businessman of the first order. According to Pete's stats on him, the man was also a CIA operative and knew the Northern Territory better than anyone. He was a key player in local and regional politics. Pete knew he was going to have to rely heavily on him now and in the future.

"Thank you, sir." Pete put his coffee and briefcase down on the last empty chair, at the end of the semicircle. He leaned over and handed Elliot his personnel file.

"Thank you, Major. Welcome to Kabul." Elliot extended a manicured hand.

Pete felt its softness as he shook it. Nothing like his own palm, which was callused by constant outdoor work. "Nice to meet you, sir."

"Excellent. Well, you look pretty rugged. Long flight?"

"Yes, sir, it was."

"Get any sleep on board?"

"Not much. Those Starlifters weren't built for passenger comfort."

Pete heard the other men chuckle indulgently and Elliot's long, narrow face broke into a sympathetic smile.

"I understand more than I care to, Major. Now, let me introduce you to the contractor who won the bid to get this power plant built."

Pete turned, his gaze automatically moving to the woman sitting in the middle of the group. She looked like a red rose in a colorless desert of men. Obviously, an assistant and probably would leave for the States shortly. Pete assumed the assistant would not be going to the job site. This was a male-dominant country and women were not encouraged to be outside the home. Hardened men with weather-beaten faces stared back at him, they regularly challenged the elements.

"If you'll give me a moment, Mr. Elliot, let me get out my roster on Roland Construction." Pete went to his briefcase and pulled out a document listing key individuals in the building of the power plant.

"Of course," Elliot said, sitting down and folding his hands in front of him.

Pete gripped the sheet in his left hand, pen in his right. "I'm ready now." He smiled slightly at the civilians. Again his gaze strayed to the woman, who sat relaxed, legs crossed, in the midst of the males. Who was she? And why bring a woman here? It would cause nothing but trouble, Pete knew, judging from his experience in Kandahar during the early phase of the war against the Taliban.

As an assistant company commander for a Marine security team that kept the airport safe from terrorists, his women Marines had caused a stir among the more conservative Islamic clerics. Pete recalled that uncomfortable time because, as commander, he had to protect all his soldiers, regardless of gender. And certain Afghan leaders disapproved of women soldiers. It had been a constant battle that had no winners, as far as Pete was concerned.

"Well," Elliot said, his voice deep and somewhat jovial, "the person running this show for Roland Construction is C. Roland, the site project engineer. You're getting one of the plums straight from the family tree."

Pete gazed in shock as the woman spontaneously and gracefully stood up . . . to her six feet in height. Gulping, he stared into her large, inquisitive green eyes. Her hair, cropped in a pixie cut, was a rich red color, the lights above displaying copper, gold and burgundy highlights. And she was no stick-like model, but as shapely as a woman painted by Titian in the Renaissance era. Her shoulders were drawn back with obvious pride and the look on her oval face was one of unspoken humor. Gold flecks sparkled in those eyes that coolly assessed him.

"But you're a woman." His comment came out sounding silly as hell, and Pete realized his gaffe when he saw the men on either side of her scowl in unison. They were Roland employees, so why wouldn't they?

"All one hundred and sixty pounds of me, Major Trayhern. I'm Calandra Roland. Frank Roland is my dad."

Though he tried to hide his surprise, Pete gawked anyway. Maybe it was the jet lag. Or maybe he was just brutally tired, having had no sleep since leaving Montana. Whatever his excuse, he just stood there staring, his pen poised over his clipboard. She was around his age — late twenties or early thirties. Calandra Roland wore no makeup, and she didn't have to. The fine, feathery bangs that brushed her broad brow softened the eaglelike look in her eyes. This woman was a powerhouse; Pete could feel it. To say self-confidence emanated from her was an understatement. He had met military women like her before, but never a civilian. Despite his clumsy manners, she extended her hand. Pete fumbled with his pen and then thrust out his hand to enclose hers. He wasn't prepared for the fact that it was strong, and as callused as his.

"Nice to meet you." He managed to choke out the words. Pete heard the four construction men chuckle indulgently.

"Is it? By your reaction, Major, you'd think I was an alien just coming off a flying saucer." Calandra measured the Marine officer from head to toe. She liked what she saw. Maybe a little too much. He had short black hair that emphasized his square face, predatory looking gray eyes and an aquiline nose. His slightly curled mouth had more of a grimace than a smile, but Cali found it appealing. Pete Trayhern was terribly good-looking, and out of habit, she glanced at his left hand. No wedding ring. Well, the dude must be divorced, then, because he was too handsome not to have a gaggle of women begging for his attention.

Her hand tingled as he released it. She saw uncertainty and confusion lingering in Trayhern's eyes. At least he couldn't hide his feelings from her. That was good. Cali didn't know what to expect from this man she'd be working with for two years. Intuitively, she felt his initial reaction to her was forgivable. After all, there weren't that many women in the construction industry, especially at the reins of a major multimillion-dollar project. Trayhern didn't know how hard she'd worked to get here, or the personal obstacles she'd had to overcome. The past belonged in the past. And with that thought, Cali allowed her mouth to curve wryly.

"Well, Major? Do I pass your inspection?"

Again, her team of foremen chortled, and Trayhern's face turned a dull red. Feeling a bit sorry for him, she craned her neck and tapped the clipboard he held. "I'm C. Roland. My men call me Cali, and you can, too, once you find your voice." She didn't want to start off on the wrong foot. On her last project, she'd fallen for a mechanical engineer — only to find out later Russ Turner was married and had been lying to her for his own manipulative reasons. Cali realized that on-site romances were never a good idea, but to have the man lie and then expose her to public humiliation had nearly undone a perfect career up to that point. Not to mention hurt her deeply. No, on this project she had to prove to her father that she could carry off an assignment and not bring shame to the family-owned company. Cali had too much at stake to be diverted by this obvious attraction.

Pete was surprised by Cali's dry wit. She wasn't taking his shock as a negative. When she touched his clipboard, he quickly scrambled. "Uh, yes, right, C. Roland. Thank you. Nice to meet you." Well, that was an understatement. Pete liked what he saw far too much. Abruptly, he remembered how women were always trouble for him. He had to be professional, keep his distance. Cali was impressive, though. A woman with command and maturity. Glancing behind her, he noticed a few of her colleagues had smirks on their faces. Construction humor wasn't lost on him; it was sometimes bawdy, but always blunt and honest.

"Really? Well," Cali murmured as she sat back down, hoping her tough, bluff tactics would work with him, "we'll see, won't we, Major? Have you ever handled a construction project like this with a woman at the helm?" Despite her steely exterior, she wondered if he'd heard the gossip about her. The construction world was large, but talk circulated. Cali's bad choice in men had nearly cost her company this job. No matter what, she had to make this project work.

Cali Roland had come out firing. Pete scowled and put a check mark by her name. "I've been an assistant company commander, Ms. Roland, and led men and women Marines. I was able to deal fairly with both genders without trouble."

Cali's smile twisted. She couldn't afford to make an enemy of Trayhern. After all, they would be working at one another's elbow, nonstop. "I wonder if your company commander was a woman, then?" Might as well get him used to the fact that she wasn't subordinate to him. As winner of the bid, her company was the most major player on this site. And Roland would then turn around and hire all the subcontractors who would then do the work under her and her company for Major Trayhern, the "owner" of this project. It was a fine line, Cali realized.

On the one hand, she was Trayhern's subordinate in that she wasn't financing the project, but the contractor who had to make it happen. The relationship between the site construction superintendent and herself required a delicate balance. They'd be like a king and queen from different countries working side by side to get the project done. Cali knew that if her company didn't meet the contract requirements, Major Trayhern could make her life miserable, and Roland Construction could lose a helluva lot of money — millions, maybe. He was her boss, but she was boss of the entire construction operation.

And if he was aware of the mess she'd created at her last job, that could be why he was looking so damn uncomfortable right now.

Biting back the urge to ask, Cali was afraid. Afraid that he knew she'd screwed up big-time. And yet, if he didn't know, she didn't want to bring it up. Her gut twisted painfully and she brushed her stomach area unconsciously in response. Feeling trapped, Cali stared back at him.

"No, my CO was male. But if it had been a woman, I'll have adjusted. I'll get over my shock, Cali, don't worry," Pete stated. Tough. She was tough. But she was beautiful, too, in a natural way he liked. Yet liking Cali for her feminine attributes wasn't in the cards. Not on a work site. And not with his bad track record with women.

"Good to hear, Major." Cali decided to

41

stay on respectful military terms with him now. To call him Pete was premature.

"You will find that Cali Roland is one of the bright stars in the global construction field, Major Trayhern," Elliot said. "Roland has a permanent office here in Kabul. They do a lot of business in the region."

"That's reassuring," Pete murmured. "Why not introduce me to the rest of your team, Cali?"

Her heart pounded with anxiety. Cali hoped the men she worked with stayed loyal and didn't gossip about her last project.

She turned to her right. "Ray Billings is our general foreman. He's the man that puts the muscle into getting things done."

Pete saw the fortysomething-year-old grin proudly, revealing missing teeth. His face looked like a road map from having obviously been exposed to a lot of harsh elements. "Mr. Billings, nice to meet you."

"Same here, Major," he growled.

Billings was built like a pit bull. He was shorter than Cali, his shoulders broad, his chest wide and narrowing into a slight potbelly just above his belt. His hands were square and scarred, the complete opposite of Elliot's pampered ones. Pete immediately liked the look in Billings's small, wide-set blue eyes. His nose had been broken in the past and hooked slightly to the right, and Pete decided he seemed like the type who had gotten into plenty of barroom brawls in his youth. Pete also noted how Billings's eyes softened whenever he looked at his boss.

The longer Cali watched the major, the more complex he seemed. Despite his military bearing and muscular frame, she could see compassion in his eyes. He was probably a good assistant company commander. The fact that he let himself show boyish embarrassment over his mistakes suggested he didn't mind revealing vulnerability. And he didn't get prickly when he wrongly assessed a person. She was pleased, for she knew a bad boss could be hell personified. In this industry, structures got built with the help of a lot of antacid tablets if it was the wrong "marriage" of titans. So far, she held out hope that she and Trayhern could hammer out a peaceful working relationship.

The bigger issues would be making sure Trayhern didn't learn about her bad judgment, and proving to her father that she was worthy of a second chance. Her family name was on the line, and she wasn't about to let her father down again.

As the rest of her team introduced themselves, her gaze strayed back to Trayhern. He had nice hands. Workman's hands. Cali could tell he was used to being out in the elements from the dark tan there and on his face. She was curious about his relationship status, but decided to table those questions. His personal life was none of her business. Was he just like Russ, the mechanical engineer she'd fallen for? He never wore a wedding ring, either, but the bastard was married with three children. Gun-shy, Cali swallowed any attraction and stuffed it deep within her.

"So this is your team from Roland," Elliot said as Pete sat down after all the introductions. "Cali is legendary as a project engineer, as I told you. She's brought in all her jobs on budget and on time." Elliot raised his thick, silver brows and held Pete's gaze. "That's impressive, Major. We know how much can go wrong at a job site — unexpected weather, worker tiffs, delivery delays, equipment breakdowns. So many things influence whether or not a project stays on schedule." Elliot smiled briefly. "And Cali's been building structures in the Middle East for the last six years. She's actually Roland's point person on any project in this part of the world. Cali is fluent in the major languages of Afghanistan and knows goat-grab diplomacy. So, Major Trayhern, you're one lucky guy."

Nodding, Pete said, "I feel very fortunate." That was a lie. He couldn't, in fact, see *any* woman handling such a job in a place like this. Still, he was familiar with the term "goat-grab diplomacy." It meant a person knew not only how to maneuver and survive, but to flourish in this ancient Middle Eastern way of life — an important skill to have.

Afghanistan was an ancient tribal country struggling to bring in democracy. Women were not tolerated in positions of authority, although Pete knew that the present Afghan government was working hard to change that. Still, one didn't take a religion-based edict that women should remain covered in a chadri from head to toe, and alter it overnight. The Taliban hadn't allowed women to hold any jobs, preferring they remain at home, barefoot and pregnant. Pete wondered obliquely if Cali had been chosen for this assignment precisely because she was female and therefore a potential role model for local village women. Probably not, because this was a U.S.A.-sponsored project and any gender bias wasn't tolerated.

Still, having a woman on his team didn't

make his job easier. Pete knew that local workmen would make up the bulk of their employees. How would a male Afghan villager take to this red-haired vixen telling him what to do? Pete could see the potential problems. "Sir, with all due respect, I don't speak any of the languages in this country. Oh, I'm a bit familiar with Farsi because of my one-year command at Kandahar, but . . . I know we're going to be working in the northern provinces, where people speak Pashto, a language I don't know. Do you have an interpreter I can use?"

"Of course, Major. I've hand-picked Ahmed to be your translator and driver. He's highly trustworthy and I know his family. Right now, he's down at the motor pool getting a Toyota Land Cruiser to drive you to the site. A bright young man. His English isn't flawless, perhaps, but he is intelligent and I'm sure he will be able to pass your orders to the Afghan workers."

"Sounds good to me," Pete said, as he checked off that question from his list.

Cali leaned forward. "Kerwin, I'm more interested in who we're going to be employing. Can you fill us in with a briefing of that area of Afghanistan? I have my own info, but anything you can add will help us immensely." Her eyes locked with Trayhern's and automatically, her skin tingled. Damn! How could that happen, when she fiercely fought the reaction? She felt a moment of panic.

"Be glad to, Cali." Elliot took six folders that had been stacked on his desk and passed them around. "This is your dossier on the region you're going to. Ahmed will lead the convoy to Dara-i-Suf, the nearest city and your jump-off point for where the plant will be built. You will be working in the Samangan Province. The regional warlord, Sheik Baider Hesam, is the man you'll be dealing with. Arm wrestling, more likely. I've already made contact with Sheik Hesam, letting him know you'll want an audience with him as soon as possible. Because Hesam is the tribal chief of this province, nothing goes on without his knowledge or approval. His official residence is in the city, though he prefers to live in his village when he can — and near the project site." Elliot frowned. "Hesam is an enlightened leader, you will find. His family has ruled the area for nearly five hundred years, and the people love and respect him. He's got great curiosity about Americans and is pro-U.S.A. In fact, he's done more in his province to support education of boys *and* girls than any other tribal leader in the country."

"Sounds like a good man," Pete said approvingly.

"Well, yes and no," Elliot countered. "He's a despot at times. He's king and he damn well knows it. Anything you need for your plant site must go through him first. You want workers, you seek an audience with Hesam. You have employee problems with a local villager, you take it to Hesam. If you try to leave him out of the core and take over, never forget he has a military on horseback that could easily murder every contractor and subcontractor onsite, including yourselves, with just a flourish of his hand. His people are loyal to him first, last and always."

"It's a fiefdom," Cali explained, looking down the row at Pete, whose forehead was creased in a frown. "Loyalty in Afghanistan is predicated upon the family, the clan, the tribe and, lastly, their imams, who are speakers for Islam. But the sheik is the core person around whom all this revolves. And we need his support." Before she got too distracted by Trayhern's good looks, Cali turned away and focused on the entire group. "The first thing we have to do, Major, is get Baider Hesam on our side. He must be made to feel an integral part of what we're doing there. Otherwise this project is doomed from the start."

"You've worked in the Middle East, so you should know," Pete replied. He wondered if he could trust her experience. But then, who else *could* he trust? Kerwin Elliot was a political operative in Afghanistan, not a construction expert.

Trust Cali Roland? Pete's heart pounded once as if to underscore that vital question. His history with women was a thorny trail filled with disappointment and pain. How could he trust this woman? Torn, he swallowed his frustration. He never attracted women who believed in trust, at least not on a personal front. In the military, professionally, he'd had no problem with them because all the women he dealt with were subordinates, as well as patriots with one focused cause. But Cali Roland wasn't a subordinate; they were more or less equals on the project, with him having the slightest edge. Pete steeled himself. He felt like he was in the middle of a field of land mines at the moment, and Cali was one of them: lethal, explosive and dangerous.

He'd be riding with her shortly to the site. During that time, Pete hoped to get to know her a little. Maybe she was married, which would make his life a bit easier. Pete refused to get entangled with a married woman; it just wasn't his style. Cali had no ring on her left hand but that wasn't uncommon. Many hard hats never wore jewelry in the field because it could get caught in equipment and they could lose a finger, a hand or worse.

Gulping surreptitiously, Pete fought his attraction to this woman. She was trouble, all right. Why couldn't she have been unappealing? Older? Nasty? Cali was none of those.

Somehow, he was going to have to harden himself against her.

CHAPTER THREE

"Pete?" As Cali gently squeezed his broad shoulder, her fingers tingled. She moaned inwardly. Her attention to him was only getting worse, she realized in despair.

With Ahmed driving the Land Cruiser, they had just arrived at the site. The mighty Hindu Kush Mountains cast deep purple shadows across the plain where a number of mobile trailers sat. Truth be known, Cali had wanted an excuse to touch Pete. Ever since their contact earlier, at Elliot's office, Cali was fascinated by him. With his face pressed against the blanket resting against the window, his lips parted, he looked so damn vulnerable. Reaching out, Cali hesitated. She wanted to touch him again, but shouldn't. Diving once more into the fire, she squeezed his arm.

"Pete? Major? We're here. It's time to wake up." Ahead of them, in the middle seat, sat Jake Barnes, the head of security.

The ex-Special Forces leader was alertly looking around out of habit.

Cali's voice was like a soft spring breeze through Pete's drugged senses. Though barely conscious, he was vividly aware of her long fingers caressing his shoulder. It wasn't a sexual touch, he realized as he slowly sat up and tiredly rubbed his face. But it was sensual as hell. Delicious. Cali had a quiet strength to her, he was discovering, much to his unhappiness. She was confident in a rare way that was a real draw for him. She was something special.

Wiping his eyes, he yawned and tried to shake himself awake. He'd slept three of the four hours they'd spent traveling the rutted dirt road they called a highway in Afghanistan. So much for getting to know Cali Roland, Pete thought. And yet a part of him was glad he was so tired, because he couldn't feel that pull toward her when he was sound asleep.

"Here," Cali said curtly, "hot coffee. Black. You need it. Jet lag is hell, isn't it?"

"It nailed me. Thanks." Pete dropped his hands from his face and took the cup. Cali was all business. *Good.* That's what he needed. Giving her a crooked smile, he mumbled, "I was planning on spending this time getting to know you better. I didn't mean to go to sleep. You're already proving indispensable." As he lifted the cup to his lips, the fragrant Afghan coffee filled his nostrils. The strong taste of it woke him up.

Cali felt heat rushing into her face as she poured herself some coffee. Why the hell did he have to give her that boyish smile? It warmed her wounded heart. Now if only she could see Pete as a virus, something truly harmful to her system. But she couldn't. As the seconds ticked by, it became more and more evident that the major was a decent guy. "Oh, I'm sure there will be times my face is the last thing you'll want to see," she countered brusquely. "I won't be offering you coffee, just problems." She gave him a long, searching look, as if throwing down a gauntlet between them.

The Toyota slowed as they approached the first terra-cotta-colored trailer. On the side was a sign that said Site Construction Superintendent. This would be Pete's home for the next two years. One end of the trailer was his sleeping quarters, the other end his office. In addition to being the color of the desert, the trailers were spaced well apart so that if the Taliban got close enough to launch a mortar attack, they couldn't strike all of them at once.

Pete knew from experience that Taliban

members often hid among non-Taliban villagers. Some communities were all Taliban, but they had been disbanded or cleansed in the last few years by the democratic Afghan government and sheiks. Most villages, though, had some members left, fanatical men who had gone deep underground, working as moles and agitators.

While Taliban members blended into village life by day, at night they gathered in secret places, planned their attacks and did damage under cover of darkness. At dawn, they melted back into the fabric of daily life, once more invisible. The shoemaker by day became a grenade launcher at night. The local baker might sell bread in the plaza, but after dark he was setting out land mines. A farmer in the fields turned into an explosives expert after sunset, placing IEDs — improvised explosive devices — along well-traveled routes where American military drove their Humvees. Knowing that, Pete sensed that this project would have to rely on the local anti-Taliban warlord to help scout out the safest workers to hire.

Sipping the hot drink, Pete smiled briefly. "Thanks for the coffee, I needed it." *Don't be too nice to her. Stay at arm's length. Be professional.* Wiping the smile from his face, he took another sip and nearly burned his tongue. Somehow, he had to divert his thundering heart and focus on impersonal things. He looked around at his new home. Cali sipped her coffee as the Land Cruiser came to a halt. She wanted so much to make Major Trayhern realize she could do the job without any problems. That she had moved beyond her unfortunate past. Her instincts told her he didn't know about it, and if so, there was a good chance he might never know. Her foremen would certainly never tell him.

Ahmed turned around and said, "Major Trayhern, we are here. This is your trailer."

Pete studied the long, prefabricated structure. Windows, two doors, two sets of wooden steps . . . Not fancy, but functional. Fancy didn't exist on a construction site. Frowning, he gazed around the flat, pebbled plain, now in shadow. There was scraggly vegetation here and there, lots of brownish-red dirt and millions of stones of all sizes, shapes and colors. "Where's the security fence?"

Cali stirred uncomfortably. "It's on its way. I'm having it flown in by commercial jet to Kabul."

Pete didn't like the idea that ten trailers sat out on this plain without any cyclone fence or razor wire, to discourage Taliban intrusion. He knew from top-secret reports that terrorists were still very active in this province despite Sheik Hesam, who held power and wanted the fanatics eradicated. Glancing to his right, Pete saw the rugged Kush Mountains, part of the towering chain of Himalayas. Their white-capped peaks soared over fourteen thousand feet, their formidable slopes covered in creeping shadows as the sun set behind them. According to his intelligence reports, that was where the Taliban hid: in caves of those mountains. They could easily ride by horseback down into this wide, open valley and attack.

Cali saw Pete's brow scrunch as he finished his cursory inspection of the site. It was her responsibility to get that fence up and provide adequate ongoing security. Knowing he didn't want excuses, she added, "I've already talked to Barnes, here, and his mercenary team will be pulling 24-7 security around the trailers until I can get that fence up and in place."

"Yes, sir," Barnes said, turning around in the seat. "We've got horses from a nearby village and we'll be riding around the trailers during the night." He hooked his thumb at two pickups following the Land Cruiser. His team of men, all ex-American military, were to be Pete's personal protection.

Giving Cali a glance, Pete said, "When is that fencing going to be here?" He didn't like utilizing his personal security team on this for too long. There weren't enough men for the job, and they'd eventually get tired of pulling long hours of duty. That's when terrorists would take advantage of the situation.

"Tomorrow at 1300," Cali said.

"Why wasn't this security fence up when the trailers arrived?" he demanded, noting how her features hardened ever so slightly at his brusque tone.

"I don't want to offer you excuses, Pete, but it's late in arriving." This was the man she wanted to deal with — the hard-nosed engineer.

"Let me decide if it's an excuse or not, Cali. What happened to the shipment?"

Cali said tersely, "We ordered the eight-foot-high cyclone fence material and concertina razor wire for the top. The commercial plane bringing it in had engine trouble and was diverted to Kuwait. We off-loaded our material, putting it on a second commercial flight that made it to Kandahar. The material was stolen out of the warehouse there before I could hire guards. The trailers, however, arrived by transport, and we got them here on time." Cali shrugged. "So now a third flight, which is on time, will arrive in Kabul tonight with new fencing material. I'm having my own security detail meet the plane at the airport. We'll put the material on waiting trucks and get them out here by no later than tomorrow afternoon."

Nodding, Pete finished off his coffee and handed the cup back to her. "I'm not happy about this. Real life happens on a job site, and I know that. But next time, let me know the details sooner." He saw her green eyes flare with frustration, then she quickly hid the reaction. His heart pounded briefly. Damn, but she was desirable. *Not now, Trayhern. Not ever.* He opened the door. "We're going to have problems all the time, and we need to pull together to solve them. I don't want to be left out of the loop."

Cali nodded. "No disagreement." Damn, Pete was excruciatingly good-looking even when he was scowling at her. Trying to recover, she said briskly, "I've worked with the good, the bad and the ugly when it comes to owners on a project. I didn't want you to think Roland was unconcerned about security. And I don't want to get off on the wrong foot with you." Not after her last project. Cali couldn't afford that. One mistake was all she got, or her career would go up in flames.

"You haven't," Pete said over his shoulder. "Let's go look at my digs, shall we?" The sooner he left her company, the sooner he'd be able to breathe. Maybe his heart would settle down then. His head knew the dangers of desiring this woman. On all levels. Pete was going to stay unreachable. It was the only way to survive two years with her. Surely, Cali had to be married. That would stop him in his tracks. How badly he wanted to ask if she was, yet to do so would be completely inappropriate.

Cali was more than willing to get out of the Land Cruiser after four hours on a bumpy dirt road less than four feet away from Trayhern. He was like a magnet to her vulnerable heart. Feeling disgruntled, she capped the thermos, pushed it into her backpack and got out. Barnes instantly followed, as did Ahmed, who triumphantly held out keys to Pete's trailer.

"Allow me, Major," he said with a flourish as he mounted the steps. The man made a dramatic fuss about opening the door and stepping aside so Pete could enter. As he did, Ahmed handed Pete the keys to his new home and office.

His boots thunking hollowly on the three

wooden steps, Pete automatically noted the construction of the stairs and enclosed porch. Roland was responsible for everything on-site, and that included little things like the setup of each preassembled mobile home that had been constructed to specifications in the U.S.A. and shipped here for use. The wood was thick, a number of sturdy nails had been driven into the planks, and on the whole, the entire structure was solid, not wobbly or made of cheap materials.

Pleased that it appeared Cali Roland's company wasn't skimping, Pete smiled and stepped through the door — and halted in surprise for a moment as he gazed into the trailer. Then he turned. Cali was standing behind him, an unreadable expression on her face. Was it a mask she wore? What was it hiding? Pete didn't know and had no business trying to find out.

"Looks like the Taj Mahal in here," he told her.

"You're the king, Major Trayhern. I figured you'd need a palace of sorts out here in the middle of nowhere. Like it?" Cali could see a ruddy color flow into Pete's cheeks. He had a five o'clock beard that made him look slightly dangerous, in an attractive way. His delicious mouth crooked

60

into that little-boy smile, and her pulse accelerated accordingly.

"Not bad," Pete murmured, cleaning his boots before he stepped inside. The trailer was pleasantly warm, and he moved aside to allow Cali to enter.

She shut the door. "Well? Does it meet your expectations?" Her gaze ranged around the room. She had had her office do some homework on Major Trayhern. She knew he'd grown up in the rugged mountains of Montana, so she'd had the trailer office decked out with a wooden table and rolltop desk. It was definitely a man's place, not a woman's. Cali knew from experience that men didn't want frills out in the field. But she also knew they missed their home. On the rear wall of the office was a large picture of a creek flowing through a mountain meadow full of spring wildflowers.

Pete stepped into the living area at the other end of the trailer. It was state-of-the-art, with a two-burner stove, microwave and small refrigerator. Everything worked. That meant Cali had brought up gasoline generators to supply power for the complex. Running his hand across the white drain board, he eyed the square aluminum sink, dish drainer, towels, small dishwasher and plenty of cabinets. "I'm impressed," he told her, twisting to look over his shoulder.

Cali stood with her hands on her hips, her mouth pursed and a rock-solid confidence radiating from her. She had the most alluring green eyes, and Pete found himself wanting to stare into them. But their relationship had to remain businesslike.

"Roland has a good name around the world, and I intend to hear only praise coming from your lips about working with us on this project." She tried to ignore that pleased glint in his eyes. He did like his trailer, and that made her euphoric.

"I appreciate that." Pete nodded. "I like all the pictures. They remind me of home," he confided.

"I thought they would." Cali followed at a respectful distance, as he explored the living area.

"That means that you did a little research on me," he said, running his hand along the wood-paneled wall. Roland Construction obviously paid attention to details. In other construction projects, the low bidder had given him trailers that were nothing but shells, filled with old, dilapidated furniture.

Cali followed him into the adjoining sleeping area. She'd personally picked out the conservative rust-red, autumn-gold and burnished-orange print for the practical cotton bedspread. To add to his comforts, Cali had hired a widow from a nearby village to clean Pete's trailer on a weekly basis. The woman had been taught how to use the washer and dryer in the trailer for his laundry. The curtains, bedspread, sheets and other linens were all washable, and nothing required ironing.

"This is nice," Pete murmured, liking the dark brown curtains hanging in the two windows. He caught himself. Would he be saying this to a male? No. Scowling, he added, "It will do." The middle panels were white lace, which lightened the place considerably.

A personal computer for his private use sat on a built-in desk in one corner, and a solid, blond-wood storage cabinet with a lockbox stood by the bed.

"I know we have the best security, but you need a safe for your important papers."

Pete didn't argue. "Vigilance pays off."

"Every time," Cali agreed grimly. She'd learned from experience, long ago, to install safes that couldn't be moved by enterprising thieves.

"I see a TV," Pete stated. "That seems out of place."

"Television doesn't work out here," Cali said, pointing to the small set on one of the cabinets opposite his bed. "I'm working on getting you a satellite feed. It has taken me three weeks to get the paperwork through channels in Kabul, something I thought would go a lot faster than it has. There's a drawerful of the latest DVDs." She pointed toward the cabinet. "I think that will keep you out of trouble and sate your appetite for a while. Satellite hookup should be another two weeks if we're lucky, I'm told."

Turning, Pete tried to remain immune to her presence, which was like sunlight shining through dark clouds. Cali's short red hair was slightly mussed by the breeze crossing the Afghan plain. There was a challenging glint in her eyes. His gaze fell to her full mouth. "You've thought of everything." What did she look like when she really smiled out of pure joy? *Don't go there, Trayhern. That's dangerous country, pardner. You should know that by now. . . .*

Feeling heat moving within her, Cali tried to cover her surprise over the intimate, burning look Pete sent her. Just as quickly, it vanished. The man was a woman magnet — no doubt about that! Accordingly, she moved away and walked quickly down the hall toward the central workroom.

"I hope so," she responded. "I already have a site radio and satellite phone installed. All four computers, office and personal, in the trailer are hooked up to a special satellite connection so you can e-mail Kabul about business, and in your spare time, your friends around the world. The commercial feeds aren't installed yet, but will be soon."

Cali felt Pete behind her, the pleasant hollow sound of his boots oddly comforting. Fighting her responses, she kept an even tone in her voice. "You can continue to talk to the outside world." She turned and motioned to the large counter. Beneath it the project drawings hung from racks, ready for use. "Last but not least, the rest of your workstation."

Pete halted near the entrance to the work area. He really liked the quarters. The main space included two desks, several built-in file cabinets and a framed print of a massive grizzly bear catching fish in a mountain river. Cali had done her homework, and that signaled that she planned to start off on the right foot on this multimillion-dollar project.

"I know Muslims don't abide alcohol," Cali told him, "but I took a chance that you were probably a wine drinker. Below the desk in your quarters, under lock and key, is a pretty good selection of California wines." Right now, she could use a drink to anesthetize herself against this man's charms.

"Good guess! And thank you. I do prefer wine over hard liquor." How much did Cali really know about him? Pete wondered. How deeply had her company dug into his background? It made him feel slightly uncomfortable. Did Cali know about his messy relationships? He hoped not. It was hard enough for him to deal with, much less have an outsider privy to his debacles.

"Roland Construction makes it a policy to know who we're working with," she said with a shrug. "We like to start off positively by letting an owner know we value the relationship. We're a team." Cali held out the keys to the safe and the wine cabinet. Although she wanted to touch him again, she dropped them into his calloused palm instead.

"Sounds hopeful," Pete said, depositing the keys in his pocket. "To some construction companies I was always the bad guy." He saw her relax slightly, resting her long fingers on her curvy hips. The only thing marring the sensual picture was the 9 mm Beretta and holster strapped around her left thigh. A beautifully long and curved thigh, at that. She was a modern Annie Oakley, and Pete was sure she could handle that weapon with ease. The fact that they were in a dangerous part of the world made him frown. The idea of Cali being shot or killed made his gut clench. Stymied by that feeling, Pete shoved it aside. If she were a man, he wouldn't give it a second thought. But she was a woman. Somehow, he had to keep that from getting in the way.

"Roland Construction has a different philosophy," Cali informed him, walking back to the door of the trailer. "We see ourselves as a two-horse team. We want to go the same direction — together — not at cross purposes with one another."

Pete nodded. He saw her implacable look become even more unreadable, if that was possible. She wasn't easy to plumb at all. Maybe, as a woman in a man's world, Cali Roland had learned not to broadcast her feelings. "Thanks for the thoughtful touches."

"You're welcome. You'll find the pantry and refrigerator well stocked with food." Cali added, "There's a village less than a mile from here. I hired an older widow who is willing to come out and clean your trailer weekly, plus cook you two square meals a day. That okay with you? Or maybe you're the kind of guy that likes to do housework?"

"Construction types don't do well at that," Pete stated, wanting to get right down to work. The whole day had been turned upside down, and he felt unprepared to deal with a woman at his site. A beautiful woman.

"How about cooking?" Cali asked a touch impatiently, wanting to get the hell out of his trailer and away from him. Being in close proximity with Pete Trayhern was like holding her hand over an open flame.

"I'm pretty good at that, so I think if this lady comes over once a week to clean up, dust and wash my clothes, that will be fine. I can rustle up grub to feed myself."

"Got it," Cali said, with a nod of her head. Looking at her watch, she said, "It's nearly 1700, and the day is done. I'm going to have security set up, and then I'm retiring to my digs, which is about four hundred feet in that direction." She pointed north.

"Good. How about radios?" All of a sudden, Pete didn't want Cali to leave. He wanted to ask her personal questions and get on a more intimate footing. All of that, of course, was folly.

"Radios and chargers for the site are in your bedroom quarters next to your personal computer. I think you'll find everything you need in there. Barnes will be on the same frequency as us. If any bandits think they can steal things out of the work trailers or from us, they won't get far." She gave a wolfish grin.

"I can tell you've done this before," Pete said. Her smile of bold self-assurance made him desire her even more. Never having met a woman quite like Cali, Pete thought his response was precisely because of that: how refreshing she was. Damning his curiosity, he dragged in a ragged breath.

Opening the door, Cali said, "A few times. I'll meet you at the main project trailer tomorrow at 0800. Ahmed will come and drive you over there."

"Sounds good." Pete lifted his hand in farewell.

Cali went down the steps without a word. She hurried to the Toyota and got in without a backward glance. Maybe that was a good sign — that she wasn't drawn to him.

Turning around, Pete closed the door and headed for the kitchen. There was a coffee-maker, he'd noticed, and he wanted a hot, strong brew. Still, as he puttered around his new kitchen, his mind and heart kept straying to the green-eyed, gun-toting Cali Roland.

She was one hell of a woman in a decidedly man's world. And they were going to be working together in very dangerous circumstances. Pete didn't like the physical danger. But the real jeopardy would be learning how to work with Cali without getting involved on a personal level. And yet involvement seemed inevitable. It was just a question of when . . . and how badly it would hurt in the end.

CHAPTER FOUR

Crack! Crack! Crack!

Cali was in a deep, early morning sleep when rifles fired loudly near her trailer. Automatically, she rolled out of bed, her hand moving to the bed stand to grab her Beretta.

She jerked on her jeans and thrust her feet in a pair of oxfords, as more gunfire erupted outside. She heard the screams and shouts of men, the thundering of horse hooves. *Bandits? Taliban?* She wasn't sure, but quickly threw on a coat over her silk pajama top. Within a minute, she was dressed and running down the hall of her trailer, radio in hand. She left the lights off for safety.

"Barnes! Report!" she snapped, unlocking the door with shaking hands.

The sky was clear, the stars so close Cali felt as if she could reach out and touch them. Dawn, a thin purple line, was just outlining the jagged hills to the east. After leaping off the stairs, she ran around the corner of her trailer toward the commotion.

More gunfire. A geyser of dirt spewed up in front of her, and Cali lunged for the ground. Heart thudding heavily, she watched as dust rose around her. She could barely make out a group of riders about a quarter of a mile away. Barnes and his team were firing repeatedly, with cool precision.

"Bandits," Barnes growled into the radio.

"Roger. Under control?" Cali scrambled from the dirt and sprinted toward the men flattened on the earth ahead of her.

"Roger," he answered. "Wounded two, I think. They're hightailin' it now. Fun's over."

Grimacing, Cali raced up as the men slowly got off their bellies to their feet. The three of them had state-of-the-art night goggles and infrared night scopes on their rifles. Cali couldn't see so well, but she could hear the thundering beat of horses retreating to the south. She gasped for breath, hand pressed to her chest. It felt as if her heart was going to explode with the fear and shock. Cali hadn't expected an attack.

Glancing down at the luminous dials on her watch, she saw it was 0400. Daylight would come soon. Breathing hard, her heart still pounding, she halted in front of Barnes, who was coolly dropping an empty magazine and slamming a new one into his rifle.

"Everyone okay?" Cali demanded, her voice husky with adrenaline.

"Yes, ma'am," he said, pushing the night goggles to the top of his head. "Everyone's fine. No wounds."

Cali heard the thud of heavy footsteps behind her. Twisting, she saw Major Trayhern barreling out of the darkness. He had a pistol in hand, and unlike her, he'd had the smarts to put on his flak jacket.

"What's going on?" he demanded, sliding to a halt in front of the group.

"Bandits, Major," Barnes drawled. "They were just snooping around and testing us. They probably wanted to see if we had security out here." Chuckling darkly, he looked at his comrades — Bobby Mills, who was thirty years old, and Gabe Willis, a year younger. Both had served with him in the Corps and were sniper trained. "I think we shocked the shit out of 'em," Barnes said, laughing softly.

"We saw them approaching from the south," Mills told Pete and Cali. "We waited until they got close enough for us to put bullets in front of their horses."

"Yeah, there were about fifteen of 'em," Gabe said, his soft Kentucky drawl belying his tension.

"Any casualties?" Pete demanded, looking to the south. The darkness had swallowed up the bandits. The plain was quiet once more, and it was colder than hell out here, almost freezing, he realized. Worriedly, he looked at Cali, whose face was etched by shadows in the grayish light. Her hair was mussed, her eyes narrowed and her mouth set. Noticing she wore a quilted jacket, he asked, "You got your flak vest on under that thing?"

"No, I don't. I forgot to have it hanging on the back of a chair near my bed. Next time," she told him brusquely. Even in starlight, Cali could see Pete's reaction. Did she see concern burning in those slitted eyes? Or anger? She wasn't sure about anything except the adrenaline making her heart hammer.

"You could have been hurt," he said, his voice heavy with warning. "You know better, Ms. Roland. This isn't the only third world country you've worked in."

Ms. Roland. He'd called her Cali before. Yeah, he was pissed, all right. "Save your scolding for another time, Major. I'm fine." She glared at him, furious that he would dress her down like a child in front of her security team. And she wasn't about to tell him about the bullet that had nearly hit her.

"Things will get easier once that fence is in place," Barnes said soothingly, running a clean cloth down the stock of his rifle. "That was just an advance team to see if we had security. So don't get uptight just yet, Major. This kind of thing will go on all the time out here, so you might as well get used to it."

Cali saw Pete scowl at Barnes, his mouth thinning. Then he glanced around the darkened plain. "Okay, let's get back to our trailers. Barnes, we'll review security later today. We may need more hardware. You did good under the circumstances."

"Yes, sir."

Cali turned and walked away, fuming, her pistol in her hand. She wasn't wearing her holster, either. Was Trayhern going to dress her down for that little infraction, too? Halfway back to her trailer, she heard someone jogging after her. Trayhern, probably to give her a lecture on desert safety. The sky was brightening above the mountains, and she could see his facial features a little more clearly. He looked concerned.

Pulling up next to her, he murmured, "I shouldn't have chewed you out like that in front of the security team."

"They work for me, Major. I'm number two person at this site." Her nostrils flared. Cali glared and she glowered at him as they walked on across the desert. "Next time you have anything to say to me in the way of criticism or critique, we do it in private, not in front of my employees. Got it?"

"It won't happen again." Okay, so he had that coming. Jet lag combined with the unexpected attack and deluge of adrenaline through his groggy system had made Pete forget himself for a moment.

Cali bridled beneath his stubborn look. He said the words, but she could tell he wasn't sure about it. Trayhern was infuriating! She halted at the corner of her trailer. "Midday, the fencing material arrives here at the site. In the meantime, I'm going to introduce myself to the regional warlord, Sheik Baider Hesam. He's got a small place in a village less than a mile from here." Cali pointed northeast. "I need workmen, and that is my priority for today. I can't hire anyone without Hesam's blessing."

"When are you going to see him?" Pete saw the banked anger in Cali's narrowed eyes. As a manager of people, he knew better than to have handled the situation with her as he had. And if he'd thought she was going to be soft because she was a woman, he could see that wasn't true.

"Sooner rather than later. I'm going to have my driver, Hakim, take me over at 0800. I'm taking my general foreman, Ray Billings, with me, as well."

"I'd like to go with you." Pete saw surprise flare in her eyes, quickly replaced with irritation.

"If you want to join me, we'll pick you up five minutes earlier at your trailer."

Nodding, Pete said, "Sounds good. How many men do you think we'll need to install the fence?"

"We've got several miles of fencing to erect, Major. Even though it'll happen in stages, we'll need a large crew initially, a smaller crew for long-term modifications and additions."

Ouch. Okay, it was no longer "Pete," but "Major." Well, he'd burned a bridge with Cali, hadn't he? The woman was as hard as the granite slopes of the Hindu Kush. He had no one but himself to blame for her tough facade and detachment from him now.

"I'll bring my interpreter with me."

"I'll pick Ahmed up at his trailer," Cali said.

"Thanks. In southern Afghanistan, we

always brought gifts to the head men when we paid an official visit." Pete sought her opinion, hoping to defuse some of her anger toward him. "Do you know what's appropriate up here?"

Cali softened toward him, seeing he was scrambling. "My company did some research on this sheik. He likes the Wild West of America. I'm taking him a Comanche war ax from the mid-1880s as a gift."

Pete nodded. "Good idea. I don't have anything to give him."

"Then tell him you have a gift on its way. You can figure out what he'd like and get it here pronto. Hesam enjoys surprises. Good ones, that is."

"Okay, thanks for the advice. I'll e-mail my father and see what he can scrounge up for me." Knowing there was nothing else he could do, Pete said, "I'll see you at 0800."

It would be too soon as far as Cali was concerned. She gave him a brisk nod, did an about-face and climbed the steps to her trailer. *Good riddance.* In college she'd been one of the few women in her class working on a civil engineering degree. When no one was looking, the male students had often tried to shame and humiliate her with sexual harassment. She never took their guff, and she wasn't about to take Trayhern's, either.

■ ■ ■ ■

The sun was bright, the cloudless sky a deep turquoise as Hakim drove the Land Cruiser toward Pai Tawa, the village where Hesam lived. Cali sat in the front seat, the map across her knees. They were like a cork on an ocean, bumbling along at twenty miles an hour over the deeply rutted dirt road. In the back seat was the major with his interpreter, and Ray, her general foreman. Although the village was less than a mile from the site, it seemed to take forever to get there. She'd sent Hakim ahead at 0600, to make sure the sheik would see them at such an early hour. Normally, business was not conducted until the midafternoon, but this couldn't wait.

Cali heard Pete talking to his interpreter. He was having him write down questions to ask the sheik. Earlier, Pete had tried to make amends to her by handing her some warm toast with butter; a breakfast gift of sorts. Surprised by his gesture, she'd eaten it. Most of the bosses she'd worked with wouldn't have been so conciliatory. Cali could forgive, but not forget. Unsure of what to think of Trayhern at this point, she wondered how the audience with the sheik would go.

"Do you have any experience with men like Hesam?" she finally asked, turning to look at him.

Pete lifted his head. "A little. We had to deal with the tribal leaders in the border region where my company was stationed. Why? Do you have suggestions?"

Good. He wanted her advice, and she was glad. Cali had been in the Middle East for many more years than he had. She eyed the well-groomed interpreter next to Pete. She didn't know why, but she just didn't trust the bearded young man. Compressing her lips, she said, "If you want, follow my actions. Once we enter Hesam's house and get to the room where he holds his audiences, you might want to introduce yourself." She glanced again at Ahmed, who was scowling at her. "Your interpreter should then take over and begin translating. Hesam knows some English, but we'd be better to speak to him in his language to ensure there are no misunderstandings. Right now, we need his blessing, his support and his men for our site."

"Sounds good to me."

Cali found herself unable to protect herself from Pete's boyish smile. A sudden vulnerability melted his outer demeanor, and she marveled at how much younger he looked. All that starch and military toughness dissolved in an instant. *This* was the man she was drawn to — that little boy with delight and impishness dancing in his eyes.

She scolded herself, reminding herself it would be a huge mistake to get personally involved with her boss. Giving him a slight, one-cornered smile, Cali turned back around. She was eager to create a working alliance with Sheik Hesam.

As Cali exited the car, she put a scarf on her head out of respect for Islamic traditions. According to her information, Hesam was pro-American, and that was good for them and the project.

"Welcome, welcome," Sheik Hesam said with a flourish. Seated against richly brocaded cushions, the leader made an impression of opulence and poise.

Ahmed, the interpreter, hurried ahead of Cali and Pete. He bowed and offered salutations in Pashto to the forty-five-year-old sheik. The translator then gestured grandly toward Pete, who had taken off his cap and left his pistol outside the room with the two sentries.

Sheik Hesam nodded deferentially to the major and motioned for him to sit to the right of him, a position of honor.

Pete was shocked and unhappy that his translator took over. Cali's advice had been correct. This was a gaffe and Pete tried to keep his irritation toward Ahmed in check. Pete touched his head and then his heart as he bowed to the warlord. Cali entered next, followed by Billings, who carried the gifts to be given to the sheik. Pete tried a bit of Pashto with Hesam, whose dark brown eyes gleamed with pleasure over the greeting.

While he went through the formalities, Pete took note of the leader's physical traits. Hesam was lean, about five foot nine inches tall. His tobacco-brown skin was weathered, with deep wrinkles around his thin mouth and broad brow. His neatly cut, black-and-gray beard emphasized his square face. The warlord wore a yellow turban, loose brown trousers, a long-sleeved white shirt that fell to midthigh and a black leather belt studded with silver and lapis lazuli cabochons.

As Pete sat down next to the powerful tribal leader, Cali waited patiently.

Pete understood that ordinarily women were not allowed in the same room with men when business was conducted. For whatever reason, Hesam didn't object to her presence. In addition to her normal construction clothing, Cali wore a dark green silk scarf that matched her eyes perfectly.

She murmured a greeting in Pashto to the sheik, who beamed in return. Her husky voice sounded lyrical, and Pete was impressed with her fluid delivery of the language.

Cali came forward and bowed deeply to Hesam. She handed him a small wooden box. "Figs from Bahrain, my lord. I hope you and your family enjoy them."

"Ahh," Hesam said, eagerly reaching for the carved box. "Figs. Thank you."

Smiling, Cali answered, "You're welcome, my lord." She turned and reached for the second gift from her foreman, Ray Billings, who had come in on her heels.

Hesam was clearly delighted when he opened the long, rectangular oak box and saw the Comanche war ax. For five minutes, Cali politely answered his many questions about the piece.

"Sit here, next to me," he finally urged her, pointing to the pillows on his left. That, too, was considered a position of honor. He asked Billings to sit to Cali's left, and treated him with equal graciousness.

Cali noticed how Ahmed positioned himself in front of the tribal warlord to translate for Pete. The damned interpreter had screwed up the entire protocol and she was furious with him. Hesam could speak English, but perhaps not so much so that they could carry on a coherent conversation. She knew Ahmed felt strongly that she, as a woman, should not be in here conducting men's business. *Tough shit.* He could glare all he wanted at her and it wasn't going to do him any good. Cali wasn't easily intimidated by such men. Besides, she'd just scored some important points with Hesam by bringing him the figs and the war ax.

In her opinion, Ahmed had not served Major Trayhern's interests at all. Pete had forgotten to tell Hesam that his gift was coming in another week or so, but the translator had bungled the important protocols in regards to this meeting. Why had Ahmed screwed her and Pete like that? Was he ignorant of local customs?

Her dark side looked at other possibilities. Did Kerwin Elliot want Major Trayhern to fail? Was giving him an inept translator a setup of some kind? If Trayhern failed, could Elliot put someone he wanted in this important post, instead? Or was Elliot's choice of Ahmed predicated solely on political connections?

Frustrated, Cali said nothing. She disliked politics, yet it was a daily part of her job.

And since she had nothing to say about the assignment of a translator for the major, she kept her mouth shut. She was in enough hot water with him right now and didn't want to bring Ahmed's inadequacies and failed protocols to his attention. Trayhern might think she was just causing trouble. Grimacing inwardly, Cali sat watching Ahmed, her lips compressed.

Hesam set down the box bearing the war ax and addressed Pete in Pashto. "I'm honored to meet you, Major Trayhern. How is your family? Are they well?"

Cali knew this dialogue was a familiar one to anyone in the Middle East. Good manners dictated that two conversants always inquire about the health of family members, first. No serious talk was ever broached until the family was discussed in adequate detail. She listened to Ahmed translate.

"The sheik welcomes you, Major Trayhern."

Pete nodded and smiled at Hesam. "Tell him, Ahmed, that I'm pleased he would see us. And thank him?"

"Of course," Ahmed murmured, then turned and rapidly spoke in Pashto.

Cali scowled as she heard him say, "The major is here on business, my lord."

What the hell was the man doing? Cali

almost interrupted. Seeing Hesam frown and stroke his goatee, she felt her gut clench. Not following correct protocol was a huge faux pas. Should she say anything? Maybe Ahmed was just nervous.

Staring at the profile of the young man, she got an uneasy feeling once more, and she wasn't one to ignore her instincts. Kerwin Elliot had said Ahmed was one of the best translators, so this didn't make any sense at all.

The door opened, and they all looked up.

"Ah, my wife, Ladan, Major," Hesam said as a slender woman dressed in a flowing gray gown with a gold-and-red sash around her waist entered.

Ahmed translated, "It is his wife. She brings us sweetmeats and coffee. That is all a woman is good for. Servant duties."

Cali glared and bit back a retort. If Ladan knew English, she didn't indicate she'd heard Ahmed's scathing remark. Hesam's wife was the epitome of hospitality. The major stared at Ahmed, opened his mouth and shut it. Obviously from where Cali sat, she could see the Marine didn't like Ahmed's statement. Hesam, too, scowled momentarily and then replaced the look with a private one. Ahmed's crack was an insult, pure and simple, and he could ruin their budding relationship with one remark. *Damn.* Ladan had an oval face and light brown eyes that flashed in welcome. Her black hair was tastefully woven in a single braid down her back.

After his derogatory comment, Ahmed stared at Hesam's wife as she brought in a shiny brass tray filled with delicacies. Behind her, two younger women carried smaller trays.

"And, Major, my two very beautiful daughters, Kimiya and Haleh," the sheik announced with pride and a welcoming smile.

"These two are the daughters," Ahmed said, his voice full of distaste.

Cali moved restlessly, anxiously watching what unfolded. The girls, both tall and slender, had dark brown hair and lively, sparkling sable eyes. One wore a blue gown and the other a pink one. When Pete got to his feet, out of deference to them, the sheik looked puzzled. Ahmed said nothing.

"Uhh, you don't need to stand up," Cali murmured to Pete. "Just sit there. Hesam's wife and daughters will give you first choice of the food, but you should turn it down and ask her to serve Hesam. That's protocol."

Ahmed glared at Cali, and she glared right

back. She'd be damned if Pete would be led into another rude and awkward situation, where Hesam could get really pissed off and throw them out because of continued botched protocols. He was a man of great power and didn't suffer fools gladly.

As if sensing his faux pas, Pete quickly sat down. The sheik's wife smiled graciously at him and knelt before him with the tray of dates, figs, yogurt and freshly fried goat meat.

Pete held up his hand and smiled. "Thank you, Mrs. Hesam, but please serve your husband first." He gestured toward their host, who sat proudly.

The woman bowed, murmured something in Pashto and rose. She then approached her husband with the tray. He smiled up at her and took some dates and figs.

"Please serve our honored guests, my beautiful wife."

"Of course I will, my love."

As if translating, Ahmed said, "You will take only a very small portion, Major. No one likes pigs."

Cali nearly choked. When Hesam frowned momentarily, she wondered if the sheik had understood the spoken English. Ahmed had just insulted his boss, but Pete didn't realize that wasn't what Hesam had said.

Nodding deferentially, Pete took the same amount of food as the sheik, no more and no less. "Thank you, Mrs. Hesam. These look delicious."

"You do not accord women any rights," Ahmed said in a frustrated tone.

"What are you talking about? This is his wife. Why shouldn't I be gracious and respectful toward her?" Pete demanded, completely irritated. Had Hesam called him a pig? Pete was unsure. He saw Cali react when Ahmed had used the word. Tense, Pete felt vulnerable. He wanted to ask Cali, but couldn't afford to shame his translator in front of the sheik.

Ahmed scowled and said nothing.

"The daughters will approach with a tray of coffee and cups," Cali murmured. "They will set it down in front of the sheik. They will offer you the first cup, but you should instruct them to give it to the sheik."

Pete did as advised and Hesam thanked him for his generosity. After his two smiling, giggling daughters served their father, they served Pete, Cali, Ray and, lastly, the frowning Ahmed. Then all three women left, leaving the trays within easy reach of everyone.

The fragrance of burta, a dish of crushed eggplant blended with yogurt, garlic, mint, cilantro, olive oil and lemon juice, filled the air. Warm flat bread was served with it. Cali inhaled the scents of fresh spices. She waited until the sheik had filled his silver plate with the appetizer before she filled her own. Ahmed glared at her again, but she ignored him.

"So," Hesam said after they had finished the social pleasantries, "what brings you here, Major Trayhern?"

Cali listened closely to Ahmed's translation. "Major, the sheik wants to know why you are here."

Pete wiped his fingers on the red linen napkin draped across his left thigh. "Please tell the sheik that we've come to ask for his help."

The conversation that followed was a flowery, long-winded one to Cali. The major would speak a couple of sentences and Ahmed would translate. The sheik would ask questions, and the process would reverse. Pete got into the who, what, where, why and how. He asked for Hesam's help in providing labor for the site.

Cali wiped her mouth and watched out of the corner of her eye for Hesam's reaction. She'd worked with tribal sheiks before. Some were arrogant about their power and family connections. Few were greedy, but some were. Most were fair-minded and had been raised from birth to be leaders of their province or clan. Where would Hesam fall?

"Major, do you ride camels?"

Ahmed scowled. "The sheik wants to know if you ride camels."

Pete grinned and shook his head. "No, sir, I don't. Why?"

Instead of translating correctly, Ahmed said, "He hates the smelly, hairy beasts, my lord."

Cali coughed. Hesam poured more coffee into the cup near her knee and offered it to her in response.

Thanking him, she sipped the thick, fragrant brew. She quirked her mouth and glanced at Ahmed, who looked back at her with hatred in his eyes. "My lord," she said in Pashto, "for whatever reason, the translator is not sharing the major's exact words with you. He said he's never ridden a camel. He did not call them smelly, hairy beasts." She held Ahmed's dark, narrow eyes. The man looked as if he wanted to strangle her.

"Ah, good, good." Hesam smiled benevolently at Pete, then turned and scowled at Ahmed. "You will tell the major that I invite him to ride with me tomorrow afternoon to see my herd of racing camels." He turned to Cali and smiled. "And you, my dear, are also invited."

Cali nodded. "I'd love to ride with you, my lord. Thank you for the honor."

Ahmed turned and muttered the English version to the major.

Pete grinned. "Well, I've never ridden a camel, sir, but I'd sure like to try. It sounds like fun. Thanks."

Cali watched as Ahmed accurately translated that message to the warlord.

"Good, good," Hesam said, rising. "I must go, but I invite you to remain, eat, drink and then leave when you feel like it. I have pressing obligations, and we can talk tomorrow as we ride to see my racing camels. Farewell." He shook each of their hands before he left.

Cali waited until Ahmed left Pete's trailer. A white Roland pickup truck, driven by Hakim, would take the translator to the trailer he shared with three other Afghan workers.

"May I come in for a minute, Major?" she asked.

Pete stood at the top of the stairs. "Sure, come on in."

"Thanks." Cali climbed up the steps, wiping her dusty boots before entering. She closed the door behind her and followed

Pete as he ambled to the kitchen.

"Listen, I may be way out of line here, Major, but I need to say something."

He frowned. "Of course. What is it?"

"I don't know what's going on with Ahmed, but he's not translating accurately. He nearly got you in hot water with the sheik and you didn't even know it." Cali watched as Pete poured a glass of water and drank it. He offered her some, but she declined.

"Okay," he said, "let's talk about this in the living room."

Cali sat down on the couch, her hands clasped between her legs as she leaned forward. Pete sat at the table. "Kerwin Elliot told you I know Pashto, Arabic and a number of other local languages, Major Trayhern. You can't run a construction site too long and not learn the languages."

"You spoke beautifully to the sheik when you entered the audience room." Pete saw her cheeks grow pink at the compliment. Cali was captivating. And he savagely reminded himself she was completely off-limits.

"Thanks. What I need to say is probably going to upset you, but your translator made you sound like an eighth grader to the sheik. Also, he left you high and dry regarding common, expected protocols." Cali launched into a recital of Ahmed's many mistakes. She saw Pete's eyes narrow, his expression grow thoughtful as she finished.

"Ahmed seems pretty intense. And I saw him glare in your direction a number of times," Pete admitted. "I wondered why he was angry at you."

"Because I'm a woman in a man's world, and around here, women don't do business with men. But Hesam knows I'm number two person on this project, and he's smart enough to let this law go and deal directly with me."

"Did you have similar problems in Saudi Arabia?"

"Yes, I did. Some tribal chiefs were more openminded about this than others. In the end, they all realized I held the purse strings, and if they wanted money to help their villagers, it was through me. So they relaxed the rules and we all got along just fine."

"Money is a language that talks to everyone and doesn't need translation," Pete murmured.

"You got that right. But tribal sheiks also have an obligation to their people, and they want to see them prosper. A happy village automatically increases loyalty to the sheik and his clan affiliations. Most chiefs are very political and have been trained to lead since they were children. They know they're responsible for the happiness of their people."

"So why do you think Ahmed translated so badly? I wasn't happy when he inferred I was a pig, either."

Shrugging, Cali said, "I don't know. And I'd bet money Hesam understood Ahmed's English to you about pigs. Hesam looked shocked at first, then angry and then I saw him cover up his reactions. You don't call anyone a pig or infer you might be one. Ahmed was way out of line insulting you like that. Elliot swears by him. Maybe Ahmed was just pissed off that you allowed a woman in there to talk business with Hesam and you." She didn't want to share her darker thoughts, since she knew she could be wrong.

"Well, that isn't going to wash." Pete studied her across the room. The morning sunlight slipped between the venetian blinds, highlighting Cali's red hair. "Since you know Pashto, can I borrow your services tomorrow on our camel jaunt? I'll leave Ahmed here, at the site. I can't afford another screwup with Hesam."

"No, you can't. Our whole project begins

and ends with this sheik. I'll be happy to translate for you. But you eventually have to get another translator. I can't do this for you full-time because I'll have my hands full with my crews. I can't spare any time to help you, too."

"Understood," Pete said. "I'll talk to Hesam about this. Maybe he has a man in his village who knows English."

"Not many know English out here, Major. But maybe you'll get lucky. Or maybe Ahmed was just having a bad day."

"We'll see. . . ." Pete said, and quirked his mouth. "For whatever reasons, Ahmed isn't going to work out. I wish I knew what his motivation was in behaving the way he did."

At that moment, Pete Trayhern looked vulnerable, and Cali found her heart opening toward him. "Don't worry, I have a box of delicious dates from Qatar you can give Hesam for tomorrow's meeting. Every time we are invited to his home, we must bring a gift. It's expected and keeps good relations. I think he's wise enough to realize Ahmed wasn't doing you any favors today. Maybe he'll forgive this one oversight."

"Here's hoping. And I forgot to tell the sheik that my official gift will be coming soon. I was nervous and forgot, but I'll mention it to him tomorrow."

Cali managed a small, optimistic smile. "Roland does background checking on all the major players, so how about if I lend you our file on Hesam today? You study it, and by tomorrow, you'll have a better understanding of him and where he stands."

"I'd appreciate it. You know, you're turning out to be indispensable, Ms. Roland."

"Roland Construction likes to make the owner comfortable, and part of the team," she answered blithely. Then she felt her heart flutter when Pete sent her a dark, intense glance. It was the look a man sent his woman, not one a businessman sent his prime contractor. Swallowing hard, Cali stood. "I gotta run. I'm going to be up half the night making sure that fence is started, using local Afghan workers."

"Okay." Cali's next responsibility was the fence, and Pete knew it. "I'll pop out every now and again to see how it's coming." That was the owner's job: to make sure things got done.

Brushing past him, Cali said, "I'd expect that." She lifted her hand. "See you later?"

Cali hated to admit it, but Pete was easy on the eyes. It was so delicious, being able to absorb his handsome, craggy features without him knowing the pleasure it gave her. And that's what it had to remain: her secret.

"You will. Send over that file on the sheik?"

"I'll get Hakim to bring it over, plus the box of dates."

After Cali left, Pete went to his office. He had a ton of paperwork to go through, plus his iridium satellite phone was blinking, meaning he had calls to answer. Yet as his mind went into work mode, he couldn't erase the excitement he felt over going camel riding with Cali tomorrow afternoon. He enjoyed her company a lot more than he should.

Remembering his past, he tried to push his hope aside. Pain and loss were not things he wanted to duplicate.

CHAPTER FIVE

"I'm glad you didn't allow Ahmed to come along," Cali confided to Pete the next morning as they drove to Sheik Hesam's village.

"He wasn't happy about staying behind." As he drove, Pete glanced briefly at her. When he woke that morning, he'd looked forward to seeing her. He tried not to like Cali, especially since he often fell for women who betrayed him.

"I'll bet his pride is hurt," she said.

"I told him I knew just enough Pashto to get by today. I have a call in to Kerwin Elliot about his credentials." Pete slowed to maneuver the Land Cruiser through some deep ruts in the dirt road. Sparse vegetation dotted the landscape, and in the distance, he saw a boy with a large herd of sheep foraging for grass or weeds. The youth smiled and waved. Pete waved back. The Afghans were a friendly people, he'd found out during his military tour. Most were hardworking, responsible and had a deep love of the land.

"I think you were right to call Elliot to see what's going on." Cali felt this was a safe statement, even though she wanted to say far more. She couldn't tell him what to do about his less-than-glorious translator. Politics always played a role in what was going on. Ahmed might be from an influential family that had ties to Kerwin Elliot.

"I'll let you know the outcome." Pete saw the worry in her green eyes, The fine lines in her forehead, partially hidden by those strands of red hair were evident. Even under duress, Cali was gorgeous. She had dressed casually in jeans, a blouse and work boots, but her small pearl earrings told the world she was a woman.

"Yes, well," Cali said, "Ahmed was complaining after he left your office."

"And you know this how?"

"Sometimes it pays to be fluent in five languages." She shrugged. "I heard him talking to Hakim as I walked over to see my driver about some other business."

"I see. . . ." Pete gave her a teasing look. "I have trouble stumbling along in English."

"That's not true, Major. I heard you try a bit of Pashto with Hesam. I believe the sheik truly appreciated your efforts."

"What little Pashto I know is from my time spent in the south with my company of Marines. I'll be talking with Hesam on a weekly basis from here on out, and it's imperative that we communicate clearly."

"That will be key," Cali agreed. "It's very important not to underestimate Hesam's power. He's a wily fox. He's had to be, since he's one of the most important political power brokers in northern Afghanistan. As you know, his family has ruled this region for five hundred years. Ruled well. The people love his family, so you don't want to be his enemy. The sheik knows a helluva lot more English than he lets on, I think. My educated guess is that he noticed Ahmed's gaffes and isn't faulting you for them."

"That's good," Pete said with relief. He saw the village coming up. It was a busy place, bustling with women in dark robes, scarves on their heads, and men wearing colorful clothing, hats or turbans. Barking dogs chased the Land Cruiser. There were no children about except for babies on their mothers' hips. Hesam was adamant about all children of his clan being educated, and Pete applauded that principle.

"So today I'll be your interpreter," Cali said brightly. "We have to patch up the disaster Ahmed created for us."

101

"I'm glad you've volunteered," Pete said, and enjoyed seeing her cheeks grow red.

"I'll try to fix what was broken yesterday."

"Knowing what I know about Afghan politics, my sense is Elliot probably owed Ahmed's family a favor, and he got this translator job by default."

Relief swept through Cali. Trayhern was sharp, she'd give him that. Of course, one look into those alert eyes and Cali knew he was a man with a steel-trap mind. The only mysteries left for her were his morals and values. Cali had run into her fair share of men who did back-room deals, manipulated, threatened and cheated to get what they wanted. Russ Turner had been one of them. He'd lied to her, saying he was single when all along he was married. Cali felt a wave of shame over how she'd been fooled.

Generally, she was an excellent judge of character, but her stupid, lonely heart had fallen into the trap Russ had set for her. A woman in a man's world of concrete and metal would always be lonely. That realization had such an awful finality.

Drawing a shaky breath, Cali shoved her own personal agony aside. Was Major Trayhern like Russ? She hoped not, but it was too early to tell. So far, he seemed to have the moral fiber and values she yearned for.

She felt the major's scrutiny. Lifting her head, she cut a glance in his direction.

"The important thing for today's outing is to establish a good relationship with Hesam," Pete stated. He'd felt Cali retreat deep within herself, and was unsure what that meant. "I believe we can do that."

Cali glowed inwardly. Pete had said "we." That showed his desire for teamwork. Then again, Russ had used "we," too.

Tamping down the glimmer of hope, Cali replied, "That's why you're bringing him those dates from Qatar. Hesam will love them. I think, with that gift, he will realize you're trying to make amends. He doesn't strike me as a man who will throw you out unless you really cross him."

"Good to know." Pete parked the Land Cruiser next to a two-story dwelling made of adobe bricks. Hesam's home looked like all the rest with its square, curtained windows, but the large door with mountains carved in the wood made the home more regal. A number of run-down pickup trucks were parked along the rutted street in front of the houses. A horse-drawn cart moved by, carrying a pile of loose hay. The driver waved to them, and Pete lifted his hand in response. Maybe it spoke highly of Hesam that he lived most of the time among his people, and not in the glittering city Dara-i-Suf, which was in his clan's territory.

"Who knew a box of dates could do so much to mend fences?" Pete shook his head.

Cali squelched a smile and climbed out of the Land Cruiser. The afternoon was heating up after the cool desert night. All the children were in school now, and a few women walked through the village. Some carried bread in a basket, others vegetables. There was a small open market at the other end of the community. A few dogs lazed about and occasionally the bleat of a goat or the baa of a sheep broke the silence. The scents of curry, rosemary and onions were strong on the breeze, and Cali inhaled deeply. Growing up, she had lived all over the globe, wherever her father had a project to build. She'd been raised on the foods of Asia and the Far East, and loved curry, in particular.

Taking a steadying breath, Cali focused on the meeting ahead and walked at Major Trayhern's side to Hesam's home. Her nerves were taut. Would Hesam forgive the Marine?

"Ah, dates . . . and from Qatar," Hesam said, sitting among several huge pillows in the audience room. "Indeed, this is a gift worthy of a king." He smiled and nodded deferentially to the Marine, who sat to his right. "Thank you, my friend." As he set the box aside, his smiling wife, Ladan, entered with a tray of hot tea and sweetmeats for all of them. When she had left, Hesam turned to Cali. "I see you are his interpreter for the day?"

Cali nodded and sipped her tea. "I am, my lord. With your permission."

"But of course." Hesam turned to Pete. "And where is the beady-eyed Ahmed today? Sick?"

Squelching a laugh, Cali set her tea in front of her and translated the statement and question to Pete. She saw the major gulp, catch himself and then try to maintain a serious demeanor.

"No, my lord. He had other business I wanted him to attend to this morning." Pete didn't want to drag Ahmed into this meeting. It was his problem to solve and not one he wanted to share with the sheik. "Ms. Roland volunteered to take his place for today."

Hesam nodded sagely and sipped his tea, his gaze sliding to the American woman. "Ahh, I see." He studied Cali. "You speak almost as a native, my dear friend."

Cali knew that when a sheik called one

"friend" it was a good sign. "Thank you, my lord. That is a high compliment."

"Tell me, would Pete be offended if I offered my sixteen-year-old nephew, Javad, as his translator?" Hesam asked her. "Javad is a bright young lad who took English courses in Kabul since he was a boy. He knows your language well. My nephew's parents were killed by the Taliban." Hesam frowned and sipped his tea. "My sister and her husband were murdered by them. He was their only son. . . ."

Cali saw the banked rage in Hesam's eyes. There was no question in her mind that he hated the Taliban. "I'm sorry for your loss, my lord."

With a wave of his hand, the sheik said, "Thank you. You must know that Javad has lost a leg. He stepped on a land mine outside Kabul shortly after the death of his parents. It ended his schooling. He was sent back here to me for his recovery, but he is bored because he's such a bright lad. I feel Javad could reclaim his confidence by working beside the major. My nephew is smart, willing to work hard and will not lie."

Cali nodded and passed on the information. Even though the major had not told the sheik the truth about Ahmed, the warlord had adroitly summed up the problem.

She instantly saw Pete's expression grow sad as she explained Javad's situation and condition. Clearly, the major wore his emotions on his face, and that once again surprised her.

Cali saw Hesam watching Pete out of the corner of his eyes as he sampled a date from Qatar.

"Let me clear your suggestion with Mr. Elliot," Pete told the sheik. "My boss must approve it." In fact, Pete could see a lot of advantages to having a family member of Hesam's on the site in that capacity. But first they had to decide what to do about Ahmed.

"Excellent," Hesam said, finishing his tea. He dipped his hands in warm, lemon-scented water in a beaten silver bowl. Taking a white linen towel to dry them, he said in English, "Major Trayhern, I know a great deal of your language, as you can tell."

Stunned, Pete raised his brows. The sheik spoke flawless English. Pete saw Cali press her hand across her mouth. Was she hiding a smile? She had suspected the man had an excellent command of their language, and she'd been right. "Yes, sir, you do." Pete realized to his horror that the warlord had heard Ahmed suggest he was a pig.

"Frankly, this was a test." Hesam gave him

a studied look. "I wanted to see if you were honorable or not, Major. Clearly, Ahmed is not the translator you want. I would advise you to look more deeply into this brigand's background. He may not be who you think he is."

"Yes, sir, I will. . . ." The sheik grasped the problem and Pete was relieved to realize Hesam wasn't holding him responsible for Ahmed's poor performance.

"My nephew, Javad, is of the highest moral fiber. You can trust him, Major. He will not lie, cheat or steal. The men I will give you to work on your project respect my nephew. He is young, but he has a good heart." Hesam touched his barrel chest with a bejeweled hand. "And equally important, he will translate your words faithfully, treat you with the utmost respect and keep you apprised of all important protocols between us." He smiled slightly. "And of course, I will decree that the men in my villages nearest to your project come for employment."

"I'm glad to hear that, my lord," Pete said. More relief funneled through him and a huge, invisible rock seemed to slide off his shoulders. Without Hesam's men, the construction could not move forward.

The sheik was looking at him, bearded chin slightly tilted, his eyes gleaming. "I'm grateful for your help," Pete said.

"I see your arrival, Major, as a blessing from Allah," Hesam said, raising his hands toward the ceiling, his voice husky with emotion. "For too long, the Taliban have tried to wreck our country. They subjugated our women, who are as strong as our men. They stopped them from being educated. I fought for their rights then as I do now. This power plant is a dream coming true for all our people of the northern provinces." His thick, black brows drew downward. "That is not to say the Taliban don't bite at our heels. They do. You are putting the power plant near the slopes of the Kush Mountains, where they can ride down from the hills and attack you. Do you realize that?"

"I was warned about that by my boss, my lord. I was hoping to get your experience and counsel on what to do about the Taliban. I know they are less active up here because your men chase them out of the villages."

Hesam popped another date into his mouth and chewed. "The Taliban want to see us fail here. In the last decade, I have worked to get rid of all fanatics who hide their allegiance from me. At night, they ride away to the mountains, meet others and then come down to attack the Americans."

He shrugged. "I have been relentless in my pursuit of ridding such individuals, but there are still Taliban members around. In the Kush Mountains above this plain there are villages that still fester with the enemies of our people. They use the caves to meet and hide in. My territory extends only so far. Another sheik has tribal power over the mountain people, not I. But I have been able to broker an agreement with him to chase Taliban out of my province. He, too, dislikes the Taliban and does all he can to get rid of them." Shrugging, Hesam added, "The Taliban are like cockroaches. You can kill individuals, but they continue to multiply, and you are never quite rid of them as you would like."

"It appears to be an ongoing problem," Pete agreed somberly.

Hesam brightened. "Democracy is what I and others want for our country." He swept his hand around the room. "The northern province tribe leaders show others what is possible. And I, for one, am your protector, Major. You can count on my men. They will not steal from you. They will put in a full day's work without complaint. They are not shirkers. So long as you pay them fairly and don't treat them as dumb animals of burden, I will be grateful."

Nodding, Pete said, "My lord, I am authorized to pay them a good wage. They will be respected. I know that they must pray six times daily, and they will be allowed to do so. I plan two shifts of workers, if you approve."

Pensive, Hesam glanced at Cali. "And does all this meet with your approval as well, my friend?"

"My lord, I represent the construction company that works for Major Trayhern. He's my boss. If he tells you that your men will be fairly paid and he needs two shifts, I believe that. I'm sure he will respect your traditions where your people are concerned. We all want to see Afghanistan get back on her feet, and her people enjoy good jobs at fair wages."

"Excellent," Hesam murmured. "Then we are in agreement." He reached out and patted each of them on the shoulder. "Come, now that we have completed our business, I want to show you my racing camels. They are the best in Afghanistan!"

As Cali rose, after Hesam had gotten to his feet, she looked across at Pete. He seemed as if the weight of the world had just been removed from his broad shoulders. She understood how important it was to have the sheik's blessing. Without the influential warlord, the area would be like lawless Dodge City without a sheriff or posse around to keep the tentative peace. Her heart beat a little harder as she tried to rein in her sudden, inexplicable joy. She quickly told Hesam that Pete's introductory gift would be presented to him as soon as it arrived. Hesam glowed.

For a fleeting second, vulnerability appeared in the major's face, and it touched Cali's heart. Rubbing her brow, she turned and followed the men out of the room.

She and Major Trayhern would have two years of working together. Two years of hell? And what would heaven be like?

Cali snorted softly to herself. Whatever loneliness she felt, she had to live with. She should stop looking for the major to become a friend — or more.

CHAPTER SIX

The next morning was clear, cool and crisp. Cali wore a dark green, goose-down jacket to shield her from the biting breeze that flowed off the Kush range just before the sun rose over the jagged, snow-covered peaks. She made it to Pete's trailer and stepped inside. As she moved toward the office, she wasn't prepared for the sight of Ahmed screaming at Pete, who'd been studying site drawings spread out across the table. The Afghan's face was livid and he was waving his arms like windmills. She nearly dropped her mug of coffee as she hesitated near the entryway, feeling like an interloper.

"You cannot send me back to Kabul, Major! I am a good interpreter! I did everything right! You are letting a mere woman fill your head with lies!" He glared down at Pete. "You would rather listen to her than to me, a man? Women are nothing!

They are slaves to serve us!"

Annoyance surged through Cali. She saw Pete's gaze turn stormy as he stood to confront the upset interpreter. Ahmed's face was frozen with hatred.

Cali realized neither man was aware of her presence. Shutting the door with more force than necessary, she saw Ahmed jump, as if shot, and whirl around. His mouth dropped open when he realized she was standing there.

"You!" he screamed, shaking his finger at her. "You have lied to the major! I am a good interpreter! You do not know what you say, woman! You have no business being here on a man's construction site! You belong at home, tending your babies!"

Cali lifted her chin, her fingers curling a little more tightly around the handle of the mug. "Ahmed, you're way out of line. Settle down. Screaming, yelling and making stupid charges like that isn't going to help anyone."

His thick black brows drew down and his eyes became slits. Nostrils flaring, he switched to Pashto. "You spawn of the devil! How dare you tell me anything! You are nothing but a worthless woman! You have no rights here as far as I'm concerned!"

Before Cali could answer, Pete came around the planning desk and stood between them. His body radiated tension. "What did he just say to you, Ms. Roland?" he demanded tightly.

Cali translated. She saw the Marine's face go very still. She was seeing the construction supervisor now, not the man. Ahmed was much shorter than him, and Pete leaned down and snarled into his face, "You're fired, Ahmed. You will not insult anyone who works for me. Particularly Ms. Roland. Sheik Hesam said the same thing she did — that you did a poor job of interpreting for me. Your services are terminated, mister. Leave right now. Go over to accounting and pick up your last paycheck."

Cali moved aside as Ahmed backed off. He cursed in Pashto, whirled and stormed toward the door.

"I will get even with you, woman!" he growled at Cali. "Count the days! I will take my revenge upon you!"

"Go back to Kabul, Ahmed," Cali answered in Pashto.

Pete winced as the interpreter slammed the door behind him. He glanced over at Cali, who took a sip of her steaming coffee.

"A helluva start to our day," he muttered. "I'm sorry he said those things to you. I'll dispatch a report on Ahmed to Mr. Elliot today."

"I'm assuming you told Elliot about Ahmed's inaccuracies yesterday?"

"Yes, he called late last night. Apparently Ahmed comes from a very rich family . . ." Pete shrugged. "You know how this political and family stuff works over here."

"I do. The rich get favors all the time. The poor never get a break."

"Ahmed will make out just fine in Kabul," Pete said darkly. He was glad to have the backing of Kerwin Elliot, but didn't share that with her. "Javad will take over as of today."

When he had the chance to clear his head of this most recent unpleasantness, Pete noticed how beautiful Cali looked this morning. Construction fashion didn't change much. Jeans, a long-sleeved white cotton blouse, a pink tank top beneath it and rough-out boots were the uniform of the day, every day. Still, Cali's cheeks were ruddy from the chill, her red hair pleasantly mussed beneath the white hard hat she wore. Those same small pearl earrings were in place. Maybe it was the dark green jacket she just unzipped that brought out the sultry color of her large, intelligent eyes.

He had to stop looking at her like that. In any case, her grim expression warned him off.

"Did Ahmed come to see you or did you call him in?" Cali asked.

Snorting, Pete went over to the coffee station and poured himself his second cup of the day. "I called him in to give him his release. The moment I told him his work was unacceptable he flew into a rage. That's when you came in. I hadn't got a chance to tell him he was fired."

Cali moved away from the major. He was too close for comfort. Her personal comfort. Last night she'd dreamed of Russ again. It was a dream filled with rage against him — his lies, his deceit. She wasn't in a good mood, as a result. Having to spend time with Trayhern was enough of a trial. To be in the same office with him was always a stress on her.

Worry gleaming in his eyes. Pete sat down at the planning desk, coffee in hand.

"The guy's a fanatic, Major," Cali murmured. Wrapping her hands around her own mug, she added, "I've occasionally run into men like Ahmed on other Middle East projects. There's a part of the Islamic belief system that is extreme, and he follows it. They think women should be barefoot, pregnant and at home. That, and out in public, women should be hidden from head to toe behind a black chadri." Cali grimaced. "The Ahmeds of the world regard women as little more than animals, and in fact, I've seen times when a camel, horse or goat was treated better than the wife of one of these fanatics. It's shameful and degrading."

Pete wanted to tell Cali to call him by his first name, not "Major." But no way could he go there. Better to stay formal, so that an automatic distance remained between them. "You handled yourself well," he murmured between sips. Seeing anger in her green eyes, he added, "Good thing you aren't easily intimidated."

"As the site project engineer I'm the last person to be intimidated. The tradespeople working under me need to be assured I'm no shrinking violet in the line of fire. I've taken the heat in the kitchen plenty of times and lived to tell about it." The only thing Cali couldn't stand was deception. Even though Pete was totally off-limits, she wondered if the major ever lied to women.

"That's true. You handled the situation with Ahmed very well." Pete hoped she had the steel in her veins necessary to run this site. Cali was a strong, confident woman, but did she have the stamina for this project? He wanted her to succeed.

Wanted her, period. The truth was Cali

hadn't given any signals that she was inter-ested in him. Pete should have felt relief, but being so close to her made him squirm. *Remember the past, Trayhern. There's no room in your heart for a woman right now.*

"Thanks." What did the major expect? Cali wondered. For her to break down in tears? To wither beneath Ahmed's vitriolic attack? Being site supervisor was a royal battle more often then not. In fact, she'd rather have Major Trayhern as an enemy than a friend, she decided. He was too easy to like. So far, Cali hadn't caught him in a lie. Not yet. She had a bad history of men lying to her to get what they wanted, how-ever. Toby, a classmate of hers in sixth grade, had talked her out of two of her valentine cookies with a story about his sick mother and taking them home to her. Cali learned later that his mom was fine and not ill at all. Toby had taunted her for weeks after that, for believing his lies. It got no better in junior high, when Cali's trusting nature had led to more embarrassing situa-tions. And then there was Russ Turner. . . .

"While you're here, I'd like an update on the fence building," Pete stated.

"We're working to get back on schedule," Cali said, holding his narrowed gazed. She finished her coffee. If he only knew the rough-and-tumble construction men she'd had to stand toe-to-toe with over the years, he probably wouldn't give her that doubtful look. As if she couldn't do the job.

"I expect a full report."

Offended by his tone, Cali did her best to keep her voice cool. "The fencing material arrived yesterday. Sheik Hesam sent over ten pickup trucks filled with workers to our site this morning. I've had Ray take them to the payroll trailer to sign them up and give them their marching orders. We plan to start crews on roads, security and fence building —" she looked at her watch "— in less than an hour. I anticipate that by noon, that fencing will start going up."

"We're already two days behind schedule," Pete reminded her, looking down at his scheduling book to make the point.

Anger simmered briefly in Cali. "I'm going to see what I can do to speed up the process." If she'd thought Trayhern was going to be a pushover, she was wrong. Already, Cali could see that she was looking through rose-colored glasses at this guy. Hadn't she learned her lesson already? A sense of failure, deep and painful, flowed through her.

"We've only got two shifts, and eight-hour days."

Cali said, "I have my methods, Major. Trust me."

Pete gave her a cutting smile. "As you know, trust doesn't enter into this. Words are cheap. It's actions that count. I have two engineers and an office clerk arriving about noon. I'll bring them around for introductions and check on your progress at that time."

Trying to be diplomatic, Cali said, "I'll look forward to meeting the rest of your team."

"Do you have more information on Hesam other than what was in your company's dossier?" Pete asked. "Is he trustworthy, do you think? Based on your experience here in the Middle East?"

"Absolutely. Hesam is a true diplomat and politico. He's a stand-up guy you can trust if you don't cross him. Have you read the dossier yet?"

Again, Pete was impressed with Roland's in-depth investigation on the main players at the construction site. It was a smart business move. "Yes, I read it. We'll see if your research is correct over time."

Cali ignored his jab. "Basically, Hesam is pro-American and anti-Taliban. What the report doesn't say is the Taliban have killed members of his family. You heard about Javad losing his parents, but Hesam has lost two younger brothers, their wives and children, as well."

Shaking his head, Pete said gruffly, "I can't imagine how awful that would be, having so many loved ones murdered like that." He vividly recalled the stories of his own parents and Jason, his older brother, being kidnapped by a drug lord. He'd been born after the terrible crisis, but had seen the results of it in his family.

"Makes two of us," Cali said. She was glad to talk about something other than the absent security fence. "I can't walk in his shoes, but I do feel great compassion for Hesam. Also, he is too worldly and cosmopolitan for the Taliban and their fanatical ways of practicing Islam."

"That's what I thought," Pete conceded.

"For example, did you know he allows women in his province to wear whatever they want? They are not confined to the imprisoning chadri. Sure, they wear a scarf on their head when outdoors, but all Muslim women do that. He has consistently schooled girls, when many in Afghanistan, under Taliban rule, stopped them from being educated at all. Hesam believes education is the way out for his people. His province has more college graduates than any other right now. And his graduates come back here to improve rural village life."

"I appreciate the extra input," Pete murmured. "Maybe I can help him in that regard."

"Oh?" Cali wanted to run. The trailer seemed to be growing smaller by the minute, and she was wildly aware of his male presence. Why couldn't she tell her heart to stop being stupid? She inched toward the door. The sooner she got away from him, the better.

"I have a good friend I made in Kabul when I was in the south of the country. She's a professor of education and a real feminist. She's had an educational model for the children from kindergarten up to K12. I'd like to put a call in to her and see if she's willing to share it with Hesam."

"Sounds good on paper, Major, but my two cents' worth is, before you call her, clear it with the sheik. It's just good manners from his perspective. Hesam may already have an educational model in place. We don't know that."

"Of course I will." Pete scowled. Not only was she verbally slapping his hand, but she seemed eager to leave.

"Major, I've seen my fair share of white

men from America show up on Middle East turf and screw things up big time. You may not appreciate my advice, but there are times I'm going to give it to you."

"I didn't just arrive, you know," Pete reminded her.

"And if I hadn't given you a heads-up on Ahmed, you'd never have known what he did to you."

Pete drew in a deep, ragged breath. This woman could be infuriating. "I'd have figured it out eventually."

Cali glared at him. Men were stupid sometimes, and she could see Pete's wounded ego speaking. Finally, some of his inadequacies were coming to light. "Not on my watch, Major. Because I don't want a problem with Sheik Hesam. You're worried about a two-day delay on the security fence schedule? Just think what would happen to your schedule if Ahmed had continued to mess things up between you and the clan leader. Protocols over here are dyed-in-the-wool and you don't deviate from them. We could have ended up with no one working at this site."

Thinning his mouth, Pete glanced down at the plans beneath his flattened hand. Damn, but she was uncompromising. And he sure as hell didn't like being snubbed like this. "Ms. Roland, you stick to your job and I'll stick to mine."

Her hand tightened around the doorknob. Welcome to another battle. Cali was used to them, but for whatever reason, she took his words more personally than she should. "You're right, Major, I have a fence to get built."

"On schedule."

Smarting at his innuendo, Cali held in the glare she wanted to give him. So, he needled back when he felt attacked. At best, she'd discovered something new today about Major Trayhern, and she mentally noted it on her checklist. Knowing the boss was paramount. Half of her job was negotiating a position with him to avoid outright train wrecks that could impact their mutual schedule.

As if on cue, Pete heard diesel engines chugging by, one after another. Glancing out the window behind him, he saw trucks filled with wire and post material. The dust rose high and thick. Turning, he said, "Looks like your trucks have arrived."

Managing a slight, tight smile, Cali stated, "Ahead of time."

"So noted," Pete replied. "With the Taliban around we need that fence up for protection."

"I'll have Hesam's best horsemen doing a 24-7 around the perimeter once we get it erected."

"The sooner the better." There was no compromise in Cali Roland's green eyes as he spoke. The way one corner of her mouth curved sent unexpected heat riffling through his body. Cali was quite the adventurer and unafraid of life, he realized. Having a strong second-in-charge on such a massive project could either make him look good or very, very bad. Grudging respect for her, as a woman in a man's job, funneled through Pete. Somehow, he'd never really expected Cali to stand up to him. She had to get the fence issue resolved, and fast. But she offered no excuses. Nor did she whine or sweet-talk to try and change his mind about the situation. That was good. And surprising. In many ways, she was just like his fraternal twin sister.

The door closed quietly. Cali was gone, though the front of the trailer would soon be filled with other busy engineers and a clerk. Pete cherished the quiet, but missed Cali's larger-than-life presence. Not to mention he had so many burning questions to ask her about her private life. Damn his curious nature for wanting to dig up information on her. Where would this get him?

Nowhere. He didn't want the massive, unrelenting pain of heartbreak, of knowing too much.

Again Pete reminded himself that he couldn't mix business with pleasure. Cali Roland was the number-two person in command of this site. Pete had to keep things separate. Still, as he thumbed through several sets of subcontractor papers, he couldn't get her out of his mind. And behind that was worry about the Taliban. And Ahmed's warning. The man had threatened Cali. Pete knew the Islamic belief in an "eye for an eye." Was it all hype? Empty intimidation to soothe the man's ruffled feathers? Cali was too alive, too vibrant, to just disappear. That thought made Pete's gut clench as nothing else ever had.

He knew it was only a matter of time until the Taliban tested them. The first attack had come from bandits, who were much less dangerous than the real foe. The Taliban didn't want to see progress; they wanted everyone in Afghanistan kept in the dark ages. The question then became not if they would strike, but *when.*

CHAPTER SEVEN

Cali pulled her gray dappled Arabian gelding to a halt. She'd taken a little-used rocky trail up the side of a barren hill now come to life with spring wildflowers. In the sudden heat of late May, she wore a long-sleeved white blouse to protect her skin from the hot, burning sun overhead. She'd covered her head with a white Roland Construction baseball cap. But even with her light clothing, Cali felt the powerful, dry desert heat. Good thing she was used to it. The Arabian caught her attention by snorting and lifting his nose to test the air. A smile tugged at Cali's mouth as she looked down upon her kingdom.

The construction site was coming online. After three weeks, it was finally starting to shape up. On a nearby hill the quarry operation was being built. The giant metal hoppers being erected would hold sand, gravel and concrete. The present work site was surrounded by a cyclone fence with razor wire. This would discourage anyone from visiting without authorization, or stealing equipment. And she'd completed the fence on schedule, so the major couldn't hold it over her. He seemed pleased that the barrier was in place.

Bees buzzed around her head and she waved them away. The breeze was scented with the fragrance of wildflowers that seemed to have popped up overnight. The once red-and-brown gravelly slopes were now covered in lush tufts of green grass and waving, colorful blossoms. It was like a miracle of sorts to see the arid area come alive like this, and Cali marveled over its beauty.

Leaning back in the leather saddle, she enjoyed the feel of being on a horse again. Sheik Hesam had given her and Pete each a purebred Arabian horse a week ago — a wonderful gift. Cali had been itching to ride since the small barn with two stalls had been built near their trailers for easy access. Horses were in her blood. When she was a child, her father had given her a dappled gray pony when they lived in India.

Too bad Major Trayhern couldn't join her. Cali had asked him if he had time to scout the hill area above the site. Oh, it had been professional courtesy, Cali told herself. He was just as worried about Taliban attacks as she was. One way to see if they were around was to look for fresh horse tracks. Security wanted to escort her, but Cali turned down their request. The major said he was mired in meetings with accountants from Kabul.

Cali felt sorry for him; she'd gone head to head with those same bean counters already, and they wanted to know where every friggin' penny was being spent, why and when. They only cared that the paperwork was in order; construction progress wasn't their concern.

Snorting herself, Cali resettled the baseball cap on her head, tugging down the bill to shade her narrowing eyes. What if Major Trayhern had said yes to her offer? Cali wasn't sure what she'd have done. Their meetings were always professional and short. Fine by her. It made her life easier, really. Taking out her small Nikon digital camera, she began taking shots of everything. Daily, she would go around taking photos, because it became a way to look at progress — or the lack of it — and what needed her attention.

Twisting around in the saddle, Cali also took photos of trails running across the slopes, each layer of hills a little higher and more rugged than the last as they flowed upward into the blue granite Kush Mountains soaring above. She could still see a lot of snow on them, and Hesam had told her they remained cloaked with white throughout the year.

It felt good to get away from the trailer. Sometimes Cali needed to break free of the intense, focused work and take a breather. Being able to ride the gray Arabian — which she'd named Bat because he moved like a bat out of hell — was going to be a godsend. Even now she found herself thinking of Pete. The last three weeks he'd worked nonstop, burning the midnight oil. And so had she.

Cali knew that start-up on a project like this was an engineering nightmare from the superintendent's point of view. Until the major could get everyone in harness, working and pulling the same way at the same time, there were hourly headaches to take care of. Cali was glad she was on the other end. Her subcontractors, who collectively resembled the United Nations, or more aptly, the Tower of Babel, were all getting along and working seamlessly. She was relieved, because it didn't always happen that way.

Bat swished his black tail as flies gathered

around him. He snatched at tufts of green grass. Cali patted the horse's thin, steel-gray neck. For much of the year, animals had a hard time trying to find anything to eat on the desert plain. Hesam had a nice herd of Arabians, and he was proud of them, but he would never think of giving them hay during the dry season. No, the hardy animals knew how to eke out an existence on nearly nothing. That was why Bat was small and slender, probably eight hundred pounds and only thirteen hands high. Still, Arabians were the hardiest breed for desert living and riding. Cali had come to appreciate the small, nimble animals years earlier in Saudi Arabia.

She noticed a trampled area and scattered prints of what appeared to be deer or sheep leading up the side of the hill. Was this a shepherd's resting spot, or was it someone overlooking the site, making a map of it? Cali decided to investigate. Even though Hesam's mounted soldiers regularly patrolled this area, there simply weren't enough men and horses to cover it all.

The slopes were slippery with loose stones. Time and again, the Arabian dug in his hooves, lurching forward up the steep ascent, dust spiraling in the wake of his arduous climb. Following the prints, they reached a rocky wash, and found the tracks petered out at a six-foot-tall bush. Mouth quirking, Cali guided Bat to higher ground.

When they reached the hilltop, she frowned, spotting more tracks. Shepherds moved flocks of sheep and goats throughout this region in search of grass at this time of year, she knew. But as she followed the prints in the dust, something else caught her attention. On a rocky butte towering above the hills she'd just climbed, she saw two caves set back in the blue-gray rock.

Moving a little closer, Cali lost the trail once more. She pointed Bat to a somewhat smoother area, where they ran into a new set of tracks: that of many horses. Who was using this trail? Shepherds never rode on horseback. They were always on foot. Maybe Hesam's soldiers had ridden over this area recently. *Probably.* The indentations looked pretty fresh to Cali as she leaned over to study them more closely.

A feeling of sudden unease prickled the back of her neck. Automatically, she rested her hand on the pistol strapped to her right thigh. Hesam had warned them that the Taliban hid in the hills, and he constantly sent out patrols to keep the roving bands at bay. As a result, the warlord handed over more Taliban members to the police in

Kabul than any other tribal leader in the northern provinces.

Bat's ears began to twitch rapidly. He became very alert, his interest drawn to the right of the first cave as they slowly approached the entrance. Cali unsnapped the holster and pulled out her 9 mm Beretta. She flipped off the safety, and held the pistol ready.

The Arabian halted suddenly. Not expecting the horse to balk, Cali nearly found herself flying out of the saddle and over the animal's head. She grabbed his mane at the last second, which stopped her forward motion. Bat snorted, but remained frozen as Cali righted herself, clamping her legs against his heaving sides. What the hell did he hear or see?

The sharp crack of a rifle reached Cali almost immediately, the sound echoing across the hills. A geyser of dirt shot up a foot away from Bat's front legs. *Where did that shot come from?* Anxiously, Cali twisted around, poised to return fire and retreat. Who was it? How many of them? Nostrils flaring with fear, Bat trembled violently, obviously wanting to turn and run. Cali could barely hold the animal in place with the reins and her legs.

Then she heard hoofbeats coming in her

direction. Like the rolling of thunder, the sound grew louder. The unidentified horsemen were on the other side of this hill. Cali couldn't see them, but she sure as hell heard them. Bat shifted beneath her, wanting to race off toward the desert plain below. Hauling him to a standstill, She quickly scanned the slope.

There!

She saw a man in tan clothes and a dark brown turban kneeling near the first cave, his rifle aimed at her. That was the shooter! Hesam's soldiers always wore yellow, orange and red when patrolling the hills, to identify them from other riders who might well be Taliban.

Cursing softly, Cali looked to see if there were any goats or sheep nearby. If this was a herdsman, she didn't want to return fire. She couldn't mistakenly kill one of Hesam's people. Since Cali wasn't a hundred percent certain, she hesitated fractionally. Besides, a rifle shot could travel a lot further than a pistol could.

More hoofbeats!

They were coming closer and closer.

Damn! Unsure of the identity of the man at the cave, Cali refused to fire, and whipped the Arabian around. Bat lifted his fine front legs and pivoted quickly. Then he leaped forward, tearing down the steep hill. Clouds of dirt and small stones flew up behind him as he dug in his hooves.

The mane of the horse whipped against Cali's hand as she jerked a look over her shoulder to see who those hoofbeats belonged to. More shots rang out, and dirt spat up on both sides of the lunging Arabian. By now, Cali was sure the man at the cave was not one of Hesam's militia or a herdsman. He had to be a Taliban sniper. Legs clamped to Bat's sides, Cali leaned back to give the animal the balance he needed as he skidded down a steep incline. Dust rose around them, choking Cali. More gunshots ripped through the air.

Dammit, she wanted to return fire, but couldn't because of the horse's speed, plus the riders were out of pistol range. She either paid attention to her mount as he leaped and skidded down the sharp incline, or she stopped him to fire her pistol. With the sound of rifle shots echoing around them, Cali knew she was outgunned and outmanned. The only thing to do was run! She holstered her pistol and gripped the reins.

Wind slapped her face, making her eyes water. She moved her hips in synch with her horse, which slid and skidded nimbly down the hill. The larger rocks were daunting. Cali didn't know how the stalwart Arabian was able to dodge them. One collision with any of those good-sized boulders and Bat could stumble, break a leg, and she'd be flipped out of the saddle. Heart pounding in her chest, Cali threw a glance back toward the crown of the hill where she'd been moments earlier. She saw ten horsemen on small Arabians with rifles.

Anger mingled with her fear. They were the enemy! Bat shifted sideways on the steep hill. Righting himself instantly, he galloped down the last slope that would lead them back to the safety of the site. How far the Taliban would trail her, Cali didn't know. She hadn't expected to run into the bastards in full daylight. Hesam had said they always struck at night. Cursing softly, she rode Bat hard down the next incline, which wasn't as steep. The Arabian knew they were being fired at. His small ears lay against his neck, his nose was thrust outward, and he clamped the bit in his teeth.

More rock and dirt spat up around them. The horsemen were continuing to fire, and Cali was damned if she was going to be a convenient target! She zigzagged the fleet Arabian down the hill, and by the time Bat leaped onto the desert floor, the firing had stopped.

Bringing the foam-flecked Arabian to a skidding halt, Cali whirled him around and scanned the hills. The horsemen were gone. Bat's flanks were heaving like a bellows, his snorts loud and harsh. He was shaking with fear. Automatically, Cali reached out and stroked his sweaty neck.

"It's okay, okay, Bat. The worst is over. You did great." She patted him with calming motions.

Cali heard an approaching vehicle and shifted to look toward the sound. Relieved, she recognized one of the four security trucks that Jake Barnes and his men drove. They must have heard the gunfire or seen the horsemen through their binoculars. Steering Bat, Cali headed toward the speeding vehicle.

To her surprise, she saw Pete Trayhern getting out of the Toyota Tundra, an M16 rifle in hand. His face was thundercloud dark, his gray eyes anxious. Hakim, Cali's driver, parked the truck and started scanning the hills.

"Cali, are you all right?" the major asked.

She nodded. It was one of the few times he'd called her by her first name. She dismounted to give Bat a well-deserved rest. "Yeah, I'm fine. You must have heard those bastards firing at me?"

Pete halted in front of her, rapidly assessing her. Cali looked a bit pale, her green eyes stressed. "Security called me. They had you in their binocular sites and saw what happened. Are you okay?" He reached out to put his hand on her shoulder. It was an instinctive reaction, Pete realized belatedly. Actually, Cali seemed fine. A little wind-blown, her cheeks a ruddy color, but no gunshot wound and no bruises. For that, he was more than grateful.

"Really, I'm okay." She gave him a slight, trembling smile, surprised at his actions. She had never expected the major to touch her. The care radiating from him staggered her.

Cali felt his fingers dig slightly into her shoulder as if he wanted to convince himself of her assurances, and her skin prickled. There was strength in his grip, and she hungrily relished the unexpected feeling.

Lifting her gaze, Cali met his concerned eyes. "I'm good, Pete." His first name just slipped out. What the hell was wrong with her? Pulling free of his grasp, she saw his eyes fill with confusion and questions.

She tried to make light of what had just happened. "Hey, you know I invited you out on this ride today. Just think, you could have been shot at, too."

Grimacing, Pete looked up at the hills, which once again appeared deserted. "That isn't funny. Next time, though, I will go with you or you'll take a security escort." Pete gave orders to his driver to ask Hesam's mounted troops to search the hills for the Taliban immediately. He cursed himself silently. Cali Roland was fully capable of taking care of herself, he told himself harshly. There was no way he could become her bodyguard. His pounding heart wouldn't settle down, however, and he scowled.

As Cali leaned down and carefully checked each of Bat's slender, gleaming legs for injury, she said, "Why? Because I'm a woman and can't handle things alone, Major? I need a man to do it for me?" She twisted to glance up at him as she lifted one of Bat's rear legs to look at his pastern. There was a small, bloody cut there. She'd have to take care of it once they got back to the stalls.

"No," Pete said, unhappily. "It doesn't make good sense for anyone from the site to ride out into the hills by themselves." He rested the M16 on his hip.

Hakim continued to gaze up at the hills, skimming the slopes anxiously, his own

M16 in hand.

Cali lifted her horse's last leg and inspected it closely. She chose not to reply to Pete's comment. He was obviously stressed, and she didn't want a fight with him. Her shoulder still tingled where his hand had briefly rested. Fighting the sensation, she said, "I'd have got off some rounds if I wasn't skidding down those hills at Mach 3 with my hair on fire." She released Bat's leg and gave him a well-deserved pat on the shoulder. Looking across the horse's neck at Pete, she added, "But I decided running was a better option. There were eleven of them and one of me."

"Did you see their faces?" Hakim interjected.

Shaking her head, Cali said, "No, not really. I saw the AK-47s they were carrying, though."

"That is the Taliban's weapon of choice," Hakim stated, frowning.

"Isn't it unusual for them to be out and around in the daylight?" Cali asked as she rounded the Arabian and checked the saddle girth.

"Yes, according to Hesam," Pete answered, dividing his attention between Cali and the hills above them. She could have been killed. Gritting his teeth, he fought the

141

harsh emotion that flooded his chest at that thought. He was not going to fall for Cali. His heart could not stand the resulting anguish. Plus, she had not worn a Kevlar vest to protect herself. Again.

"I think," Hakim said, "that because so many of Sheik Hesam's men are working on the power plant site, there are far fewer patrols in the hills than before. The Taliban knows that and is getting bolder." Shaking his head, he muttered, "And that is not good."

"No kidding," Cali said, remounting. She settled into the saddle and looked at Pete, who still seemed anxious. "Well, now we know, huh? Maybe we should drive over to Hesam's village and tell him what happened. He might have a plan or something up his sleeve."

Sighing, Pete said, "I'm going to have to." He glanced at his watch. Dammit, his time was at a premium. But he couldn't have Taliban horsemen harassing the site, either. Trying to tamp down the terror he felt over Cali's near miss with death, he looked up at her. "You want to come along?"

"Love to. I'll ride Bat back to the site, clean up a bit then join you, okay?"

"You weren't even wearing a flak jacket to protect yourself, Cali," Pete said, motioning toward her. "Again." The time when bandits had attacked the trailers, she hadn't been wearing one, either. Anger laced the concern Pete didn't want to feel.

"So sue me. I didn't think —"

"I know you didn't, dammit. But I need you alive, not dead." Pete wanted to add that he wouldn't tolerate such a lapse of security by one of his people, but he didn't. He'd broach this topic with her later, when both of them were calmer.

Cali watched him spin on his heel and growl at Hakim to get in and head back to the security trailer. Brows rising, she picked up the reins and nudged Bat forward with her heels. Pete's voice was laced with something other than exasperation. On the way back across the busy construction site, Cali had time to ponder over that last look the major had given her.

If she wasn't wrong, it denoted a man who cared more than just a little for her. Now, how did she feel about that discovery? Maybe she was mistaken. Cali had been known to read men wrong in the past. Russ had fooled her completely. . . .

Her pulse accelerated with fear. Fear of intimacy. With a shake of her head, Cali refused to believe the major cared for her at all except as a business partner.

CHAPTER EIGHT

Kerwin Elliot thumped his index finger on a report lying on his desk. "According to this, Major Trayhern, you're asking for a helicopter."

"Yes, sir," Pete said. "We're two months into this project and, frankly, having to come to Kabul every two weeks to give progress reports is costing us a lot of time."

Elliot's thick gray brows rose. "Oh? I consider these meetings essential to tracking the various projects I'm responsible for."

Hearing the banked anger in his tone, Pete was glad Cali was with him for support. "Sir, with all due respect, I think we may have lost sight of the mileage to and from Kabul. Ms. Roland and I spend four hours, one way, on a dirt road rough enough to jar a person's teeth loose. Then we spend another four hours driving back to the site. That kills a whole day."

"So you're wanting to add an unbudgeted

helicopter to your supplies list? So you can fly here to see me bimonthly?"

"Yes, sir, I do." Pete felt sweat running down his rib cage.

"I can see the handwriting on the wall, Major. If I give you a helicopter, every other project team will want one. Your request is not within budget, and I can't authorize it." Elliot glanced at Cali. "How about you, Ms. Roland? Why doesn't your company provide a helo, instead?"

Cali stirred. "Because a helicopter was not in our budget, either, Mr. Elliot."

The man grunted and gave them each a hard look. "What you're suggesting is a money hemorrhage, as far as my accountants are concerned. Sorry, Major. You're going to have to bite the bullet on this one."

Frustration thrummed through Pete. "Sir, I don't like having our management team spending two whole days away from the site each month."

Shrugging, Elliot said, "I can't help it, Major."

Damn. Pete nearly mouthed the word. "Perhaps we can send our report by courier instead? Or see you once a month instead of twice?"

"Major, these meetings are crucial for my team to follow the various projects. You know that."

"Yes, sir, I do. But I'm sure you can appreciate my dilemma."

Elliot gave him a faint smile. "Yes, I can appreciate your concern, but there's nothing to be done about it."

"Thank you for your time, sir." Pete glanced over at Cali. "Do you have anything else to discuss with Mr. Elliot?" He saw her green eyes widen. Strands of red hair dipped rebelliously across her brow. Pete's heart always took off at an unsteady gait when Cali's gaze met his.

"No, nothing more, Major Trayhern." She rose and shook Elliot's hand. "We'll see you in two weeks."

"Where are we going?" Cali asked as she walked at Pete's shoulder down the crowded street in Kabul. The afternoon sun was brutal, the July heat unrelenting. Desert-camouflaged Humvees, manned by U.S. Marines, moved slowly up and down the avenue. Horses and donkeys pulling carts clip-clopped along, their heads down, ears twitching. The odors of Kabul were half intoxicating, half revolting to Cali. The refreshing scent of mint warred with the sharp tang of lemons. Both were used in many dishes. Diesel fumes from passing trucks made her choke.

"I'm going to see an old friend of mine," he said. They wove among streams of women carrying baskets of bread and other items from a nearby market. Children of all ages roamed the streets. Taking a left down a narrow alley, Pete added, "I'm not done trying to find us a chopper."

Cali grinned. "I didn't think so." The walls of the three-story buildings rose around them. The alley was dirty, human and animal fecal matter clearly present. Paper and other debris littered their dusty path. When the fragrant smells of curry and tomatoes filled the air, Cali looked up. A second-story window was open, and a woman was cooking over a brazier on the balcony. A breeze stirred, feeling good against Cali's damp skin. After wiping her brow, she settled her hard hat back in place.

"While I see my friend, you can do some business at the Roland Construction office down the next street. How about we meet at a little restaurant near here. I found it when I was coming up here on company business while stationed near Kandahar." He took out a pad and pencil from his pocket and wrote down the name and address. Ordinarily, he'd never suggest such an intimate place, but they'd missed lunch and his stomach was growling with hunger.

"Oh." Cali hesitantly took the piece of paper. "Dinner?"

"We'll pay separately, don't worry."

She smiled and tucked the paper into her jeans pocket. "Of course. What time, Major?" Cali could spend an hour in the small company office and contact her parents plus hand in some paperwork to the manager who ran it.

"An hour? Will that give you time to handle your paperwork?"

"It should." Cali almost said, *Take me with you,* but held back. Blantant curiosity — and possessiveness — flared inside her. Everything about Pete Trayhern intrigued her, but she had to let him be. She lifted her hand and waved. "See you later."

They sat in Fatima's Place, an open-air restaurant off the beaten path in Kabul. The sun was low in the sky, causing ribbons of red, orange and gold to streak the western sky. No traffic disturbed them, since the restaurant was not on a main, paved road. Locals came here to enjoy simple meals of basmati rice, kebabs or curried lamb. Cali and Pete ordered Kebab Murgh, chicken marinated overnight in yogurt, turmeric and garlic, with just the right touch of cayenne pepper. The black tea served just before the meal was dark and delicious, with a bit of honey stirred in.

"Heck of a day, huh?" Cali said to Pete as they were served their food. The round table was covered with a red-and-white-checked cloth. To add to the ambience, a small alcove housed clay pots filled with brightly colored flowers, and a small fountain spewed out erratic jets of water.

"Yeah, but a good one, I think." He sipped his tea and gave her a triumphant look.

"You look pretty happy. Something happen?" she ventured, savoring the spicy seasoning on the well-cooked chicken breast.

"Do I look happy?" Pete was surprised, since he prided himself on keeping his emotions off his face. As Cali watched him, he tried to stop dwelling on her glistening lips. He forced himself to pay attention to cutting up the fragrant chicken on his plate.

"A little. Pleased, maybe?"

"Do you always mind read?"

"Only when I have to."

"Now I *am* in trouble." Pete chuckled, then looked down at his food again. Did Cali realize how beautiful he found her? How perfectly shaped her mouth was?

"Relax, Major. I'm a great keeper of secrets."

He chewed thoughtfully and allowed himself to meet her sparkling green eyes. "You are. We've been working together for some time now, and I know very little about you." God knew, he wanted to know everything. When she raised her hand gracefully to wipe her lips with her napkin, he swallowed hard. Beauty in motion.

As she debated how much to tell him, Cali saw the interest in his eyes. Was it professional or personal interest? She didn't want to misread him as she had Russ. And she didn't dare show Pete how nervous she was. "Well, I don't play golf. I know a lot of execs do, but I find chasing a little white ball around on a green silly."

"Finally we agree on something." Pete grinned. Their jobs at the site had them at loggerheads on a daily basis. He had come to respect Cali's way of resolving problems.

"Red-letter day."

"Possibly. So, you don't like golf. I know you like to ride horses."

"I grew up riding."

"Why do you enjoy it?" Pete wanted to know so much more.

"It gives me a sense of freedom. I love nature. I like being out in it, rain or shine. I notice you like to ride, too." Although he never rode with her, Cali had seen Pete riding with Hesam's security almost daily. He was good at forging loyalty with Hesam's men, who obviously felt the major was one of them.

"Two things we agree on."

Shaking her head, Cali finished off her chicken. "Frightening, isn't it?" Squelching laughter, she looked up to see his eyes gleaming with merriment. For just an instant, Cali found herself wishing they didn't work together. Why couldn't she have met him somewhere else?

"Don't let it go to your head, Ms. Roland."

"Not likely," she answered dryly. The waiter came over to their table, dressed in baggy, dark red pantaloons and a white shirt and apron. Cali handed him her plate and thanked him in Pashto. The young man bowed and removed Pete's plate. A minute later he was back, serving them steaming coffee and dessert.

Pete dipped his spoon into his firni, a custard pudding flavored with cardamom and rose water, and topped with ground pistachios. "I got us a helicopter." He didn't mean to sound as if he was gloating.

"What? You did? How?" Cali's eyes widened.

"An ex-gunny sergeant of mine, Joe Ha-zeltine, married a local woman here in Kabul. He runs a garage and is the world's best scrounger. I told him about our problem of time and distance, and he said he knows of a Canadian merc team that has a helo. He said they're crazy as loons, but he can talk them into letting us hitch a ride a couple times a month. They work up in the north as well." Pete smiled. "I won't tell you what the deal was, but he said they'll go for it." In case the matter ever became public, Pete wanted to protect Cali and her company. This idea was his alone, and if Elliot found out about it, he'd be damned unhappy.

"Wow," Cali whispered, impressed. "You scrounged around among the locals and came up with a Band-Aid fix."

"Something you've done many times on jobs yourself, I'm sure."

Cali grinned and sipped her coffee. "Construction in foreign countries often makes for strange bedfellows. Yes."

"I like the idea of not wasting two days of our time twice a month," he growled. He watched as a soft breeze lifted strands of hair across her smooth brow. His hand fairly itched to reach out and thread his fingers through them. Cali was all-business. There

152

was no flirtation, no come-hither looks. And hell, maybe what he felt was just an unfulfilled daydream on his side of the aisle. After his disastrous history with women, why the hell would he want someone as powerful and confident as Cali Roland to return his fevered yearnings? He had to be crazy. Or maybe lonely. Yeah, that was it.

"You look like you're daydreaming," Cali said. "A penny for your thoughts?" She saw Pete's cheeks turn a dull red. *Oops.* Had she stumbled onto some of his secrets? Mouth curving, she asked, "Are they X-rated? If so, you can plead the Fifth."

"I'll take the Fifth."

Cali decided to hell with it. "You look lonely. Maybe you have a significant other waiting at home?" She had no right to be nosy, but her curiosity was eating her alive. Someone as good-looking and intelligent as Pete Trayhern *had* to have someone. Heart beating strongly in her chest, Cali held her breath waiting for his answer.

Turning the cup slowly in his hands, Pete murmured, "No, no one. Relationships aren't my thing."

"I see." Cali nearly choked on the cooling coffee. Furthermore, she knew she was blushing. Oh, would she ever get over that teenage trait? "I don't know of any relationship that's easy."

Shrugging, Pete said, "I seem to draw women who like to betray me."

Placing her cup on the table, Cali tried to tread lightly. "Betrayal? As in lying to you?"

"Yes, that." Pete scowled. "Go figure. One of the things I value most in life is the truth. So what do I do? I get involved with women who lie to me."

She heard the hurt in his tone even though he was trying to be flippant about it. "You tell the truth and they lie?"

"Yes." Pete fought against the softness that came to Cali's green eyes. He had to resist, dammit. But the hard walls around his heart weakened as he drowned in her compassionate gaze. His words came out haltingly, as if torn from him. "When I was in Annapolis, I fell in love with someone, a midshipman in my class. Her name was Barbara. We agreed to get married when we graduated, but after graduation, she told me that she loved someone else. I asked her how long the other relationship had been going on." Pete shook his head. "Barbara had been seeing the other guy for six months and I never knew it, never caught on."

"Ouch."

"Really."

Cali saw the wounded look in his eyes.

"People can fall out of love. Maybe she was afraid to tell you?"

"No, not Barbara. She was — is — an opportunist. I finally figured that out about a year after we split. The other guy's father was a corporate multimillionaire. She was after money. She wanted to marry power."

"Well, my track record isn't much better," Cali admitted.

"I was wondering if you were married."

"Me? No." She gave him a sour look. "I'm a global tumbleweed. There aren't many men who want to give up their careers for mine."

Relief, sharp and deep, moved through Pete. Finally, he'd found out that Cali Roland was single. "Surely you have someone waiting at home for you."

"Home?" She snorted softly and looked around. "*This* is my home, Major. Wherever I am, that's home. I'm married to my job. At least it's honest and doesn't lie to me." Cali wanted to add, *Like Russ Turner lied to me and used me.* But she bit her tongue.

"I imagine it's tough being a woman in a business like this." Yet his heart was jumping for joy because she wasn't married. Pete tried to tamp down his excitement. It was a stupid reaction, but oh so real. He simply could not imagine Cali without a man in her life, someone completely in love with her — mind, body and soul. She was so unique and rare.

"It can be," Cali said. She really didn't want the conversation to go in this direction. Her loneliness had gotten her into so much trouble that she'd sworn it never would again. Not ever.

"Well, we're a fine pair," Pete said. "Reasonably intelligent, well-off and not bad looking, and without a serious relationship."

She fought the desire to reach over and comfort him. Touching him would be so dangerous. "Maybe it was just as well you found out about Barbara's lies. You wouldn't want to be married to someone like that, would you?" Cali stared at the dark hair that covered his forearms. Would Pete feel as strong and firm as she suspected? Her entire hand tingled. And then there was the sad look on his face . . . No matter how much Cali wanted to be a robot without feelings, it was impossible. And this unexpected personal sharing made her even more vulnerable to him. Fingers curling into her palms, she fought her own inner demons on this issue. She didn't want Pete to mistake her intentions. Uneasy and confused, Cali didn't know how to show her compassion for his pain. Judging from the look in his gray eyes, he appeared caught up by the past in that moment.

"You're right. I've more or less made my peace with Barbara." Pete reluctantly glanced at his watch. "Thanks for listening. I didn't mean to delve into ancient history." He didn't, but something about this woman made him want to spill out his wounded heart to her with an abandon he'd never experienced before. Stymied, Pete saw her give him that soft, understanding look she usually sent everyone but him. Warmth flowed through him, erasing his pain.

"I hear a lot of stories," Cali told him, her voice husky with feeling. "Men get lonely out here. Their wives and families aren't nearby. Sometimes I think our work exaggerates our wounds. We have a lot of time to think about them, without much 'real life' around to distract us."

"Truer words were never spoken," Pete agreed. "Our work *is* lonely." He was damn lonely. And Cali was single. And available.

Refusing to admit he was lonely for her insightful company, he said, "It's time we go." He rose.

Cali was glad he wanted to leave, since she was so close to reaching out and grazing her fingertips across his arm. Pete Trayhern had somehow gotten through her defenses. "I think we'd better hail a cab and get back to our Land Cruiser parked at Elliot's office."

Pete settled his utility cap on his head. "We can probably get one down on the corner." He saw what he thought was regret in Cali's green eyes. Was it? Unsure, he paid his part of the bill. Cali laid money on the table, as well. Dammit, he didn't want to leave the quiet, personal space they'd created with one another. But he had to. Already, he'd made a mistake in having such an intimate dinner with her.

Pete wished they could spend the whole evening here, talking and exploring one another's pasts. But that wasn't going to happen. He saw Cali settle the white construction hat back on her head. Back to business.

It was the last thing he wanted right then. Even after being repeatedly burned by women who had betrayed his trust, Pete found himself in the uneasy position of wanting Cali Roland. What was he going to do? How did a man stop himself from wanting something he could never have?

Chapter Nine

Everything was looking good to Cali. They were making excellent progress at the site. She drove her white Toyota Tundra outside the enclosed power plant area. The August heat was nearly unbearable, and she was glad to have air-conditioning in the truck as she did her daily drive-by inspection. Work was in full swing, with earthmovers and bulldozers pushing dirt to pave the way for the actual buildings. The gravel quarry was operating efficiently. Stockpiles were being maintained.

The concrete plant hoppers could be seen near the hills, about a hundred yards inside the perimeter fence. Cali had had her people carefully train the Afghan workers who would operate the concrete plant. They were learning the rhythm and timing of making cement in order to begin pouring the large foundations.

Clouds of reddish dust rose in the dry,

hot air. Water trucks routinely trundled along, sprinkling the parched ground in order to keep the choking dust to a minimum.

The construction road around the site was not in great shape. Afternoon thunderstorms routinely rushed down from the mountains, delivering monsoonlike downpours that rutted the road. Cali had to drive carefully to avoid the axle-deep pits and gullies. Under no circumstances did she want to rip out the belly of her truck by driving into one of those deep trenches. The red clay was hard as steel when it dried.

Today, she wanted to reach the south corner, stop and take digital photos of the progress. Very early in her career, Cali had learned to document her work with pictures. They never lied. And if the accountants from Pete's side ever questioned anything, Cali would have an array of photos to back up her side of the story.

She pulled over at the far end of the site. Massive thunderheads had formed over the mountains and were now moving toward them. She could see semiopaque, purplish veils of rain darkening the rolling hills coming in her direction. These storms were fitful, powerful and no one could accurately forecast them.

After turning off the engine, Cali threw on her hard hat and climbed out. She reached in and picked up the roll of blueprints. The breeze was fitful, the afternoon air as stifling as an overheated oven. As Cali shut the door and walked around the truck, she made sure her radio was on her belt, as well as her pistol, which she carried everywhere. She flattened the blueprints on the hood of the truck and began a critical study of progress at the site.

Sliding on a pair of sunglasses, Cali looked up. The Taliban were omnipresent. They'd proved that time and again by night forays around the fence. At least twice a month there were raids.

After her meeting with the enemy on horseback, Cali hadn't slept well. It was one thing to be on a construction site in a third world country, and another to be a constant target. Here, fanatics struck without rhyme or reason. Her nerves were taut and she was far more jumpy than she'd ever been on any other project. Cali didn't know which was worse, the danger from the Taliban or the danger of working with Pete Trayhern.

She waved to a group of sentry guards patrolling inside the fence. The small Arabians they rode were different colors, from brown to black, gray and white. Dressed in traditional Afghan costume, the riders rode proudly, their shoulders back and heads held high. They were consummate horsemen, Cali acknowledged.

A breeze gave her momentary respite from the suffocating heat. Breathing deeply, Cali smiled to herself as she took out a red pen and started noting progress on her blueprints. She also dated each entry. Once she'd recorded the changes for the day, she unsnapped her digital camera from the leather case hanging on her belt and began taking the mandatory photos.

Cali was halfway through her shots for the day when she heard a truck approaching far faster than it should. Frowning, she lowered the camera and looked in that direction. Instantly, she went on guard. The truck, a dark blue Toyota with crunched fenders, raced toward her. Dust rose behind it like a rooster tail, indicating its high rate of speed. She saw at least six men in the bed of the pickup, all Afghan and carrying rifles.

Cali didn't like what she saw. Normally, she had a sentry with her, but the guards' truck had had oil-pressure problems and was in the garage for repair. Quickly putting the camera away and gathering up her blueprints, she climbed back into the cab. The blue truck was speeding her way. She grabbed a two-way radio as she started up her Toyota Tundra.

"Major Trayhern, are you there? Over."

Glancing around, Cali saw the speeding vehicle round the corner of the fence and continue toward her. It was less than half a mile away. Who were these men? She knew none of the Afghans who worked on the site would ever speed like that. The potential of tearing out the oil pan on a truck was too real. Yet this blue Toyota was flying toward her as if the driver didn't care.

"Trayhern, here. Over."

Relief drenched Cali as she forced her pickup back onto the rutted road, clasping the radio with her free hand. "Do you have anyone in a blue Toyota out here?" Sweat dribbled down her face. Cali drove her truck toward the eastern side of the work site. Apprehension sizzled through her as the unfamiliar vehicle came closer, gaining on her. The men in the back were standing up and aiming their rifles at her.

"No, no one," he muttered.

She could hear him riffling through papers. More than likely he was in the construction trailer. "Okay, I've got a problem. I see Afghans with guns, and they're aiming at me. I don't have a security truck with me because it broke down. I'm going to make a run down the eastern side of the site, outside the fence. Call out the guards. I may need some help. Over."

"I'm on it, Cali. I'll call the head of security to get out there. And I'm climbing in my truck right now. Be careful. . . ."

She heard the concern and tension in Pete's tone. The worry. They always kept one pickup for security needs at the construction trailer, and she knew Pete would use it to come after her.

The first rifle shots cracked the air like a whip, passing too close to her head. Cursing softly, Cali gunned the engine and jerked the radio to her lips. "Pete, they're firing at me!" It was too late to take back use of his first name. Cali addressed him formally to keep that distance between them, but right now she was scared. Scared she was going to be killed.

After dropping the radio on the seat, Cali wrapped both hands around the wheel and stomped on the gas. The blue Toyota kept gaining on her, and she tried to think beyond her panic. And then, like a storm of hail, bullets slammed into her vehicle.

Son of a bitch! As Cali sped toward the curve, red dust rose behind her. Good! If they couldn't see her through the thick cloud, they couldn't fire accurately at her.

Grimly, she kept her attention riveted on the dangerously rutted road. She purposely straddled the deep trenches, knowing that she'd have to slow down to take the corner. It wasn't a banked curve, unfortunately. No, if she didn't brake now, she'd go skidding off the road and into the desert. If that happened, she was dead meat. She didn't have to guess who was behind her. It was a Taliban attack. In broad daylight.

Damn them! The Tundra groaned and skidded as Cali hit the curve. The truck bumped and jostled. Knuckles white on the wheel, she forced the growling vehicle to stay on the road. Oh God, if she hit one of those ruts at this speed, it could flip her over. Sweat ran down Cali's rib cage. Her fingers ached as she held on to the wheel and guided the Tundra across the hazardous terrain.

More bullets struck her truck. The pinging sounds were so close! Gasping, Cali felt a moment's relief when the vehicle hugged the corner and came out of it without sliding off the road. Up ahead, at the nearest security gate, she saw a white pickup speeding in her direction. Pete! It had to be! Cali suddenly ducked and winced as the windshield blew inward on her. A well-aimed bullet caused thousands of sparkling bits of glass to explode all around her. She squinted to protect her eyes, feeling the sting of glass striking her arms and neck as wind roared into the cab.

Cali had no choice but to keep going. Through her rearview mirror she saw the blue Toyota lunge toward the corner. The driver nearly lost control, the truck bumping wildly and nearly skidding off the road. She had half a mile to go before she reached help. The security guards were standing up in the bed of the white Roland truck; she saw their M16s at the ready.

Suddenly, she heard a sharp sound, and her Tundra began to sway drunkenly. *Shit!* The Taliban soldiers had hit one of the tires. Riding on three wheels, the truck was no longer controllable at this speed. Eyes widening, Cali fought to keep the vehicle straight. If she hit one of those ruts . . .

"No!" The scream tore from her lips as her vehicle listed. And then, at forty miles an hour, the flat tire on the front left side sank into a deep rut. Everything went into slow-motion then, as if Cali were viewing a film. She felt the jarring slam as the wheel hit the deep groove. The next second, the truck was lifting as if it had wings. Like a slow-moving nightmare, it leaped upward, its motor growling, then bounced nose-first on the road. In the frenzy of movement and sound, Cali saw Pete's truck speeding toward her. She caught a glimpse of the security guards answering Taliban fire. But none of this mattered now. She was in the air, and careening off the side of the road into a desert littered with brush.

Since she hadn't had time to fasten her seat belt, Cali knew she was in trouble. Her mind raced with ideas on how to survive this. She didn't want to die. As her truck sailed off the road, slowly rotating to the left, she gripped the steering wheel with every ounce of strength she possessed.

Pete let out a curse as he saw Cali's truck jam its left front tire into an unforgiving rut. Seconds later, it was flying skyward. His heart screamed out in protest. He didn't want her hurt! Or killed. Tromping on the accelerator, he heard the security guards firing at the approaching Toyota, and saw the vehicle suddenly veer to the right. Five men were flung out of the bed like rag dolls as the vehicle struck the deadly ruts.

Acting on pure adrenaline, Pete slammed on the brakes and yelled out the window, "Go after them!"

Desperate to get to Cali, Pete stopped the pickup and bailed out, his pistol raised. As he sprinted toward Cali's truck, now un-moving, a myriad of images ran through his mind. Was Cali okay? He was afraid of what he would find, yet desperate to get to her. In the background, he heard his guards clambering out of the pickup, screaming in Pashto at the dazed and stunned Taliban scattered nearby.

Running hard, air tearing raggedly from his lungs, Pete reached the small rise where the Tundra sat. Relief flooded him as he saw Cali move. At least she was alive! The door swung open. She fell out and landed on her hands and knees.

"Cali!" he yelled, putting his pistol away. Pete dropped to her side and gripped her shoulders. "Are you okay? Talk to me."

Her face was ashen and the bloody cuts on her neck and arms shocked him.

"I'm okay. Give me a minute." Cali sat up and leaned against his hands. At once, Pete's nearness steadied her. She felt him embrace her and hold on to her.

"My God, I could have flipped over. . . ." Closing her eyes, Cali raised her hand to her head.

Pete divided his attention between Cali's injuries and his guards. They'd rounded up all the attackers and disarmed them. They were settling the prisoners in a tight circle and placing plastic handcuffs around their wrists.

Reassured, Pete leaned down, his face inches from hers. "Look at me, Cali."

She lifted her chin and drowned in his stormy gray eyes. "I'm okay, really. I just bashed my head against the window." She pointed to a growing goose egg on her brow. Giving him a crazy smile, she added, "No concussion. My pupils are fine." His touch felt more than just stabilizing to Cali. The shock from her brush with death began to dissolve beneath the fierce caresses of his trembling hands across her tense shoulders.

"You sure?" Pete studied her beautiful forest-green eyes. The urge to sweep her into his arms nearly overwhelmed him, but he fought it. Damn, but he wanted to press his mouth against her parted lips. He wanted to taste Cali. Feel her.

The thoughts were shocking to him. Galvanizing. What the hell was wrong with him? Angrily shaking off his desire, Pete abruptly leaned away from her.

"You look fine. But we need to get you to the doctor. Can you stand?"

Cali was unprepared for the sudden gruffness in his tone. "Uh, yeah." Pete helped her up, and she was grateful because a wave of dizziness assailed her. Unexpectedly, she

169

swayed against his warm, hard body. Oh, how many times had Cali wanted to do just this? Wanted to touch him? Feel his strong, vibrant form against hers? *Too many times.*

"Easy. . . ." Pete breathed, his mouth pressed against her hair. "Take it easy, Cali. Let me help you to my truck. . . ."

It was heavenly to be tucked protectively against his side, Cali decided. Her vision blurred, then cleared as she walked forward drunkenly. Maybe she'd hit her skull a little harder than she'd thought. Maybe her hard head, as her father called it, was not so hard, after all. Her boots seemed to have a mind of their own as she stumbled through the soft sand. Pete kept his arm around her shoulders and held on to her as if she were a priceless work of art. Cali's mind reeled and tangled, along with her fast-beating heart. She could smell the sweat from his body, feel the dampness of his T-shirt.

Pete ordered his guards to stay with the prisoners. After tucking Cali into the truck, he made a call to the office trailer. Javad, his right-hand man, would inform Sheik Hesam, and would get another company truck out here to transport the raiders. Grimly, Pete waved to his guards, who held the scowling, bleeding prisoners at gunpoint.

Once in the truck, Pete turned to Cali. The dark, ugly blue bruise forming on her forehead undid him. "You really need to be checked out by Dr. Hakimi."

"I know." Cali's voice sounded hollow to her own ears. She struggled to latch the seat belt around her. Too bad she hadn't done that earlier. But then, banging her head against the window would have happened anyway, due to the pickup almost flipping over.

Pete drove at a moderate speed toward the gates in the fence. "Tell me what happened."

Cali told him bits and pieces. By the time they reached the entrance, a number of site security men on horseback were galloping out to help bring in the Taliban prisoners.

Lifting her hand to rub her forehead, Cali murmured, "Hesam isn't going to be happy about this. The Taliban have been attacking us regularly. I know he's trying his best to find them up in the caves in those hills, but there are more of them than he counted on. This is getting crazy."

Nodding, Pete drove straight to the medical trailer. "I agree. We need to talk to him. Get more of his men making trips up there in the hills to root them out. We can't have people attacked right outside our site like this."

Now Cali's head began to ache in earnest. She'd been injured before and knew the routine: first shock set in, followed by pain. "Are you going to put a call in to him this afternoon?"

"I will after we get you to the doc." Worried, Pete glanced over at Cali. Her face was ashen. She'd closed her eyes and her fingers were pressed against her brow. With her lips parted, she looked excruciatingly vulnerable. As he parked the truck, he tried to swallow the feelings for her that had only grown over the last three months. Climbing out, he said, "I'll come around and get you. Stay put."

No problem there, Cali thought. She felt like jelly that had been dumped out of a jar. Relying on Pete's guiding hand, she inched out of the truck and allowed him to shepherd her up the wooden steps and into the trailer. As Cali eased onto the awaiting gurney, she heard Pete call for the doctor. Hurting everywhere, feeling frayed and vulnerable from her experience, she tried to ignore his gentleness and concern. But it was impossible. When Cali had least expected it, Pete Trayhern had come to her rescue.

CHAPTER TEN

Pete couldn't curb his worry about Cali and her injuries. He'd just taken care of the Taliban prisoners and had driven back to the medical trailer to check on her. The nursing assistant told him that the doctor had seen Cali, and she was at her own trailer, resting for the next twenty-four hours.

The day was hot and he was sweating profusely. As he drove down a two-lane dirt road toward the western side of the complex, he noted dust was everywhere, despite the water trucks on duty. The trailers in this section were used as homes for the main construction people. The units had been spaced far enough apart so no mortar round or grenade launcher could hit more than one at a time. Being bunched together wasn't a good idea in a war zone. And this was turning out to be a constant battlefield.

Pete knew by heart where Cali's trailer was located. It was a standard terra-cotta color, like all the rest. In the window nearest the door, however, a large, healthy potted plant was hung. As he pulled up and turned off the ignition, he noticed that the plant had bloomed. The blossom looked like a pink hibiscus — a touch of beauty in the desert. Just like Cali.

How was she? He wondered if he should stop by to see her or just leave her alone. Pete didn't want to keep second-guessing himself, so he climbed out of the truck and locked it. If she were a man, he wouldn't hesitate to visit, make sure she was okay. He took the wooden steps two at a time, then knocked on the white aluminum door. Maybe Cali was asleep. Maybe he should have called her first. His heart roiled in his chest, and he wiped sweat off his face with his shirtsleeve.

The door opened and his heart picked up in beat. Cali was dressed in pink linen trousers and a dark green, formfitting top. Her left arm was wrapped in white gauze and tape. Pete saw the darkness in her eyes and figured she had to be hurting. The warmth in her gaze, however, quieted his anxiety.

"Come on in. I was just going to pour myself a well-deserved shot of whiskey to settle my nerves. Not exactly doctor's orders, but I know it will help." Cali grimaced as she stepped aside so he could enter. "I'm getting the shakes now. Adrenaline letdown."

"Pour me one, too?" Pete asked, turning and shutting the door. At once the delicious coolness of air-conditioning enveloped Pete. He took off his cap and stuffed it into his back pocket, grinning tentatively. "I wanted to make sure you were all right."

Cali tried to keep her tone light as she went to the kitchen and fetched the liquor from beneath the sink. Her hand trembled slightly while she poured the amber liquid into two shot glasses. "I'm just shook up right now. I guess I didn't think the Taliban were so bold or stupid to try and attack us like that. I know they've been aggressive, but never like this. And am I ever sorry I didn't have that security pickup with me today. It's the last time that will happen." She reached for one glass, turned and handed it to Pete. Their fingers touched and Cali tried to ignore the resulting tingle. Impossible.

Pete nodded in thanks. "This is a new type of attack," he agreed wearily.

Cali lifted her glass in a toast and quickly downed the contents. "Let's drink to life." The liquid burned like fire in her throat and gut. She set the glass aside and walked to the couch, tucking one leg beneath her as she sat down.

Pete downed his own whiskey and set the empty glass on the counter. His lips drew away from his teeth as he sucked in air, trying to reduce the fiery sensation of the liquor.

"Mind if I join you?" he asked, gesturing to the leather sofa. Cali looked so fragile and he ached to take her into his arms. Dammit, he couldn't protect her, and that realization was a brutal one. Nor could he show his emotions as he had out there at the accident scene. And yet there wasn't a thing he would have done differently.

"Sure, sit down." Cali was surprised that he wanted to stay, but her head hurt too much to think about it. This wasn't the time to explore her feelings for him.

Pete joined her, settling a few feet from where she sat. He wanted to move closer, but that wouldn't be right. He planted his elbows on his thighs and clasped his hands together. "I just wanted to tell you about the conversation I had with Hesam earlier. This is an entirely new style of attack. The sheik said the Taliban were pretty quiet in his province until we came. It's one thing for them to lob rocket-propelled grenades into our site at night, but quite another to attack you in a truck along the perimeter road in daylight."

Cali leaned back, feeling the effects of the alcohol soothing her jittery nervous system. "They were out to get anyone who was there. I'm sure they didn't know who was in the truck," she said. Pete's closeness helped. Right now, she wanted him around, and somehow, he must have sensed it. Or maybe he was just making a house call because he was superintendent at the site? Cali wasn't sure, and really didn't want an answer to that question.

"I'm not certain I agree. They were after a high-value target. Why else would they risk a daylight attack against our security?"

"I don't know." Cali was afraid to think they might have purposely targeted her.

Shaking his head, Pete studied his callused hands and the many small scars on his fingers. "How are you doing now?" He glanced up and held her gaze.

"I'll live. The doc gave me a tetanus shot, antibiotics to take and —" she pointed to her bandaged arm "— he picked fifteen shards of windshield glass out of my arm. And found three more pieces here," she said, gesturing to her neck.

"Thank God you didn't get any in the

face. If one of those splinters had hit you in the eyes . . ." Pete's voice trailed off at the horror of that possibility. He tore his gaze from hers and frowned down at his fisted hands. *You have the most beautiful eyes in the world. I could lose myself in them. . . .* He wanted to tell her. But he didn't dare whisper those words. This close call had brought feelings to the surface he'd not been aware of before.

"I got lucky and I know it," Cali agreed softly. "I wonder if they'd have attacked if security had been with me? Were they waiting to catch someone out on the perimeter without a guard, or was it just the luck of the draw?"

"Security will interrogate the prisoners. We'll know more soon. I don't like what happened, Cali." Pete didn't care if she objected to his use of her first name. Somehow, he couldn't call her "Ms. Roland" now.

"I'd like some answers myself." She could tell Pete was wrestling with a lot of emotions just by looking at his chiseled, bronzed face. His straight black hair was closely cropped, a few errant strands dipping rebelliously over his furrowed brow. He was intensely handsome, and Cali felt a delicious sense of desire for him as she absorbed his strong profile. What was there *not* to like

178

about this guy?

Plenty, her head told her. *Think about Russ. Think about what he did to you.*

"From now on, Cali, you will have security with you. If the truck breaks down, you'll wait until it's fixed before you leave the site. Have you ever been shot at on other projects?" Pete asked.

He saw her lips part. Lips he so badly wanted to taste, touch and make his own. Obviously, he couldn't act on his desire.

Shaking her head, Cali said, "No. First time. Oh, I've been in a lot of dire straits on other job sites. Even had a gun aimed at my chest by a pissed-off sheik. But we managed to calm things down, and cooler heads prevailed." Cali smiled, feeling her tension beginning to dissolve. "If I'd been thinking, I'd have just pulled out my pistol today and started shooting back instead of running from them."

Pete straightened in alarm. "No, Cali, you did the right thing. It was five of them against one of you. Besides, hindsight is always twenty-twenty." His terror over what had happened — what could have happened — made his gut feel as if it were burning. "You can't outgun these bastards."

"I didn't know who they were. At first I thought they were some of our people, driving too fast on that friggin' road. I swear, I'm going to find some extra gravel and get a dump truck out there and fill those ruts. They are just too dangerous for anyone to drive on, never mind the damage they cause our trucks, which are not in endless supply out here."

Hearing the grimness in her tone, Pete said, "We have to get some culverts across that road before we put gravel on it. We need to drain off the rainwater." He'd have to eyeball his budget to find extra money for the tons of gravel and pipes. Expenditures like this often popped up on a construction site. Still, his budget was tight and he had to be careful where he spent any cash. He had approval to do some drainage projects in town. He'd take some of that material, and pour open concrete channels there instead. Kerwin Elliot and his bean counters back in Kabul made him go over the budget every two weeks. Pete didn't give a damn what this would mean. Cali had nearly been killed, and was lucky even though her truck had flipped over.

"I'm feeling better now, Pete — I mean, Major." Cali's eyes were growing heavy. "I think the whiskey helped."

"I don't mind if you call me Pete," he said in a gruff tone.

Cali had closed her eyes momentarily. Her hair was mussed, red strands burnished with gold highlights. Her pixie-style haircut was perfect for someone who wore a hard hat all day long. She didn't need a fancy hairdo to look beautiful to him. No, she was a natural product of the earth, and Pete liked that about her. She never wore perfume or makeup. Lip balm, yes, because the desert air was brutal. And lip balm simply enhanced those elegant, soft lips of hers that he wanted so badly to kiss.

Cali sighed and opened her eyes. "Thanks, I will. You can call me Cali if you want, too." The man had just saved her life. She couldn't continue to be so standoffish under the circumstances. Through her lashes, she studied his strong face. There was something so clean and powerful about Pete Trayhern. Her defenses were weak, so she let herself study his features.

"Listen, can I call anyone for you? I'm sure your parents might like to know what happened and that you're okay."

She winced. Not only was she dizzy and tired, but she couldn't avoid the issue. Yes, her parents should be contacted. "If you could just call my dad . . ."

"Are you sure about not contacting anyone else? I know you said there was no one special in your life. . . ."

"There's no guy you have to call." It hurt to say the words, and she saw Pete frown. Uncertain what emotion flitted briefly across his face, she said, "Look, my past with men is awful and I'm tired of getting hurt all the time." Cali shrugged and touched the center of her chest, above her heart. "I seem to pick the wrong guy every time. Neanderthals in disguise are what I call them. They pretend to want to see me as strong, confident, a leader in my own right, but after a while, their mask falls away and they try to control me. I won't put up with that anymore. I'm twenty-nine years old and I've been around the block one too many times." There, the truth was out. Or as much as she was going to say about it. Russ had been the worst of all of them.

Pete rubbed his hands against his thighs and sat up. "I see." It was all he could think to say. He wanted to comfort her, but knew they had to keep some distance. Instead of reaching for her, he leaned back on the couch.

"It's not something I'm proud of," Cali told him, touching her aching head briefly.

"I've already told you I don't have a sterling record with women, either." Somehow, Pete wanted her to feel better about her honest admission. He could see suffering in Cali's eyes, along with real pain.

"The women who lied to you?"

"That's right. My parents taught all their kids about the honor of telling the truth. I just can't figure out how I always draw women who don't."

Cali felt for Pete and heard the rawness in his tone. "Maybe the right woman just hasn't come along yet," she said softly.

"I've sort of given up," Pete admitted guardedly. Why was he telling her what lay in his heart of hearts? The words just tumbled out, unbidden. Uncontrolled. What kind of power and influence did she wield over him? Pete felt almost naked in front of her.

"I told my dad last year that there wasn't a man on this earth that could reach the bar I'm insisting on."

"And what did he say?"

"Well, you have to put this into the context of his marriage, Pete. My dad fell in love with my mother on a construction site. I guess they fought like cats and dogs. They tamed each other, he said." Cali gave a careful one-shoulder shrug. "They're going on thirty-five years of marriage now. They still love each other. That's amazing to me."

"Yeah, throwaway marriages are a dime a

dozen nowadays," Pete said unhappily. "People cohabit and they don't even think of weddings anymore. My own parents married around age thirty. My mother said that she'd been hit by a car at the Reagan Airport in Washington, D.C. The accident blinded her. My dad rescued her, stayed with her and took care of her until she regained her sight."

"Wow," Cali murmured, "that's a helluva story."

Pete felt infinitely better discussing his family instead of himself. And he sensed Cali needed someone to talk to after her near brush with death. That was understandable. He'd had many such experiences with his Marines after they engaged the enemy and needed "let down" time afterward. As an assistant company commander, he was used to listening to his officers and people. Sometimes just listening provided a monumental healing for a soldier who had survived combat. "Over time my parents just gravitated to one another. My mother finally got her sight back, and she told me, when she saw my father for the first time, she fell in love with him even more than before."

"So, what's wrong with us, then? Why can't we find a love like that?" Cali looked unhappily around the trailer. Outside, she could hear the throaty rumble of bulldozers at work, the deeper growl of earthmovers. All of it was somehow calming and re-assuring to her.

"I don't know, Cali. I've fallen in and out of relationships so many times I just can't take it anymore." Staring down at his scarred hands, Pete added, "My parents have a relationship based on mutual admiration and respect."

"Like my folks," Cali agreed. "It's a generational thing, maybe. I mean, look at our contemporaries. We can't keep a relationship going for three months, much less thirty years!"

"What does that say about us?" Pete mused, more to himself than her. It was so easy to talk with Cali. "What's in us that we can't make a relationship work? Are we so narcissistic and into ourselves that we lack the selflessness it takes to make a relationship fly? Are we so scared of making a commitment that, at the least hint of one, we find something wrong with the person we're with and force them to leave?"

"Or," Cali added thoughtfully, "are we trying to live up to an impossible standard our parents set for us? Maybe we lack the grit and heart that real love demands from both people to make it work."

"If I had those answers, I wouldn't be where I am." That was the truth, and Pete didn't like admitting it.

"So," Cali wondered out loud, "do we demand such perfection of our partner that they'll never reach that bar?"

"Maybe," he replied. "I know I look at every woman I date and compare her to my mother, to my parents' relationship."

"So do I, with men," Cali said. "Probably a fatal mistake. I know better. All people are different."

"Are we aiming too high, then?" Pete asked her. Cali's face was less tense now, he noticed with relief.

"Maybe we are as unable to forgive our imperfect partner as we are unable to forgive ourselves for our daily mistakes."

"You might be on to something."

Cali was hungry for personal conversation with Pete. Maybe because of the combination of whiskey and being in shock, she felt brave enough to ask him deeply personal questions. "So, what are some of your warts?"

Pete felt his guard go up. He'd wanted to be a good listener for Cali, but now he wasn't sure what to say. "Oh, no, you first. You brought up this topic."

"Chicken heart."

"Yeah, I am."

"Men. You want to be seen as so tough and capable, and yet you're like melted butter in a skillet about some things. I've watched your face change when one of the Afghan workmen brought his baby son for you to meet, Pete. What is it about men showing their soft underbelly? What stops you from being just as vulnerable and open as women are?"

"Social training, maybe?" he suggested. "Is that what you look for in a man? Vulnerability?"

Cali sat up and uncurled her legs. "I want to be able to express, share and feel every emotion with the man in my life. He doesn't have to cry, but he can. I want him to be in touch with his emotions, and more importantly, I want him unafraid to share them all with me — the good, the bad and the ugly. I don't think that's asking too much, do you?" Cali gave him a scrutinizing look.

"No, but it's asking a lot. Most men can't do that, Cali." Pete shifted uncomfortably. This was the first time they'd had a personal conversation, and it mattered to him more than he wanted to admit.

"Can't or won't? From where I stand, it's a social conditioning process that definitely needs to be thrown away," Cali said, frustration in her voice. "Men can feel just as deeply as any woman. You can't tell me you don't. But if a man can't share his feelings with the woman he loves, then there's a loss of intimacy. And if a man can't be intimate with his partner, what's the use of getting serious?"

Pete felt compelled to move the conversation to safer ground. "My parents have that kind of intimacy. So I know it's possible."

Cali pressed her palm to her brow for a moment as a wave of dizziness came and went. "You're right, Pete. I watched my parents growing up, and they were always intimate with one another. They would sit down every night at the dinner table and talk about their day, problems, triumphs and failures. I had good training on what it takes to keep a marriage together. And so far, I haven't found one man on the planet who has the guts to just be an ordinary human being who feels things and can share them with me." Russ had pretended to be that way, but she didn't want to reveal this debacle with Pete just yet. The radio on his belt squawked suddenly, and if Cali didn't know better, she would think he looked relieved.

He straightened and answered the call.

Hesam had arrived, and questioning of the Taliban prisoners would begin. Pete had to get back to the security trailer pronto.

"You heard the call." He rose, tucking the radio back into his belt. Truth be known, he was glad to be leaving. The spell between them was broken, and Pete was thankful in one way. In another, his lonely heart had absorbed this quiet, honest moment, possibly more than he liked.

"Keep me in the loop on this. And would you call my dad?"

"That's a promise. I'll call him first and then go to the security trailer, where Hesam is waiting." Glancing down, Pete studied her hands, which were almost as callused and scarred as his. Cali earned her living by being one with the earth, just as he did. He wanted to reach down, squeeze her fingers reassuringly and make her feel better. He couldn't do that, but his heart accelerated with sudden, unexpected joy. Pete felt incredibly light, as if he were lifted on invisible wings. The look in Cali's eyes, however, was solemn and dark. She was a pensive, intelligent woman who dug into the enigmatic corners of herself and others. That scared him. And that was good, he told himself. Cali expected too much of a man. Based on what she'd said, he certainly

189

couldn't fill her needs. Pete should have felt relief over that, but he didn't.

"Tell my dad that after I have a nap, I'll call him," Cali said. The sudden, crazy desire she felt to stand up and step into Pete's arms surprised her. The part of her that apparently hadn't learned the lessons Russ had taught her wanted to throw herself into Pete's embrace, kiss him until they melted together in a scalding pool of desire.

It had to be the whiskey and the adrenaline, Cali told herself. Right now, she felt weak and almost out of control. She'd never had two close brushes with death and wasn't sure how to cope with them.

"I'll reassure him you're okay," Pete murmured. He pulled the cap from his back pocket and settled it on his head. If he didn't leave, he'd be treading on dangerous ground — a big mistake. Patting the radio, he said, "I'll see you later. Call me if you need anything."

"I won't need anything." Cali was lying, but that was okay. "I think I'll lie down for a while."

"It's a good thing to do, after shock," he agreed softly. "I'll let you know what we find out from the prisoners."

"Thanks. I'd like that."

Cali watched as he walked toward the

door. Pete's shoulders were incredibly broad. And he carried many responsibilities on them with the ease of a born leader. She knew men who could never handle what Pete did here at the site. He was a damn good manager and the Afghan workmen truly respected him. Even liked him, which was unusual. Heart glowing, she fought the feelings. Right now, she was exhausted. And her boundaries with Major Trayhern were at an all-time low. Somehow, Cali knew she had to repair them and get some distance. She'd never expected him to rescue her, much less hold her. And the walls she'd erected against him had dissolved like putty when he'd unexpectedly embraced her out there. Confused and in pain, Cali was glad to see him leave. She had to have time to heal herself emotionally to remain immune to Pete Trayhern.

CHAPTER ELEVEN

The late-August heat was blistering as Cali stood off to one side of the cement operation with Pete. This was the first test run on mixing concrete. The three hoppers, large steel cylinders with sloping bottoms, stood upright in their sturdy steel frames. One held cement, another sand and the last one gravel. The screw assemblies at the bottom of each fed just the right amount of each material into a large metal mixing drum — or were supposed to. There, a measured amount of water was added to create the specified concrete blend.

Cali's heart beat a little harder in her chest. Roland Construction was responsible for supplying the different types of concrete for the foundation pours. She'd labored long hours with engineers of the German company that had won the subcontracting bid to erect and operate the plant. Making concrete was like mixing up batter for a cake, she thought, smiling to herself. A number of workmen were moving about, including Albert Golze, the head of the company.

"Looks good," Pete said to her, giving her a sideways glance. The hot Afghan sun burned overhead and he was sweating freely. So was she. Her green eyes, glimmering with excitement and anticipation, tugged at his heart.

"Yes. Fingers crossed. First pour. Let's see how today goes." Cali lifted the radio to her lips and told Golze to start the process.

The machinery began to rumble and roar. The mixing drum turned, and water splashed as it rotated. Cali watched the process with great interest. Today was an important day, a make-or-break moment. A passing breeze cooled her sweaty skin momentarily, under the long-sleeved white blouse protecting her arms from the sun. It had been a smart move to wet down the pink bandanna she always wore around her neck. It acted like a mini air conditioner of sorts.

"Here come the delivery trucks," she told Pete, pointing to four big vehicles slowly backing down into the area where the drum would release the first batch of concrete. Worry laced her anticipation. This was a nerve-racking ordeal for any contractor wanting to impress her boss.

Pete nodded at her. "I liked your jury-rigging on that dump, since we only have two real concrete mixers out here."

Cali arched inwardly, relishing his praise. "Lessons learned from other sites in third world countries." Pete, as owner, was responsible for furnishing six concrete mixing trucks. But two trucks had disappeared en route to the site and two had been damaged beyond repair in road accidents. Replacements were ordered, but no one could guarantee when they would be delivered. They'd had to improvise or fall months behind schedule. Four dump trucks had been requisitioned by Cali, and their beds rebuilt by her welding crews to carry concrete around the site. It was jury-rigging at its best, but in a remote, rural environment like this, she had to have cards up her sleeve to ensure the job came in on time.

Pete watched the lead dump truck ease down the incline, the driver following hand signals of a German construction worker. Pete had to give Golze credit — he and his men had worked their asses off converting four of their best dump trucks into concrete carriers in lieu of the specially designed mixers. Golze and Cali had worked for weeks designing a steel container to fit in the bed of each truck. It was nail-biting time for Pete. He hadn't been sure what she could come up with as a fix for the problem.

"Think we'll ever get the required number of mixers out here?" Cali asked. The truck was now ready to receive a load of concrete, and she tried to remain patient. *Let it work without a hitch. . . .* Unconsciously, she held her breath again.

"Doubtful," he responded.

Golze himself was in the control house above the waiting truck bed. If one of the three hopper feeds didn't work properly, the load would have to be dumped and lost. Not to mention this would slow down the entire schedule, which Pete knew she wanted to avoid. He was tense for her and for himself. Since the Taliban attack a couple of weeks ago, the whole site had been riddled with tension. Today, it was either going to dissolve or stretch to its limit, depending upon what happened in the next few minutes.

Pete saw the different hoppers delivering their ingredients. The sounds of the mixing drum groaning and grinding continued as it slowly turned. He could see the gray slush from where he stood. "So far, so good," he murmured. Taking a water bottle from his belt, he slugged down half of it. Staying hydrated in a hot desert like this was essential. Cali followed suit.

Pete enjoyed gazing out the corner of his eye at the curve of her long, graceful neck. She was attractive no matter what way she moved or what angle he viewed her from. And since her scrape with death at the hands of the Taliban, his protective nature had been working overtime. He saw the three pink scars on her neck where glass shards had been removed. He'd also noted shiny scars dotting her beautifully tanned arms. It hurt him to see what the bastards had done to her.

The interrogation of the attackers had confirmed they were Taliban. They refused to answer any questions except to tell Pete they hated Americans and would kill them on sight. Hesam's guards had taken them away for further interrogation. The sheik had discovered the men were part of a larger ring operating from a high mountain village in the Hindu Kush range. With the help of another sheik, Hesam had sent fifty of his soldiers on horseback up to that faraway cave. They had captured twenty-five more Taliban fighters, who were now in custody in Kabul. Since then, there had been no more attacks on the site, and Pete hoped the lull would continue. His mind turned back to the woman standing at his side.

How different Cali was from others he had known. She shrugged off the scars, saying that they were just medals of valor for living life. He liked her attitude. Wisps of red hair clung damply to her temples as she put the bottle back into her belt. Pete had wanted another in-depth conversation with her, but site demands stood in the way. Yes, he was with Cali for up to eighteen hours a day, off and on, but the project took precedence. Often, Javad was at his side, and Pete was grateful not to have to deal with his deeper feelings.

And thinking of Javad, he saw the young man smiling and waving as he limped up the hill toward them. Javad always carried a radio, to communicate with Pete and translate orders to the work crews when necessary. He had a new prosthetic leg, thanks to Pete's intervention with a Kabul hospital. No longer did the boy have to hobble around on crutches.

Pete nodded a greeting to his approaching assistant, then turned back to watch the operation.

Everything took time and skill. Golze came down off the platform where the operations shed was located — the structure housing the instrument panel that controlled the mixing process. He threw Pete a thumbs-up, grinning broadly.

"He's confident," Cali said hopefully. *Oh please, let this pour go well.* How badly she wanted to show Pete that she had what it took to do the job. Russ had hurt her confidence, and Cali saw this project as a way to prove to herself she still had the goods.

Pete crooked one corner of his mouth upward, and heat suffused her body. That little-boy smile of his was so precious. She ached for just one hour alone with him, such as they'd shared three weeks ago in her trailer. Since then, they'd returned to their usual impersonal, professional behavior. That hour had nearly been her undoing. Under no circumstance could Cali let down her guard like that again.

"I think confidence and construction go together. Both start with a *C*," Pete said. "You can't have one without the other." His pulse beat a little harder as he watched Golze walk over to the hoppers. So much hinged on this effort.

Cali nodded. She lifted her hard hat, wiped sweat from her brow and settled it back on her head. Golze was giving orders to the hopper operator, an Afghan who was being trained by the knowledgeable concrete foreman. Eventually, all these functions would be handled by locals.

Pete had his own people ready to take test cylinders of the poured concrete. The samples would be cured and then tested at specified standards by junior civil engineers working alongside the German crew. They would check the concrete, not Golze. Pete had his own men on the job because the concrete crew might be tempted to fudge on the numbers and say the mix was fine, when it wasn't. That way, good concrete got poured and bad batches were rejected.

Again, Pete's nerves fluttered and his stomach tightened. Bad concrete was a nightmare he didn't want or need.

Cali watched with anxiety as the drum containing the concrete slowly released its load into the waiting truck. When the gray slush started running into the metal vat, the jury-rigged dump truck groaned and settled on its shocks. Cali knew such vehicles were not specifically designed to haul the monumental weight of several cubic yards of wet concrete. She and Golze had calculated meticulously, matching capacity with material poundage.

"Here we go," Pete said warily. "Come on, let's watch the first foundation pour."

The banked enthusiasm in his voice ignited her own nervous tension. She saw worry and excitement in his face. Mouth dry from anxiety, she took another swig of water, then followed him across the dusty, graveled parking area to their trucks. They would drive the short distance to the actual power plant foundation site.

The dump truck groaned, coughed and backfired. Then slowly it chugged up the dirt incline from the mixer area. Gears ground as the Afghan driver learned firsthand about carrying heavy, wet concrete.

By the time Cali arrived at the pour site, Pete was already feeling hopeful. He watched, mesmerized, as the truck bed lifted with groaning protest. Gray concrete oozed out of the makeshift hopper and ran sluggishly into the waiting forms below. Five German crew members, with Afghan counterparts, were armed with concrete vibrators to insure the mix flowed evenly around the steel reinforcing bars. It was important to get the concrete well distributed; air bubbles took a lot of work and money to correct. The process would continue for four straight hours, the dump trucks interspersed with the two mixers.

"Looks good," Pete said finally. A sharp drop in tension allowed his stomach to relax. It had been only twenty minutes and that was good for a first pour. Since the concrete would have another slab right above, it wasn't necessary to steel trowel the surface.

He watched his people put the last of the test cylinders in their boxes. They would be moved to the curing room later, to be crushed at seven-, fourteen- and twenty-one-day intervals to ensure the concrete met specifications. If the samples passed muster, it meant the concrete was good. If they didn't, concrete that had just been poured would have to be taken out and the process started all over again.

"Yeah, looks real good," Cali agreed, relieved that things were going so well. She looked up at Pete, who was squinting against the sun. "I need a few minutes to discuss some other things with you. Your office?"

He swung his attention to her. "Sure. We have to celebrate placing two hundred cubic yards of concrete today." His happiness over their success was tempered by the serious look on Cali's face. He glanced at his watch to check the time, then told Javad he'd be at the office trailer for about thirty minutes, in case he was needed. The young man smiled and nodded.

Cali walked beside Pete to their trucks.

The breeze caressed her hot face, and she took off her damp neckerchief and wiped her dusty cheeks. "Do you look forward to a cold shower every night like I do?"

Pete laughed shortly. "Yeah. Truth be known, I'd like to take one three or four times a day. The grit gets into my clothes and chafes the hell out of me."

"Ditto," Cali agreed. "We're certified dirt balls, there's no question." Heart lightening with each step, she felt as if she'd just been released from a dark prison. The converted dump trucks were a triumph.

Glancing over at him, Cali wondered if he was as excited by the success. He was deeply tanned, with strands of black hair plastered to his skull beneath the dark blue hard hat he wore. His mouth held her answer; she could see the corners lifting upward, as if ready to grin. And his gray eyes had lightened considerably.

"Well, while we talk, let's clean the dirt out of our mouths and throats with some cold Pepsi," he offered.

Pete drank nearly half a Pepsi before putting the can down in front of him. Wiping his mouth as he sat behind the planning desk, he watched Cali pour her soda into a large plastic tumbler filled with ice cubes.

The office staff was in the field, the trailer quiet for once except for radio chatter that didn't directly concern them.

"Masochist. Now your stomach is going to knot up because it wasn't prepared for all that cold stuff," Cali warned him. She took a sip and tried to brace herself for the coming confrontation.

Rubbing his flat, hard belly, Pete said, "You know what? My mouth and throat are very happy now." He poured the rest of his Pepsi into the glass in front of him. Cali had taken off her hard hat and laid it on the desk behind her. He'd hung his on a peg near the door. "What do we need to cover?"

Cali took several more sips of the icy liquid before speaking. "It concerns my need for an electrical subcontractor."

"Okay." Pete hesitated, unsure where this talk was going to go. Not to mention he was distracted by her beauty. Cali's white blouse was open at the throat and revealed the length of her neck and her delicate collarbones. He shouldn't notice these things about her. Not now.

"So what about electric?" He held her widening emerald eyes and saw a faint blush sweep up into her cheeks. Damn, but she was alluring. And he wanted her. All of her. But only in his dreams.

Taking a deep breath, Cali gripped the glass. "I want to use Wharton Electric to lay the conduit beneath the concrete foundations that will eventually be poured."

Frowning, Pete reached into a drawer and pulled out the contractor file. His brows dipped as he opened it. "I don't see Wharton on the approved list, Cali."

She grimaced. Why was it so hard to confront Pete on these things? She'd never had problems doing this before. Maybe her career would plummet, after all, due to Russ and his lies. Unsure, Cali compressed her lips. "No, Wharton isn't on Mr. Elliot's approved list."

"What's wrong with Hartman Electrical? They're on the list here," Pete said, tapping his finger on the sheet.

"Have you done any background check on Hartman?" she demanded.

"No, but I'm sure Mr. Elliot and the team in Kabul did. You know contractors who want to work on a project have to submit their data one to two years ahead of time. If their stats and past performance are good, they're put on the list."

Right. Cali bit back the retort. Her heart was speeding up noticeably. "Hartman is a small company, Pete. I don't see how your boss could have okayed a firm whose biggest job to date was a hundred thousand dollars." She shrugged. "The electrical bid for this project is in the millions."

"So what's your point?" Shifting uncomfortably, Pete realized where this was going. Everyone in the industry had their favorite subcontractors.

"My point is that Wharton is a known entity to me, to Roland Construction. They've worked around the world on multimillion-dollar projects. Hartman has not."

Frustration thrummed through Pete. He saw the set of Cali's jaw and the tightness in her mouth. A delicious mouth that he badly wanted to explore. . . . The thought was completely out of place, and he shoved it away. Leaning forward, he picked up the list and held it toward her. "But Hartman has been approved. You know I can't just let a contractor walk in here and ask for someone else. Front office won't allow that."

"Hartman doesn't have the trucks, the machinery or men to properly handle this project, Pete. I don't know why Elliot put them on the list at all. We need someone who brings in all the equipment and men needed. Someone who doesn't have to scramble to find it in-country."

"I don't do the background research on

these contractors," Pete told her. "That's not my job. My job is to make sure this site runs with what is given to me."

"And that's all well and good," Cali said, trying to keep the tension out of her voice. "But Hartman isn't up to the task. They're a fine contractor for a small job, not something this size. And if you allow them to come in, there will be delays."

Delay was not a word Pete liked to hear. In every contractor's legal agreement there were clauses stipulating hefty amounts of money would be paid out for every day the project went over the end date. And Pete knew his reputation would suffer if this site and building went overschedule. Rubbing his mouth, he dropped the paper back on the desk.

"Hartman will come in here," Cali warned, "and will realize they don't have what's needed. They'll scramble to hire men and supervisors. But from where?" She lifted her hand. "Electrical is a highly complex field. Finding qualified men to lay the conduit and wire is one thing. To get good supervisors who know what to look for, what is right or wrong, is another thing, Pete. That will cause us a lot of time loss."

Cali wasn't wrong, and he felt trapped. "I'm sure Hartman can step into the job."

His boss back in Kabul expected him to stick with the preapproved list of contractors. Oh, Pete knew there was a lot of politics in this, and that Kerwin Elliot was a consummate player. It was no secret that every political operative had his favorites for projects. And for whatever reason, Elliot had approved Hartman as one of the potential electrical contractors despite any shortcomings.

"Look, Cali, I don't okay these contractors. I get handed the list just like you do," Pete repeated.

"I understand that," she said, keeping her voice soft yet firm. She saw the frustration in his eyes. Her heart twinged at having to put him in a stressful position, but she couldn't help it. "If Hartman is allowed to come out here, they will be stretched. They'll start hiring hacks. I'm worried about the quality of workmanship."

"I'm not forcing you to use Hartman," Pete stated. "But I am requiring you to use contractors from this list."

Damn. Cali wanted to mouth the word but didn't. The air was taut and nearly crackled between them. Outside, she could hear the graders, bulldozers and other machines roaring and chugging. Only the radio calls back and forth between supervisors in the field broke the brittle silence between them.

"And if I use one of the contractors on the approved list and have them subcontract to Wharton? What will Kabul do?"

Pete shrugged. "Kabul doesn't care if you spend your money for extra overhead." He knew Roland would have to pay additional costs to get it done. This was a game played by all contractors to get their favorite subs to do work on a project for them. And he could see Cali's point and didn't disagree with her. Hartman was too small and would have problems here, but it was out of his hands to control.

"If I do it that way, Roland will spend roughly fifty thousand dollars. And we'd like reimbursement for that amount."

Ouch. Pete pushed his fingers through his short-cropped hair in frustration. Even though he sparred with Cali on site problems all the time, he always found her desirable. Times like this just reminded him how impossible any personal relationship would be. Corporate ethics wouldn't allow it. "I can't authorize additional payments to you just because Roland wants a different electrical company. You're going to have to take it out of pocket."

"That's not fair," Cali protested. Why, oh why, did she have to take Pete's tough words so personally? She wavered internally, her confidence crumbling.

"An owner can't have the contractor calling the shots on who works on-site, either," he added. "That's why we use a pre-approved contractors list. We have to maintain a budget and set procedures. You know that."

Nostrils flaring, Cali knew Pete couldn't magically dip into some account back in Kabul for the extra funds. "Okay, then I'm willing to eat the overhead costs if you agree to pay the cost on the concrete mixers that never arrived." She advanced to his desk, her arms across her chest. "By contract, your company was supposed to have six concrete mixers out here for us to use. Four did not show up, as you know. I went and jury-rigged a bunch of dump trucks with my time, men and money to compensate for that problem, Pete. And because of my ingenuity, we are on schedule."

"I realize that," he told her. Her body was radiating tension, but so was his. Seeing Cali's eyes soften a bit at his compliment, he added, "And it's working."

"Look, Pete, I need wiggle room here. I know some mixers were stolen and some were wrecked on that damn road from Kabul. Is that my problem? No. You guys have your problems, and you have to cover them. When it came to Roland not having the fence up for security because of delays beyond our control, you still made me accountable for getting it out here and getting it up. Which I did," she added. "Within schedule."

"Yes, you did get that fence up in record time," he admitted.

"Mr. Elliot cannot keep asking Roland to absorb extra costs. You and I agree to waive some of these costs, but there comes a point when your company has to stand up to their obligations, Pete."

She was right. Taking a pencil, Pete fiddled with it distractedly as he pondered the situation. The jury-rigging Cali came up with was not in the contract. Roland had put out a lot of money to get dump trucks refitted to haul concrete. Plus, the dump trucks weren't going to be available for any other use after the pours were done. It was a huge monetary loss for Roland.

"I'll call Elliot this afternoon and I'll make clear the costs Roland has incurred. We'll get this straightened out, Cali."

Pete knew that Roland could send in a team of lawyers to fight for every overcharge not in the contract. That could drag the project out for years. Lawyer fees alone made it wise to settle these skirmishes in the field and not in court.

Her arms fell to her sides. "Thanks."

"I'm sorry we have to come to blows like this sometimes."

"Me, too," Cali said, backing away from the desk. The apology in his eyes melted her, and she wished she could be immune to him. Just see him as the boss and nothing more. She picked up her hard hat and settled it on her head. "If Kabul wants to follow procedures, so does Roland. I'm going back to the hoppers to make sure things are running smooth."

The door shut and the trailer grew quiet except for the sounds outside. Pete sighed and sat back in his chair, the pencil still in his hand. The last thing he wanted was an argument like this one. They occurred daily over little or big issues. Still, his heart wasn't into this particular fray. Cali was right; his boss had made a mistake in qualifying such a small electric company. Pete knew such mistakes were part of the construction business.

The hurt lingering in Cali's green eyes tore at him, and made him feel badly over having to lay down the law. She deserved better than what Kabul was dosing out to her company. And somehow, Pete was go-

211

ing to see that it got fixed in this one skirmish.

For whatever reason, he wanted to see her smile. She didn't do it often, but he waited for those rare moments. It was like getting a glimpse of the real woman beneath the hard hat. Even after months of working together, he ached to know her on a more personal level. But to go there meant ignoring his past history, and Pete couldn't do that. When their two-year commitment was over, would he still feel this connection to Cali?

Pete set the pencil back on the desk. He already knew the answer to his silent question.

CHAPTER TWELVE

"You have a female for main contractor?" Brad Parker, the project's newest engineer, asked his boss. "That's an interesting plus. It will be the first time I've ever worked with one."

Pete sat at his desk and tried to keep from snarling at the man. Thirty-two-year-old Parker had just arrived on-site and didn't know Cali's reputation. He wasn't in the military, nor would his employees be. "Ms. Roland knows her business," Pete responded, a tinge of warning in his voice. He didn't like the fact that another Taliban attack had necessitated this change in personnel.

Three weeks ago, in mid-September, their owner's chief structural engineer had been driving on the outer perimeter road and had hit a roadside bomb. Teddy Hanson had suffered major injuries. Pete was eternally grateful that the Canadian helicopter crew had been coming in that day to pick them up for their bimonthly flight to Kabul. They were able to whisk Teddy to the hospital, and an operation saved his life. But that left a hole in Pete's supervisory force, and Brad Parker, a civilian, was Teddy's replacement.

Chuckling, Brad leaned back in the chair, seeming far too pleased with himself. He had his legs crossed, a clipboard in his lap. "Listen, women at a site like this are rare, anyway. I've banged around Asia and the Middle East a bit, and women are off-limits because of all the religious beliefs." He grimaced. "Hell for me. I like women. I like their company. That's the only thing I *don't* like about jobs out in the middle of nowhere."

Pete couldn't disagree with him. He handed Parker the rest of the reports, plus his duties, which were clearly spelled out in the standard operating procedure manual they all used.

"Teddy Hanson won't be coming back, and you've signed a contract for one year. I think by the end of that time you'll know whether you've had your fill of our site or not," Pete said.

"There's always Kabul. If you let me escape one or two weekends a month, I'll be okay."

"If you want to drive four hours one way to reach the city, that's fine by me." The guy looked like a leading man in a movie. The errant thought that Cali might be attracted to this easygoing, smiling structural engineer bothered Pete.

"Well, let's see how it goes." Parker picked up the clipboard and the manual and rose. "I came out of a nasty divorce a year ago. Women are nice, in their place. But I'm not interested in making a home with one soon."

The two men shook hands, sealing the start of Parker's tenure. "I know Ms. Roland is out at the building site. They're waiting on you, Parker. We've got a lot of work backed up that needs inspection and your recommendations."

Putting his dark blue hard hat on his head, Parker grinned. "I'm on it. I'll give you an update at the end of the day."

"Sounds good. Thanks." Pete watched the man leave. He was six foot three inches tall, well-built and in vital health. As the door shut, Pete wondered again if Cali would be drawn to this man armed with charm, poise and a flashing smile.

Scowling, he shoved the thought aside and got to work.

Cali was looking at the steel rebar that had

been put into the bottom of the square foundation. The September sunlight poured warmth down upon the dry plain. For a moment, she lingered there, enjoying the heat and surveying the progress.

"Ms. Roland?" The deep male voice came from behind her.

"Yes?" She looked up into the glimmering blue eyes of a stranger. An intensely good-looking stranger. Behind his square jaw and handsome face she sensed a keen intelligence.

"I'm Brad Parker, the new structural engineer." He extended his hand. "I'm Teddy Hanson's replacement."

Cali reached out and gripped the man's broad and callused hand. "Nice to meet you, Mr. Parker."

"Call me Brad."

Sometimes, when Cali shook hands, men tried to crunch her bones. Over the years, she'd learned this was a subtle test to see if she was really a strong woman. Parker seemed to monitor the amount of pressure he exerted, however. He was gentle with her.

She grew uncomfortable under his intense gaze. Heat sprang up in her face as he gave her a long, appreciative look. Releasing his hand, she stepped back, unnerved.

"I think 'Mr. Parker' will do," she answered coolly. A warning went off deep inside her. A sense of fright. She didn't have time to analyze why. For now, she would focus on the rebar inspection. Turning, she gestured toward the foundation. "We're glad you're here. You've got a lot of inspecting to do in order to catch up. Right now, we're running a week behind schedule because we lost Teddy to that roadside bomb."

"Well, don't fret, Ms. Roland. I'm here and I'll get us back on schedule. Guaranteed." Parker gave her a confident smile.

His smile reminded Cali instantly of Russ — the man who had taken her down at the other project. He, too, had possessed a killer smile to go with his drop-dead-gorgeous looks. It was obvious that Brad Parker thought a lot of himself, and she couldn't ignore the sense that he was coming on to her. Maybe she was making this all up. Running scared because of what Russ had done to trick her. Without thinking, Cali dropped her gaze to Parker's left hand. No wedding ring. But that wasn't unusual. Construction hard hats didn't usually wear jewelry. Asking about his marital status would give the wrong impression.

"Well, let's take all your unbridled energy and put it to work," Cali said, stepping aside as he moved closer to her. But instead of allowing a safe distance between them, Parker got in her space. Cali automatically stepped away again and shot him a dark look of warning.

The man smiled and glanced down at the construction schedule. "Well, have no fear, Parker's here, Ms. Roland. We'll get this baby back on schedule in a snap."

Cringing inwardly at his bravado, Cali said, "Unless you're prepared to work 24-7 for a week, that won't happen, Mr. Parker."

"Let me impress you."

Cali's stomach knotted. "You don't need to work at impressing me, Mr. Parker. You need to impress your boss, Major Trayhern."

"Oh, him. He's a real serious type, isn't he?" Parker walked down one side of the dug foundation and looked closely at the rebar.

"Major Trayhern does a damn good job on this site, Mr. Parker," Cali snapped. "If I were you, I'd reserve any early opinion of him and let him impress you with his knowledge and experience."

Lifting his hand, Parker laughed. "Yeah, maybe you're right. Well, time to get down to business. I've got a lot of rebar to inspect, it looks like."

The wind gusted and a cloud of dust

swept across the area. Cali took off her damp pink bandanna and wiped her face. She was sweating in the autumn sunlight. So was everyone else. The Afghan workers, who were learning the correct way to place rebar, chattered in their own language. Bulldozers rumbled in the distance, and the familiar sound soothed Cali's frayed nerves a bit. She wanted to run from this guy, but couldn't. She had to make sure his inspections were thorough and met her criteria as well as Pete's.

Cali followed, keeping a safe distance from this engineer who obviously thought he was going to flirt openly with her. What a contrast to the sense of safety she felt with Pete Trayhern. Pete wasn't flashy like this character. He was responsible and stable in comparison, something Cali had always wanted in a man.

As they moved to the second side of the foundation, Cali watched Parker lean down and test the wire ties that held the rust-colored rebar together. He had a workingman's hands. As he ran through his checklist, he seemed to forget she was trailing him like a shadow, and that sent a wave of relief through her.

She tried to forget how similar Parker was to Russ. And because these circles tended to be small, she wondered if he knew Russ. That thought sent a shaft of terror through her. Pete didn't seem to know of her past, and she was anxious to keep it that way. He respected her, and Cali never wanted to lose that precious bond with him.

"Hey," Parker called, twisting to look over his shoulder, "how about we get a soda together later at your office trailer, and celebrate my coming to the site?"

She gave him a flat look. "The only time I need to see you in my office, Mr. Parker, is if there is a problem with your inspection of my people's rebar placement." She saw him grin slightly, shrug and turn back to the work at hand. This guy didn't know when to quit.

Cali had never thought of herself as a woman to be chased at a construction site. Maybe that was due to her assumption that she was "one of the boys" in a male-dominated profession. She wanted the men to treat her as an equal. And then Russ had come along and laid his elaborate trap for her. She'd fallen for it blindly — and stupidly. And now, Parker was trying to chase her. Well, to hell with that. She was off-limits and he'd better get the message. How she wished for Pete's quiet company instead.

■ ■ ■ ■

Near quitting time, Pete happened to be walking out among the newly dug foundations when he saw Cali with Parker. The shadows were deep as the Kush Mountains grew purple in the evening light. It would get cold and blustery now that the daytime heat was gone.

He had wondered how Parker was doing. Was he as good as Kerwin Elliot had said? The only way to tell was to see him at work. Pete was a hands-on manager, not one to stay in his office all day. He pined for the outdoors — the sun, the rain, the elements. It was where he felt at home.

His kept his eye on Parker, who was down in a foundation checking newly laid rebar. There seemed to be a problem, and Cali had crouched down to look at the section. What Pete saw next shocked him. He was a good two hundred feet away, walking between foundations, when it happened. Cali always wore gloves to protect her hands in this environment. Her current pair had dropped to the ground between her and the new structural engineer. As she reached to retrieve them, Pete saw Parker grab Cali's hand.

221

It was a deliberate act. Pete halted, his mouth going grim. For an instant, he wanted to run over and yell at Parker to get his damn hands off her. Cali could have retrieved her gloves on her own. Parker hadn't reached for them but he'd reached for her hand, instead.

Rage funneled through Pete. She couldn't see him, with the angle he was approaching. And he couldn't see her expression. But her body language was clear. She yanked her hand out of Parker's, stood up and uttered sharp, curt words. Judging from the surprised look on Parker's face and the censure in her voice, Pete figured she was angry. And well she should be. Who did Parker think he was?

As Pete pushed forward, his steps deliberate, puffs of dust rising where his work boots landed, he wanted to curl his fist and slam it into the engineer's smug face.

"Problems, Ms. Roland?" Pete asked as he neared them. When Cali snapped her head toward him, anger and frustration were evident in her clear green eyes. Her cheeks were a heated red and her mouth was pursed.

Cali fumbled with her leather gloves. She was a case of nerves from Parker's unexpected touch. "Major, er, no." She found her professional voice as she saw the banked anger in her boss's eyes, aimed at Parker. The structural engineer was still crouched, clipboard resting on his thigh.

Cali was so glad to see Pete show up. She didn't need rescuing, but his presence was an immediate comfort. What a difference in personality between these two men. She longed to be near Pete, not egotistical Parker, who clearly thought he was God's gift to women. Even now, Parker seemed unconcerned about his behavior, and that made her even angrier. But this was not the place or time to tackle it. They were surrounded by Afghans who could see everything, and Cali knew, from a managerial standpoint, that one didn't drag dirty laundry out in front of employees. She gave Parker a warning look that spoke volumes, then returned her attention to Pete.

"We're inspecting the rebar," Cali told him, her tone now calm and collected.

Pete looked intently into her upturned face. More than anything, he wanted to ask if she was all right. She had gone from angry to all-business. Maybe later they could talk in private.

"What have you found so far? Any problems?" Pete asked his new hire.

"None, Major Trayhern," Parker called.

"From everything I can see so far, Ms. Roland's men are doing a fine job. Of course, we're only on the second foundation, with eight others to go, but it's looking consistently good."

Pete wondered if the engineer realized his faux pas. Pete could tell Cali was shaken, even though she tried to hide it. Her hands trembled slightly as she jerked her gloves back on. This made Pete all the more protective of her. "I want to see you in my office before quitting time today, Parker." Looking at his watch, Pete added, "That means within the next thirty minutes."

"I hear you loud and clear, Major. I was going to come in and see you shortly, anyway."

Pete nodded and turned to Cali, who avoided his gaze. The panic and fear seemed so out of character for her. "You okay?" he asked, his voice quiet and probing.

"Y-yes, I'm fine, Pete."

Every time she used his first name, he felt his flesh react as if stroked by a warm, moist breeze. Cali compressed her full lips and adjusted the white hard hat on her head.

"Thanks for asking," she added.

How badly Pete wanted to talk to her. But that was impossible right now. "Well, I've got a few more stops to make." He didn't want to go. Instead, Pete ached to put his arms around Cali and tell her it was going to be all right. But that was not to be, and sadness flooded him.

"So do I," Cali muttered. Swallowing hard, she turned on her heel and walked away. She wanted to run. Parker was a copy of Russ Turner in every way, and dread wound through her. This guy worked for Pete, so she couldn't fire him. She couldn't refuse to work with him. And worst of all, she was going to have to deal with Parker day in and day out. He was so damn bold and sure of himself. And he was chasing her. Cali could taste it. She wiped her sweaty brow with the back of her gloved hand. Escape. That was all she wanted at this moment. Pulling down the brim of her hat, Cali tried to breathe fully. She was breathing shallowly, as if scared. Well, wasn't she?

And then her quick strides slowed. She wondered if Pete had seen what Parker had done. If he thought she'd encouraged Parker's actions. What if he had? Would he blame her, the way she'd been blamed at the other project? In her experience, Cali found that men stuck together. When one woman came against all of them, hers was the reputation that got shredded and ruined.

Russ had walked away laughing.

"Mr. Parker, what did you think you were doing, holding Ms. Roland's hand like that earlier?" Pete stared hard at Brad Parker. The structural engineer had just gone over his notes with him, and their meeting was over. It took everything Pete had to keep his voice low and unruffled. He felt nothing like he sounded. Inside, he was furious. And as he appraised the shock in Parker's darkly suntanned features, he waited for an answer. An answer he practically wanted to shake out of him.

"Why . . . I was just reaching down to grab Ms. Roland's glove. The wind blew them off the rebar."

"Really? That's not how it appeared to me from where I stood."

Parker shrugged easily. He picked up his reports and clipped them back on the board resting on the table. "I was just trying to be a gentleman, Major Trayhern."

He was lying and Pete knew it. Yet the innocent look on Parker's face would fool a lot of people. Maybe because he yearned for Cali, but could never have her, Pete saw Parker as a huge threat. Maybe he was just jealous. Okay, he damn well admitted it, but only to himself. "Next time, Parker, keep your hands to yourself. It looked like you deliberately reached out to catch her hand as she bent down to pick up her gloves."

Parker chuckled. "Hey, she'd been wanting her hand held all day, Major. I was just complying."

Rage funneled up through Pete. "Complying? As if she was wanting you to do something stupid like that?" He ached to curl his hand into a fist and put it right through Parker's smiling features. The guy was brazen, bold and arrogant.

Parker picked up his hard hat and placed it back on his head. "Major, with all due respect, I don't have to go out and chase women down. They come to me." His mouth curved faintly.

"Let me be very clear," Pete said, his voice deep, "I don't *ever* want to see you out on my site touching Ms. Roland in any way at any time. I don't care what the reason is. You got that?"

"Not a problem, Major. I can't help it if she was flirting with me all day long. But I'll refrain and make sure it doesn't happen again. Are we done? I've got some reports to type into the computer."

"We're done." Pete held on to his rage. He watched the man stroll out of his office as if he didn't have a care in the world. Rubbing his jaw, Pete wondered if it was true. Did Cali ask for his attention like that? Every cell in his body exploded with a screaming *no.* Cali had never flirted with anyone at this site. Not ever. Not even with him.

Sitting down on a wooden stool, Pete tried to focus on a set of blueprints. The sounds of earthmoving equipment provided a back-drop of noise as he unrolled the scrolls outward and flattened them. Try as he might to focus on his work, thoughts of Cali assailed him. His heart insisted Cali had not invited the advance, but jealousy ate at Pete. He was so deeply in turmoil over the possibility that she was drawn to Parker that bitterness coated his mouth. He reached for a soda, chugged some of it and set the can down a little harder than necessary. What was he going to do with these feelings?

CHAPTER THIRTEEN

Pete reached Dara-i-Suf, the largest town in northern Afghanistan, just at dusk on the blustery mid-November evening. Cali was with him. He pulled into Sheik Hesam's resplendent "other" home. The two-story adobe structure was large, covered with ivy and surrounded by a ten-foot-high wall of the same material. This was Hesam's official headquarters, Though he preferred a simple, quiet village life to the city. Only in winter did he stay here, Pete had discovered.

The sentries were on horseback and heavily armed. As Pete and Cali drove up to the black, wrought iron gate, the guards recognized them immediately, smiled and allowed them into the compound. Roiling gray clouds, pregnant with rain or a mix of snow, threatened.

Pete tried to quell the anxiety fluttering in his chest as he braked the Tundra in the gravel parking area. The IEDs, or roadside bombs, were getting to be a regular and dangerous intrusion at their site since the Taliban had renewed their attacks. These threats were slowing down the project. Hesam had invited them to a crucial meeting on how to deal with this menace.

Cali had an almost permanent scowl on her brow these days. More restless than usual, she kept crossing her legs or folding her hands in her lap. Oh, she'd make remarks about things they passed as they drove along the only asphalt highway in this area — birds, animals or people in carts drawn by horses or donkeys. Small talk, he thought. Nothing personal. He didn't know whether to be relieved about that or not.

Pete climbed out and saw Javad, his interpreter, come walking through the main doors. The young man was dressed in dark burgundy pants, a white, voluminous shirt, cinnamon-colored vest and an astrakhan hat on his head. He smiled and waved exuberantly. Pete grinned in greeting.

"Javad. I didn't expect to see you here," he said. He ambled around the front of the Tundra, carrying a carved chest made of elm wood. The wind was biting and he was glad to be wearing his Marine field jacket.

"Hello, Pete. I decided to hitch a ride to town and visit my uncle's home. I hope you don't mind if I ride back to the site with you tomorrow?" Javad shook his hand, then turned and greeted Cali warmly. She smiled and shook his hand, too.

"Of course you can ride back with us. Not a problem." Damn, but he'd wanted to drive back alone with Cali, maybe get a handle on her recent change in behavior. She was edgy all the time now and a lot less communicative. Something was eating at her, but he couldn't guess what it was. Normally an owner never discussed personal issues with the main contractor, just business. Now, with Javad riding back with them, Pete definitely couldn't bring up such a delicate topic with Cali.

"Excellent!" Javad said, and escorted them into the house. "Come, my aunt and cousins are about to serve us a wonderful dinner. My uncle is eager to see you." He led them through ornately carpeted rooms to a cream-colored stucco archway.

Inside, Hesam sat among pillows on a brilliant blue, yellow and red handwoven rug. The sheik's face beamed with undisguised pleasure as he gestured for them to enter. "Come in. Welcome to my humble abode. Sit, sit. My wife and daughters will serve us shortly. Javad, come and sit on my left?"

"Of course, Uncle."

Cali smiled and tried not to let her strain show as she conversed in the sheik's language with him. Working nonstop with Brad Parker was getting to her. He'd never touched her again, but his flirtatious looks made her stomach clench. He was trying to wear her down. Just as Russ had done. She was wiser this time, but didn't have the luxury of firing Parker. For now she had to live with it.

Cali sat on a comfortable turquoise-and-crimson pillow opposite Pete. There was little time to chat before Ladan, Hesam's wife, entered, bearing a silver tray filled with steamy, spicy food. Her daughters, in traditional dress, brought fruit and drinks. For the next several minutes, Cali focused on greeting the entire family. After the women politely excused themselves, the rest of them got down to the serious pleasure of eating. Even though she was upset, Cali found herself hungry. The Qorma-i Tarkari, a dish of cauliflower, carrots and potatoes topped with lamb sauce and seasoned with turmeric, cumin, saffron and dill over basmati rice, was delicious.

"So," Hesam said to Pete in English, "my nephew intimated that you had a special package arrive at your site last week. Can you tell me about that?"

Pete wiped his mouth on his napkin. Hesam was key to the site being built. His men provided the very necessary workforce. Some things Pete would not divulge to the sheik because it was company business. However, this was an easy subject to talk about, and he looked over at Cali. She gave him a nod.

"The package was very important, my lord. And Javad was there in my office when it arrived." He smiled at the teenager. "You can't keep a secret, can you?"

Flushing, Javad bowed his head. "Major, I saw how excited you were, and when you told me what it was, well, I just dropped a hint to my uncle." He raised his hand and pressed it to his heart, giving Pete an earnest look. "I did not tell him what it was, Major. I swear to Allah."

Smiling wryly, Pete said, "Thanks for that, at least."

Everyone chuckled.

Pete waited until the food was cleared away by the women and the four of them were alone once more. He picked up the elm box and presented it to Hesam. "Sir, these are a gift from me to you. They were late in coming, and I apologize. But the intent is heartfelt."

"Ah, a gift." Hesam eagerly took the long,

rectangular box and set it on the floor in front of him. "You are a very generous man, Major."

Eager to see his reaction, Pete grinned. "I've been waiting for these to arrive for some time, my lord. Please, open the latch."

Hesam did so and opened the box. "Oh, I do not believe this!" Stunned, he looked up at Pete. "Can this be so? Do my eyes deceive me?"

"Your eyes do not deceive you, my lord. Those are two Colt .45 replicas. The real deal. And I have the holsters for them, out in the truck. Please, look at the pistols. They're created from originals found back in the late 1800s of our Wild West era."

Hesam murmured with undisguised pleasure as he picked up one pearl-handled pistol and looked at it. "This is indeed a *great* gift, Major. Thank you."

"You had mentioned at one time that you were interested in our cowboy era."

"Yes, I am. You see, we still ride horses here in my country," Hesam said, turning the piece over and over, looking at the fine detail and workmanship. "And since I am a gun collector, one of my dreams was to own a pair of Colt .45s." He gave Pete a look of incredulity. "This is an amazing and gracious gift. Thank you very much. I shall cherish these pistols."

"You can fire them, too," Pete said. He asked Javad to go out to the truck and retrieve a wooden box containing the leather holsters. Grinning, Javad sat up and practically ran out of the room.

"Then I will wear them daily," Hesam declared. "I will become a cowboy of the Old West."

"I've provided a great deal of ammunition for them, my lord. That, too, is out in the truck. It's a pretty heavy box, and you may want some of your men to carry it into where you keep such things."

"You have thought of everything, Major." Hesam beamed with pleasure. "You are truly a good man with a generous heart." He waved the Colt .45 and watched the glint of light bouncing off the silver surfaces. And then, as if struck by a brilliant thought, he turned to Cali and spoke to her in Pashto. "Are you sure you do not want this man as a husband? He's very generous."

Coloring fiercely, Cali shook her head. Her heart thudded at the unexpected words from Hesam. "My lord, I like Major Trayhern very much, but not as a husband. That just wouldn't work in our situation."

"Pity," Hesam said. "For he is a man among men. My daughters are very interested in him." He chuckled. "But I told them that he was not of our faith and therefore unavailable to them."

"I understand," Cali said.

"Besides, I'm sure the major has someone back home?"

"Not that I know of, my lord."

"Pity." He turned and switched to English. "Will you both come with me? To my office? I have some strategies to stop the Taliban from being so bold. I need your thoughts and ideas on how we can work together to keep your site safe for the future of my people."

It was near midnight when Hesam was done laying out elaborate plans to keep the site safe. Scratching his head, Pete sat opposite the sheik at the large, highly polished mahogany table. Intricately hand-carved, the oval piece had the legs of a lion — an impressive table for an impressive leader.

Cali sat to his left. She looked drawn and tired. So was he. His only wish was that they could steal a few moments together.

"The Taliban is gathering force up in the Kush Mountains," Hesam said wearily, sipping the last of his coffee. He set the delicate, white china cup painted with roses on the saucer at his elbow. "I fear they are only going to get bolder. My friend the tribal sheik of the next province is low on men and horses. He has asked me to take over more distant forays into the mountains for him. I said I would try, but could not guarantee to provide the number of soldiers he needs to keep the Taliban out of the caves and valleys of his land."

"With most of your men employed by us," Pete noted, "you don't have the usual resources to hunt them down."

"It's more than that, Pete," Cali said. She tapped the map spread before them with her fingertip. "Sheik Hesam may control this province, but the mountains are more of an obstacle than flat plains."

"Very true," Hesam said sadly. "There are pockets of Taliban who get together in these high mountain valleys to plan and plot. They then lure the youngest men, sometimes mere boys, to trek over the mountains and plant the roadside bombs. Few suspect boys of such carnage."

Glumly, Pete agreed. And he wasn't going to start shooting every youth he saw outside their perimeter fence as a possible Taliban suspect. "I need to try and get your security guards to stop more of these boys and find out if they are from local villages or not."

"One way around that would be to issue

everyone a photo identification," Cali suggested. She glanced toward Hesam, whose black brows rose with surprise. "Anyone, and I mean anyone, coming around or into our site, would have to wear this photo ID. Those caught without it would be immediately suspected of being Taliban."

"That's a cost I'd have to determine, and then run by my boss in Kabul," Pete warned them heavily. They would need thousands of dollars in time and people to pull it off. "I personally like the idea and will back it, but I can't guarantee that it will be approved."

Hesam waved his heavily ringed hand. "Major, I will absorb the cost."

Pete stared in surprise at the sheik. "Sir?"

"I'll bear the cost." Hesam frowned and propped his hands together in front of him. "After all, I'm just as concerned about this as you are. Any incursion into my province is a threat to my power here. My people must see me as proactive. I can hire those with photographic experience, buy the necessary equipment and have women of the villages within thirty miles of the site get people lined up for identification cards. What do you think of that?"

"That is an incredible offer, my lord," Pete declared.

Cali heaved a silent sigh of relief. "I'd back the plan with your ideas."

Rubbing his hands together, the sheik said, "Excellent." Peering over at Pete, he added, "And I assume you must still seek approval for this identification card process from Mr. Elliot?"

"Yes, sir. But I don't think he'll balk at it, since we aren't having to put new money into our budget."

"Let me know when he approves it. In the meantime, I will ask my beautiful wife to contact women leaders in our villages to begin making the necessary arrangements. Hopefully, by the time Mr. Elliot approves this, we will have much of the infrastructure in place and be able to move quickly." Plucking at his black-and-gray beard, Hesam said, "With winter coming on, there will be fewer attacks. The heavy snow in the Kush will slow or stop most Taliban maneuvers. That is their pattern — rest in winter, attack vigorously from spring through autumn. So we can use the winter to get the identification process defined and completed."

"It's good to hear the Taliban will ramp down for a while. Our teams need a rest," Pete said.

"We do," Cali agreed, feeling weary from

the long day. "It would give us some breathing room."

She saw the hope in Pete's shadowed gray eyes, too. How she ached to talk to him privately. Cali needed to talk to someone about Brad Parker. But who? With winter approaching and snow threatening to fall heavily within weeks, she was going to be very busy. Everyone would be scurrying, because winter always caused setbacks in schedules and planning due to inclement weather conditions. Still, as she glanced at Pete, silently absorbing his presence, she wished she could simply talk with him — woman to man.

The mid-December weather was sunny for once. Cali was bundled up in her sheepskin coat, heavy jeans and waterproof boots as she sloshed through an area checking rebar. Brad Parker would be around sooner or later, and she dreaded his arrival. She tried to avoid him as much as possible. Her breath white with each exhalation, and she eyed the hundreds of men busily working around her. They were all dressed in thick fleece robes and heavy dark trousers, their heads protected by their warm turbans. Work never ceased at a large building site. It always reminded Cali of bees humming around a hive, ever active.

Tugging at the skull liner inside her hard hat, she brought the flaps down to keep her ears warm. Cali squinted up toward the noontime sun. To her right the beautiful Kush peaks were clothed in their winter finery. The snow was thick and deep, glistening like millions of shards of glass in the bright sunlight. The sky was lapis lazuli blue, dark and dramatic looking. The snow-covered plain stretched out to the left, an unbroken field of white. Beyond the perimeter fence, Cali watched as sentries in trucks slowly prowled the road where she'd almost lost her life last summer.

The breeze was sharp and cutting. The red mud was thick, as always, and gathered like awkward weights under her boots. Most of the clay fell off when she stomped her feet, then continued toward a foundation where the assistant responsible for placing rebar waited for her. Most of the Afghans were highly skilled at arranging of rebar and wiring it together now. They took great pride in their work, and Cali wasn't surprised that Parker had little to gripe about regarding the necessary reinforcing steel in the foundation. Good thing, because she wanted to avoid that guy like the plague.

"Hey, fancy meeting you here, Ms. Roland," Parker called as he sloshed eagerly toward her.

Cali frowned and noticed the engineer was bareheaded, his thick black hair short and emphasizing his good looks. Fear rattled through her. She said nothing as he flashed his megawatt smile, however. What the hell was he doing out here without a hard hat on? Parker knew the rules. But then, he seemed to consider himself so damn important in the command structure that he could sidestep regulations whenever he felt like it.

"Where's your hard hat, Mr. Parker?" she asked when he approached.

"I don't need one." He flexed his arm muscles beneath the coat he wore. "See? I'm tough."

"I'm not impressed."

"Most women are."

"I'm not most women, Mr. Parker." Cali looked around and spotted a small supply shed nearby. The shack was a place to keep extra gear like dry gloves, which quickly got wet and frozen in winter weather. A lot of skull liners were hanging on hooks, along with different colored hard hats and tools. She reached in and she found a dark blue hard hat and pulled it off the hook.

"Wear this," she ordered him, and threw it in his direction.

Parker was caught off guard. The hard hat struck him on the chest and bounced. If not for his fast reflexes, it would have tumbled into the mud. Snatching it up, Parker shot her a disgruntled look.

"You wear it on my site, Mr. Parker, or you leave. You come out here without it again and Major Trayhern will be notified." Cali wasn't going to give this guy an inch, because he'd take a mile if she allowed it. Time spent with the man had taught her to keep him on a very short rein.

"For you, Ms. Roland, I'd do *anything*." Parker grinned contritely and threw the hard hat on his head. Settling it so that the brim shaded his eyes, he smiled widely. "Now, do I look even more handsome than I did before?"

Cali turned away. The engineer was always testing her. Pushing her to see if she was going to be as tough as a male boss would be. She didn't have time for games, but had played them too many times on other sites with men who questioned her authority.

They moved toward the foundation together. Every time Parker got a little too close, Cali automatically moved away from him, her gloved hands stuffed into the pockets of her coat.

"Beautiful out, huh?" Parker gestured to

243

the sun overhead. "We don't get enough of these kinds of days, do we?"

Forced to answer, Cali said, "No, there aren't many sunny ones here in the winter, Mr. Parker."

Halting near where the new rebar had been placed, Cali spoke briefly in Pashto to the supervisor. He was an older man, in his fifties, with a gray beard and black, smiling eyes. At one time he'd been a high-iron man, a worker who walked steel beams and girders six to ten stories above the ground on projects in India. Cali had a lot of respect for high-iron walkers; it took guts to do that, especially without any safety net to catch them if they fell.

Parker didn't wait; he hopped down into the five-foot-deep foundation trench where the new rebar was located.

The arrogant engineer should have waited since the Afghan supervisor might have had something to tell him. But he didn't and this was a sign of disrespect as far as Cali was concerned. After thanking the supervisor, she walked over to another wall and eased down into the muddy area. Rebar was placed every eight inches and then wired to another layer going the opposite direction. There were four double rows in the base of this particular foundation. As soon as the rebar was inspected and passed, they could begin pouring concrete, provided the temperature cooperated.

"I just got back from Kabul," Parker said to her as he walked along, checking the wire ties. "Found a helluva party being thrown by a Canadian contractor." He grinned at her. "I have a helluva hangover even today. Too bad you didn't want to come along, Ms. Roland. There were a number of American women, secretaries, at the party, too."

"Parties aren't my gig, Mr. Parker, and you know that."

He brought the dark blue hat down a little more firmly on his head as a stiff breeze whipped through the trench. "Yeah, I know, but I'm going to keep trying. You've been out here a long time and you never take time off."

"The nature of the beast, Mr. Parker." She continued to check the wire wrapping. It looked very good. Cali made sure to keep her distance from Prince Charming. Hadn't he gotten the message by now that she wasn't interested? Let him go sow his wild oats at parties in Kabul. That was fine with her. He thought he was a babe magnet of the first order. To her, he was a royal pain in the ass.

"I don't see you as the nonpartying type,"

Parker said, a bit thoughtfully. He straightened up and filled out the form on his ever-present clipboard.

"I don't care how you see me."

"Can't help it, Ms. Roland. To me, you're a standout." He chuckled over his own joke.

She didn't smile. Opening her own clipboard, Cali filled out the number of the foundation and scribbled her own notes. "I like nature, Mr. Parker. It's a far more pleasant diversion than what big cities offer."

Shrugging, Brad tucked his pencil into his coat pocket. "My younger sister is a real party animal. She lives in San Francisco. I like to go visit her because she knows all the in spots, and we have a good time from dusk to dawn. How about your family? I know you have several older brothers, all in construction. Are they like you? Allergic to big-city fun?"

Glancing up from her notes, Cali sent him a warning look. Parker was always snooping, always trying to find out something personal about her. "Mr. Parker, my life and my family are off-limits to you. Got that?"

Giving her a grin, he said, "You can't blame a man for trying. You're like the Sphinx, Ms. Roland. Any man worth his salt is going to be interested in you because you don't give up much of yourself to anyone.

You're a beautiful, enigmatic mystery."

With Russ as her teacher, Cali had learned that lesson the hard way. "Being the boss means exactly that, Mr. Parker. Business is business. That's as good as it gets. Are you done with your inspection?" Her voice was calm and authoritative.

"Yes, ma'am, I am." Brad signed the form and looked around. "I'll be going to the next building to check out the rebar there. Coming along? Maybe I could buy you a cup of good, thick Afghan coffee at the local eatery?"

Since autumn, Hesam had allowed several village women to set up a small shed where they offered coffee, tea and food for the men. It helped the women's families monetarily, gave them status, and Cali had applauded the strategy to have them hold important jobs at the site. She liked the idea of hot coffee now, but not with this guy. "No, thanks. I have other things to attend to." She climbed out of the foundation with the help of the attentive supervisor standing nearby.

"Pity," Parker called to her, flashing her a smile. "Why, I'd even let you buy your own cup, Ms. Roland."

Taking a deep breath to keep her patience, Cali glared down at Parker, who stood confidently in his knee-high rubber boots, red down vest and sheepskin jacket. "I'm not interested." She'd bit out the words to let him know he was overstepping his bounds — again.

Glad to be leaving Parker's galling company, Cali started walking toward the white Roland truck parked in the distance. Her pulse picked up in beat when she spotted Pete striding across the site. Her crazy heart practically lurched out of her chest when he saw her, too, and changed course, heading toward her. The ache in Cali's throat continued as she slopped through the ankle-deep red mud to a firm gravel path.

The wind was cold and sharp, but somehow, with Pete's gaze locked to hers, Cali didn't feel it. His cheeks were ruddy from the slicing breeze, and beneath his dark blue hard hat, he wore the wool inner liner over his ears. As always, he had on his winter desert-camouflage uniform. Under his left arm was a clipboard, his right hand swinging freely. Pete had such broad shoulders. Her attraction to him was like a driving force screaming within her. If only things were different. If only . . .

"Hey, is this a beautiful day or what?" Pete called in greeting. Cali looked earthy and gorgeous in the bright sunlight. The dark pink goose down vest she wore beneath her opened coat emphasized her face and flushed cheeks. The joy glimmering in her green eyes made him feel as giddy as a teenager.

"It is," Cali said, coming up to him. They kept a good distance between them as they halted to talk. "I feel like an old turtle climbing out of the cold mud to sit on a log and let the sun warm me," she chuckled. Pulling out her clipboard, she got ready to discuss the rebar with him.

"Hey, you sound like a down-home girl, not a city slicker." Pete had seen a thawing in Cali's attitude toward him. Was it because of Parker? She'd started changing after the engineer arrived at the site. Pete had seen her avoid the guy time and again. Was there a problem? Pete could do little but watch the structural engineer, keeping an eye out for trouble.

"Oh, give me Mother Nature any day," Cali said.

Pete eased a little closer as she held out the clipboard for him. His desire warred with retaining a businesslike demeanor with her. He watched as Cali took off one glove, held it between her teeth and pointed to several figures on her form. Leaning down, he caught a whiff of her feminine fragrance.

Cali never wore perfume, but she had a sweet, heady smell that he automatically inhaled anytime he got near her.

This was pure torture, Cali thought as she tapped the clipboard. Pete was so close. On one level she reacted to his presence, on another, she was hyperfocused on keeping him informed. "These are the stats on the rebar tests. They're looking good," she said.

Pete nodded, doing his best to ignore her incredible-looking lips. The lower one was slightly fuller than her upper one. What would it be like to kiss them? The thought was forbidden but irresistible. Trying to listen to her explanation, Pete fought his body's reaction to her, like warm melting snow in spring sunlight — Cali's sunlight.

"I think the Afghan workers are incredible," he said, straightening. Unfortunately, he and Cali had to step apart. He watched as she briskly settled the papers back into order on her clipboard. She pulled on her glove and faced him. "I've never seen such good stats on rebar placement in my life," he told her. A wisp of red hair had peeked out from her ear flap. Cali was allowing her hair to grow longer during the cold of winter. Though he had a maddening urge to tuck that rebellious strand back into place, Pete curled his hand at his side. No, he couldn't go there. He couldn't do that.

"I'm so proud of them, Pete. They get better every day. The sheik was right, they take great pride in their workmanship."

Pete looked past Cali and saw Brad Parker down at a foundation checking rebar. "Parker gripes that he doesn't find enough errors. He tells me he's getting bored."

Snorting softly, Cali kept the derision out of her tone as she said, "But he's thorough. Doesn't miss anything, that I can see. The workers know their stuff, and that's why Mr. Parker isn't giving you a bunch of reports on errors."

"Hmm . . ." Pete glanced at her again. He saw a darkness in her eyes that hadn't been there before. How to broach the topic with her? She seemed unhappy every time Parker's name was brought up. "I got the first identification badges, for the nearest village, this morning. They look real good."

"That's great!" Cali exclaimed. "Hesam was right about the Taliban leaving us alone when the snow started falling."

"Yes, but that means come spring, when the ground gets solid again, they'll be back."

That sent a shiver of dread through her. "I know."

"This site is a lot more dangerous for everyone than I first realized," Pete said, looking around, his voice revealing his worry.

Although she wanted to reach out and reassure him, Cali kept her arm at her side. "I knew it wouldn't be safe. I didn't know how bad it was going to be."

"I worry for you." Pete gulped. Good God! Where had that admission come from? The words had flown out of his mouth without censure. He saw Cali's eyes widen with surprise, and a different emotion he couldn't name. Then her gaze grew shuttered and he could no longer read her.

"That's funny," Cali said softly, "I worry about *you.*" For a moment she felt so close to him. His expression exuded warmth — for her. But just as quickly, Pete allowed that professional mask to fall back in place over his face. He was so handsome, strong and kind. Heart beating in her chest, she hungrily soaked up his unexpected admission. He cared about *her.* Even though Cali was frightened by that realization, she didn't have the same panicked reaction she got when Parker was pursuing her. "I mean —" she faltered slightly "— because you're the boss here, I'm sure the Taliban know who you are. I think you would be a target because of your status on the site."

Seeing the worry in her eyes, Pete managed a wry smile. "Listen, they aren't going to take on a U.S. Marine." He added soberly, "I've had the same thought about you. I'm sure they don't like the idea that a woman is the number two boss here on the project. That has to chafe, given their fanatical ideas about Islam and women. I was afraid they'd target you because of that."

The wind swept between them. The sun was inching westward, and Cali saw deepening shadows on the white slopes of the mountains behind where Pete stood, so strong and proud. "Don't worry about me. I've been in and out of a lot of scrapes, Pete." The worst one, she wanted to say, was with an engineer named Russ Turner. But she didn't. He'd dishonored her, shamed her, and there wasn't a man on the project who'd respected her after Russ had got done telling his lies about her. Grimly, she said, "I'll survive anything the Taliban wants to throw at me."

"Well . . ." Pete hesitated ". . . okay with you if I still worry?"

Managing a one-cornered smile, Cali knew it was time to get going. As much as she wanted to stand and talk to Pete, she couldn't. "That's a nice thought — someone worrying about my skin. Usually, it's the other way around."

Her skin. Pete longed to reach out and brush his fingertips against her smooth, flushed cheek. Would Cali feel like velvet, as he imagined in his torrid dreams? "As boss of this site, it's my job to worry," he told her teasingly. "I'll see you later."

Cali turned and headed on to her muddy white truck. Buoyant because of the private thoughts she and Pete had exchanged, she felt as if she were walking on air, not across heavy, sticky mud. Funny how a few huskily spoken words from Pete made her feel so buoyant, while a remark from Parker brought her down like a rock.

Parker was adroit enough, smooth enough to start rumors that others would believe. That was how Russ had gotten even with her: gossip. Malicious lies that the men on the site believed. Having so many fine lines to tread with Parker was sapping Cali's energy and enthusiasm for the job.

She climbed into her truck and started it up. As she drove toward the other end of the site, she instead honed in on the warm look Pete had given her. What was she going to do?

Right now, Cali felt like she was standing at the fulcrum of a balance scale. On one side was Parker, who was immature and cocky. On the other was strong, quiet and responsible Pete Trayhern. Both wanted her. Well, she knew Parker did. But did Pete? Cali wasn't sure. She should have felt relief if he only had platonic thoughts about her, but she didn't. Yet if Pete was attracted to her, how in the hell could she handle his attention? Panic struck Cali, and she tightened her hands on the wheel.

CHAPTER FOURTEEN

It was closing in on midnight and Pete didn't know what to do. He sat at the desk in his living area, mulling things over. Outside, a December wind howled and the ping of icy sleet pattered like a hailstorm on the trailer. Not even the ugly weather distracted him from his core issue: Cali Roland. Whether he liked it or not, Brad Parker was forcing him to look at her in a new light. That realization had shaken him as nothing had in a long time.

Running his hand through his short hair, Pete turned to his computer. With satellite connection, he was in touch with the world even out in this remote spot. Every night, he put notes about the job into a daily journal on his Dell business computer. Then he traded it for his other one, an Apple G5, which was his personal computer. Any job notes were considered legal documents in a court of law, so Pete kept personal things off the business computer. Tonight, much of what he was feeling spilled out onto the twenty-inch G5 computer screen. Sent via military satellites, his e-mails were encrypted and protected, just as he wanted. That way no one could hack into them and know the contents. Privacy was becoming rare in cyberspace and every option guaranteed his messages would be read by only those at the other end. The e-mail message he struggled with was to his parents. He was telling them about Cali, how his past haunted him like a good friend and how fearful he was about having another relationship.

Easing upright in his chair, Pete finally sent the message to his mother. It was time he got some outside help on his dilemma.

"Morgan, did you read Pete's e-mail from last night?" Laura asked as she put a bowl of steaming oats with blueberries in front of her husband.

Morgan glanced up from his seat in their cozy breakfast nook. A storm overnight had coated the oak trees with powdery snow that sparkled like diamonds. Wintry sunlight lanced through the floor-to-ceiling windows to the round yellow table where he sat. "No," he said, sprinkling brown sugar into his bowl.

"It's different," Laura stressed, settling across from him with her own bowl of cereal. "I think he's interested in someone, Morgan."

Raising his brows, he muttered, "Again?"

"Oh, darling, don't take that tone."

He spooned oats into his mouth and gave her a skeptical look. After wiping his lips, he spread his pink linen napkin back across his lap. "Listen, I've never seen any of our children have as many disasters in relationships as Pete has."

Sending her husband a beseeching look, Laura buttered her toast. "He's had a few disappointing relationships, that's true. He's trying to understand and learn what love is about."

Snorting, Morgan said, "He has train wrecks when it comes to the women in his life."

"Morgan, don't be so hard on Pete. He's tried. He really has. He just doesn't pick the *right* women, is all. Give him time. He's learning what he does and doesn't like."

"Laura, that son of ours has absolutely no sense about women. I don't know who he got that from."

She grinned briefly. "Probably me. I was always the romantic idealist."

Snorting softly, Morgan said, "That's true."

She pushed the printed e-mail toward her husband. "Do you have time to read it?"

Morgan heard the hope in her voice and dutifully picked it up. The e-mail wasn't long but it snagged his interest right away. Setting his spoon aside, he devoted his full attention to it. "Well, looks like he met someone."

"Oh, Morgan, you're using that tone again."

"I don't know when his bad luck with women is going to end, Laura. I really don't. It hurts us to see him hurt. I wish he'd get some perspective on women in general."

"Didn't you see? He's asking *us* for advice regarding his dilemma. That's new. At least I think he's trying to not make the same mistakes." Laura bit into the piece of whole wheat toast she was holding and gave her husband a pointed look.

"I guess you're right. Before, he just jumped off the plank into shark-infested waters."

"Oh, darling! That's unkind. All children go through awful times in relationships. They will make mistakes, and all we can do is be there to support them and hope they learn from the experience." Laura finished off her cereal. "Besides, I think Pete is being cautious this time. He's trying to analyze things before jumping in. That's also new."

"Pete always thinks he's in love." Morgan took a piece of his sourdough toast, wiped the inside of the bowl clean and then popped the piece into his mouth. He picked up his mug of coffee. "That's his problem — he thinks too damn much and it all gets rolled up in a ball inside him. He doesn't talk to the woman at all. Communication is such a key in any relationship. And he's very bad at it."

So maybe her husband wasn't going to look at the bright side of this new development. Laura pushed her bowl aside, enjoying the warmth of the sun on her shoulders. She was glad to have on woolen slacks and a sweater. Winter in the Rocky Mountains came early and hard. "Then take heart, because Pete is communicating with us about this, Morgan."

Morgan sighed, put the coffee down in front of him and wrapped his large hands around the mug. "Laura, he's in a pickle. He thinks he might be drawn to Cali Roland. But she's the lead contractor on this project. He can't mix business with pleasure. Everyone knows that. If the people he works for get wind of this, he can kiss his job goodbye, because he'd have crossed lines you don't cross." Morgan frowned in consternation.

"Well," she said pertly, picking up her napkin, folding it and placing it on the table, "I think we should counsel him, Morgan."

"To do what?" He grimaced. "Darling, as much as I want to see Pete happy, this isn't a situation that's going to give him that."

"Do you think he likes Cali Roland?"

"I can't really tell from his e-mail. He's in angst over past relationships and worried about getting burned again. At least he's wary this time, as you said."

"Yes, he is reacting differently this time around. Age and maturity are coming into the picture."

"I wonder if Ms. Roland knows about Pete's interest in her. He didn't say if she's single, has a relationship or is divorced. I wonder if he's checked her out yet."

"You're such a sourpuss about this, Morgan! Don't you want to see Pete happy?"

"Of course I do, but he's in a jam on this one." As if he hadn't been with the others! But Morgan bit back that comment because he didn't want to annoy Laura.

"What would you advise him to do, Morgan?"

Realizing how stubborn his wife could be

261

when she cared about something, he murmured, "Have patience. If he really is drawn to Cali Roland, he has to wait until he's reassigned to another project before he pursues her. He can't have a blatant affair with the woman who's running his construction project."

"Okay," Laura said tentatively. She watched as a blue jay hopped from one branch to another of a snow-clad oak. "Just wait."

"Yes. You should point out to him that their mutual careers could be at risk if he steps over that invisible line from business to personal."

Frustrated, Laura chewed on her lower lip. "But if Pete waits, it would be for over a year. When he gets reassigned, he could end up halfway around the world. Cali is there in Afghanistan for three years to ensure completion of that power plant."

Nodding, Morgan finished off his coffee. He set the mug aside and looked lovingly at his wife. "Pet, there are no easy answers on this one. If they really do love one another, a year is nothing. You know that." He reached out, gripped Laura's hand and gave it a gentle squeeze. "Look at us. We met at the airport. You were hit by a car and ended up temporarily blind."

"Yes, and you stepped in and took care of me through that awful time."

"It was a pleasure."

"I was so scared," Laura admitted, returning his squeeze. "I couldn't see, and my whole life was upended. You were the only stability I had — a stranger who walked into my life and took pity on me."

Grinning, Morgan reluctantly released her small, fine fingers. "Oh, I didn't feel pity for you. It was lust."

Laughing, Laura sipped her coffee. "It was not! We were falling in love with one another, whether we knew it or not."

Pushing back his oak chair, Morgan grinned. "Lust and love. All tied together, pet."

Archly, she said, "Well, love won out."

"And I've been lustfully happy ever since." Morgan picked up their dirty dishes and carried them to the kitchen counter. Laura chuckled and followed. She busied herself at the sink.

Giving her a quick embrace, Morgan murmured next to her ear, "Write to our son and tell him to be patient. Praise him for waiting this time, watching and hanging back. Tell him real love takes time to develop."

Laura leaned back against her husband

and said, "I think he should do more than that. I think he should let Cali know that he has a long-term commitment in mind."

Morgan bussed her soft cheek. "And how is he going to do that?"

"Well," she said, smiling up at him, "Christmas is always a good time to let a special person know you like them."

"Merry Christmas, Cali." Pete hesitantly handed her a small gift. They had just celebrated with all the contractors at the main headquarters trailer. The home office had given each contractor Girl Scout cookies as a gift. Out here in Afghanistan, little things like sweets meant a lot. Pete's idea had gone over big with Kerwin Elliot.

Most of the contractors were still celebrating as Pete and Cali had left, heading over to his trailer. Cali sat on the edge of the chair now, stunned by his gesture. She took the small, gaily wrapped gift. Outside the window, snow twirled and fell in lazy patterns, already ankle deep on the site. "Thanks. I didn't expect this, Pete." She looked up into his weary gray eyes, almost at a loss for words. Cali had never expected a gift from her boss. Not a personal one.

Pete had invited her to come over and share some mulled wine with cinnamon sticks. They sat at his office desk, across from one another. He looked terribly handsome in a red alpaca sweater he said his mother had knitted for him. Cali's heart lurched as he sent her a nervous glance.

"I don't have anything for you," she murmured, turning the gift around in her hands.

"I understand," he answered. Gift-giving between the owner of the plant and the contractors was discouraged. But for holidays like Christmas, employers could give all contractors a common gift as a way of saying thank you. Big, expensive or personal gifts were outlawed, because they might be misconstrued as a bribe.

"I like the cookies you gave us," Cali said as she set the box on the table. Her fingertips tingled. Should she even accept a personal gift from Pete? The bribery rules screamed *no.* Picking up her tall mug of warm, spicy wine, she tried to sound lighthearted. "You're brilliant, Pete. There wasn't a man in that room whose eyes didn't gleam with hunger for those cookies." Oh, how Cali wanted to let down her professional demeanor and be herself.

Hands clasped on the table, Pete smiled tentatively. She had set his gift aside. Well, what did he expect? If she accepted it, she could be in hot water. And yet he was the one who had initiated this. If she turned him in, he could be out of a job. So what the hell was he doing?

Truth was, he was lonely for a woman's company. They'd both been nearly a year at the site and Pete hungered for her softness. He was sick and tired of business, and longed for personal downtime. A mindless force was driving him to take this small, experimental step.

And yet Cali could reject him. Pete tried to emotionally prepare himself for such a possibility. His heart started hammering. He was so unsure of how she really felt toward him. "Actually, the Girl Scout cookies were my mom's idea," he said. "My boss liked it, too, and so we ran with it."

"I like the fact you have a good relationship with your parents. And you go to them for ideas?"

"I sure do. Don't you go to your parents at times?"

Cali set aside the mug and glanced again at the foil-wrapped gift at her elbow. "Of course. I wonder, though, if father-daughter relationships are more common than son-mother-father relationships. I've found men sometimes have problems communicating." Cali couldn't stop looking at her gift, try as she might to curb her curiosity. She felt a mix of giddiness and fear. To have a relationship with any man on this project could be a fatal blow to her career, she knew. Cali was using this project to prove to everyone that she wouldn't turn into a moon-eyed woman in love with the wrong man. And she wasn't about to drag her father's good name through the mud twice by having a fling with this handsome Marine. It was the right decision, but Cali paid for it daily.

"Guilty as charged when it comes to talking," Pete said, holding up his hands. He saw Cali giving the gift another long, careful look. A feeling of dread poured through him as he waited for her to decide whether to open it. His parents had been right: any important relationship took time. It was like the wine he was drinking presently; it hadn't been made overnight. The wine had to age before it bloomed. That gave him some solace, but not much. That he was even thinking of a relationship scared the hell out of him.

"Yes," Cali murmured, "you are much better at talking with me than Mr. Parker is. And I appreciate that about you." She stole a glance at him. His features were closed, but that quirk at the side of his handsome mouth gave away his real feelings. Her own mouth grew dry and her pulse accelerated. Cali was going to hurt him, and he was the last man on this site she wanted to do that to.

"As much as I'd like to, Pete, I can't accept any personal gifts from you — or anyone. You know, the bribery laws and all." Her voice trembled slightly when she saw him wince ever so slightly.

"I realize I overstepped our business relationship," he said, the words sounding hollow and robotic. Cali was declining his gift. This hurt a lot more than he'd thought it might. Unconsciously, he rubbed the center of his chest. "I'm sorry to put you in this position. You don't have to take it. I never intended it as a bribe."

He heard Cali sigh. Her green eyes had turned lustrous and soft with some unknown emotion, and her delicious mouth flexed. Oh, if only he was a mind reader. "Whatever you decide to do about this, I'll back you. I know I was out of line."

It pained her to see the haunted look in Pete's eyes. "Listen," Cali said tiredly, "give yourself a break, Pete. We're out in the middle of nowhere. We can't go home to be with our families for Christmas. I think it's kind of natural to think of gifts for the people you work with, don't you? At one time, we used to be able to give presents to whoever we wanted. But construction has gotten so complex that even the hint of a gift between owner and contractors smacks of bribery." She managed a slight smile. "I know you're not trying to bribe me."

"I'd never do that to you, Cali," Pete admitted, defeat in his tone as he studied his clasped hands. "And yes, I do miss my family. Christmas was always a special affair at our house. I guess the holiday got the better of me. Thanks for understanding."

"It was a nice gesture. Just wrong time and place," Cali said forlornly.

They always tiptoed around one another. So much was left unsaid. Sometimes, when Pete was tired after a long day, Cali would see his professional mask slip for just a second and he would look intently at her. The heat in his eyes would set her flesh on fire and start her pulse pounding. How she wanted to respond. And then she'd remember work and how a relationship wouldn't bode well for either of them.

Lifting her mug to him, she added, "Rest easy. I won't say anything to anyone. I know you did this out of the goodness of your heart, not to sway me into making certain decisions on your behalf."

Sadness filled him. Pete lifted his own

mug and gently touched the side of hers. "Thanks." Cali was always good as her word. He had come to truly appreciate what she brought to the construction table; she was one of the easiest supervisors he'd ever worked with. They had their confrontations, but Cali didn't put her ego in the way as men did. No, they hammered out solutions and compromises that had kept the project on schedule and within budget. People like Cali were a rare find. And Pete quietly tucked away his feelings for her.

As often happened, the past came back to tap him on the shoulder and make him remember all the gutting, searing pain he'd experienced. He could live with Cali's rejection. What Pete couldn't live with was the blistering torture of once again losing someone he thought he loved.

CHAPTER FIFTEEN

"Hey," Pete called to Cali as he drove up in his pickup, "are we going to celebrate our one year here at the site tonight?"

He saw her turn toward him and smile. Her white hard hat was coated with a light film of dust. She looked beautiful in her jeans and longsleeved white blouse rolled up at the cuffs. That pink handkerchief that was always around her neck was soaked with sweat. It was hotter than usual on this May afternoon.

Cali halted her progress with the three hoppers that loomed above her on tall steel supports. Her heart beat harder. Pete's smile was always a boost to her spirits. Wiping the sweat off her brow, she stepped up to the open window of his truck. "A small celebration?"

"Yes, a little one. No gifts involved," he teased, remembering his faux pas last Christmas. That seemed so long ago.

"No gifts," she laughed. "Sounds like a plan to me." How she wished it could be more! But over the last five months, Cali had tried to stuff away her dreams and concentrate on the harsh reality of her job. Besides, they'd had a handful of IED attacks from the Taliban. Just as Sheik Hesam had warned, their enemy was far more active now that it was spring.

Her green eyes held such warmth that Pete found himself staring into them hungrily. "How about at my office? I've got a special wine from a Montana vineyard called Rattlesnake Creek. Compliments of my parents."

"Sounds great!" Cali looked at the watch on her darkly tanned wrist. "It's 3:00 p.m. now. I've got to try and figure out what's wrong with this damn hopper assembly. What time do you want to meet tonight?"

"Is 2000 good?" And then Pete corrected himself, because Cali was a civilian. "How about eight?"

She patted the truck door. "I'll be there. First, I'll want to clean up and look decent." She pointed to her dusty white blouse and filthy jeans. Crawling around the materials hoppers was a dirty, thankless task.

Nodding, Pete put the Tundra in gear. He spotted Kabir, the team leader for the day shift. The Afghans were now operating the plant for Roland Construction. Kabir didn't look happy, even at this distance. "Sounds good."

"What kind of wine?"

Her smile went straight to his heart. "It's a sauvignon blanc. My mother visited a vineyard over in Missoula. She was impressed with their variety of organic wines and sent me a bottle. I kind of like the name of it — Blind Curve."

"Intriguing," Cali agreed, lifting her hat to wipe her perspiring forehead with the back of her arm. She could feel the grit on her skin.

"Yeah, sort of like our lives, isn't it? Blind curves?" Pete wanted to say more, but they both had to get back to work. The desire to connect with her had only increased, and he looked forward to these precious moments with Cali.

"Oh, no argument from me on that one. I feel like my life has been one huge blind curve since coming here. We never know what will happen next." Cali meant that on a personal level as well, but she couldn't admit it to him. Pete would think she was talking about the unexpected Taliban attacks.

"Speaking of which, I'm going to touch

base with security. We're looking at different ways to ensure fewer IEDs along our perimeter road. See you later." Pete nodded to Cali and drove on.

She got back to work, trying hard not to anticipate the precious hour she would spend alone with Pete. Settling her hard hat back into place on her damp hair, Cali continued toward the hoppers. Tongues wouldn't wag if she went over to his trailer at that time of night. With the project cranking up to full gear because of the land drying out, she was up until midnight every night working and planning with him.

The day's heat was stifling. And excessive for this time of year. The winter had been milder than usual, which helped them in digging foundations, building new roadways and pouring thousands of yards of concrete. They were even a little ahead of schedule. As expected, the concrete pouring had been slowed last November because of cold winter temperatures. Placement of concrete had come back on schedule in mid-April. But for whatever reason, the three hoppers hadn't been working right. Lately, the feed mechanism kept jamming.

Cali was spending most of her time on the problem, since the Afghan crews could not figure out why it kept occurring. Getting into the open hopper assembly was perilous, and Cali respected that safety was most important.

As she walked quickly down the road, her thoughts moved to another problem. The leader of the day team, Kabir, was a man she didn't trust. Cali didn't know why. He lived in a nearby village and had a large, extended family. Hesam felt the thirty-year-old Afghan was a trustworthy and competent leader. But for some reason he made Cali think of a weasel.

Even now, she saw a flash of anger in his eyes as she reached the site. His arms were wrapped tightly against his chest, showing his defensiveness.

"Did you find anything during your inspection, Kabir?" Cali looked up at the three hoppers.

"Nothing."

She felt his dislike of her, and yet suspected Kabir didn't like anyone who wasn't an Afghan. More than once they'd tangled on issues involving the plant and its maintenance. Kabir seemed to think he could let some of the oiling and cleaning of equipment slide, and Cali had caught him at it several times.

"Where are the maintenance records, Kabir?" She wasn't going to be pushed around.

"In the shack."

"Get them for me, please." Cali saw him glare at her. "Now." It wasn't a request. It was an order.

"I think you should come in and see them. I've put them all out on the desk for you to inspect, Ms. Roland."

Shrugging, Cali said, "Fine." Her boots crunched on the gravel as she made her way to the small wooden building behind the hoppers, where many tools, and all the maintenance records, were kept. They were not pouring concrete tonight or tomorrow, so the plant was quiet. All the workers had been sent home nearly an hour ago. Only Kabir remained at Cali's request.

She spent the next ten minutes poring over the records, while Kabir sat on a wooden stool nearby, glowering at her.

The shack was stifling, even though the door and all three windows were open. How she wished that an afternoon breeze would sweep down from the mountains and cool them off. Hard hat set aside, Cali leaned over the desk, her eyes narrowed as she went through the records one entry at a time. She'd brought out her ever-present notepad and pen and set them beside the paperwork. As she began to pick up a pattern of missed maintenance, she vaguely realized the light was growing dim.

Glancing up, Cali looked out the window toward the hopper assembly. The sky was turning a dark gray, from gathering thunderheads.

"Turn on the light, please, Kabir?" she said, bending over the desk. The stool scraped the wooden floor behind her as she focused on the records.

Suddenly, Cali felt a strong hand wrap around her mouth, and she gasped. She was lifted off her feet and jerked back against Kabir's hard, lean body. Shock and terror surged through her. What the hell was he doing? Fighting to free herself, Cali brought her steel-heeled boot down on his foot, but barely grazed it.

Kabir grabbed Cali as she twisted and jerked. Her breathing was harsh and choked. She knew she was in trouble, so she lifted her foot and pushed against the heavy wooden desk with all her might, trying to upset his balance. Kabir was the same height as her, but heavier. His hand slid roughly against her mouth, and she bit him.

With a yelp, he released her.

Cali spun around, disoriented. The door. She had to get past Kabir and scream for help! But the Afghan leaped forward, blocking off that escape. *Damn him!* What was going on? Why was he attacking her?

Making a leap for the door anyway, Cali slammed directly into his chest, bouncing back like a ball off a wall. She crumpled to the floor, then scrambled to her feet again. When Kabir advanced on her, his slitted eyes filled with rage. Seeing his arm swing back, his fist cocked, Cali threw up her forearms to protect herself from the coming blow.

Why was he attacking her? Was he angry she was a woman? His boss? The thoughts collided violently with her instinct to survive.

His fist slammed into her elbow, and pain arced up Cali's arm. The jarring blow threw her back onto the wooden floor. Lifting her legs, she kicked out as Kabir started to lean down, his fingers curved like talons, to grab her by the shoulders. *Yes!* The impact of her boots connecting with his chest made him gasp. He was thrown backward, his arms spinning like a windmill as he tried to break his fall.

When he crashed heavily against the wall and dropped to the floor, Cali scrambled away on all fours. Breathing hard, half sobbing, she headed toward the open door. *Escape!* She had to get out!

Everything became like a slow-motion

movie to Cali as she staggered to her feet. Out of the corner of her eye she saw Kabir leap up with amazing agility. He grabbed for a wooden club leaning near the door — a two-foot-long wooden handle for a sledge-hammer.

Terror sizzled through Cali as she dug the toes of her boots into the rough shack floor and launched herself forward in a last ditch attempt to escape. But as she reached the door, she heard Kabir's footsteps behind her. *No! Oh, no!* He was going to hit her. As Cali bounded out the door, her world suddenly exploded. Stars, lights and fireworks went off inside her head. It was the last thing Cali remembered.

Where was Cali? Pete stood impatiently on the porch of her trailer and knocked once more. It was 9:00 p.m. He turned and scanned the plant site, visible in the glow of security lights that had been put in place last year. The sulfur beams cast a yellowish hue over everything they touched. Pete saw Hesam's security guards on horseback, conducting their normal rounds outside the fence. Everything looked quiet. But where was Cali?

After knocking again, Pete waited for a response, yet heard nothing. This was strange. She was always in her trailer at this time of night. He'd tried calling her on the radio, but there was no answer. Sometimes radios wore down and needed a recharge. Maybe hers wasn't working, and that's why she hadn't returned his call. Worried, Pete hurried to his Tundra and drove down to the concrete plant. There were security lights around the area, but no light in the operator's station.

The shadows were inky and deep as he pulled the truck to a halt near the building. Getting out, he heard the crunch of his boots against the gravel as he hurried toward the maintenance shack. That was the last place he'd seen Cali.

The door was wide open and it was dark inside. Once he flipped the switch and the light came on, Pete looked around the small space. A lot of papers were scattered over the desk and across the floor. His eyes narrowed. Cali's hard hat sat on the desk, too. How could that be? She'd never leave her hat behind.

Pete's heart beat harder. Something had gone wrong; he could feel it. He saw a wooden sledgehammer handle lying on the floor and picked it up. The light was poor, so he moved under the one naked bulb hanging from the ceiling and closely in-

280

spected the wood. As he looked at it, he saw something that made his breath hitch; strands of red hair matted with dried blood.

His mind spun. The first thing he could think to do was go to his truck and pull out his radio. Selecting a channel, he waited impatiently.

"Hesam here."

"My lord, this is Pete. Is Cali at your village visiting, by any chance?"

"Er, no. Why?"

"I think I have a problem. Can you get over here right away? I might need your help."

"Of course. My horse is saddled. It won't take but twenty minutes to reach you."

Pete knew Hesam preferred riding his black Arabian stallion to driving his car. His clan had always been horse people. "Okay, that's fine. Come to security headquarters."

"I will."

After hanging up, Pete grabbed Cali's hard hat and the sledgehammer handle, then started back to the truck. He drove to the security trailer and contacted the chief, advising him to have guards check the entire site for Cali.

Within twenty minutes, Sheik Hesam reached the plant site. Pete tried to be patient while the sheik galloped toward the trailer, and handed one of the security teams the reins to his mount.

Not wasting any time, Pete said, "My lord, I think something has happened to Cali. I can't find her anywhere." He relayed what he'd found.

Hesam scowled as he eyed Cali's hard hat. "She goes nowhere without her hat. It is a matter of safety to her."

"Exactly," Pete muttered. "One security team has looked everywhere and not found her, nor have your horseman outside the fence."

Hesam turned to his guards and exchanged quick words in Pashto. "Who was around when Cali came down here?" he added in English, addressing the Roland sentries.

"My lord," one sentry said, "the only man here was Kabir. I saw him myself. Miss Roland was going to meet with him about 3:00 p.m. Everyone else had been sent home."

"You are positive of this?"

The guard nodded solemnly.

Pete listened to the translation by Hesam. He said, "The security people logged out the hopper crew one hour earlier. Kabir was the only one left, according to the records. Why do you ask?"

Stroking his beard, Hesam looked around and then dismissed the guards. He turned to Pete. "Kabir has always been rebellious."

Anxiety began pumping through Pete's entire body. "What does that mean?" he rasped. Staring into the sheik's shadowed eyes, he felt a wave of fear.

"Unfortunately, Kabir's nephew is a member of the Taliban. I never questioned Kabir's own allegiance. He has been faithful and true to me, his village, his family and my clan."

Mouth dry, Pete looked toward the mountains, faintly illuminated by the rising moon. "Kabir is a member of the Taliban?"

"No, I do not think so. I hope not."

"You *hope* he isn't?" Pete stabbed a finger toward the floor. "That was one thing I asked of you, sir — not to let anyone with known Taliban members in their family work here on our site."

Hesam gave him an apologetic look. "Kabir has never spoken out against Americans, or against me, for that matter. I've never caught him in a lie."

"So what does that mean for Cali?" Pete's voice became hoarse. "She's gone, and Kabir was the last one here. If we assume he *is* tied in with the Taliban, why would he try to kidnap Cali? Does he want money?" Pete couldn't stop the wobble in his voice. Emotions deluged him as he stood tensely in front of the sheik. *This can't be happening.* Pete had paid so much attention to security, to keeping everyone involved in this project safe. *Why Cali?*

Shutting his eyes, he took a deep, ragged breath. He knew the answer: she was a woman in a position of power, and the Islamic terrorists could not stomach that dynamic.

"My friend," Hesam soothed, patting Pete on the shoulder, "let us not panic. If Kabir is a member of the Taliban and he was the last one to be seen with Cali, then, yes, she could be kidnapped. I will have my guards here go to Kabir's village and look for him. If he is there, he will be brought in, held and questioned."

Gulping, Pete opened his eyes and stared down at Hesam. "Why would he do that?"

"I cannot read minds, my friend. But he might have been given orders to try and kidnap you or Cali because you are the leaders of this enterprise." Stroking his beard again, Hesam walked out of the security office and stared up at the dark slopes of the Hindu Kush. Pete followed him.

"The Taliban hide in caves up there," Hesam continued. "You know that as well as I.

Kabir could have kidnapped her and handed her over to our enemy. They would have taken her by horseback up into the mountains."

"To what end?" Pete couldn't keep the desperation out of his voice. A terrible, deep trembling began within him and he wanted to scream in rage and fear over Cali's disappearance.

Hesam turned and looked up at him unhappily. "You know that they behead Americans. . . ."

Pete staggered backward. Pain, serrating and swift, closed in, making him feel as if he was suffocating. "Not Cali," he rasped. "They couldn't do that to her." And yet he knew of another captured woman, from Ireland, who had spent thirty years in Iraq helping the poor. Iraqi terrorists had threatened beheading, but at the last moment had saved her from such a fate and put a bullet in her head instead. Either way, she had suffered terribly for months and then been murdered. Oh, God, that couldn't happen to Cali.

He needed her.

There, it was out. Pete bitterly acknowledged that in the last year he'd come to need Cali. He'd never admitted that to anyone. Certainly not to Cali, who insisted that their relationship be only about business. Pete hadn't told his parents, either, too afraid that such an admittance would somehow jinx the relationship he dreamed of having with Cali someday.

Wiping his mouth, he turned away and repressed a sob that tore up into his throat. Pete wanted to cry. He wanted to vomit. Feeling Hesam's firm, steadying hand on his shoulder, Pete lifted his head.

"My friend, do not go there, at least, not yet," the sheik said. "I have a plan."

CHAPTER SIXTEEN

Cali's head hurt like hell. Each jostling movement of her horse made it worse until it felt like sledgehammers were pounding her brain. Hands tied with rope in front of her, she held the reins in numbed fingers. Her captors rode in front and behind her. Dizzy, she gripped the front of the saddle.

Cali realized she was helpless. It wasn't something she'd felt often in her life. Just one other time — with Russ. Bitterness coated her mouth as that awareness permeated her foggy state. Anger mixed with fear began to seep through her as she became more conscious of her surroundings.

In the faint light of dawn, she saw other horses in front of hers. A single line of Afghan riders, all with AK-47 rifles slung over their shoulders, moved at a slow, plodding pace up a narrow dirt trail littered with stones. To her left rose a long, smooth slope of rock. To her right was a thousand-foot drop-off to a chasm far below. As she recognized the mountainous terrain, terror radiated through her. Taliban. She'd been kidnapped by them!

Blood trickled down the side of Cali's head, where she'd been coldcocked by Kabir. She couldn't lift her hands to touch the area, could only feel the warm fluid still leaking from the wound and dribbling downward. Most of the bleeding seemed to have stopped, and blood was now drying on her left temple and tense jawline.

Horses snorted and breathed heavily, for they were, Cali estimated, over ten thousand feet. It was an effort to breathe, so she knew the elevation had to be high. Eyes squinting from the constant agony, Cali struggled to get her bearings. But each time she moved her neck, pain shot through her skull.

Numbly, she noted that evergreens appeared as scraggly dark shapes on the steep, rocky slopes far below. It was cold at this hour and this altitude, and she was glad of the woolen burka she was wearing. Who had put it on her? She was still wearing her construction clothes beneath it. Trembling, Cali couldn't stand the thought of being unconscious and having some man or men touching her, pulling the burka over her body. Nausea rolled in her stomach.

Straining to look out through the criss-crossed netting in front of her eyes, Cali tried to determine how many men were in the raiding party. There was no mistake about it: Kabir was a Taliban member. He must have dragged her out to the fence, unseen. Someone had to have cut a hole through it — his Taliban friends, no doubt. Kabir could never have gotten Cali through the security gate; the guards would have discovered her.

How long she'd been slumped over the neck of the horse, Cali had no idea. Her watch was missing. She'd awakened to find her mouth gagged, her hands bound and her body covered in the black burka.

The steady movement of the thin, small Arabian beneath her was somewhat soothing to the fear eating away at her. Where were they going? What where these men going to do with her? She thought of trying to escape, but on this narrow path, it would be impossible. Furthermore, there were several riders behind her, and someone had a lead on her horse. She was boxed in with no place to go.

Her mind gyrated crazily back to Pete. Had he realized she was missing yet? What must he be feeling right now if he knew she had been kidnapped? The metallic taste of blood coated the inside of Cali's mouth. The rag forced between her teeth was tight around her neck, and her jaw ached. How she longed for water!

Her back molars felt loose, thanks to Kabir's blow to her head. *The son of a bitch.* If she got any chance to escape, Cali resolved she would get even with that traitor.

Again, she thought of Pete. For some reason, she desperately needed the handsome Marine, who had always reminded her of a courtly knight from the olden days. They had never kissed, or touched one another as lovers would. So how could she want him like this? Was it due to the terror of dying?

Didn't everyone need someone in a crisis? Of course. Her heart pounded, underscoring the feelings that now raced with an agonizing awareness through her. She wasn't sure which was more painful — the threat of dying, or discovering her need for Pete.

Oh, what Cali would give to be free! She twisted her wrists, which were bloody and raw from the ropes. She tried to loosen them, but the coarse strands only cut deeper.

Miserably, Cali closed her eyes, the ache in her heart even worse than the physical pains haunting her. Somehow, Pete had slowly, over time, worked through her armor and touched her.

Cali was sure she had a mild concussion, because her nose had bled off and on throughout the ride. Right now, there was no bleeding, but she could feel caked blood pulling at the sensitive flesh around her nostrils and upper lip. If she got out of here, what was she going to do about Pete? She would still be working with him. . . .

Everything seemed so bleak and hopeless to Cali. If only she got a chance to escape! Right now, she wanted to be racing down the gravelly, rocky slopes of the Kush Mountains to freedom. Back to the building site. Home to Pete. . . .

Rattled by these deep feelings, Cali continued to rock forward and back with her horse's movements, her head bowed, the hammering pain unrelenting. What she'd give to stop and rest for just a little bit. They'd been riding all night. In the pale light of dawn, she had no idea where she was. No landmarks looked familiar as they made their way across the steep, dangerous terrain. Where were they heading? And what would her captors do with her? Rape her? Torture her? Hold her for ransom? Behead her? The last thought nauseated her.

All around Cali rose the silent Kush

Mountains. If only she could find one familiar landmark. Oh, she'd done a lot of riding up in the hills around the site, but never this far or this high. Dizzy and confused, Cali couldn't even tell directions, except that the sun rose in the east and set in the west.

At the top of a steep rise, the narrow trail flattened out. Cali caught sight of a huge cave just ahead. That's where they were going.

Twisting her bonds, Cali worked and worked to loosen them. Her wrists were numb and she felt no pain, but fresh, warm blood ran down her hands and she knew the rope was cutting into her flesh.

The string of horses wearily moved into the cave and halted at the rear. Cali saw two men in turbans, with bandoleers of ammunition across their chests, waiting. A small fire deep within the cave lent just enough light to see. The fragrant odors of coffee, curry and lamb wafted, mouthwatering smells that reminded Cali of just how hungry she was.

A posting line was strung across the back of the cave. Cali saw the lead riders dismount and tie their weary mounts to it. She did not see Kabir among them. Was he a mole, a hidden implant in the village and at the site, giving the Taliban information? Cali thought so. It would explain why he wasn't among this group. Kabir had probably gone on home that night, faded back into village life, and no one knew what he'd done — except her.

She stiffened as the tall man at the front of the group came striding toward her. Twisting her head, she saw four other riders near the opening, waiting. Were they there to stop her from turning her Arabian around and racing out? Probably.

"Get down," the man snarled to her.

Shock bolted through Cali as she got a good look at his upturned face. It was Ahmed! Pete's first interpreter! Her surprised reaction earned a cocky grin from the man. He reached up and grasped her arm.

"You!" Cali rasped through the gag. Instinctively, she jerked her foot out of the stirrup and thrust it forward. Her boot slammed into Ahmed's chest as he tried to haul her off the horse.

He grunted and careened backward. Dust rose around him when he fell.

Another Taliban soldier who had just dismounted ran up and grabbed hold of the burka Cali wore. With one hard jerk on the material, she was wrenched out of the saddle. She tried to brace herself for the fall, but air whooshed from her lungs as she landed hard on her right side. The horse danced around, his hooves barely missing her. The pain in her head was so intense she cried out. Blindly, Cali struck out with her feet, but the man was faster. In the enveloping burka, Cali couldn't maneuver. The thick fabric twisted around her legs, preventing her from lashing out once again.

"Get her!" Ahmed thundered, scrambling to his feet. He quickly dusted off his trousers and strode over to where Cali was being jerked to her feet. Grabbing the top of the burka, Ahmed yanked it off her. Then he leaned down and jerked the gag from her mouth.

His hand was like a claw, digging painfully into her shoulder. Cali spat out the rag and wrenched herself from his grasp. She was glad to be rid of the damn, hampering burka. How any woman could live in such a prison was beyond her. Tossing her head, regardless of how much it hurt her, Cali glared up at Ahmed.

"You son of a bitch! You're a traitor!" she spat. Cali saw him snarl and lift his pistol out of its holster.

Her eyes widened. Her breath stopped as he jammed the gun into her face. Staring up into the dark barrel, only inches away, Cali felt her world grind to a halt. Ahmed grinned savagely down at her, hatred burning in his dark eyes. Slowly, he cocked the gun.

That sound was the only thing Cali heard in her narrowing universe. All other noises ceased to exist. She heard the alarming click and saw the lean, brown fingers on the pistol. And Ahmed's index finger slowly pulling back the trigger — to kill her. *Die. I'm going to die . . .* In that moment, her life began flashing before her eyes.

Cali stared fixedly at the gun barrel hovering inches from her face. Wanting to live warred with the fact that she was going to die within seconds. Something vital snapped within her. Air rushed out of her lungs and through her parted lips. Ahmed's eyes burned like those of a demon who was going to suck her life away from her. She was going to die . . .

"Ahmed! Leave her be!"

"But, my lord, Arsallah —"

"No! Go about your business, Ahmed. Put that pistol away! Now."

Cali flinched as Ahmed angrily jammed the pistol back into the holster. Breathing hard, her arms gripped by the guard who stood behind her, Cali jerked a look to her right, toward the man who had just spared her life.

Arsallah walked quickly over to them. He was a tall man, as lean as a starving greyhound. In his silver-studded leather belt he carried a curved knife in a jeweled case, and he grasped an AK-47 in his left hand. Cali sensed he was the leader of this group.

Glaring up at him, she growled, "Let me go, dammit! You have no right doing this to me! I'm an American citizen."

"Enough, woman. Keep it up and I'll gag you once more. Wouldn't you rather have some hot coffee? Some lamb and curried rice? Surely, you're as hungry as we are. Now, be quiet. Ahmed!" Arsallah turned to the man, who stood nearby. "Take her and sit her down over there by the picket line. Keep one guard on her and feed her."

Ahmed bowed, though his teeth were clenched. "Yes, my lord." Although rich, Ahmed obeyed because Arsallah came from a very old, rich family himself. By day Arsallah ran his family's oriental rug business. By night he rode for the Taliban like himself.

After he dragged her to where the horses were tied, he roughly shoved her to the ground. Cali collapsed on the camp floor, her shoulder striking the rough granite wall. Pain flared again up her neck. She felt so weak. Her legs were like Jell-O. Adrenaline was pumping hard through her, and she was shaking not only internally, but physically. Fear of dying flooded her, along with the serrating terror of the unknown to come.

"Stay there," Ahmed hissed, shaking his fist in her face. "You aren't going to live long, anyway." Then he grinned savagely. "One last meal, you yapping dog. You are going to be a symbol to any female in Afghanistan who dares to defy Islam. No woman will show her face when we get done with you."

With a look of triumph, Ahmed muttered fiercely, "I've been waiting for this moment, Ms. Roland. I helped plan this kidnapping. Oh, it took a long time and much patience on my part. No one fires me from a translation job. It has been a pleasure plotting to capture you." Wheeling around, he snapped an order to a Taliban guard to watch her closely. Then he stalked back to the fire, where all the men were sitting down to eat.

Breathing raggedly, Cali tried to settle herself. She leaned against the wall and slowly straightened her weakened legs. Her heart pounding like a sledgehammer in her breast, she closed her eyes momentarily, trying to deal with her avalanching emotions. Ahmed had threatened a year earlier to get even with her, and now he had. Why hadn't she been more alert? Taken his threat more seriously?

Stomach churning, her heart racing, Cali tried to think coherently. She had to figure out if she could escape. Quickly memorizing the layout in the cave, she began to grasp just how large it was. From the piles of dried horse dung, she realized they must use this cave often. A wind blew into it, making smoke from the small fire drift back toward her. That meant there was another entrance behind the horses.

Craning her neck, Cali tried to pierce the grayness. It was impossible. Her eyes kept blurring, a sign of a concussion. Despite this, she did the best she could in studying the space. From her position, most of what Cali could see were countless legs of horses. She could also detect the dancing, wavering shadows of men on the rough cave walls, cast by the light of the fire.

Every few minutes, dread and terror paralyzed her. Ahmed kept stealing dark glances in her direction. Time and again he stroked the pistol at his side. That memory of his gun barrel staring down at her made her nauseous with fear.

Cali watched a younger man, probably in his late teens, tending to the horses. He quickly unbridled all the animals and slipped soft cotton halters on them. One of the soldiers at the campfire called to the lad.

"Zalmai, come get some hot tea. Then feed the horses."

The youth ran to the fire, where the men huddled. He brought his tin mug of tea back to where the horses stood. After setting the steaming cup aside, Zalmai brought in piles of dried grass and threw it before the eager animals. The Arabians quickly bent to the task of eating.

Cali wondered why he hadn't unsaddled them. But then she realized that, if they were discovered, the Taliban could quickly slip on the bridles and ride hell-bent-for-leather and escape. Cali felt sorry for the horses. Having a saddle on for long periods didn't do their backs any good.

Stomach growling, she watched as Zalmai walked back over to the fire. He brought her a wooden bowl and a cup of coffee. Her mouth watered in anticipation.

"May I have some water? Please?" she asked him in Pashto as he set the food down beside her.

Glowering, he nodded and spun away.

Cali looked longingly at the bowl of food. There was rice, vegetables and bits of lamb

299

in the curry sauce over them. Despite her situation, she was starving. And she realized that if she was going to stay strong, she had to eat.

Zalmai brought back a flask of water. He then took the knife from the sheath at his side, leaned down and sliced through the thick bonds around her wrists.

Groaning, Cali felt sharp pains pulse up her arms as they fell away. The ropes had cut deeply. She sat there feeling the blood begin to flow back into her numbed hands. Flexing her fingers was an agony.

"Eat," the boy commanded, sheathing his knife. "And do not try to escape or he will shoot you." He pointed to the guard who stood scowling at her across the way.

"I won't escape," Cali said, reaching for the water. "Thank you."

Zalmai sneered at her and turned away. His tasks done, he could now sit with the men around the fire.

Cali ate ravenously with her fingers. There were no utensils. All the while, she kept glancing about furtively, checking out the cave as the light grew brighter. Eventually, as the sun rose higher, she realized that the cave faced east. And west was where the plant site lay, somewhere far, far below them.

Despite the constant pounding in her head, Cali tried to compute the miles they'd traveled. From the time when she'd been knocked unconscious to their arrival around dawn, their trek would have taken twelve to fourteen hours. At no time did she think the party had trotted or galloped, for the slopes they'd climbed were slippery and far too dangerous for any kind of speed. A horse could walk roughly three to five miles in an hour, depending upon the terrain. That meant they might be anywhere from thirty-six to fifty-six miles away from the power plant.

Cali's legs slowly strengthened and her wrists began to burn in earnest as the blood flow returned. She'd rather feel pain and know there was no permanent circulation damage to her hands from the tight bonds she'd worn. She glanced at the horses, which were voraciously eating. Perhaps she would be able to steal a mount. The Arabian would have to run far enough, fast enough, to outdistance her captors. But, she didn't know the trails and she'd be lost. *Damn.* Finishing off the flask of water, she sat back, sated.

The murmuring of the men around the campfire continued. The soft snorting of the horses, the smell of the sweet hay all conspired against Cali. She slid downward, tucked her hands beneath her head and closed her eyes. There was nothing she could do right now. The horses were exhausted and so was she. No, she'd have to try and make her escape later.

Right now, Cali just wanted to sleep. Sleep and dream of all Pete Trayhern had meant in her life.

"Come, Pete, this way," Hesam urged the engineer, jabbing his heels into the flanks of his black Arabian stallion as they climbed the steep, narrow trail.

Pete urged his gray gelding up the slippery slope. They were forty miles into the Kush, following a sparse, sometimes nonexistent trail. Ahead of Hesam were his best trackers — two older men who had hunted snow leopards, wild goats and deer throughout the region. Amazingly, despite their age and gray beards the men walked most of the time, the reins of their horses in their hands, as they hunted for signs that the Taliban had passed this way.

Pete rode up beside Hesam. The sun was low in the west, and at eight thousand feet on this spring day, the air was cool. Pete was glad he had on his camouflage jacket to stave off the chill. Behind them, he heard the scrambling of ten other horsemen, for the sheik had come with his best men, all heavily armed, to find Cali.

"These two men," Hesam told him, pride in his tone, "can find spoor where no one else can. Trust me, my friend, they not only know the shape of each horse's hoofprints, they can follow them anywhere."

Pete looked down at the barren gray rock. It was impossible to find prints on this. Yet these trackers had. "I don't know how. . . ." he murmured. He felt a small trickle of hope. His heart wrenched in his chest every time he thought of Cali missing — kidnapped by their enemy. Tears pricked the back of his eyes time and again, and he kept gulping to keep them from showing.

He knew the warlord could have chosen not to get involved in the hunt for Cali. Personal pride, Hesam had told him, would not allow him just to send his soldiers to look for her. Cali was a friend, and friends did not abandon one another in a time of need. Pete was grateful that the sheik was riding with them.

"You see the shrubs here and there?" Hesam said. "Those long tuffs of grass? If a horse walks by, there are changes. Blades get broken. A bush may snag strands of a horse's tail." Hesam grinned confidently and looked around. He kept his AK-47 handy, the butt resting on his left thigh. "I know of several deep, large caves up there." He pointed toward the craggy rocks that loomed far above them. "I believe the Taliban use those caves. My trackers have often found horse dung, cold campfires and bits of hay in them. So we know they are occupied. And there's a good chance that is where they hide out."

"But would they still be there? Wouldn't they move on?" Pete asked. He felt his throat close up again with emotion. Oh God, he couldn't control his feelings no matter how hard he tried. This had never happened before. After he realized Cali was gone, a new, shocking revelation had occurred to Pete: he cared deeply for her. Because he'd never experienced such complex emotions with another woman, he didn't know what to call them. Whatever they were, they made his soul ache.

When and how had this happened? Pete had fought attraction to Cali for a year now. This connection to her must have grown silently in the small moments they'd shared. As he remembered those times, so few and far between, Pete felt his whole being contract with feeling. One moment he was filled with hope, the next, despair that she could be dead. Gone. And he'd never see her smile again. Never hear her husky, rich voice, which always soothed his fractious moods. Never experience that unexpected, soft touch of her fingers grazing his flesh. *Oh God, it's too much to bear. . . .*

Pete struggled to get out of this maelstrom. The sky was an intense lapis blue, streaked with thin, fine cirrus clouds like strands of a woman's hair. Below, he saw the valley where the plant sat. It seemed so far away. Another world. And his heart was an open wound, bleeding constantly each time he thought of Cali, pictured her face or those beautiful, warm green eyes of hers.

The sheik's voice interrupted his thoughts. "They might still be there, who knows? They traveled all night, that we do know. After fifty miles of trekking, most horses, even Arabians, must rest several hours before they get their strength back. No, I'm sure they reached those caves. The question now is whether they're still there or have moved on."

Grimly, Pete pulled his cap a little lower to shade his eyes from the sun as they turned up the trail. Hesam felt the Taliban had taken her to make a statement about women being in charge, and that it would not be tolerated. Whatever the truth, Pete was helpless in his panic. Gripping the barrel of the horse with his long legs, he pulled behind the sheik as the path narrowed once more. So far, no one had called him to demand money. In his gut, Pete knew they were going to kill Cali.

Please let her still be alive. Let us find her in time. . . .

CHAPTER SEVENTEEN

Cali quietly but intently worked her wrists against the cotton bonds that had been placed around them after the meal. Sunlight was just leaving the cave now, and she estimated that it was midafternoon. The sky was a cobalt blue and cloudless. The dry heat that rose from the desert plain below made the cave stifling, even though she was sure they were over ten thousand feet in altitude.

Fifteen of the twenty Taliban had left an hour ago. She'd overheard them saying that Sheik Hesam was following some miles below. They'd ridden off to create a false trail in another direction, so their cave would remain undiscovered and secure.

Zalmai, the teenager who'd been left to watch her, was busy unsaddling the other horses. He'd been given orders by Arsallah to rub them down, brush them and dress any scrapes or nicks they'd gotten on the journey. Only two horses were near Cali. And two sentries guarded the entrance to the cave, rifles across their laps as they watched the trail.

Her ears picked up an odd noise. Cali looked out of the cave and heard a helicopter. Her heart began to thud as she wondered if Pete was responsible. Could it be a U.S. Army Apache? Cali knew that with the heat and infrared sensing equipment on board, it would have the ability to ferret out humans and animals. The noise grew in volume, indicating there was more than one helicopter. The guards rose and quickly moved back inside the cave. They pressed themselves against the rough stone walls to remain hidden from prying eyes, rifles ready to fire.

The whapping sounds intensified. The helos were very close to the cave! Licking her dry, cracked lips, Cali frantically tugged at her bonds, but Zalmai had tied them tightly. The guards at the entrance exchanged worried glances. She heard the teen speak softly to the horses, which moved restlessly.

The whole cave began to shake and shudder as the helicopters slowly flew past the entrance. Sure enough, two desert-camouflaged U.S. Army Apache helicopters appeared. Jerking frantically at her bonds,

Cali finally felt them give. Within seconds, her hands were free! No one was watching her; they were watching the Apaches fly by. Could the pilots see anyone inside the cave? Cali didn't know.

Suddenly, a horse reared at the end of the line. By accident, it kicked over the metal pail holding the brushes and comb that Zalmai had used earlier. The accompanying sound was like an explosion echoing through the cave. The horses lunged forward in terror, their eyes rolling wildly. The picket line snapped.

Cali saw her chance. A small bay gelding, the one nearest her, realized he was free. The whites of his eyes showed the depth of his fear as he lunged forward. Cali shot to her feet. The Arabian careened drunkenly by her, his halter lead rope flying in the wind. She made a grab for the saddle horn.

In seconds, she had swung aboard the horse. Leaning low, she kicked him repeatedly in the flanks with the heels of her boots. Alarmed, the guards tore their attention from the Apaches, back to her. Cali kept low, hand outstretched to retrieve the loose, flapping halter lead. She caught it! Swinging the bay to the right, she lashed out with her boot as one guard stepped out from the cave wall and tried to stop her.

Her heel slammed into his chest. He let out a groan, knocked off his feet.

Shots were fired behind her. As she yelled at the Arabian, Cali yanked on its lead so that the careening animal turned down the rocky trail they'd come up earlier. Wind screamed past her while she hunkered over his neck. The black mane whipped her face repeatedly, stinging her skin. More shots whined around her. Cali heard them echoing off the barren mountains.

Eyes watering, barely able to see from the horse hair slapping in her face, Cali coaxed the Arabian to full speed. They crossed the ridge and dived down a narrow gravel trail. Cali knew the guards would follow her. She gasped for breath and slowed the horse a little. At least they couldn't fire at her here. The trail constricted suddenly, to less than one foot in width. On one side, harsh black-and-white rocks rose steeply upward, on the other was that thousand-foot drop. One slip by the frightened Arabian, and Cali knew she could die. She didn't want to. She'd come too far. *No way!*

By urging the Arabian to a ground-eating trot, Cali was taking a terrible chance, she knew. There were so many stones on the path that if the sure-footed horse mis-tepped, it would be the end for both of them. Cali held her breath as terror zig-zagged through her.

In the background, she heard the Apache helicopters. They seemed to be flying away from where the cave was located. How could that be that they hadn't seen her? Her frustration mounted.

She sensed that Pete was around here somewhere. Who else in this province had the authority to call in Apaches? No one but Pete. Her hopes rose. He'd come after her and was trying to save her. Could he sense her need of him?

The steep trail suddenly widened as they reached a flat gravel stretch. Relief, sharp and clean, raced through her, and she hauled the horse to a skidding stop. The trail split in two just in front of her. Which branch to take, Cali wasn't sure. Her head pounded with fiery pain and her vision blurred, then sharpened. She had to fight the effects of her injury because if she didn't get the hell out of here, she would have no life at all to worry about.

Clamping her legs around the horse's heaving, sweaty sides, Cali jerked the halter lead and coaxed the Arabian onto the upper trail. The other path led downward, and there were too many places where the Taliban could halt their horses, get her in the bead of a rifle sight and kill her. No, she was going to take the trail that climbed upward. At the very least, she'd be safer from gunfire.

The sun was hot and Cali perspired heavily as the Arabian scrambled up a slope of loose stones and damp soil. At the top, she twisted around in the saddle. Her pursuers would try to find her, but she couldn't see them. Perhaps the riders who had left earlier were in the cut down below her, on the other trail. Cali just didn't know, and was afraid of running into them, especially since she had no way of defending herself.

Standing up in the stirrups on her restive and uncooperative horse, Cali anxiously searched the rocky, unforgiving terrain. She must be over ten thousand feet in altitude, for nothing was growing on the bluish granite that surrounded them. Snow covered the mountains, no matter which direction she looked.

The Arabian snorted in fear, his ears nervously flicking back and forth. For safety reasons, Cali wished she had a bridle on the animal and a bit in its mouth. Still, the horse seemed to do pretty well on just a halter and lead.

Her gut told her to follow the path across

the granite escarpment in front of them. Knowing that the power plant site was to the east, Cali hoped she could find another trail leading in that direction. She clapped her heels to the horse and the Arabian lurched forward once more, its hoofbeats sounding hollowly on the gray stone.

"Did you hear that?" Hesam skidded his foam-flecked stallion to a halt.

Pete cocked his head, and everyone on the trail stopped. "That was rifle fire!"

"Yes, gunshots," the sheik muttered, pointing upward. "Your pilots have seen nothing?"

Pete held his radio and kept contact with the two Apache helicopter crews. They had been looking nonstop since arriving on the scene. "No, nothing. . . ."

"Can they pick up on noise?"

"No. Just body heat."

Hesam studied the trail in front of them. It forked, one going up and the other continuing down the sloping incline. Pulling his black stallion around, he called sharply to his twenty men, "Follow me!" His horse leaped forward, gravel and stones spraying from beneath his hooves as he clambered up the steep trail.

Pete followed, leaning forward and racing

up the narrow path. *Gunshots.* A horrible vision flashed before him, of Cali pushed to her knees, blindfolded, hands behind her back and a rifle held to her temple by the Taliban. No matter how many times he gulped, he couldn't stop the burning sensation in his heart or his wild, untrammeled grief. The wind tore around him, the tears drying on his cheeks as his horse topped the ridge.

Ahead, the sheik galloped at high speed, the mane and tail of his black Arabian flying like flags in the wind. As he urged his own mount forward, Pete tucked the radio away in his belt. He saw Hesam pull out his AK-47 and get it ready. Ready for what? Without another thought, Pete yanked the M16 strapped across his back and got it ready for use. He was trained for this, but God help him, the stakes had never been so high. He had to save Cali, if she was still alive.

Soon, Pete was surrounded by Hesam's fleet horsemen. They were on a smooth, granite escarpment that sloped gently upward.

More gunshots! *Closer!* Pete urged his gelding up alongside the sheik's black stallion. "This direction!" he yelled, pointing to the east.

"Yes!" Hesam responded, and dug his heels into his Arabian.

As they crested the slope, Pete's eyes bulged with disbelief. There, on the lower escarpment, Cali was riding a bay horse for all it was worth. Right behind her were three men on horseback, firing at her.

"Taliban!" Hesam roared. Twisting, he gestured sharply to his men. "Try and take prisoners! Save Ms. Roland!" He whirled his stallion around and careened recklessly down the trail to intersect the oncoming Taliban soldiers.

Pete veered his Arabian to the left. As he made a beeline for Cali, he began to see her weakened state. And yet she was riding hell-bent-for-leather. The horse didn't even have a bridle, just a halter and lead rope. Shots filled the air once more. She leaned low, hugging the neck of her horse and guided it ever upward toward him.

Pete's horse slipped and skidded awkwardly on the slick granite. After a moment of panic, Pete steadied the gelding. Cali was less than a mile away. For one second he glanced at the approaching Taliban soldiers, who weren't prepared as Hesam and his men who swept like eagles down upon them. Startled, the Taliban pulled their mounts to a halt and lifted their weapons toward the attacking group. A hail of bullets peppered the air in return. Pete was glad to be wearing a flak vest but his chief concern was putting himself between Cali and the Taliban.

He aimed his thundering horse straight toward her and saw her surprise when she finally noticed him. His heart lurched into this throat. She was so close, yet so far away. A bullet could find her any second now . . . Her relief was evident, and Cali guided her fleeing Arabian directly toward him. Pete wove through thick brush, the gelding leaping a fallen timber, and then he was right where he wanted to be: a protective barrier between Cali and her pursuers. If any bullets were fired, they would hit him or his horse now. Not her.

In a matter of seconds, one horseman on a bay Arabian turned away from the sheik's men and aimed directly for Cali. Pete didn't even think, but yanked his horse to a halt, shouldered his M16 and fired. The butt thumped repeatedly into his shoulder, ramming against it as he squeezed off several rounds.

The Taliban soldier was lifted off his horse, flipped over backward and slammed facedown onto the rock. He didn't move.

Satisfaction thrummed through Pete. The

sheik's men grabbed the other two Taliban soldiers, who had thrown down their weapons, their hands held high in surrender.

With the danger over, Pete turned his attention back to Cali, who had halted a half mile above them and was watching the fray. As he galloped toward her, his gaze clung to hers. She slid weakly off the horse, fell to her knees and pressed her hands to her head. Oh God, how badly was she hurt?

As soon as he reached her, Pete flew out of the saddle, dismounting even before the animal had stopped. He bolted across the granite, fell to his knees and threw his arms around her hunched shoulders.

"Cali, tell me where you're hurt." His words came out in gasps. Breathing raggedly, he ached for any kind of response. Finally, Cali lifted her head. The left side of her temple was bloody and the flesh torn open. Her red hair was matted around a swollen, ugly wound. Flinching in horror, Pete gripped her sagging shoulders more securely. He noticed tears tracking down her dusty features. She had to be in horrible pain, and he felt helpless.

"Cali?"

"I — I'm going to be okay, Pete . . ." Cali's words sounded hollow to her, as if she were a thousand miles away. Maybe it was the concussion, and her hearing was off. She wasn't sure. But Pete's strong arms gave her stability and solace. He had come for her, saved her in the final stretch. Dizzy, she reached out, her bloody hand touching the flak vest on his chest.

"I . . . have a concussion, Pete. A bad one. I'm dizzy but I'll be okay. Just give me a minute . . ."

Pete gently cupped one side of her face. "You're safe now, Cali. It's all over." When she lifted her head, her eyes were glassy with pain. "It's okay now," Pete said roughly as he held her in his arms. "You're safe, Cali. God, I almost lost you and I can't, I just can't . . ." He gulped and blinked at tears stinging his own eyes and blurring his vision. Looking down at her wan, bloody face, he choked out, "I'll call in a medevac from a forward base. One will land here and take us to a hospital. Just hold on, okay? I need you."

Those were the last words Cali heard before she fainted in his arms. She was safe. She'd seen the terror banked in his stormy gray eyes, the way his mouth tensed with the pain he felt for her. The world had been spinning, and now, as she was sucked into an invisible tornado, his last words were a balm to her frightened soul.

■ ■ ■ ■

"Cali's sleeping just fine now," Dr. Jason Wright assured Pete. The doctor quietly closed the door to Cali's private room at the Kabul hospital. He took Pete by the arm and led him down the long, quiet hall. At the end was a large window and a set of stairs.

Pete was bone weary. After Cali had fainted in his arms, he'd called on the radio for a medevac helicopter. It had arrived an hour later, and they had finally been airlifted to Kabul. All the while, Cali was in and out of consciousness, and that scared the hell out of him. The nurse on board had told him that a doctor could determine the amount of damage Cali had sustained from the concussion. All Pete could do was sit next to her as she was blanketed and strapped to a cot. She was given an IV, and the nurse checked her vital signs every fifteen minutes.

The darkness of night stared back at Pete as he looked through the window. Dr. Wright, a U.S. Army physician, had taken Cali from the ER, through the X-ray process and then made her comfortable in the private room. Pete had told him he was

Cali's boss, so that he could know what was going on.

As soon as she was admitted to the hospital, he had called Cali's father. Needless to say, Mr. Roland was upset, and Pete tried to allay some of his fears. The elder Roland had said he'd fly to Kabul right away, along with his oldest son, another engineer.

Wiping his gritty, dirty face, Pete asked the doctor now, "Aren't you worried that Cali might die if she sleeps?"

Dr. Wright smiled briefly and clapped Pete on the shoulder. "No, Major, I'm not. Cali has a concussion, for sure, but her vitals are stable and improving. We have her on a medication mix that is going to reduce the swelling in the area where she was struck. From what she told us, she's very sleep deprived. We'll wake her up from time to time just to be on the safe side, so don't worry. The nurses are packing dry ice around that head wound every thirty minutes, and monitoring her vitals. Cali's in the best of hands. Why don't you go get cleaned up? We have a men's shower and locker area down in the basement. I could loan you a pair of scrubs if you don't have anything else to wear."

Touched by the doctor's concern, Pete nodded and dropped his hand from his face.

He desperately needed a shower. "Thanks, Doctor. I think I'll take you up on your offer."

"Good, come with me," Dr. Wright said, gesturing toward the stairs. "Then you can go to the cafeteria, get something to eat and catch some shut-eye in the interns' room. Cali isn't going to wake up for probably eight hours. She has to sleep off her trauma, Major. An ordeal like this would exhaust the strongest person. We'll come get you when she awakens. So you can rest easy, get some sleep."

Nodding, Pete could feel hope flooding back into his heart. Relief made him light-headed. "Sounds good, Dr. Wright. Thank you."

A minute later, that joy was followed by exhaustion. *Cali is safe. She's going to live.*

CHAPTER EIGHTEEN

When Cali awakened, her father was at her bedside, along with her oldest brother, Logan. Each was holding one of her hands. Their faces were grim and anxious.

"Dad?" Cali's voice cracked. She desperately wanted some water. "What are you doing here?"

"Why else? To make sure you're okay." Frank Roland smiled down at her. "Logan and I arrived an hour ago. The doctor says you suffered a nasty concussion, but you're going to be fine, thank God."

As if reading her mind, Logan went to get her a glass of water. He eased his arm beneath her shoulders and lifted Cali just enough so that she could thirstily slurp the cool liquid.

"Welcome back, Sis," he said warmly.

"Thanks, Logan. It's good to see you."

"We're glad you're among the living. More?" he asked, gently supporting her head and shoulders.

"Please." Cali looked around, her vision not quite normal. After she finished the water, she focused once more on her father. "Dad? That damned Ahmed, the translator, was behind this. I saw him in the cave." Her voice dropped to a frustrated whisper. "He put a gun in my face. He was going to pull the trigger. I thought I was going to die."

"He's dead now, Cali. Major Pete Trayhern told us everything earlier. There was a big shootout below the cave after you escaped. One of Sheik Hesam's men took him down," her father said. He patted her hand. "When you feel up to it, the Military Police want to take a full statement from you. But not right now, Cali. You need to rest and regain your strength."

"Kabir . . . one of the Afghan workers . . . hit me on the head."

"Pete told us he found a sledgehammer handle in the hopper shack. It had blood and strands of your hair on it. That's how he knew you were in trouble. I'll make sure the MPs know all this."

"Where's Pete?" Cali whispered.

"He had an emergency back at the site." Squeezing her hand gently, Frank Roland said, "He didn't want to leave, but we told him you would be in good hands with us."

Frowning, Cali realized her mind wasn't functioning very well. "What kind of trouble?"

"Cali, just rest," Logan soothed as he gave her another refill of water. "Don't worry about the site right now."

"Thanks, Logan." Cali lifted her hand and wiped her mouth. She felt very weak. Bit by bit, in flashes and pieces, the kidnapping trauma started coming back to her, terrifying her all over again. "I'm in Kabul?"

"Yes," Logan murmured, shifting the chair and sitting back down. "Pete said you escaped the Taliban, rode like hell until they met you on the trail. You fainted after they found you. Pete called for a medevac to pick you up, and they brought you here."

As she studied her brother, Cali noted he hadn't shaved. His dark brown hair was short and neatly cut in a military style. Logan had been in the Marine Corps for six years before he came to work with their father in the construction company. The military had rubbed off on all three of her brothers, that was for sure. How handsome Logan looked despite the toll the flight had taken on him. Too bad he'd just recently gone through a nasty divorce. It had left him gaunt, without the usual glimmer of joy in his blue eyes.

"It's all starting to come back." Cali pointed to her bandaged brow. "I'm having flashbacks." She turned her head toward her father and gazed into his dark blue eyes. She didn't want to concentrate on her trauma. *Pete* . . . Cali felt a clawing sensation in her chest. She needed him as never before, even though having her family with her was comforting.

Her thinking was slow and spongy. She felt nearly incoherent. "Dad . . . you said Pete had an emergency back at the site? What happened?"

"There was an earthquake in that province — 4.5 on the Richter scale. The hoppers came down."

"Oh, no," Cali murmured. It hurt to frown. Her headache intensified and she pressed her fingers against the bandaged area. "Not the hoppers."

"Now, don't fret," Frank told her gruffly. "He'll handle it."

"Hoppers can be rebuilt," Logan reminded her.

"I should be there to help him. The concrete plant is Roland's responsibility."

"You aren't going anywhere for at least three days," Frank told his daughter firmly. "Dr. Wright said you need that time to recover here at the hospital." He smoothed the gown across her shoulder. "Your mother nearly came with us but we had an emergency at the house and she couldn't make it. I told her you would speak with her once you woke up so she wouldn't worry so much."

"Sure, Dad, I'll talk to Mom."

"Good, good."

Logan smiled down at Cali. "You slept through the quake. Things were rocking a little around Kabul, too."

"Where was the epicenter?" Cali asked. She struggled to sit up, with her father's help. Logan rearranged the pillows behind her back.

"About ten miles west of Dar-i-Suf," Frank told her.

"Oh, dear," Cali whispered worriedly. "That's Sheik Hesam's territory. Were there casualties?"

Logan handed her a fresh glass of water. She felt weak but capable of holding it, an improvement from minutes earlier.

"Nothing serious. Just a lot of abode huts losing a wall. Small stuff," Logan assured her. "There's no word of casualties, just scared a lot of people, sheep, camels and goats."

Frank glanced over at his son. "Why don't you go back to the hotel and get some sleep?

We haven't had much of late."

Logan ran his long fingers through his hair. "I think I will, Dad." He gave Cali a quick look. "We're staying at the hotel next door."

"Great. Thanks for coming, Logan. This is a nice surprise." And Cali watched him flush slightly. Logan was such an ice castle, so remote from normal human emotions. She hurt for her big brother, because the divorce had been hell on him. She'd watched him suffer, but he never cried. He never confided in anyone, not even her, and she was the closest of all his siblings.

"Yeah, I'll bet it is," Logan teased. Going to the door, he said, "Dad? Are you coming?"

"I'll be along soon," Frank replied.

Cali watched Logan leave, then turned to her father. The light from the window made his gray-streaked hair look nearly luminous. Frank Roland was the stuff of legends. He'd built dams in the Amazon jungle, pushed roads through Laos, Thailand and nearly every country in the Far East. He was like Indiana Jones, and Cali loved him fiercely. He constantly let his children know how much they meant to him.

"I can see you're disappointed Pete isn't here," Frank said.

"I am," she admitted, holding the glass tentatively between her hands. Its coolness felt good in the warm, stuffy room.

"He didn't want to leave, Cali. I thought he was going to cry after he got that emergency call." Frank looked at her intently. "He was very shaken by your kidnapping."

A ragged sigh tore from Cali's lips. "Oh, Dad. Everything is so complicated."

"Life usually is."

Her eyes narrowing, she whispered, "After that mess with Russ at the other site, I swore off men."

Frank gripped his daughter's hand. "I know how much that relationship hurt you, honey. And I know you saw this project as a way to vindicate yourself. You have, so relax, all right?"

Cali felt shaky and uncertain. "I crouched in that cave after I was told they were going to kill me." She sent her father an anguished look. "And who did I think of? I thought of Pete and how much I needed him, Dad." Gulping unsteadily, she closed her eyes. "I just feel so torn up, so unsure of myself right now, of my life."

"You're traumatized, Cali," Frank said gently. Rubbing her shoulder, he added, "And you've worked a year with Pete. I don't think it's strange you'd need him in a crisis. You've been a team there at the project. Seems like a pretty natural and normal reaction to have."

"Okay." Cali bit down on her lower lip, afraid to look her father in the eye. "Dad, you know we can't mix business with pleasure in our world. You don't fall in love with your boss. Especially the one who holds the purse strings to Roland paychecks. I did that once and look how it hurt all of us, our reputation, my reputation."

"We all make mistakes, honey. You weren't the first to fall in love with a hard hat. Right now, from what Dr. Wright said, you're suffering from PTSD, post-traumatic-stress disorder, because of the kidnapping. He warned us that you might be a lot more emotional than usual for a while." Frank gave her a brief hug and released her. "Dr. Wright said it may take months for you to recover from this life-and-death incident. Pete may be central to your healing. There's nothing wrong with that. He cares for you, Cali."

"I — I'm just so confused, Dad." Cali stared down at the glass in her hands. "I can't want Pete. Not in that way." She glanced up into her father's dark, worried eyes. "Do you know what I mean? I've got Brad Parker, the structural engineer, chasing me like I'm a piece of meat. I'm running scared, Dad. I keep Parker at arm's length, but I have to work with him. I don't want Pete thinking I'm causing problems because I'm a woman."

"So you haven't gone to Pete about Parker's actions toward you?"

"No. I'm afraid Pete will hear about the mess I made with Russ at the other project. I live in terror of that happening. I don't want to stir up muddy waters here at this site. I just deal with Parker by keeping him at bay. It's not the best solution, but it has to do for now." Cali winced and blew out a long, unsteady breath. After drinking the last of the water, she turned and placed the glass on the bed stand.

Her father's face was composed but tired looking. She saw a glint in his blue eyes and knew he wasn't going to let her off the hook. In a way, despite her roiling emotions, it felt good to confide in someone about her angst.

"Judging from what I've seen of Major Trayhern, I think you can trust him, Cali. I would ask him to transfer Parker. Get this guy off your back and out of your sights for now. You don't need that extra pressure, plus trying to handle this project for us."

Hearing resolve in her father's gruff tone, she murmured, "Trust . . ." Frowning, Cali stroked the side of her aching, bandaged head. "That's the real issue, isn't it, Dad? Russ destroyed my trust in men. Completely."

"Cali, you have to learn how to trust all over again. The major doesn't strike me as another Russ. Do you agree with that?"

Slowly, Cali whispered, "Yes. Pete's always been there for me. Any problems we've had, we hammer out. He's not a liar or a cheat, like Russ was. I've spent a year working with him and he's never tried to be anything less than honest and straightforward with me, Dad."

Leaning back in the chair, Frank crossed his jean-clad legs and put his hands in his lap. He smiled slightly and looked up at the ceiling in contemplation. "Is there more to this, Cali?"

"What do you mean?" Her heart plunged as she felt her father watching for a reaction. The man knew her too well. Feeling raw and vulnerable, she just didn't have the energy to ward off her father's gentle, persistent probing.

"Pete was upset over your being injured. More than I would expect a site superintendent to be toward his second-in-command. Is there . . ." Frank opened his hands and looked at Cali ". . . something more between the two of you that you aren't telling me about?"

A shudder worked through Cali, and her head began to ache even more. "I — I don't know, Dad. I'm afraid . . . afraid to look at it, at us, because of my past with Russ."

"Well, you know the story of how I met your mother. One kiss did it for us. We knew after that that we loved one another."

"I've never let him know how I feel, Dad."

"Have you wanted to?" he asked quietly.

Terror sizzled through Cali. It felt as if something inside her was screaming in agony. "It's silly, I know. He's the diametric opposite of Russ and Parker. Pete has such honor and integrity, Dad."

"You sound unsure. And the best antidote for that is just to wait and see. Answers come with time."

"Right . . ." Cali hung her head, hiding her face. Tears welled up behind her tightly shut eyelids. "I'm not sure of anything anymore, Dad. I'm afraid. I feel so ungrounded, spacey . . . and that's not like me."

He reached over and squeezed her elbow. "You were going to die, Cali. How you're feeling right now is normal after being given a death sentence and surviving it."

Lifting her head, her eyes awash with

tears, Cali croaked, "I feel out of control, Dad. Completely."

"And Pete gives you a sense of stability? Security with his presence?"

"Y-yes."

"I don't think that's a bad thing."

"I do. Out there in that cave, I found out how badly I wanted Pete. My heart felt like it was being ripped out of my chest. I was so surprised by the sheer power of my wanting."

Frank studied his hands, which were weatherworn and scarred. "Well, darling girl, Pete's care and concern for you is special, I think. And you mumbled a lot in your sleep. It was all about Pete."

Cali's heart plunged. "What did I say, Dad?"

"You kept calling for him." Her dad patted her hand. "And it was obvious to me that you feel more than a boss-to-employee kind of thing. But maybe I'm wrong. I've had a lot of close, friendly relationships on my projects with various owners. Granted, they were all men, but we became fast and lasting friends. And maybe that's what has happened between you and Pete. You became good friends."

Closing her eyes, Cali felt the pain in her heart more than she did the unremitting throbbing in her head. *Friends.* "Oh, God, Dad. I don't know. I've run this through my mind so many times that I lie awake some nights."

"I know, I know," Frank murmured.

Cali opened her eyes and held her father's gaze. "What's the answer here?"

"Answers don't always come when we want them, honey. When we arrived at the hospital, Pete was beside himself with worry over you. He stood there in the hall and told me that he was sorry he hadn't told you so many things. I agreed that life is short and should be acted upon, not set on the shelf until some convenient moment comes up." Giving her a slight smile, Frank added, "I think my comment gave him a lot to think about."

Frustrated and weary, Cali whispered, "It's impossible under these circumstances to be on anything but a business footing with Pete. You're the one who taught us you never mix business with pleasure at a construction site."

"That's true, I did," Frank said, his tone contrite. "But in your case, a woman in what's nearly a one hundred percent male-dominated field of work, it doesn't necessarily apply. You aren't a robot, Cali. You have feelings, needs and dreams. You're young and beautiful, and relationships are going to be a part of your life and experience."

She didn't feel very beautiful right now. More like an unraveling ball of yarn. "I'm so afraid . . . Sometimes I want a relationship so bad I can taste it, and other times it scares me to death."

"Your mother and I knew there was a good possibility you'd fall in love with a hard hat someday. But for all we know, you could fall in love with an accountant, or maybe a man in another field altogether."

"Bean counters?" Cali scoffed. "That would be the day."

"Or a pilot —"

"I want a man with his feet stuck in the earth."

"Or —" Frank smiled gently "— any of a hundred other careers. There's no telling where you'll meet the guy of your dreams." Sobering, he added, "I understand the many fine lines you're walking at this project, Cali. I know you're hurting from that sordid affair with Russ. But he lied to you and we all support you and are working to help you repair your reputation. And not all hard hats are like him. I think right now you're working your way through all that stuff. Don't you?"

"You're always able to put how I feel into a sentence or two," Cali said softly. Her headache was receding a little.

"It's easier to see someone else's life clearer than our own. I'm not so adept when it comes to your mother and me and our stresses, travails and problems over the years. It takes time to see them, Cali, and it's not easy. That's part of life — learning how to understand, cope and change. It doesn't happen all at once, usually. It's a process of discovery and communication."

Wearily, Cali sank back against the pillows. "Right now, I feel like a raw lump of emotions, Dad. Nothing but confusion." Her life, her relationships, her plans for the future all seemed scattered like a thousand jigsaw pieces around her feet.

"Those are PTSD symptoms, honey." Frank held her bandaged hand. "They'll be pretty loud in volume for a while, Cali. Maybe you should take some time off, a month of rest. Dr. Wright said that after a life-threatening experience like this, you'll feel the effects powerfully for many months, until you can work through them. What do you think? You haven't taken the vacation you have coming since being at this site. Go to a favorite place you like to vacation in and get away from here."

"I can't leave now. There's just been an earthquake. I'm needed back at the site as soon as possible." Frustration tinged her tone. "I'll get over these crazy feelings, Dad. I will."

"Well, just think about it," he counseled her gently. Picking up the satellite phone on the bed stand, he rose to his feet. "And as for all the other dilemmas you're wrestling with, sleep on it, Cali. In the meantime, will you talk to your mother? I know she's worried sick about you."

Cali's throat closed, choked with tears. "I really want to talk to Mom." Talking to her mother would comfort her and give her time away from her jumbled thoughts.

Pete had admitted he needed her. Cali wasn't sure how to respond to that. Or if she dared say anything at all. Stymied, she didn't know what to feel toward Pete, or what would happen between them. Everything was a roiling mass of contradictions inside her.

She had three days here at Kabul to recover, and then she would get back to work. Work with Pete. Good God, what was she going to say to him when she saw him? Surely he realized she'd heard him say those words. What was he expecting to hear from her in return? There was no way to avoid

the fact that something had changed between them.

CHAPTER NINETEEN

The late May sun beat down on Pete as he inched his way to the top of a hopper. Albert Golze, the foreman, was on the controls platform next to the opening. Trussed up in a sling that cradled across his hips and thighs, Pete flexed his gloved fingers and jammed his hard hat down on his head.

"Ready, Major Trayhern?" Albert asked.

Glancing down into the yawning chasm of the hopper, which was roughly thirty feet deep and twenty feet in diameter, he nodded. "Yeah, let's do it." He gripped the rope above him and steadied his booted feet against the scraped and scarred metal wall.

Sweat trickled down Pete's temples. The breeze was hot. At least ten Afghan workers crowded tensely at the various openings to watch what was going on. Because of the earthquake, one of the three hoppers had fallen over. The sand hopper, in the middle, had sustained serious damage to its auger feed. In the past two days, Pete and Roland's welding team had worked nonstop to get the downed hopper erected again, and this one repaired.

The grinding, whirring sounds of the winch began and Pete was lowered in jolting movements downward. He kept his left hand outstretched as he "walked" down the wall with his booted feet. The inside of the hopper was stifling, and Pete longed for any breath of air, any breeze. His short-sleeved camouflage shirt stuck to his body, dripping with sweat.

For a moment he thought he heard a helicopter approaching, but that was impossible. The grinding noise of machinery drowned out all other sounds. His thoughts swung from the auger below him to Cali. She'd been gone two days. And it had been hell on him. At no time had Pete been able to get through to Cali by iridium satellite phone.

When the quake occurred, the site had sustained minor damage, except for the concrete plants. And without the hoppers in operation, no concrete could be mixed. That threatened to put them behind schedule, and Pete could not allow that to happen. He'd had no choice but to come back and provide the leadership needed to get the hoppers up and running again.

His boots scraped the steel wall, and he extended his arm to keep himself upright and balanced. The sloped bottom of the hopper was below him. Spreading his feet, Pete dangled directly above the newly fashioned shutoff gate Roland's men had just installed. He gave Albert a hand signal, and the winch jerked to a stop. Pete felt as if he'd just been rear-ended and suffered whiplash.

Sweat ran into his narrowed eyes. Breathing hard, he leaned over and ran his gloved fingers across the new welds. They appeared solid. After wiping his face with the back of his glove, he moved to the opposite wall. Everything looked good, so he called Albert on his radio. "Open the gate."

A groaning and clanking started. Pete remained spread-eagled over the huge gate as it rumbled open.

"Good," he shouted into the radio. "Now shut it."

The gate closed, Pete noticed a number of workers looking off in one direction. What was going on? From his vantage point deep in the bowels of the metal monster, he couldn't tell. Pete asked for the feed auger to be operated while the gate was again opened and closed. This completed the testing, and he silently heaved a ragged sigh of relief. Giving Albert a hand signal to lift him out of the hopper, Pete prepared to ascend.

The ropes jerked, then grew taunt. More than happy to get out of the hopper, Pete breathed in fresh, hot air as he was pulled to the lip. Albert stopped the winch and then held out a strong hand in his direction. As Pete gripped the foreman's powerful arm, he was easily hauled back to the metal grating of the access platform. In no time, Pete had shimmied out of the harness and handed it to an awaiting worker. Turning, Pete lifted his hard hat and wiped off his sweaty, grimy brow.

"Let's load this hopper half-full with sand, Albert. We'll see if those new gates will hold."

"Yes, sir, Major Trayhern." Golze gave orders to the workers below by radio. A number of Afghans scurried toward the front-end loaders to begin dumping the material. Piles of sand they placed on the long, narrow conveyor belt would then spill into the hopper.

"Hey," Golze said, "did you see that helicopter land?"

Shaking his head, Pete wiped his mouth. "No. Who was it?"

Grinning, the German said, "If my eyes didn't deceive me, it was Fräulein Roland. And the guy with her, I think, was her brother." Pointing to his eyes, Golze continued with humor, "At my age, I don't see so well at a distance, but I couldn't miss Fräulein Roland's red hair. She's back a day early from the hospital. I wonder if she was bored to death?" He chuckled indulgently.

"Knowing her, she wanted to be back at the job." Pete's heart leaped in anticipation. Cali was home!

"Why don't you go welcome her, Major Trayhern? I'll take care of the sand-feed tests. I'll report via radio when we're done. Yes?"

"Thank you," Pete said, grateful for the man's understanding. Golze looked tough, but beneath that rugged exterior was a heart of gold. The German smiled widely and lifted his hand in farewell.

Could Golze see how he felt about Cali? Gazing into the foreman's dancing blue eyes, Pete thought the older man might have answers he presently did not.

Did Cali need him? That was the sixty-four-thousand-dollar question that had hung like a scimitar over Pete's heart. He had told her he needed her. Where had those words come from? He'd not been aware of the violent emotions buried deep inside him until that crucial moment when Cali fell into his arms.

Once he climbed down the metal ladder, Pete bounded over to his Tundra pickup. Just feeling the cool air-conditioning on his hot, sweaty body was a godsend. Pete opened a bottle of water and gulped down half of it before driving out of the concrete plant area. *Cali is back home. Here, with me.* His heart pounded with joy and dread. She might not remember him saying those words to her, but if she did, he'd find out soon enough how she felt. Fear churned in his gut as he drove toward the center of the site and headquarters. All the trailers had, over time, taken on a pinkish-red cast thanks to all the dust.

Trying to ignore his racing pulse, Pete parked the truck. As he got out, clouds of billowing dust blew by him.

Taking the trailer steps two at a time, he gulped hard, twisted the knob and walked into the cool comfort of the Roland headquarters. He immediately saw Cali seated to his left. If he went on impulse, he'd go over and put his arms around her. But to his right, standing at the drafting table, was a tall, dark-haired man in familiar construction clothing. Logan, Cali's brother.

Shifting his attention back to Cali, Pete closed the door and took off his hard hat. He tried to smile. "Hi, stranger. Welcome back," he said. Cali looked so wan. Her left temple was bandaged and her red hair tousled. Despite this, she looked beautiful.

"I was trying to find out where you were." Cali smiled weakly.

"At the hoppers," Pete explained, filling her in on the details as he approached her desk. His throat closed up with emotion. He wanted to tell her how he felt. But then he turned and saw the man at the end of the trailer approaching him.

"Pete, this is my oldest brother, Logan. Logan, meet Major Pete Trayhern, my boss."

Shaking Logan's lean hand, Pete felt the strength in the man's grip. "Nice to see you again, Logan," he said. "I'm sorry I didn't get to chat with you at the hospital. Are you babysitting your sister here?"

Pete saw the man's serious expression thaw a little, his mouth curving slightly. "Nice seeing you again, Major." Logan smiled. "Let's put it this way — my sister is bullheaded and didn't want to be in that hospital room one minute longer. So I told her that I wanted to make sure she got here in one piece."

Nodding, Pete released the man's hand. "Thanks. We've probably called Cali bull-headed, too, but only behind her back. . . ."

Everyone politely laughed.

Pete turned and studied Cali. She had already started working on the in basket, which was piled high with papers. "How are you feeling?" He heard his voice go husky with concern.

"Oh, headache is all." Cali pointed to the bandage on the side of her head. "Doc says I'll have them off and on. It's no big deal." For whatever reason, Cali felt tears prick the back of her eyes. Why? She kept remembering Pete's words: he needed her. With all the uncertainty in her life, she didn't know how to take his confession.

"Do you need some aspirin?" Pete asked, concerned. He could see her copper freckles standing out against her pale flesh. Cali shouldn't be here; she should be in bed, resting.

"Yeah, I took some, but they're running out of steam. I could use a few more."

"Hold on," he said, heading for the bathroom at the end of the hall, "I'll get you some."

Cali gave him a grateful look when he returned with two aspirins along with a cup of water. "You are truly a knight on a white horse. Thanks, Pete." He had been that and more for her out there in the mountains. Cali would never forget his efforts to find and save her.

When their fingertips met, Pete felt his heart lurch with such powerful emotion that for a moment he was dumbstruck. It felt as if he were a shy teenager with a crush on a girl he could never have. He cleared his throat, more than a little aware of her brother watching him.

"So, what's the plan here?" Logan casually asked his sister.

After finishing the water, she set the cup down and faced both her brother and her employer. "Pete, the doctor told me I wouldn't be fit for duty for about two weeks. My father asked Logan to come along so that he could temporarily replace me at the site."

"I see." Pete hid his surprise. From a tactical standpoint, he agreed with the elder Roland's plan. They couldn't afford to be without a site project superintendent. And it was common sense to replace Cali with someone of equal or greater status. But he sure would miss working with her on a day-to-day basis.

Giving him a wry smile, Cali said, "Can you put up with Logan tailing me around

347

for two weeks? I'll direct his work and nothing will fall behind schedule, I promise."

"Sure, no problem." He looked at Logan. "Welcome aboard."

"Thanks. This is only temporary, Major. I know my sister's penchant for perfection in getting things done on time, but she needs to heal now. Roland Construction doesn't want the job falling behind schedule because of what happened."

"Sounds like a solid plan to me. And call me Pete."

Logan nodded and smiled briefly. "I can do that. Most people call me Logan."

Cali sighed. "Phew. Glad that's over with."

"You were worried I'd say no?" Pete eyed her quizzically. That was an odd reaction from Cali. She was obviously not her normal gung ho, confident self. The seriousness of her injury was just beginning to seep into him. There was nothing he could do, however, and this just about killed him.

Cali shrugged delicately. "I wasn't sure, Pete. We're a good team and we've worked well together. I know it can cause problems to bring someone in to pinch-hit for a while. If these darn headaches would stop, I would be a hundred percent."

"But the doctor says you'll have them off and on for a while?"

"Yes," Cali said unhappily. She drowned in Pete's dark gray gaze, which held so much turmoil. She could sense his tight control. What was he feeling? While she ached to fall into his arms again, Cali knew that couldn't happen with her brother around. She certainly didn't want Logan to know how awkward and bewildered emotionally she felt toward Pete, either. Her father knew and had promised to keep her secret.

"Cali, you're looking peaked. How about I drive you over to your trailer?" Pete suggested. Then he turned to Logan. "I can get you up to starting speed in about an hour. Will that do?"

"Sure. I'll go meet some of our people and let them know I'm going to be working with Cali for a while," Logan answered.

Her head pounding, Cali rose slowly and picked up her hard hat. "Take me home, Pete. I think I've had enough for today."

Home. Pete opened the door for her. He wanted to cup his hand around Cali's elbow because she seemed so much more fragile than usual. But he resisted the impulse since he knew she was highly independent. Instead, he followed her to the Tundra and insisted on opening the door for her.

"Thanks." Cali climbed into the hot,

stifling cab.

Pete got in and turned on the engine. Instantly, the cooling breeze of air-conditioning bathed them. As he backed the truck up, he saw her close her eyes and briefly touch her bandaged temple.

"You okay?" he demanded, turning the truck and heading for her trailer.

"Yes, fine. Just tired. Stressed out, if you want to know the truth." The doctor had said she had symptoms of PTSD. Cali had heard the term used for those who survived combat. But how could she get those symptoms from a kidnapping? She hadn't bothered to research the syndrome while at the hospital, even though Dr. Wright had encouraged her to read up about it. Her heart had screamed at her to get back here to the site. Why? To go back to work? To be close to Pete? A combination of fear and trepidation churned within her. She was just too tired to search for answers.

"Hey, being kidnapped by the Taliban, narrowly escaping death and then being stuck in a hospital would stress out even the strongest person," Pete said gently, keeping both hands on the wheel as he drove. He tried to go slowly and avoid potholes, because he realized Cali had a splitting headache.

"I guess it would when you stack up all the details of my last few days. I really missed being here," Cali admitted. Through narrowed eyes, she watched Pete's profile as he drove. "The work is my life, and my life is the work. A real type A . . ."

Heart twinging in his chest, Pete swallowed hard and kept his face from mirroring his sinking feelings. Based on what she'd just said, he doubted Cali had heard his words. And shouldn't he be relieved?

Yes, Pete supposed he should. He never should have uttered those words that had been torn from him. And somehow, he was going to have to bury them again in a deep, dark place inside.

But how?

CHAPTER TWENTY

Cali's uncertainty and hesitancy haunted Pete. He saw the pain in her eyes. After helping her into her trailer, he stood at the door, hand on the knob. Cali moved slowly, one hand raised to the bandage on her temple.

Once she was safely inside, Pete didn't want to leave her. He felt welded to the ground, and words came flying out of his mouth. "What else can I do for you, Cali?"

Cali hesitated, then murmured, "A hot bath, Pete. Can you turn on the water for me? It hurts like hell to bend over. I feel like my head's going to fall off."

Heartened, he closed the door and said, "Sure, no problem. A hot bath solves a lot of problems."

Moving down the carpeted hallway, Cali whispered, "Yes, it does. Thanks, I really owe you." Something deep within her responded to his enthusiastic reply. Now that she was alone with him, she didn't want him to leave. It was a stupid feeling, but Cali didn't have the strength to fight it. Just having Pete near was salve to her tattered emotional state. He gave her hope that someday she'd be her old self once more.

"Did the doc give you pain meds?" Pete wondered as he lingered at the bathroom door. She was even more pale, if that was possible. He wished he could stop all her pain.

"He gave me morphine derivative drugs, but I hate taking them because they will knock me out cold." Her mouth tensed as she pushed open the door to her bedroom. "I just think I overdid it today. If I take a hot bath, relax and then hit the bed, I think I'll feel fine in the morning."

"Sounds like a good prescription to me," Pete murmured. "Let me get your bathwater started." Even doing something so trivial for Cali made him feel useful. He didn't want to look too closely at these bubbling feelings of euphoria. Just having her back immeasurably improved his mood.

Due to the throbbing pain in her head, Cali's movements were slow and disjointed. Normally, she could shimmy out of her boots, jeans and tank top in a matter of seconds. Not today. Just hearing the water running in the tub made her yearn for the warm, relaxing liquid.

There was so much Cali wanted to discuss with Pete, but she didn't dare. Every time she talked, she could hear her voice echoing oddly in her left ear. The doctor had told her she might have some hearing loss or changes due to the blow by Kabir. *Damn.* Cali had found out from Logan on the flight here that Kabir had been picked up in the village where he lived and taken into custody. Right now, Sheik Hesam had him in jail in Dara-i-Suf, and he would stand trial for his attack on her in the next few months. That suited Cali just fine.

With much fumbling and frustration, she was able to wrap herself in her bright green organic-cotton robe, which hung around her knees. She padded down the hall, the nubby texture of the carpet feeling good beneath the soles of her feet. Pete emerged from the bathroom just as she arrived. Her heart leaped at the intense, burning look he gave her, before quickly hiding the expression. Her body responded automatically. She felt heat flowing from her toes to her head and then settling deep in her abdomen.

"Good timing," he murmured. "How are you doing?" Even though she was frail, he couldn't help but notice every lush curve of her body was there for him to ache for. Pete swallowed hard and forced his hands to remain at his sides.

"I feel like hell warmed over, Rough Rider." Consternation flowed through her. Now where had that nickname come from? She was too exhausted to explore the question.

Chuckling, Pete stepped aside. He liked the endearment. Like Teddy Roosevelt, the original Rough Rider in the Spanish-American War, engineers in their business were always out on the front lines in third world countries. Preening silently over the name, Pete said, "Come on in. The water's ready. I poured a little bit of apricot bubble bath in there for you."

He marveled over the way the soft green fabric fell across Cali's womanly form. Her breasts were full and pressed against the material. Looking back up at her face, he saw darkness mixed with pain in her eyes. Even so, the urge to kiss those pursed lips was nearly his undoing. Cali's freckles stood out starkly against her pale skin. Without thinking, Pete lifted his hand and gently touched her wan cheek.

"Listen, if there's anything else you need, call me." Why had he reached out like that? Oh, God, why couldn't he keep his hands to himself? Pete felt a pang of guilt stab his heart. He shouldn't have touched Cali. He *shouldn't*. And yet she looked so lost and helpless. He wanted to protect her somehow. . . .

Cali's skin tingled hotly where his work-roughened fingertips had feathered across her skin. Her surprise over his caress made the pain in her head momentarily subside. Or had Pete's unexpected touch been a healing one? Unsure, Cali whispered, "You'll be the first to know, Pete. Thanks. You can expect me back at HQ tomorrow morning — just like before."

"Only if you're feeling better, Cali. I can run this place with Logan and your foreman, Ray Billings. Just get rested up. Please." Turning, Pete forced himself to leave before he became emotionally dismantled around Cali. He strode down the long hall. Oh, he'd seen the flare in her emerald eyes when he'd spontaneously grazed her cheek. How badly he wanted to lean over, embrace her gently, pull her to him and kiss away all her pain. A burning ache glowed hotly in his lower body.

If he had his way, he'd stay and help her bathe, gently dry her off, take her to her bed and then lay there holding her while she slept. Maybe that's what needing a person meant. Pete wasn't sure. Cali was pressing buttons in him no woman had ever hit before. Maybe needing someone made him more compassionate, rather than just lustful. This was all new territory for him.

He let himself out of Cali's trailer. The day was still hot, the wind like a blow-dryer. The site was a beehive of activity, the constant noise and movement soothing his fractious, distracted state over Cali's condition. As he climbed back into his Tundra to drive to the concrete plant and check on repairs, Pete's hope grew. Cali had come back early. She'd wanted to be here. Was it because he'd said he needed her? Or because of her sense of duty to the site and her father's company? Though unsure, Pete decided to let happiness lift his spirits without analyzing it to death. Two days without Cali in his life had been pure, unadulterated hell.

As he drove slowly down the dirt road toward the hopper assembly, his mind worked feverishly to figure out a way to see Cali — alone. Without her brother around. Something wild and free was pushing him to do it, and he was helpless to stop it.

"Hey," Pete called to Cali from the back of his gray Arabian gelding, "how about lunch up in the hills today?" His heart raced with anticipation. He told himself it was okay to do this, that this was a pleasurable way to conduct business.

"A picnic?" she asked, grinning. She couldn't help but notice how handsome Pete locked in casual civilian clothes. The dark green baseball cap on his head shaded his narrowed eyes. She was both excited and terrified to be alone with him.

"Sort of an unofficial welcome back. A business lunch between supervisor and project engineer." Pete pointed to his saddlebags. "I had Javad make us some beef sandwiches, round up some sweet pickles, a bag of Frito-Lay's and chocolate pudding for dessert. Interested?" He relished her look of surprise and the glow of health in her face. After two weeks, the bandage had been taken off her head. Red, glinting hair covered most of the scar that had been left in its place. She seemed to be healing, at least physically.

"Do I need a horse?"

"Nope. Climb up behind me. You're headache free now and I know how you like to ride. The sheik's men have already cleared the way for us. They've made sure there're no Taliban lurking where we're going. We'll ride over to that little creek flowing down the side of the hill near the western gate. There's some nice shade there, a few tough old olive trees we can sit under." Lifting the saddlebags, Pete added, "You can carry the food over your arm."

"A business lunch, huh?" She'd alternately hungered for time alone with Pete, then wanted to avoid him altogether. Parker seemed to sense her vulnerable state and was acting like a bad cold. He'd grated on her exposed nerves since her return to the site. Emotions still swinging widely, Cali had never before had to ride such a daily roller coaster. On top of her internal chaos, Pete's words about needing her whispered her to sleep every night.

Logan seemed to sense her bond with Pete and was acting like a big bad guard dog. The first week after her return from the hospital, Cali had worked mostly from her trailer, catching up on mountains of paper-work, while her brother took over site demands with Pete in the field. Every time Cali had tried to dodge Logan to see Pete, her brother insisted on coming along.

Pete extended his hand to Cali now and removed his foot from the stirrup so she could mount up behind him. She was incredibly athletic, swinging easily into posi-tion. The Arabian danced nervously, and

Pete pulled the horse to a halt. Cali took the saddlebags from him, then wrapped one arm around his narrow waist. Her breasts felt good against his back. Pete absorbed the intimacy between them like a thief. Turning the horse toward the hills, he said, "Ready, kemo sabe?"

"Ready, Rough Rider. Let's hightail it out of Dodge."

Laughing, he nudged the gray gelding into an easy lope. The late May wind moved around them, hot and dry. The Arabian snorted with each stride, neck arched, ears shifting alertly back and forth.

"This was a creative idea, Pete," Cali exclaimed. Oh, how she loved moving in synch with him. Keeping his back erect and strong, Pete flowed forward naturally with each movement of the cantering horse. The breeze fanned her face and lifted her hair against her neck. Unaccountably, Cali's depressed spirits rose. Pete was like sunlight to her since the kidnapping.

"Then you aren't going to worry what the workers think?" he teased, guiding the horse through the gate. The guards smiled, raised their hands and waved.

"Not today," Cali said, waving back at the sentries. Maybe she'd been through too much. Maybe she needed this unexpected time alone with Pete. Feeling needy and vulnerable, Cali had yearned for his presence. And so often, he would miraculously show up wherever she was, as if knowing she wanted, needed his strength.

Cali saw the narrow trail that led down into a small pasture. Often, boys with sheep or goat herds came to this oasis for water. Today, there was no one around. Five olive trees hugged the green banks of the small creek, where ice-cold meltwater cascaded. Compared to the heat of the desert plain, it was indeed a Garden of Eden. Cali had often wanted to come to this place and eat her lunch, but never had time to do it.

Reaching their destination, she slid off the horse and stepped away. The grass was cropped short, courtesy of the sheep and goats, and resembled a nubby velvet carpet. Pete dismounted with grace and placed hobbles on his Arabian's front legs. After removing the bridle, he hung it over the horn of the saddle.

"Come on," he coaxed, excitement in his tone.

"You did reconnoiter? Right?" A shiver of dread wound through Cali as she warily looked around. Pete had assured her earlier all was safe, but her nerves jangled. Because of the kidnapping, she hated going outside the perimeter fence. It gave her a sense of safety she desperately needed, and she rarely ventured outside.

Pete slowed his stride so she could keep up with him. "It's safe here, Cali." He heard the fear and trepidation in her tone. And when he saw her looking around, as if afraid she might be attacked, Pete knew these were elements of PTSD she was experiencing. "I've been wanting to come to this place for a long time. Especially in the summer, when it's so hot out there on the plain."

He and Cali walked down a slight incline toward the grassy bank. Pete could see multicolored rocks beneath the clear, bubbling water. The olive trees provided welcoming shade from the strong sunlight.

"I've wanted to come here, too," Cali told him. Silently, she breathed a sigh of relief. They *were* safe here. No one was going to jump them.

When Pete gave her that boyish smile of reassurance, she felt her pulse speed up. Taking the leather saddlebags from her arm, he led her to where the trees converged in a shady triangle. "Have a seat."

Cali settled down on the springy grass. Her tension began to bleed off by degrees. After all, she was with Pete, and he represented protection. She watched as he knelt down in front of her and opened the first saddlebag. He pulled out a bottle of white wine, an opener and two paper cups.

Cali reached out and took the chilled bottle. "Drinking on the job? Some business lunch." Giving him a teasing look, she opened the bottle.

"Ordinarily I wouldn't drink during the day, but this is a special celebration, Cali. This looks like great chardonnay."

"You're bending the rules, Mr. Owner." In a way, Cali didn't mind. Perhaps she should, but it wasn't in her heart to protest right now.

He watched her pour the golden wine into the awaiting cups. "Sometimes business rules need to be bent a little here and there. This is one of those days." Pete wanted to add that having Cali back at the site was a celebration of life unlike anything he'd ever experienced. But he couldn't.

Cali recorked the bottle and set it aside. "I follow the rules set by the owner." When Pete handed her a cup, she held it up to him. "Here's to us."

"Us?"

"Why not? You helped save my life out there." Her voice shook with feeling. "And if this is a way to celebrate doing that, then I'm all for it."

"You saved yourself, Cali. We just happened to arrive in the middle of your escape. Even without us, I know you'd have managed to get home to us alive." Pete touched her cup with his and took a long sip of the fruity wine.

"Mmm, nectar from the goddesses of Mount Olympus," Cali purred, relishing the cool drink. Any mention of the kidnapping brought back a stomach-numbing fear that she tried to avoid.

"Especially good on a hot day like this," Pete said. Setting his cup aside, he sat down and crossed his legs. From the second saddlebag, he pulled out sandwiches, sweet pickles and a plastic bag of corn chips.

"I can't believe we're here," Cali said, unwrapping her sandwich as she slowly looked around and absorbed the beauty of the place.

"I wanted to wait until you felt better. Logan seemed pretty intent on guarding you." Pete smiled over at her.

"Yeah, my big brother . . ."

"Was he like that when you were growing up?" Pete asked, then took a hungry bite of his beef sandwich.

"Logan is protective of women in general." She sighed, appreciating the crunchy sweetness of a pickle. "And I think that's what landed him in hot water with Sue, his ex-wife."

"Oh?" Pete met her thoughtful green gaze. He loved how the fitful wind lifted strands of her hair. After a year, they were finally alone. Together. There was such a guilty pleasure in being with her. Pete was helpless to fight the warm feelings flowing through him, touching his lonely soul.

"Yeah, Logan was firstborn. He was charged with taking care of the three of us. I'm glad I didn't get to be first. Sometimes he'd suffocate you with his presence, thinking he knew what was right for you."

"I see trouble on that one," Pete murmured, sipping more of his wine. They sat side by side, less than six inches separating their knees. The fragrance of the grass, the crystal water splashing across the stones all conspired to make him relax for the first time since Cali had been kidnapped.

"Bingo. He wouldn't let Sue be herself, let her escape from his considerable presence. They were married five years. She finally told him she wanted out, that she felt like a prisoner."

Nodding, Pete watched the play of sunlight and shade across Cali's tousled hair. Her eyes were bright. This was the healthiest she'd looked since her ordeal. But he knew she hadn't fully healed. He had seen her grappling with her emotions. There had been times when Cali lost her temper at the site, or flared unexpectedly at one of her coworkers, which wasn't like her at all. Logan had said Cali was suffering from PTSD. And that was something Pete knew a little bit about. They would all need to be patient and supportive. "No one likes to be crowded like that," he quietly agreed.

"I know," Cali said, sounding sad. "Logan cared so damn much, but I think he believed being protective was the same as loving someone. And it isn't."

"Sometimes you can be too protective and it turns the other person into a weakling. That's not good," Pete commented.

"Not that I'm an expert on love. Hell, all my relationships crashed and burned, and it wasn't because I was being like Logan. I have my own unique set of problems." Did she ever. Russ Turner haunted her, and now she had a new obstacle that would make a romantic relationship that much more difficult.

With a groan, Pete said, "I'm guilty of that, too. I haven't had one good relationship yet. I'm beginning to think I'm cursed or have a black cloud hanging over my head."

Cali held his frustrated gray gaze. "Why is that, do you think?"

"I honestly don't know, Cali." Pete finished off his sandwich and sipped more of the wine. "I've discussed it with my parents — that's how bad off I was. Not that I figured it all out."

"What was your mom and dad's conclusion about your relationship issues?"

"My mother said I just hadn't met the right woman yet. That I was learning about relationships just like everyone else did — by going through many of them."

"And how would you know this special woman from the rest?" Cali finished her sandwich and nibbled on some of the salty Frito-Lay's. Right now, Pete looked incredibly relaxed. His eyes were light and filled with warmth — toward her, she thought. That scared and lured her simultaneously. Her wounded emotions screamed at her to open up to him, to be vulnerable and available. Yet the terror of intimacy, of having this turn into another fiasco like the one with Russ, warred violently within her.

"Mom told me I'd dream about this woman, or in the middle of the day, even when I'm busy, she would automatically pop into my head. And that every time I thought of her or pictured her face, my heart would swell with such happiness I'd feel like I was going to explode." Pete sipped the last of the wine and put the cup aside. Holding Cali's interested gaze, he added, "And when we were apart, I'd feel like I'd lost my other half. I would hear her voice in the breeze around me and hear her laughter in the tumbling of a brook. Mom said that when I was in love with the right woman, all these things would happen."

"That's beautiful, Pete." Cali wondered if any man would ever see her that way. She was a hard hat. A woman in a man's world of steel and concrete. Sadness filled her heart as she sat there realizing that no one would ever likely see those possibilities in her.

Pete held her gaze. His voice dropped to a rasp. "Cali, I know things have been rough for you since the kidnapping. You've struggled daily since your return. I'd like to help you if I can." Something shifted. Cali felt it. As if Pete's husky, emotion-laden words had just unlocked the key to her heart that had been a prisoner for so long.

CHAPTER TWENTY-ONE

Drowning in the caring warmth of his eyes, Cali began to melt. There was such vulnerability in Pete's tanned face, the way his mouth curved to validate what he'd just whispered to her. He wanted to help her.

Without thinking, Cali reached out and touched his cheek. His gray eyes grew dark and stormy with desire. Just as quickly, she withdrew her hand and tucked it in her lap, her fingers tingling wildly. The tension mounted between them and Cali found herself, for once, without words.

"The kidnapping has changed you, Cali. I'm concerned for you."

Voice wobbling, she managed to whisper, "Pete, I don't know what's happening to me. I've been so emotionally unstable since coming back here." In a corner of her mind she wondered if this was an owner telling her she was going to be released from her job because she wasn't performing up to par. That struck terror in Cali. *Not again.*

"I know," Pete said sadly. He captured her tightly balled hands between his, then released them. "And I think I know why. You were afraid to come to me about all of these changes brought about by the attack. I fought not saying anything, Cali, for as long as I could. I saw you wrestling with a lot of feelings. And I wanted to try and help."

Looking down at her hand, Pete saw how long and supple her fingers were as she spread them out after he'd touched them. There was something strong and beautiful about Cali's hands, and he'd always been drawn to them. She was an engineer, someone who built megalithic structures that cost billions of dollars. She was one with the earth. She had to be in order to be a builder. All those things were such positives in Pete's view.

There had been such strength and yet an incredible gentleness when he'd squeezed her hands, Cali thought tearfully. "Are you going to fire me?" she blurted. There, the worst of her fear was verbalized. Stomach knotting painfully, she saw surprise flash across his eyes. His mouth opened and then quickly closed.

Pete gazed deeply into her emerald eyes.

"Why, no. Of course not. Is that what you thought? That I'd brought you out here to release you from the job?"

Tears blurred Cali's vision. "Oh, Pete. I don't know what to think." She choked back a sob. Pressing her hand against her lips, she battled the powerful emotional response to his simple question. Finding her voice, she rasped, "I know I haven't been a very good manager since coming back from the kidnapping. I battle anger, fear and anxiety every hour. They come and go unexpectedly. I have lost my temper and yelled at workers and supervisors when I shouldn't have. I try so very hard to stop it from happening, but I don't know what's going on or why. I feel almost out of control. I've never felt like this and I don't know what to do about it. Or how to stop it."

"I have a story to tell you, Cali," Pete answered quietly. "I want to share something very personal with you about my parents. My father, Morgan Trayhern, worked for a secret organization within the government. He labored tirelessly to put a lot of South American drug lords behind bars. To halt the drug trade to the States. He thought our family was safe." Pete grimaced. "What he didn't expect was that the cartel would kidnap not only him, but my mother and my older brother, Jason."

"Oh, no," Cali whispered. She pressed her hand to her lips and stared at Pete. His face was dark and filled with memories of that painful event.

"They were kidnapped. My parents were drugged, separated and taken to different countries in South America. My brother, who was six years old at the time, was taken to Hawaii, to another drug lord's estate." Pete picked some blades of grass and tore them apart between his fingers. "My father was tortured daily. My mother was drugged and raped."

"My God," Cali said. "How horrible." She couldn't begin to understand the impact that would have had on his parents, much less their children. "How did they escape?"

"Several months later they were rescued. My father was nearly dead when they found him." Pete shrugged painfully. "My mother, well, she was frank about the rape. She said a part of her died and was taken from her, that it forever changed how she looked at men, how she looked at her husband. And herself."

"The injury to their marriage must have been horrendous, Pete. I simply can't wrap my mind around such an awful experience."

"It's impossible to imagine," he agreed

quietly, sifting the bits of grass between his fingers and watching them drift to the ground. "I was born after all of this, of course, but eventually, my parents told me, when I was old enough to understand." He gazed at her, his tone hushed. "My parents suffered major PTSD symptoms. So did Jason. I grew up, more or less, with that poison in our family. I came to recognize it, since my parents grappled with it daily. So did my brother. In fact, Jason was so wounded by the experience that it nearly ruined his military career. We were all scarred by what happened. I saw the damage PTSD does to a person, to a marriage and to a family."

Cali took a deep, ragged breath. "Why are you telling me all of this, Pete?"

"Because I see the same symptoms in you, that my parents once had." He gave her a searching look. "And I'm sure I'm overstepping all boundaries here with you, but I just can't stand seeing you suffer anymore. I want to help you, not fire you."

Closing her eyes, her hand pressed against her pounding chest, Cali fought back hot tears. Voice quavering, she said, "Dr. Wright said I would have PTSD. Logan told me to get help from a therapist. I didn't want to believe that the Taliban had hurt me that much. I fought everyone on this. I didn't want the enemy to win, didn't want to admit they had taken a chunk out of me, out of my life." Opening her eyes, Cali glanced over at Pete. "And now you're bringing it to my doorstep. I can't fight a third person on this. I'm just too tired, Pete. I used to look forward to my time at the site, but now it's a daily nightmare that just keeps going and going."

Choking down the tears, because she didn't want him to see her cry, Cali added, "I'll do what I have to do to get well. It's enough that you aren't going to fire me."

"I have a solution, Cali. One that I hope you'll agree to." Pete reached into the saddlebag for two airline tickets and handed them to her. "Come home with me for the first two weeks of June. To my parents' home in Montana. They will help you understand your feelings. My mother will be your guide, if you want."

Stunned, Cali stared at the ticket. They were for first class seats on a major airline, from Kabul to Anaconda, Montana. She read the departure date, then searched Pete's face.

"Go home with you, Pete?" Her world shifted. Cali felt an array of disjointed feelings, along with a sudden, unexpected ray of hope produced by his offer of help.

Sheepishly, he said, "When your father came to the hospital and you were still unconscious, I had a long talk with him before they called me back to the site. I'd already talked to Dr. Wright, who warned me that you'd have PTSD to battle afterward."

"You told my dad about this plan?" There was disbelief in her voice. Her father hadn't said a word to her about that particular conversation!

Pete nodded. "Yes, I did. I wanted to let him know that I supported you getting well. That your work on the site was superior and I believed you deserved my help. And —" Pete smiled hopefully "— he was the one who suggested we take two weeks off and go to my parents' home. Your father said that learning from people who have already had the experience is the best way to heal."

"Yes, my dad believes that." Cali sat there digesting the plan. Her father was very good at evaluating people, and he had an eye for quality. Turning the tickets over in her hands, she looked down at them for a long time. Compressing her lips, she finally lifted her head, and saw genuine concern in Pete's eyes.

"Okay, who is taking over for us if we leave?"

"Logan will take your place. And my number two, Captain Lane Johnson, will do my work while we're gone."

"Logan? He left already."

"Not as far away as you think," Pete told her. "He's in Kabul right now."

"But he said he was going home."

"Logan is working with my bosses and the accountants to get up to speed regarding the project. If you agree to take the time off, he'll come back here and be able to keep everything on schedule. More than anything, Cali, your brother wants to see you get well."

"I wondered why he was acting so funny. He was so overly protective of me."

"Logan saw the changes in you, Cali. He came to me about it. He was worried I wouldn't understand, but I assured him I did, and that I'd create a plan of action to help you."

Shaking her head, Cali sighed and looked around the quiet glen. "Does your home have running water like this?" she asked, gesturing toward the creek.

"Does it ever," Pete said, excitement in his tone. "So will you fly home with me, Cali? Give yourself a chance to heal?"

Her heart in turmoil, Cali whispered, "It would be a professional vacation of sorts, okay?"

"I understand. This trip is about your health. I want you well. And I want to continue to work with you here at the site when we get back." His spirits rose as he saw Cali study the tickets in her hand. "Listen, at worst you'll be spending two weeks with my family in the Rockies. You aren't required to do anything you don't want to do."

Mulling it over, Cali said, "The truth is, I could use a break." She touched her temple, which was rapidly healing. "And I think I'd rather talk to people who had PTSD than see a therapist right now." Because she was emotionally fragile and Pete made her feel safe and more stable, Cali saw the trip as a positive step. *Together.* But she didn't say that. Cali didn't want to promise Pete anything, although she could see concern in his gaze and hear caring in his roughened voice. "I'm willing to talk to your parents about the kidnapping and what it's doing to me. But if that doesn't work, then I'm going to have to see a therapist. I can't stand this up-and-down emotional drama inside myself. It is taking my focus away from work."

"I'll bet my parents can help you understand it, and you'll get a lot out of this trip. If you need a therapist afterward, that's fine, too. We'll do whatever you need to heal from this, Cali."

"Thanks for the vote of confidence, Pete. That means a lot to me." In all honesty, even though Cali had worked with Pete for a year, she had no idea what he was like personally, on a day-to-day basis. The extra dimension of having him with her during this most vulnerable time scared her. But what was she going to do? Cali knew she desperately needed support and guidance right now.

"Logan said you wouldn't come to me," Pete said softly. "He didn't say why, but that it had something to do with your past."

"Logan was right," she admitted. "If anyone but you had wanted to do me this favor, I'd have turned the offer down." Cali was too frightened to tell him about Russ or the subsequent hell her professional life had become. Logan knew all about the debacle and he had never told anyone. Her big brother was a guard dog for her, and Cali was grateful. Right now, she needed protection.

"That's a compliment I'll accept," Pete said, taking the tickets back from her and stuffing them into the saddlebag. Cali trusted him enough to go home to heal. That sent a wave of euphoria through him. "You'll get to meet my whole family and you can size them up and decide if you want to work with them. If you don't, they'll certainly understand. You're not going to a prison, Cali. I want you to feel as if you're having a vacation of sorts. This isn't mandatory, nor will it affect your job status here or with me. If you'd rather handle this another way, I'm open to that, too."

"Thanks for giving me choices, Pete. I guess I'm in shock over the idea, that's all." Staring down at her clasped hands, Cali added, "My dad knows about your suggestion and thinks it's a good one, so I'm not going to argue with that. He's been a guiding light in my life and has never led me astray."

Pete said, "Speaking of parental support, my mother is jumping up and down for joy because I'm coming home. Frankly, we're both needing to cash in our vacation time, anyway. This is one way to do it." Pete gave her a crooked smile. "I think you'll like my mom. People trust her instantly. Everyone automatically opens up to her."

"Okay, Rough Rider, I'm willing to try this," Cali said, picking up her paper cup and drinking the last of her wine. "Any man who thinks his mother is great has my vote of confidence." Her pulse was fluttery. Her stomach churned with anticipation, fear — and what else? Every time Cali looked into Pete's strong, tanned face and those laughter-filled gray eyes of his, she felt helplessly drawn to him. And afraid to call what she felt for him anything other than her crazy symptoms.

"That's great, Cali." Pete rose and dusted off his rear. "I have a good feeling about this." And he did. But he couldn't delve too deeply into the fact that Cali was going to be home — with him. In a strictly personal environment. Unable to erase the anxiety he felt, or the raw yearning for her as a woman, he went over and bridled the gelding. Then he leaned down and unhobbled the horse, reins in hand.

As Cali rose from their picnic site, she picked up the cups and handed them to Pete to stuff into the saddlebags. How did he really feel about her coming home with him? Trapped? Obligated? The way his mouth crooked upward told Cali he was very happy right now. And she didn't wish to spoil the moment with all of her hard questions. *One step at a time,* Cali cautioned herself as he mounted the Arabian, which was eagerly eating grass. *One step at a time.*

"I've never been to Montana," she confessed as Pete held out his hand and helped her mount behind him. Settling into place, she took the saddlebags over one arm and wrapped the other around his waist.

Pete reined the gelding around. "You'll love it. We live in the Rockies, in a beautiful area. As a kid I always liked waking up in the morning and inhaling the scent of pine coming through my open window."

The Arabian picked its way along the trail. Sunlight beat down on Cali and she felt a contentment she'd never experienced before. Listening to the birds calling out to one another, the stream gurgling noisily, Cali sighed. "I think that going home with you is going to help me so much. You've become so important to me."

She spoke the words so softly. They came unbidden, without her thinking first. Was it the prospect of the trip stopping her normal mechanism of holding the secret, personal feelings inside? Cali didn't know. This honesty and intimacy with Pete was so new that it made her feel like she was walking on the thinnest of ice and at any moment could fall through

CHAPTER
TWENTY-TWO

"My family adores you," Pete confided to Cali as they stood thigh-deep in the rushing waters of a wide, cold trout steam. He swung his fly rod back and forth with rhythmic precision. The June day was perfect, the sky a deep blue, the scent of pine wafting in the air.

"They're a pretty great group," Cali agreed, smiling at him. The clear water, a dark green, swirled slowly around them. She heard the call of a golden eagle circling above. The screech of scolding, noisy blue jays mixed with the babble of the creek created a wonderful symphony to her ears.

"Who's your favorite so far?" Pete teased. He released the reel, and the line went snaking out a good hundred feet in front of him, into a quiet, deep pool of water halfway across the creek.

"That's a tough question. I love all the kids. Jason and Annie have two beautiful children. And I think Kamaria — Kammie — is special. You said she was adopted by your family?"

Nodding, Pete reeled in and began flicking the line back and forth once more. "My parents were out in Los Angeles on business when the big earthquake hit. After they dug out my mother, and she was recuperating at Camp Reed, the U.S. Marine base south of L.A., a Marine team with a dog found Kammie and her dead mother buried under apartment rubble. My mom was helping out by feeding the babies at the hospital. When she saw Kammie, she fell in love with her. As things developed, my father found out Kammie was adopted because she had no other relatives. So they ended up bringing her into our family."

"What a happy ending to such a tragedy," Cali said softly. She looked down at the creel they'd brought. Inside the woven wood basket were two nice, fat trout. Pete wanted to cook them for lunch after hiking in the Rocky Mountains. The willow container was half-submerged in the cool water to allow the captured fish to live.

"Kammie is a favorite," Pete told her, grinning. He began to wriggle the fly at the end of the line once more. Again a pine-scented breeze embraced by him. "And I

know everyone likes you." How could anyone not like Cali? he wondered. His family
had warmly embraced her from the beginning. And her PTSD symptoms were already dissolving, just from the outpouring
of love they effortlessly bestowed upon her.

Chuckling, Cali said, "Thanks for letting
me know." They'd flown a long haul of connecting flights from Kabul to Seattle, Washington, and then picked up a commuter
flight into Anaconda. From there, Annie
Trayhern, Jason's wife, had piloted them by
helicopter to the small town of Phillipsburg,
nestled deep in the Rockies. It was there
that the entire Trayhern family had met
them. Cali was overwhelmed due to jet lag,
and worried that she might not fulfill their
expectations. But she shouldn't have been
concerned. Blond-haired Laura Trayhern,
the matriarch of the family, came forward,
threw her arms around Cali's shoulders and
hugged her.

"Your family is a lot more open about
showing their feelings than mine is," Cali
confided to Pete now.

"Well," he countered, slowly reeling the
line in again, "when you're the only girl with
three brothers, I can understand where
you're coming from. Men don't tend to be
too effusive." He laughed lightly.

"True," Cali murmured. "But my mother is very open, a true hugger by nature. I think she's taught all the Roland men to open up a little and show some emotions."

"And that doesn't hurt," Pete agreed. "Well, I don't think there's another trout that's going to bite." He pulled in the line and glanced over at her. "Can you settle for two trout instead of three for lunch?"

"I hate to kill them, Pete." And Cali opened the creel to show him the gleaming rainbow trout. "Could we let them go? Would it hurt your feelings too much if we ate those peanut butter sandwiches we packed instead? These fish are so beautiful."

Seeing the look on Cali's face, Pete couldn't help but abide by her wish. "Sure, no problem. But you do like fish, right?"

"I do." Cali offered him a slight smile and pointed to the trout. "It's just that these two could go back to their home and be free. Maybe because of all the violence during the kidnapping, I just don't want to see anything else killed or trapped."

Agreeing, Pete put on a glove. If a trout was picked up by hand, bacteria would be transferred and the fish would eventually die even if it was released back to the wild. Gloves prevented this. Pete gently picked up each large trout and eased it back into the cold stream. Both fish promptly zoomed off, hightailing for that deep, quiet pool down below.

After pulling off the glove, he dropped it into the creel. "Okay, let's wade to shore and chow down on our peanut butter sandwiches."

"Thanks for the reprieve, Pete."

He saw the warmth in her green eyes. Since they'd arrived home, he'd made no attempt to touch Cali even though he wanted to. Pete had been clear with her that this was a business vacation. In the last week, he'd watched her slowly begin to relax. There had been an amazing change in her demeanor. Cali was more open, laughing easily, joking and rapidly becoming a child in nature.

As they slowly made their way out of the stream, Pete saw her lift her hand toward him. She squeezed his arm. Inhaling her special womanly fragrance, he didn't have time to react. She stepped back, her cheeks flaming.

"What was that for?" His skin tingled where her hand had rested like a butterfly, fleeting and sweetly unexpected, on his jacket.

"Just thanking you for continuing to be a knight in shining armor. You didn't have to release those trout. I know how much catching them meant to you."

Shrugging, Pete slogged slowly toward the bank beside her. "I don't want to make you unhappy, Cali. You're right, we've seen enough violence. You nearly got killed by the Taliban when they kidnapped you. I understand."

"Yeah, you respected my request." She glanced at him.

They reached the pine-needle-covered bank, where colorful red columbine swung lazily in the breeze. "My ego doesn't hinge on whether I keep or eat the two fish I caught." Pete climbed out of the water then turned and offered Cali his hand. Would she take it? She did, and he hefted her up the incline to his side. Reluctantly, he released her hand. Something magical was occurring between them. He couldn't define it, but honeyed moments like this were sweeter than any he could recall in his life.

"Acts of mercy become you," Cali murmured. They both shed their hip-high rubber waders and hung them over some low limbs to drip dry. Farther away from the bank they'd opened a dark green wool blanket, and a picnic basket awaited them. Slipping off her no-nonsense brown oxfords, Cali knelt by the wicker basket. Pete joined her and wriggled his toes.

"You have a hole in your right sock," Cali pointed out as she opened the basket.

"Oh." Pete pulled up his foot and inspected the black, thick fabric. "So I do."

"Do you darn your own socks?" Cali asked, handing him a sandwich wrapped in plastic.

"Thanks. Yes, my mom taught me how a long time ago. She said the boys in the family had to know how to take care of themselves, that they shouldn't be relying on a woman to do things like that for them. I'm a pretty good darner. This sock just missed my scrutiny, was all." Pete chuckled as he opened the sandwich. Cali handed him a bag of corn chips, a plastic container with some of his mother's chocolate cake, plus a can of Pepsi.

Sitting down opposite him, their feet inches apart, Cali hungrily ate her whole-grain bread sandwich. "Your mother and mine are similar," she confided between bites. Lifting her Dr. Pepper, she took a sip and set it down. "When I came along, Mom saw the boys asking me to do 'woman's work' for them. That came to a screeching halt in a hurry. She told my brothers they were responsible for themselves. I wasn't."

"Good for her. Men aren't as helpless as

they think they are." Pete gazed around. They had chosen a small clearing where sunlight poured down like liquid gold between the mighty Douglas firs. With the chirp of chickadees, the piney fragrance in the air, he'd never been happier than right now. And it was all due to Cali. She looked beautiful in her orange tank top, blue jeans and that perennial pink handkerchief around her throat. He'd never seen her as exhilarated as she was now. But given the responsibility and pressure of building that power plant, he'd never seen this relaxed side of her. Taking this vacation had been the smartest thing he'd ever thought of.

After finishing her meal, Cali lay down and rolled over on her stomach, her chin resting on her clasped hands. "I love being here, Pete. It's so peaceful, with the sound of the water, the wind through the pines. . . ." She wanted to add, *You make me happy, and this time has been so healing,* but she stopped the words from leaving her lips.

Munching the last of his salty Frito-Lay's, Pete gazed at her lithe, strong body. How badly he wanted to reach out and caress Cali. The thought lingered, hot and burning. After all his terrible mistakes with women, he found Cali's nearness calling him like a compelling siren he could barely resist. Unsure, Pete said, "I was lucky. I got to grow up here. And —" he pointed toward the stream as he gazed down at her half-opened eyes "— my father taught me trout fishing here when I was seven years old."

"You were very fortunate," Cali said. The day was slightly chilly because the Rocky Mountains didn't heat up until late June. The warmth of the sun upon her body, the soft sounds of the creek, all conspired to make Cali feel sleepy. "I'm going to take a nap, Pete."

"Go ahead," he urged, reaching over and retrieving the basket. "I'll clean up and then I'm going back to the creek. See if there's any more trout in there that want a good fight with me. I'll catch and release them."

Since coming home with him, Cali had been sleeping eight hours a night. At the site, she worked eighteen hours a day. Pete was sleeping in late, as well. This was a time to slow down and catch up on a lot of things.

Smiling softly, Cali closed her eyes. How peaceful she felt. The sun was like a warm blanket across her body. The earth felt supportive beneath her belly. Turning her head to one side, she sighed softly and started drifting off to sleep. It wasn't like her to take naps like this, but she was beginning to realize that the trauma of the kidnapping had stressed her out in ways she hadn't fathomed. Grateful that Pete seemed to understand, she drifted in the netherworld of sleep and newfound contentment.

"Cali is a lovely person, Pete," Laura Trayhern confided to her son as they sat at the redwood picnic table, eating freshly roasted ears of corn. The whole family had gathered at Jason and Annie's new home for a barbecue. "And our daily talks over coffee have been helping her, I think. Do you see a difference in her yet?"

Pete glanced to his left and saw Cali at the barbecue with Annie. Together, they were brushing the beef and chicken with a thick, tasty-looking sauce. "I sure do, Mom."

"How are you two getting along?" Laura asked, buttering more of her corn.

Pete shrugged. "Fine. It's just that, well . . ." Frustration thrummed through him and he wiped his buttery fingers on a paper napkin. "We only have a week left. I see a lot of positive changes in Cali since we've come home. Now I realize that the kidnapping really stressed her out. More than I ever imagined. I wish we had more time here."

Around them, Jason and Annie's two children, Alex and Rachel, were running, laughing and playing tag. The other adults were chatting, drinking beer and standing in a loose semicircle around the barbecue.

Laura nodded and kept her tone low. "Time heals all things. And even though you only have two weeks here, it's a good start. I know from my own kidnapping experience that at first you don't realize how traumatized you really are. I'm sure you've seen Cali in many different moods because of it. And I believe she's starting to make those connections within herself. The time here is going to make her more aware, reflect more, and that's not a bad beginning."

Relief flowed through Pete as he finished off his ear of corn. "I'm glad you understand all of this, Mom, because I didn't know how to approach Cali about it. As a kid I saw you and Dad struggling through it off and on, even when I was young. I felt helpless then, and I feel helpless now."

Caressing Pete's arm, Laura gave him a sad smile. "We wrestled with our symptoms for nearly fifteen years after they occurred. It was a deep wounding for us. That was a terrible period for our whole family, Pete. I knew it was affecting you, too. And yes, I'm sure you felt helpless. It's an awful thing to see someone you love in pain and you can't ease it for them. All you can do is stand there and watch them suffer."

"That's exactly how I felt," Pete admitted. He caught his mother's hand and gave it a squeeze. "Lessons of life, Mom. I'm old enough to look back on that time and understand it now."

"I'm glad, Pete. I'd like to think that we grew as a family through those trials and tribulations after we were rescued. And it was hard on everyone. No one escaped the pain." She brightened a little. "But look how it has helped you with Cali. Because of your experience with us, you knew what was happening to her, even though she didn't. You devised a plan to help her. We learn and develop compassion by going through an event and coming out the other side. And you've used your experience well to support her."

"I hope I have, Mom."

"Cali needs to decompress from that event, Pete. It takes months. Sometimes years. Everyone heals from such a crisis at their own time and pace. There is no such thing as a normal time period to heal such a wound. Right now Cali is experiencing all kinds of emotional swings. Being here with us is new and strange to her, too. That can add stress, not necessarily remove it."

"Maybe I should have taken her back to her own family."

Reaching over, Laura patted her son's large hand. "Honey, you gave her a choice. She didn't have to come here at all. She could have turned down your airline tickets and told you she'd rather go home to her family. But she didn't."

Pete gazed over at Cali. Clearly, she and Annie were getting along like sisters. There was lots of laughter and joking between them. Jason stood off to one side with their father as they talked over cans of cold beer. Pete turned back to his mother and searched her softly lined face. "I guess I'm in a hurry. It eats me alive to see Cali suffering, Mom. I feel like I did as a kid when you and Dad were going through your pain and struggles. Déjà vu all over again."

"Pete, you have to be patient," Laura whispered gently. "The fact that Cali came here with you says a lot. She's tussling with this PTSD, on top of being the head of that project over in Afghanistan with you. That's double stress in my book. Give her room, Son. I know you have high expectations, but healing isn't a straightforward process." Laura smiled, placed the finished cob on her plate and wiped her mouth with her napkin. "Let Cali initiate. If she wants to talk, then be there as a witness for her. Don't try to fix it for her, Pete, just sit quietly. A good part of caring for someone is listening to what their needs are, what they're saying. Not always having ways to fix it for them. They have to learn that for themselves."

"You ought to know. You've been married to Dad for a long, long time. You know what it takes to heal from something like this."

Chuckling, Laura said, "Yes, and I've had to train him constantly on what a good relationship is all about. We never hid our arguments or our love for one another from you kids. So use what you learned and apply it to Cali. Right now, Pete, she doesn't need to feel like she's being expected to turn a corner on her wounding. Don't put out vibes that you expect that at all. People pick up on those invisible demands. Give her space and room. That's what she needs right now. Look to see what makes her happy and relaxed. That's what you should be doing for her."

"As always, you're right," Pete murmured, a catch in his voice. He tore his paper napkin into pieces and watched them fall haphazardly onto the table. A breeze moved through and he captured the pieces before they were blown away.

"Real healing takes time," Laura cautioned. "Cali's got a lot to juggle, Pete. Plus, you're leaving the project in another year. What's Cali to do without your support as she heals? You'll be off and assigned somewhere else in the world, and she's there at that site, alone. Have you thought about that?"

"Yes to all the above, Mom. I don't have any easy answers. I see her trying daily not to lean on me, on any of the family, but she needs to. She needs to reach out for the help we want to give her. I just don't know how to emphasize that to her."

Lifting her chin, Laura said pertly, "Just give her the time she needs. I can't stress that enough."

As usual, his mother knew just what to say. Pete shifted his gaze toward Cali, who was turning the chicken breasts now with a pair of tongs. Annie was expertly flipping hamburgers. They made a great team and Pete enjoyed their combined laughter and camaraderie.

Frowning, He looked down at the pieces of shredded napkin in his hands. *Time. We need time.* Suddenly the fact that he was going to leave Cali in a year really began to eat at him. Why hadn't he looked at this more closely? Was that why she still refused to lean on him? Absorb his strength when she had little available within herself right now? His heart contracted at the realization. Deep down, Pete didn't ever want to be parted from Cali. Churning at that sudden knowledge, he rubbed his aching gut with his hand. Life was so damn complicated.

Grateful for his mother's counsel and farsightedness, Pete examined several options in his mind. Understanding Cali's condition only clarified his feelings toward her. On any given day, she was moody, sometimes smiling, other times remote and unavailable. His mother had handed him a valuable piece of information. What to do with it?

"Mom, do you *need* Dad?" he asked.

Laura gave him a long look before she answered. Moving her plate aside, she said, "Need? Of course I do. Why do you ask?"

"Well, you know my track record with relationships. I can't define love. I don't know what it is, obviously. I thought I was in love with women before . . ."

"Pete, we all go through relationships to find and define ourselves. We've all done, more or less, what you have. I know you've had a lot of disappointment with women."

"Disasters." His jaw tightened as he glanced apprehensively in Cali's direction. Right now, she was having a good time, and he could see how relaxed her features were. At any given moment, Pete could tell instinctively what Cali was feeling. "Is needing a person right?" he asked finally.

"Oh, honey, need can be positive or it can be an unhealthy thing. In what context are you asking this?" Laura tilted her head, studying him closely.

"I don't really know," he hedged.

"Okay," she said. "Did you need the women you had relationships with?"

Pete studied the grain of wood on the table before him, his brows drawing together. "That's a fair question. I wanted them, but need? No, I never needed them." Not like he needed Cali. Sighing, he said, "There's a difference, isn't there, Mom?"

"I feel you floundering around, Pete. You're wrestling with something. Want and need are different. If you love someone, you need them. I feel it's a natural combination."

"So, need *is* love?" He searched his mom's dancing blue eyes.

"Sometimes. Not always. An unhealthy need would be two people who lean on one another, acting as crutches to the other. That isn't healthy. That's clinging because you're afraid of individual growth or life."

"Clinging is something I can recognize," he admitted ruefully.

"In my generation, a woman was taught she needed a man for security and money. Thank goodness it's not like that now," Laura said. "Women today can go out and be power earners like any male can. The need for a man as a security blanket has pretty much disappeared. That would definitely be an unhealthy way of needing someone."

"Women married for security, then? And not for love?"

"In my day, women mixed these two up into one. I don't think many woman 'fell in love' just for security. I have friends my age who did marry for security and monetary reasons. Most of them never separated this stuff out. It was all stirred into the same pot — you married for love, which gave you security and money."

"That doesn't seem logical."

Laughing softly, Laura said, "It's not. Not really. But society didn't encourage women in my time to work outside the home. So what were they to do? How would women of my day see things? It's very different now,

Pete. Women of Annie and Cali's generation aren't hamstrung by those confinements and expectations like past generations of women were. It was a general brainwashing, if you ask me. Today, in other parts of the world, women are still held down like that."

He gave her a long look. "Did you marry Dad for security? For need?"

Chuckling, Laura shook her head. "Honey, I was a wage earner in my own right before I met him. I had a good life as a writer. So, no, I did not marry your dad for security or monetary reasons. I fell in love with him as a person."

"And you needed him?"

"After I fell in love with him, he became my best friend, Pete. You *need* your best friend, someone to talk to, be held by, listen to when you're confused or undecided. And your dad needs me, too, for the same reasons."

Pete shook his head. "Mom, I never needed anyone in my relationships." *Not until now.* Not until he'd blurted out the words to Cali after she fell into his arms had Pete realized it.

"Then why are you asking me about this?"

"I was just wondering, Mom."

He saw her intent look, and then she trained her gaze on Cali. Nodding, Laura returned her attention to him. "Maybe for the first time in your life you've met someone you need, Son?"

"I — maybe, Mom. I'm not really sure yet." That was a lie, and Pete hated lying to his mother. "Life is really complicated for me right now. I'm just trying to figure out some things."

Laura patted his broad shoulder. "In a healthy relationship, Pete, need is a part of loving a person. You like to need them and vice versa. It's natural. And if you find yourself needing someone now, I think that's good. You're maturing as a person and maybe you're seeing women and relationships on another, more evolved level."

"Maybe," Pete said, fighting back the desire to confess all to his mother. She was so easy to talk to, but he had to keep his need for Cali secret until he could figure out his feelings. As an engineer, he was trained to come up with answers to complicated problems. All his life he'd done so. As he sat there, he let his mind roam. Would Cali ever need him? Pete didn't know, but hoped she would. It was a terrible dilemma for him. He felt like those trout trapped in the creel: living but not free.

CHAPTER
TWENTY-THREE

Cali jerked awake, a scream tearing from her lips. Sitting up, she quickly pressed her hands against her mouth to stop the awful sounds. She gasped for breath and anxiously looked around. *Where am I?* Everything looked strange to her. Unable to shake the recurring nightmare of the kidnapping, she jerkily climbed out of bed. Shafts of moonlight filtered through the open window and lace curtains. It was chilly in her room, but the fresh pine-scented air momentarily stabilized her.

Still breathless, Cali oriented herself to the here and now. *I'm with Pete. His parents' home. Montana. Oh God, I'm scared. So scared . . .* She grabbed her pink silk robe and she shakily pulled it over her nightgown. As she tied the sash with trembling fingers, Cali felt an icy sensation in her bones. Her body was hot and sweaty, her heart thundering in her chest. Had she awakened anyone in the Trayhern home? Heavens, she hoped not. Wiping her damp brow, Cali felt the need to escape the bedroom. Coming to the Trayherns' hadn't stopped the nightmares. And every morning she felt more eroded, less in control and more frantic to stop them from invading her sleep.

Cali stepped out into the hallway. The guest room was located at one end of the two-story home. Luckily, there were no bedrooms right next to it. Breathing raggedly, she padded down the hallway, the cedar wood cool and smooth beneath her bare feet.

She had a driving urge to go to Pete's room, located at the other end of the long, curving corridor. Cali's head spun. Her heart somersaulted violently in her breast. *Pete.* She Needed Pete! Dazed, she collapsed against the wall, her hands pressed to her cheeks. This nightmare had dissolved the last of her fight to deny her feelings toward Pete. Flashbacks of him smiling warmly at her in the trout stream flooded into Cali like warming, life-giving blood. The heated, vital impression soothed her jangled nerves.

For a year she had denied her attraction to Pete. Her need of Pete. Shaken to her core, Cali felt scalding tears running down her face. Should she go to Pete's room? Wake him up? Ask for help? How many nights had she lain awake wanting to do just that? Every night. Pulverized by the violence of the flashbacks, Cali no longer had the strength to resist him.

The realization was like a brutal earthquake through all her carefully programmed systems and responses. Cali pressed her back against the cool wood, wanting a respite from her crazed inner world. What would Pete think if she knocked quietly on his door? He'd said he needed her. For so long, she had tried to forget that remark, or convince herself that she'd dreamed it. But in that moment when he'd confessed how he felt, Pete had become her protector. Her sanctuary.

Sobbing, Cali repeatedly wiped her cheeks, but the tears kept pouring out of her eyes as if a dam had burst. Hadn't it? The warmth of the June day at the trout creek had nearly been her undoing. Had she imagined desire toward her lingering in Pete's eyes?

Unsure of anything, Cali lifted her head, her vision blurred. Pete. She wanted him so badly she felt paralyzed by it. Her feet wanted to go straight to his room. If she did that, she'd risk everything: her job, her father's good name, her honor or what was left of it. Pete could spurn her. And then what?

Her mind reeled with possibilities, all bad ones. She needed to go somewhere private and think. For now, Cali couldn't bear to go back to her room and face going back to sleep. Looking down the hall in the other direction, she thought of a place where she could go and no one would hear her: the gym.

There was a Jacuzzi just inside the entrance. Putting one unsteady foot in front of the other, Cali made her way toward the cedar door. Maybe just sitting next to some water would help ease her torn state. Oh, when would these nightmares cease? When would she get a good night's sleep?

Pushing open the door, Cali halted, surprise widening her eyes. With his back to her, Pete stood by the floor-to-ceiling windows, looking out at the night. He turned and his own eyes flared in astonishment.

"Cali?"

"Oh, Pete . . ." she hesitated. "I didn't know you'd be here."

Gazing at her deeply shadowed face, Pete realized something was terribly wrong. "I couldn't sleep. I came out here to think."

He walked over to her. "You don't look good, Cali. What's wrong? Another nightmare?" He saw such terror in her eyes and in the contortion of her wet lips. Cali had been crying. It tore him up inside. Something old and painful wrenched within him. And then, amazingly, it dissolved and left him clearheaded. Without thinking, Pete opened his arms to her.

"Cali, let me hold you," he rasped thickly.

Hearing his whispered words, seeing his eyes burning with unaccustomed intensity, Cali wavered, too shocked to move.

"Am I dreaming?" She searched his darkened face.

"No way are you dreaming, Cali. I'm here. I'm real. Please, let me help you." Too shaken by her wild appearance, Pete felt all his defensive walls crumbling. He'd never seen Cali so vulnerable as right now. Her pale face glistened with tears. Her luscious mouth tensed with an agony only she knew and carried within her. Hair mussed, she looked more a waif than a confident construction supervisor. He understood what trauma did to people and how it could shatter their world. His heart would no longer allow him to step away from Cali. The words he'd longed to whisper to her once again slipped between his lips. "I *need* you,

Cali. Come here. . . ."

It was as if her entire world altered, split and cracked open. She felt momentarily faint, sensed that her life would forever change from this moment onward. Never had Cali experienced such reactions. Pete's whispered words had moved her heart, her world, her spirit. Hope funneled through that crack in her inner being. It filled her, fused her back together again like a flash of lightning.

Without another word, Cali stepped into his beckoning arms. Pete needed her. She needed him. "Hold me," she quavered and wrapped her arms around his lean waist. Driven by fear and yearning, she fell into his arms. Cali didn't care what Pete thought of her actions. *He needed her.* Those words sang through her like a trumpet, making her glory in life, in ecstatic possibilities she'd never ever entertained before this moment of epiphany.

As she rested her head against his chest, Pete felt as if this single act were the most delicious, most important of his life. Feeling his body respond to this unexpected intimacy, Pete ran his fingers gently through her hair. The strands were tangled and damp. When he eased his fingers across her shoulders, he could feel her trembling.

"Cali, you're shaking like a leaf."

She squeezed her eyes shut and tears trailed down her cheeks. "Oh, Pete, I had this horrible nightmare again . . . the kidnapping . . . Ahmed cocking his gun and holding it in my face. I knew I was going to die! I just knew it." Cali bit down hard on her lower lip to halt a sob punching up through her chest and into her aching throat. Wanting to scream, she buried her face against Pete's chest instead. His arms were strong, caring and warm.

Grieving over Cali's anguish, he hungrily drew her strong, supple form against him. He had never heard Cali as shaken and distraught as right now. His heart contracted with her pain and he pressed a chaste kiss to her hair. His mother's words from the day before came back to him: *PTSD nightmares . . . The worst kind. The type that take a person back to relive a trauma, making it as real as the day it happened . . .* Yes, that was what Cali was experiencing.

Most of all, Pete recalled his mother saying that being held and gently rocked was the most healing thing of all to her when she had one of these awful, gutting nightmares. And God knew he wanted to do this for Cali now. They'd gone way beyond professional boundaries. Pete felt a driving ache tunnel through him, demanding that he be true to his feelings for her, no matter how raw. No more mind games, no more trying to rationalize things with this strong, heroic woman who had escaped death. As he stood there supporting her, Pete closed his eyes and simply absorbed Cali into him. Never had he felt so happy. Or so scared. He'd whispered those words to her again: he needed her. Yes, God help him, he did. She had asked for his help and he would give it to her without hesitation.

And so Pete allowed her sanctuary in his embrace. Oh, he wanted to kiss her senseless. He wanted to fix this situation for Cali so she would no longer feel the pain. But he couldn't do that, and he knew it. As she sobbed against his chest, her wet tears tearing at his heart, Pete remained strong for Cali. Little by little, he began to rock her as he might a hurt, frightened child.

Cali's special fragrance filled Pete's flaring nostrils and he began to lose track of time. For now, he was content just to hold her, feel the warmth and lushness of her silk-covered body pressed against his. She could have turned away once she'd discovered him out here. Instead, she'd chosen to walk into his arms. Grateful for her unexpected trust, Pete wasn't about to blow this by trying to drag her into his bed. *Not a chance.* And maybe, he realized, his feelings for her were different from all those he'd felt in his past relationships. She was a sensual woman and he wanted her in that way. But he also wanted her mind. Her heart. Her ideas. Yes, this was a very different reaction than he'd ever had to any woman before Cali. Better. Heady. Scarier. What was he going to do?

Gradually, Cali's sobs lessened. Pete gently pulled away enough to look down into her wounded green eyes. Her lashes were thickly matted with tears. Lifting his hand, he gently wiped her cheeks.

"Cali, you know what I want to do? I want to take you back to my bedroom. I want to lie down with you and just hold you. No funny stuff. Right now, you just need to be held. I want to do that for you. May I?" Cali had entrusted him with her vulnerability, her pain. He wasn't about to destroy the tentative, fragile trust strung between them.

Nodding, Cali whispered brokenly, "Yes, I — I need you, Pete. I do want to be held." No longer could she dodge the central question of Pete in her life. All she was going through had worn her down, and paved the way for that startling truth. As she gazed up into his tense, shadowed features, she saw his eyes burn with an emotion that caught

410

her completely off guard: love. Or was it just general caring for someone in pain? Need wasn't necessarily love. Cali wasn't sure, but she felt so desperate in that moment, it was impossible to analyze anything. Right now, she needed Pete. His arms. His strength and tenderness.

"I understand." There was that word again: *need.* Now, Cali was admitting she needed him. Pete's heart soared with such tumult and joy he felt as if he were caught up in a tornado, spinning out of control. Curving his arm around her shoulders, he guided her toward the door, down the hall to his room.

Cali choked on a sob from time to time, her hands pressed to her face, making Pete want to fiercely protect her. He knew his love for her could help her heal. It was a knowing from his heart, not his head. And that was a vital difference, he realized. For the first time in his life, he was in touch with real love. Now he understood his mother's words and what she'd meant. He loved Cali. She was the woman he wanted in his life forever.

His bedroom door was ajar. Pete ushered Cali into the quiet, moonlit room and toward the queen-sized bed. While he turned and shut the door, she climbed in and lay down, pulling her legs up beneath her silk robe in a fetal position.

Easing down beside her, Pete pulled the quilt over both of them. Cali's curved back was toward him, and when he moved closer, she nestled against him. Pete ached to love her, but right now, she needed his care. Sliding one arm beneath her neck, he curved his other hand around her waist, beneath her breasts.

"There," Pete breathed into her silky hair, "now you can go back to sleep, Cali. Just shut your eyes. The nightmare won't come back. I'm here and I'll hold you safe." He whispered these words against her neck and her hand moved against his.

"Thank you, Pete. I'm so tired. I've been waking up so often, every night. . . ."

Bothered that he hadn't known, Pete gently embraced her. "You'll sleep now, Cali, because you're safe. No more bad dreams. Just good ones. I'll protect you."

Almost instantly, he felt the tension begin to drain away from Cali. Her hips were softly aligned with his, her supple spine followed the natural curve of his chest and torso. Her head was pressed trustingly beneath his jaw.

How long Pete lay awake in the silvery moonlight, realizing the gift Cali had just bestowed upon him, he didn't know. Eventually, his lids grew heavy. And sometime just before dawn, he dropped off into a dreamless sleep with the woman he'd needed all his life. She was in his arms, and he'd discovered real love.

With Cali.

CHAPTER TWENTY-FOUR

Cali awoke slowly. Calmness inhabited her, not terror. That was new and different. Every morning she woke up feeling jittery and frazzled. Not today. She heard the melodic call of a robin outside the window. Barely opening her eyes, she realized the first rays of the sun had come over the horizon, setting the tips of the Douglas firs ablaze with gold fire.

Something was different. And wonderful. Sighing softly, she felt Pete's heavy arm around her waist, secure and comforting. His other arm rested beneath her neck on the pillow they shared. She was sleeping in Pete's embrace. The realization was sweet, poignant and filled with promise. As Cali listened to his sonorous breathing against the back of her neck, felt his moist breath flowing across her skin, a tender smile pulled at the corners of her mouth. Instead of waking this morning with death inhabiting her soul, she felt lightness and hope.

A miracle had occurred last night. Out of the raw, tortured darkness, Cali had not only found safety in Pete's arms, she'd discovered the sweetness of her real feelings for him. Pete could have tried to kiss her, grope her and taken her to bed for sex. Instead he'd held her, rocked her and tried to assuage the pain she was going through.

Once more, he had shown a maturity that few men would have in the same situation, and it blew Cali away. A dulcet heat flowed out of her heart and rippled through her body. She felt an ache, primal and intense, building within her. Pete was asleep, and yet they curved and flowed against one another like puzzle pieces, fitting perfectly together.

She lay there listening to his breathing, relishing his male strength holding her as if she were a priceless, fragile object. She couldn't bring herself to reestablish the defensive barriers her mind wanted her to erect. Before, Cali had always been able to logically explain away her hunger for Pete, her need of him as a friend and confidant. Russ had been that reason. But not now. Closing her eyes for a moment, Cali realized she had no answers to the dilemmas that faced them back at the job site, or the fact that Pete would leave in a year for another assignment. Just the thought of separation sent a terrible, ragged pain through her heart.

Opening her eyes, Cali understood something her mother had taught her. "Honey," her mom would tell her very seriously, "life isn't for cowards. You have to step out on the plank and leap off, even though you can't see where you'll land, or if it's safe or dangerous. Living life is about taking risks and chances. It's about surrendering and having faith that whatever you decide, there's an invisible safety net out there. But you'll never know it before you make that leap, Cali. You'll only see it appear after you've shown the cosmos that you have the heart and blind faith to go ahead and make that jump."

Well, Cali was going to do exactly that right now. She was going to take the greatest gamble in her life: love Pete. She was going to risk everything — her heart, her soul, her career and life as she knew it. Cali was going to let him know that she loved him so fiercely it stole her breath every time she tapped into that core energy.

Turning over, she slowly sat up. The quilt fell away. Pete shifted onto his back, his right arm flopping down beside his body.

He stirred. Taking off her robe, Cali then pulled the nightgown over her head. She watched as Pete's black lashes fluttered. His mouth was beautifully shaped, strong and male. After dropping both silk garments to the cedar floor beside the bed, Cali eased down beside Pete and faced him. Her fingers moved slowly and sinuously up across his flat, hard belly to his wide, thickly haired chest.

It was so easy to lean closer, until she was touching his warm, firm flesh. Cali sought and found Pete's parted mouth. The moment her lips met his, she felt him come fully awake. She saw his lashes lift and those dove-gray eyes grow intense with new awareness. As her lips caressed his mouth, lingering and exploring, she felt his arm wrap around her.

"I want to love you, Pete," Cali whispered against his mouth, trailing her tongue across his lower lip. "Right now, right here . . ." And she pressed her naked form fully against his tensing, muscular body.

"Cali, are you sure?"

Pete's voice was still thick with sleep, but his words carried an urgency in them. Lifting her head so that she could look down at him, Cali said, "There has been one constant in my life this past year, Pete, and that's you. Last night, I made a break-through of sorts." She gazed deeply into his stormy eyes. "My need for you is really about loving you. Love. And that's why I want to be with you now. If you don't feel the same, it's okay. I'll understand."

Cali tried to steel herself for his rejection. She saw so many emotions, vivid and read-able, pass through his widening eyes. It was the last look, one of tenderness, that made her heart melt. Pete reached up and framed her face with his callused hands.

"Cali, I love you, too. I don't know when it happened, or how. I fought it just as hard as you did." Pete slid his fingers across her smooth, soft cheek. "Last night I couldn't stand by and watch your pain or your tears. I realized then I was just playing a mind game with myself about how I really felt toward you. I was scared, though. I have one hell of a past to be wary of. I didn't want to make the same mistakes as before. You are . . . too precious to me, Cali. I was afraid to call what I felt for you anything except need, for fear of screwing up again."

Giving her head a shake, Cali shared a smile with him. "I felt the same, only for different reasons. Right now, I need to love you, Pete. We've denied ourselves for so long. You're a part of my healing process, and I know it. How I feel toward you has been there from the day I met you, not just since the kidnapping. All that brush with death did was bring my feelings for you to the surface. I want to love you, if you want to love me in return, Pete."

His arm tightened around her, and Cali felt the air rush out of her lungs as he crushed her against him. His body hardened beneath her own and he hotly returned her fevered kiss.

Wordlessly, Cali moved her palm in a caress across Pete's torso to the elastic waistband of his pajamas. With a few simple movements, she pushed them off his narrow hips and down his legs. Pete kicked them aside. Now he was completely naked, taut and hard beneath her eager body. As she pressed insistently against his hips, Cali heard him groan. The wonderful sound reverberated through her like thunder on a hot summer afternoon. His mouth was demanding, and she opened fully to him.

His hand wove teasingly down her spine, leaving a trail of fire in its wake. He grasped her hips and positioned her against his demanding length. Drowning in his stormy gaze, Cali wrapped her legs around his and moved down upon him. As he slid into her hot, eager depths, her eyes closed. Lips caressing her breast, Pete began to suckle her nipple and heat erupted throughout her hungry form. She surged rhythmically against him and felt the moorings of her mind disintegrating as the two of them fused into a fiery oneness.

All Cali wanted in this moment was to love Pete as fully as her heart, soul and body had yearned to do for so long. Absorbed in their passionate union, she felt an incredible explosion occur, sending white-hot fire emanating from her womanly core. Seconds later, she felt Pete's body grow rigid, bending like a taut bow against her own. Together, they rode the volcanic eruption that each had been wanting to share for so very, very long.

How long Cali clung to Pete and rode that crescendo of heat and blinding light, she didn't know. Finally, sobbing for breath, she felt Pete tuck her beside him. She smiled up at him and slid her arm around his damp shoulder. Pete was so strong. So male. And so gentle with her. "I love you, Pete Trayhern."

The words, husky and filled with rich emotion, flowed through Pete like the brightness of a rainbow after a fierce, transforming storm. He grasped her hip with his hand and gazed deeply into her half-opened emerald eyes. Cali's mouth was soft and well kissed. Feeling drained and hot at the same time, glorying in the look she was giving him, Pete returned her smile.

"And I've loved you from the day I set eyes on you, Cali Roland."

Pushing her fingers through his damp hair, she whispered, "I did, too, Pete, but I was too much of a coward to admit it."

He caressed her tousled hair. "You've never been a coward, Cali. Not ever."

She trembled and said in a low voice, "Pete, I have something about my past I need to share with you. It was the reason I fought so hard and long against loving you." Taking a deep breath, Cali launched into the explanation. "Russ Turner was a mechanical engineer on my last project, over in Bahrain. He worked for the owner. Over time, he courted me. Oh, he said and did all the right things, Pete. Brought me flowers, candy and the rest. I fell for it. The whole dance was nothing more than a manipulation to get me into his bed. Afterward, he started to ask me to lie on some paperwork between my father's company and the owner. I refused to do it. I couldn't believe he'd cheat on specifications. When I said I wouldn't, he produced a videotape of us making love."

Pete scowled, seeing the anguish in her eyes, "He *what?*"

"He wanted to blackmail me. He said if I didn't cheat on the specs to cover up mistakes he'd made, that he was going to put the tape on the Internet and ruin not only my career, but my family's company."

"That son of a bitch," Pete breathed, gently moving strands of her red hair behind her ear. "What did you do?"

"I was panicked. I went to my dad. It was so scary, Pete. I knew I had to tell him and I felt so ashamed, so embarrassed."

"Anyone would, Cali." Pete lay back and stared up at the ceiling. No wonder she had been so formal and standoffish at the site. Cali had to have been reeling from this awful experience. It all made so much sense now as he replayed those early months they'd spent getting to know one another at the job site.

"At the time," Cali admitted, pain in her hushed tone, "I wasn't sure of anything. I was running scared. I'd never encountered someone so manipulative or controlling. My father listened without judgment. I was so grateful for his understanding. He said he'd take care of it."

"How?"

"My dad went to the owner and told him

everything. They had been long-time friends in the field, so he was able to persuade Mark Stilwell that Russ was the culprit, not me. Stilwell got the videotape from Russ and fired him on the spot."

"That was good," Pete said, relieved. Stroking her hair, he added, "The damage had been done to you, though, sweetheart."

Arching at the softly spoken endearment, Cali said, "Russ was vindictive, Pete. He was fired from the job, a letter of reprimand put in his personnel file. Wanting to get even with me, with my father's company, he stayed outside the site gate and told anyone who would listen lies about me, and how I'd gotten him fired."

"Damn . . ."

"Yes, and for two months after that, Russ hung around and spread all kinds of lurid gossip about me in the nearby villages, about what we did in bed together, and how bad Roland Construction was." She shook her head and avoided Pete's sharpened gaze. Finally, forcing herself to face him, Cali added in an anguished voice, "So many of the hard hats believed him. I couldn't defend myself, I was one woman in an Islamic country and they all believed Russ. I had so many management problems with our subcontractors because of that. It was the worst nightmare of my life. Well, I'll amend that. The worst was the kidnapping, and thinking Ahmed was going to shoot me in the head."

"I didn't know, Cali," Pete said apologetically. He cupped her face and saw the tears swimming in her eyes. "What did you do about Russ? Someone — the owner — should have stopped that gossip." Pete sure as hell would have. In a heartbeat.

"Stilwell finally acted and sent Russ back to the States." She turned her face and pressed a kiss to Pete's callused palm. His touch was so steadying.

"Finally! I wouldn't have let that bastard hang around to do that kind of damage to you, to the project." Pete kissed her lips. "It's over now, Cali. There are people like Russ in our world. And not just in the construction industry. You did the right things, though. I'm sure it was a managerial hell for you, with men thinking you were the reason for Russ being fired. But it's over, Cali. You're here with me. This connection we have is more than I thought I'd ever have in my life. I hope you feel the same way."

"We had so many problems to overcome."

Pete whispered against her lips, "Whatever problems are thrown at us we'll handle together, Cali. Last night when you were standing there in such tortured pain, I recalled my mother's words and wisdom about need. I knew then my need of you was based upon love. That's what love is all about, I realized. We can hold one another through the storms that swirl around us." Pete lifted his head and met her teary eyes. "And we can share the joy, just as we are doing now, during the good times." Caressing her hip, Pete gazed down the length of her firm, womanly body. "You are so beautiful to me, Cali," he said, his heart expanding with a fierce love for this courageous woman.

The words were like a warm, soothing balm to her soul. Cali lay there wondering why she'd fought loving him for so long. Pete was nothing like Russ. Yet Cali knew that her wound had been so fresh and deep that she had been projecting her hurt onto Pete, who was the diametric opposite of Russ. Understanding that she needed time and space to see the difference, Cali felt at peace with the year-long process that had brought them to this place. "Sometimes, Pete, I get hardheaded."

Cali watched his mouth curve boyishly. "No kidding."

"Come on, I'm owning up to it now." She

playfully hit his shoulder.

He laughed and nodded.

"We've loved each other for over a year. We've worked well together at the site. And now . . ." Pete looked toward the window, where sunlight was spilling into the room ". . . we've finally admitted our love for one another." Sobering, he caressed her flushed cheek. "And we're good together, Cali. We make a great team. We always have. We were just too scared because of our individual pasts."

Cali slid her palm up his damp, strong biceps. Pete could carry the weight of the world on his shoulders, Cali knew. "Your mother said you were running scared, but she felt that when the right woman came along, you'd recognize love, real love, for the first time."

Pete nodded. "My mom told me that time and again. I was just too jaded, too scarred to believe her, even though I wanted to," Pete confided, his voice husky with feeling. "But after so many wrecks, I was beginning to think that I was just unlucky in any relationship."

"You were never that to me." Cali smiled deeply into his luminous eyes. "You treated me with respect. So often, I fantasized about you being my best friend, someone I could really talk with, Pete. I saw how honorable you were toward everyone, including me. What was there not to fall in love with?"

"Putting it that way," Pete said wryly, "I can see your point." He caught her hand and slowly kissed her palm. "We've come a long way in a year, Cali. I think we both needed that time to heal up from our wounds and get over our pasts."

"It was your stability, Pete, your way of handling things with me and everyone at the site that must have finally convinced me, on an unconscious level, that you were the man I wanted to spend my life with." Cali gave him a wry smile and touched her head. "Only I didn't get it here."

"You were too scared, sweetheart. You've had a lot piled on you in the last couple of years. I think I'm lucky that you saw through all of that stuff and trusted your heart — and me."

He was more than right, Cali realized humbly. "I've never met a man who could see so deeply into me as you have. And I'm not frightened by it. Instead, I feel good about it, safe with you."

"And protected," Pete growled as he kissed her. Cali's lips were sweet, soft and hot beneath his hungry, searching mouth. The sunlight was a warm, delicious addition to the heat generated between them. Tearing himself from the embrace, Pete looked into her burning green eyes. "I want to protect you from the hurts in our world, Cali. I know I can't always do that, but I want you to know I'm sure as hell going to try. No matter what, I'll hold you through it all."

Pete's rasping words touched her pounding heart, which was wide-open with love for him. Her lips tingled and she ran her hand across Pete's sandpapery cheek. "You've always been my knight in shining armor, darling. I know you can't always protect me. We'll stand together, back to back, and do the best we can for one another. Fair enough?"

He gave her a tender look. "Fair enough."

Cali captured his face between her hands and kissed him for a long, long time. She gloried in the maleness of his mouth, in his power and skill as a lover. Finally easing her lips from his, Cali whispered, "And we've got an awful lot of things to work out because we do love one another. Like the project. What are we going to do, Pete?"

He nodded, hearing the anxiety as well as the hope in Cali's tone. "I've got some ideas that I'll pursue about those issues in the next few days." Stroking her cheek, he added, "First things first. Let's tell my parents. I know they'll be happy for us. And you might want to call yours and tell them about us?"

"I'll call them today," Cali said. "But my father is going to have a ton of questions he'll want answered."

Chuckling, Pete nodded and pressed a kiss to her forehead. "We'll know some of the answers fairly quickly, I promise. And as we get info back from my sources, we'll keep them in the loop."

Worried about what was to come, Cali didn't share his obvious confidence. But as she drowned in his lambent gray eyes, problems of business dissolved. This man she loved so much gave her hope over seemingly insurmountable obstacles. Cali leaned her head on Pete's chest and was soothed by his strong heartbeat. She had faith in their future — together.

Chapter
Twenty-Five

"What did you find out?" Cali asked Pete as he sauntered into the bedroom. She sat on the edge of his bed, tension thrumming through her. He had been on an hour-long call to Kabul with his boss, Kerwin Elliot. She could barely contain her curiosity over what he'd discovered.

"Plenty," Pete said softly as he shut the door. He came and sat next to her on the bed. His hand was rough and callused as it reverently stroked her cheek.

How had three days flown by so quickly? Her world had changed remarkably in that short span of time. The whole Trayhern family was celebrating her and Pete's newly admitted love for one another. Laura was beside herself. Morgan smiled a lot. And Pete's siblings were convinced that Cali was the right woman for him — finally. Her own family was equally thrilled. Her father, of course, had more questions than they had answers to right now.

Cali and Pete lay down on his bed, the quilt's colors muted by the darkness of midnight. Everyone in the household was asleep except them. A stained glass lamp on the tiger maple dresser emitted a soft glow in the corner of the bedroom.

Cali knew Pete had finally talked to his boss, Kerwin Elliot. How would Elliot react to him being in love with the site's main contractor?

Nuzzling his jaw, she asked, "What did you find out, Rough Rider?"

Content as never before, Pete propped himself up on his elbow and gazed down at her. Cali's breasts were tempting, and so was she. Every night, they made love two or three times. Right now, however, more important things were at stake. Leaning over, he kissed her furrowed brow. Lips against her skin, he whispered, "I asked Elliot if I could remain with the project until it was completed. I told him I didn't want to be rotated out after two years. That I'd want a stay of orders because I loved you and wanted to be with you."

Cali leaned back and held his darkened gaze. "What did he say, Pete?"

Easing her to a sitting position next to him, Pete curved his arm around her waist.

She wore a particularly attractive, jade-colored nightgown that brought out the color of her sultry eyes. The neck, a plunging V, revealed the swell of her breasts. "I had to pull in some favors owed me," he told her wryly. "Elliot told me to talk to General Edwards. He said he didn't have a problem with me remaining on the project, but because I was in the service, it was ultimately the military's call. I talked to my father two days ago and he also suggested I speak to General Edwards about our plans. I have two more years of active duty owing, Cali. When you go through the academy, you have so many years you must give back to the service before you can leave."

Stroking his tousled hair, she smiled at him. "Did the general say yes? I'm on tenterhooks, Pete. I live in fear of your bosses telling you I can't be at the site any longer, now that they know we have a serious, ongoing relationship." Oh, how Cali wished they could remain together. But everything she knew about the business convinced her they'd have to separate. Her heart doubled in beat to underscore the dread she felt.

Frowning, Pete touched her lower lip. Such a wanton mouth. A mouth he loved. "I'm sorry, Cali. I know you're anxious, and so am I."

"We're breaking some ironclad rules, and I know the military doesn't take such things lightly. So what did General Edwards say? Will he allow you to stay that extra year to bring the plant online?" The hope in her voice was obvious. Without thinking, she held her breath.

"Yes, he did. Finally." Pete saw her luscious mouth curve with such joy that he felt his heart expand to the breaking point.

"Oh, Pete! That's wonderful!" Cali threw her arms around his shoulders, hugging him happily.

Laughing, he pulled her down beside him. He liked the way their bodies fit together, his strong and lean, hers incredibly soft and supple. "Can you stand more good news?"

Breathless, Cali murmured, "Could I? Of course. It's about time we've had some good things happen to us."

Cupping her face, Pete leaned over and whispered, "I've talked the general into allowing me to choose my next assignment. Not without a little help from my very influential father, of course. It doesn't hurt that Edwards and my dad have been good friends for decades."

"Friendships can often pave the way," Cali agreed.

Chuckling, Pete said, "I also talked to your father about your next career move, by phone earlier today. He said there's an assignment coming up in Qatar after we're done building the plant in Afghanistan. It's a big desalination project to turn ocean water into fresh water. Your father said he's earmarked you for the assignment because of your Middle East experience." Pete grinned mischievously. "There's a military base nearby, and General Edwards promised that they'll assign me to a huge airport construction project. We'll be less than ten miles apart. On two different job assignments, but close enough to live together. How about that?"

Stunned, Cali blinked and assimilated all the incredible information. "Unbelievable. Wonderful."

Pete's smile disappeared and he became serious as he leaned over and kissed Cali's parted lips. "I told your father that I love you. And I wanted to try and work out some kind of agreement with him about our construction work, so we can be together."

Sliding her hand down Pete's torso to his hip, Cali shook her head. "You know, yesterday when I called my mom to chat, she sounded odd. I asked her if anything was wrong and she said, no, there wasn't. That

434

everything was fine." Giving him a probing look, Cali muttered, "Now I know why. You'd talked to my father earlier."

Preening a little, Pete said, "Don't be upset with them. I made them promise that I could share the news with you when the time came. I had to clear everything with the general first."

"You're such a sneak, Trayhern."

"Oh, come on, Cali. I had good reason to be a little undercover about all my maneuverings."

Chuckling, Cali sat up and crossed her legs. She pulled the quilt across Pete's hips and her own. Clasping her hands on top of the fabric, she asked, "And what did you tell my father? That you wanted to be with me on future projects?"

"Sure I did. Your dad asked me what plans I had after leaving the service."

"Don't be so stingy on the details, Trayhern."

"He offered me a job, Cali." Pete saw her eyes flare with surprise and joy. Embracing her, he added, "I told him as long as I could kick around the world for Roland with you at my side, I'd accept his more than generous job offer."

"This — this is wonderful, Pete!" Cali shook her head and shared his smile. "I was hoping Dad would make you a job offer. I hinted at it with him, but he didn't say much."

"That's because he knew I had to talk to General Edwards and get things settled on this project first."

"My father has always been a planner of the first degree, so I'm not surprised about all of this." Cali leaned over and placed a long, lingering kiss on Pete's mouth. "I like the idea of being together."

Pete reached across her to open the small drawer on the cedar bed stand. Pulling out a red velvet case, he held it toward her. "Maybe this will convince you of my intentions, Ms. Roland. Go ahead, open it up."

Surprised, Cali took the small jewelry case. "What did you do, Pete?" She carefully unlatched it.

"I talked to your parents several times in the last few days. I told them that I love you with my life, Cali. I assured them my intentions toward you were honorable. They knew I'd be giving you this engagement ring . . ." Pete held his breath as she opened the case. Watching closely, he saw Cali's eyes light up with awe and then turn warm — with love for him.

"This . . . is beautiful, Pete." She carefully took out the gold ring inlaid with flashing pink stones.

"They're pink diamonds, Cali. You love the color pink. I don't think there's a day that went by when you weren't wearing a pink tank top, socks or a blouse." He grinned. "Or that hot-pink bandanna that was always around your neck." Gazing deeply into her eyes, he said, "Well? Would you consider becoming engaged to me? And marry me when the time feels right?"

Holding the ring between her fingers, Cali studied the flawless, scintillating gems, which flashed with dramatic fuchsia high-lights. Lifting her eyes, she met Pete's. He looked terribly worried, as if she'd say no to his offer. There was such vulnerability in him. And that was one of the many facets of him she loved. He wasn't afraid to show his softer side with her. Pressing the ring into his hand, she whispered, "Of course I'll marry you, Pete. Slip it on my finger."

Nothing in Pete's life had prepared him for the deluge of joy that poured through him as he eased the gold, channel-cut ring onto Cali's extended finger. His voice was husky and uneven as he murmured, "Cali, I want to marry you. You've been my best friend and confidante for over a year now." He closed his hands over hers. "There wasn't a day when I didn't wake up looking forward to seeing you. Oh, I know we have wrestled with a lot of problems at the site, but we were never adversaries. We always talked, and that's what got me. You communicated so easily, and it wasn't hard for me to explore any situation with you." Squeezing her hand, he added, "I want us to always be able to do this. My mom and dad both agreed that being able to talk to one another is the strongest tie that will bind us."

Caressing his hand, Cali agreed mutely. Tears came to her eyes, and she was no longer afraid to let Pete know how deeply touched she was. He lifted his hand and brushed the tears from her cheeks. "That's so funny, because that's what my parents have said about their marriage, too. And they've been married for thirty years now." Cali's smile was wobbly. "I like what we have, Pete. And I think we've earned this with one another. We've had a year to see who and what we are. Time has been on our side. You are confident, but you don't let your ego run you, which is good. So many men have such a big ego they can't admit they're wrong or listen to anyone else. I've seen pride tear so many relationships apart."

"I'll always listen to you, Cali. You're intelligent. You're creative. And you make me laugh. Your sense of humor has saved me so many times. With you, I don't have pride. It will never stand between us or tear us apart."

"Dad always said I had the gift to make others smile when things got bad," Cali said, laughing softly. She lifted her hand and watched the light refract through the pink diamonds. "And you aren't so bad in the humor and joke department, you know."

"Cali, I'm looking forward to laughing and playing together," Pete told her. "We have our work, which is serious, but now we can let these other facets of ourselves shine through, too."

"So many surprises and good things all at once," Cali whispered.

"I have one more."

Cali's eyes widened. "What?"

"I managed to talk General Edwards into giving us four more weeks off."

Four weeks! Cali couldn't believe her ears. "You're a miracle worker, Rough Rider."

"You inspire me, Cali." Pete pressed a kiss to the back of her hand. "My mom made me realize that the kidnapping had wounded you a lot more than I first suspected. She's the one who talked me into trying to get you more time off." His voice turned grim as he stroked Cali's work-worn hands. "I saw how my mother has struggled over the years to get back those missing pieces of herself that were taken from her."

"Laura is incredible," Cali whispered, suddenly emotional. More tears leaked out of her eyes. "And she's right, Pete. I've felt so off-kilter, seesawing with feelings I never thought I could have. And the nightmares every night, about being in that cave . . ." Her voice dropped off. Looking away, Cali closed her eyes and shook her head. She felt Pete gently squeeze her hands. "I never told you," she said softly, turning and holding his concerned gaze, "how glad I was to see you ride over that hill. I was so afraid of dying, Pete. And what made me mad as hell was that I could never tell you that I needed you. I couldn't bear the idea that you'd never know, that we'd never have a chance to be together."

"Well," Pete said, his voice husky with feeling, "that's exactly what we're going to do. Your folks would like to have us come for a visit. What do you think? Would you like to go home, too?"

"Oh, I'd love that," Cali said, yearning to see her parents. "Now, it's possible."

"Yeah, and now it's my turn in the hot seat. Your parents can watch me 24-7."

Giggling, Cali said, "How do you think I felt here? Like a bug under your collective family's microscope!"

"You passed their inspection with flying colors," Pete reassured her.

"Thanks, but I think I figured that out."

"They love you, Cali. They can see us married."

"And your parents are okay with us becoming engaged?"

"You bet. In fact, my mother is already bugging me about when we'll set a date to get married," Pete chuckled.

"That's something we should think about," Cali told him seriously.

"I'm open to suggestions."

Giving him a dirty look, Cali said, "I'll bet you are. . . ."

"Hey, I'm the guy who fought you all the way, and finally capitulated to the fact I love you." Pete pulled her back into his arms. "I can't conceive of a day without you, Cali. You brighten my life, you make me laugh and you make me happy."

Nodding, she curled her hands around his arms, which held her snugly against him. "What about a winter wedding at the end of this year? Most of the outdoor work will be finished at the site by then. Logan and your assistant could easily continue the schedules without us at that time."

Pete leaned over and pressed his lips to her soft cheek. "I like that idea. Let's discuss it with both sets of parents."

"I want a small wedding, Pete. Just close family and friends. No huge extravaganza, okay? I'm a simple kind of girl."

"Whatever you want, sweetheart. As long as I'm with you when we say 'I do,' I don't care. You, your mom and my mother can plan whatever works. I'll just make sure to show up on the appointed day."

Laughing breathily, Cali gazed at him. Pete's gray eyes were velvety with love and longing for her. "I never thought I'd fall in love, Pete. I had such a bad experience with Russ that I'd given up on having anything personally fulfilling like that."

Caressing her arm, he said, "Me, too, for different reasons. But the first time I saw you, Cali, the doors of my heart just flew wide open. I thought I'd been in love before, but I hadn't. Not until you crashed into my life. Over the last year, I've discovered what love really is. Before, I didn't know what the word meant, or could mean. I guess I had to mature, go through a lot of rough experiences in other relationships, to appreciate what I finally have with you."

Cali pressed a kiss to his rugged jaw. "And

I had to go through that experience with Russ to appreciate you, Pete. Come on, let's take a shower together." She looked at the clock on the bed stand. It was nearly 1:00 a.m. "We'll have a huge surprise for your family come breakfast tomorrow morning."

Easing her out of his arms, Pete pulled the quilt aside. "My mother will be jumping up and down for joy. My father will just sit there and say, 'See? I told you so.' "

Sliding her feet to the cool, polished wood floor, Cali stood up. Pete joined her, and when she leaned up against his tall, solid frame, he slipped his arms around her. The boyish gleam in Pete's eyes sent a wave of tenderness through Cali. "I have a feeling that we're going to live a very exciting life together, Major Trayhern."

"Oh, I think you're right, Ms. Roland." He sought and found her willing mouth. Just the way Cali moved against him made him want to forget the shower altogether.

"You know what, Cali Roland?"

"What, Pete Trayhern?"

"I'm going to look forward to a globe-trotting life with you. Forever. . . ."

ABOUT THE AUTHOR

A homeopathic educator, **Lindsay Mc-Kenna** teaches at the Desert Institute of Classical Homeopathy in Phoenix, Arizona. When she isn't teaching alternative medicine, she is writing books about love. She feels love is the single greatest healer in the world and hopes that her books touch her readers on those levels. Coming from an Eastern Cherokee medicine family, Lindsay was taught ceremony and healing ways from the time she was nine years old. She creates flower and gem essences in accordance with nature and remains closely in touch with her Native American roots and upbringing.

The employees of Thorndike Press hope you have enjoyed this Large Print book. All our Thorndike and Wheeler Large Print titles are designed for easy reading, and all our books are made to last. Other Thorndike Press Large Print books are available at your library, through selected bookstores, or directly from us.

For information about titles, please call:
(800) 223-1244

or visit our Web site at:
www.gale.com/thorndike
www.gale.com/wheeler

To share your comments, please write:
Publisher
Thorndike Press
295 Kennedy Memorial Drive
Waterville, ME 04901